MW00874453

Being WEST IS Best

A GINNIE WEST ADVENTURE

Book Four

MONIQUE BUCHEGER

Secret Sisters Club: A Ginnie West Adventure
Text Copyright © 2013 Monique Bucheger.
Illustration Copyright © 2013 Mikey Brooks.
Cover design by Lost Treasure Illustrating.
Published by True West Publishing.

All rights reserved. No part of this book may be reproduced, scanned, or distributed
in print or electronic form without written permission. Brief quotations in printed
reviews are acceptable. Please contact the True West Publishing for further
information.

All characters appearing in this work are fictitious. Any resemblance to real persons,
living or dead, is purely coincidental.

Printed in the United States of America
Charleston, South Carolina
ISB-978-1-939993-19-9

DEDICATION

This book is dedicated to the many people who helped me weave my story. It would not have been the same without you.

Hillary Straga--I love how you give "reality" to the voices inside my head and make them sound so amazing outside of it 😊

Mikey Brooks--Thanks for the amazing covers. They really make my books stand out.

Gracie and Jessie--Thanks for lending your beautiful faces to Ginnie and Tillie on the covers of my books.

Gary--"Scoot Merritt" Thanks for the collaborative creativity. I love what you add to my series.

And to my husband, Kurt... your support has been sustaining and incredible and I love you even more than I did thirty years ago when we started our married journey together.

WEST FAMILY TREE

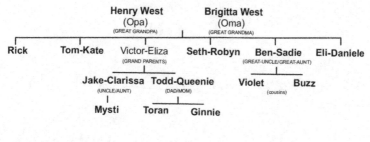

Henry West
(Opa)
(GREAT GRANDPA)

Brigitta West
(Oma)
(GREAT GRANDMA)

Rick **Tom-Kate** Victor-Eliza **Seth-Robyn** **Ben-Sadie** **Eli-Daniele**
(GRAND PARENTS) (GREAT-UNCLE/GREAT-AUNT)

Jake-Clarissa **Todd-Queenie** **Violet** **Buzz**
(UNCLE/AUNT) (DAD/MOM) (cousins)

Mysti **Toran** **Ginnie**

Jasper **Amanda**

Tillie Bold denotes living family members

v

FREE GIFT

To claim a set of FREE downloadable

Ginnie & Tillie paperdolls,
go to:

TheHeroInsideMe.com

1

GIDDY

*G*innie swung down from the saddle and landed in the pasture grass with a soft thud. Her leather riding boots creaked as she straightened. Joy bubbled through her, erupting in a happy squeal.

"Can you believe it? Dad actually proposed to Tillie's mom. My best friend and I get to be sisters—for real!"

Her horse, Calliope, nodded, rippling her jet-black mane against the rich chocolate sheen of her coat. "Even though I don't need a new mom, Miss Amanda is pretty cool. Maybe she'll help Dad be cooler—he's kinda lame." Ginnie laughed, and then hugged her mare. "Of course, he did take all of us in a hot air balloon to propose, so maybe she's helping already."

Calliope whinnied, nuzzling her velvety lips against Ginnie's elbow just below her mint-green T-shirt sleeve.

"Hey, that tickles." Ginnie clicked at her horse and led Calliope to the water bucket.

She unfastened the lead and draped it over the pasture fence. Next, she uncinched the saddle, slid it off, and hefted it onto the nearest post.

Ginnie freshened Calliope's drinking water. "I'll be back soon, girl." She gave her horse a final pat and swiveled, grinning as she ran to the gate.

She slipped through, closed it, and bolted toward the redbrick farmhouse, nearly running into her great-uncle. "Oops, sorry."

"No harm done." Uncle Ben's kind gray-blue eyes twinkled as he motioned to the open kitchen window behind him. "Did you enjoy your ride? He shook his head and chuckled. "I guess that's a silly question. I think you would live on Calliope if you could."

"Yes, sir ... I sure would."

"Like your mama. Riding her horse always fixed the wrong in her world and made the right even better." He smiled. "I left you a piece of cake on the counter. See you in a bit."

"Thanks." A sweet warmth showered over her as she let Uncle Ben's words repeat in her mind.

He was right, riding Calliope always made her feel better when life got her down and intensified good feelings when life was going well ... like today ... when her best friend would soon officially be her sister.

2

Ginnie waved at Uncle Ben as he headed up the hill to the main barn.

The phone rang as Ginnie passed the kitchen window.

She quickened her pace and glanced up the hill.

Her great-uncle was closer to the barn than the house. The phone rang again.

"Coming." Ginnie hurried through the side porch door, reaching the kitchen as the answering machine picked up.

The slice of red velvet cake caught her eye. She snatched up the clear glass plate from the counter and walked toward the phone, listening for the speaker to start talking. When he did, her feet grew instant roots in the doorway between the kitchen and family room.

"U-Uncle Ben? Hey, it's Jasper." Ginnie's chest tightened at Tillie's birth dad's name. They hadn't seen him for six years. "Uncle Ben? Aw, man. I really need to talk to you. Okay, here's the deal ..."

A few seconds passed like fudge sauce through a strainer. "Today's the one-year anniversary of my sobriety. I want to celebrate by coming home. I know I've been an idiot, but I've gotten help." Two seconds of silence passed before he spoke again.

"Uncle Ben ... w—will you help me get my family back? I miss my little girl. I'm ready to be the husband and father Amanda and Tillie deserve."

His voice lost some of its confidence before sounding determined again. "I've really changed this time ... for good. I'll do right by them, I swear it. This is a borrowed phone, so I can't leave a callback number. Please, Uncle Ben? Will you help me? It would mean ..."

Be-e-ep! The machine cut off the rest of his message.

Ginnie spun toward the kitchen. Her hands turned to cooked spaghetti. The glass plate tumbled to the hardwood floor, shattering around the blob of red velvet cake.

As if hit by an immobility spell, Ginnie stood paralyzed, considering what this phone call would mean to her family.

Her ostrich-like dad had finally allowed a new woman into his heart, a woman Ginnie had begun to love with all of her heart.

Her best friend was supposed to become her sister, and although

3

Ginnie didn't *need* a new stepmom, Miss Amanda was fun to be around.

Of course, what none of them needed was the man who had hurt her best friend and abandoned her when she was six.

Tillie needed him least of all.

The phone rang again. Ginnie raced to it, determined to squelch the shrilling. She snatched up the handset, ready to inform Jasper Taylor that there had been a change of plans and his presence was neither required nor desired.

"Who is it?"

Ginnie jumped, surprised to see her twin brother standing in the archway. She pushed the "off" button and twisted to face him. "I—I don't know."

"Then why do you look so freaked out?"

She shrugged. "Where's Dad?"

"Outside." Toran hitched a thumb toward the side porch door. "He said something about getting oil from the barn."

Maybe Toran could help. He had a way of solving tricky problems without complicating the issues. Ginnie blew out a worried breath. "We've got a problem, Houston."

"That's my line." Toran's blond eyebrows scrunched with concern. "What's wrong? And why is there cake on the floor?"

"That's the least of our worries." Ginnie glanced at the broken glass and flattened cake. "Jasper's back."

"Jasper who?"

"Jasper *Taylor*." Ginnie rolled her eyes. "You know—Tillie's lousy excuse for a dad. He wants Miss Amanda and Tillie back."

The color drained from Toran's face. "No way!"

"Yes way!" Ginnie pushed "play" on the answering machine and did her best to swallow her rising fear as her best friend's worst nightmare repeated his crazy plan.

Toran's eyes widened.

Ginnie backed against the kitchen sink, hoping to steady her legs, which were now doing a very good imitation of a bowl of Jell-O.

4

SUGAR BEETS!

*P*lease, Uncle Ben? Will you help me? It would mean ..."

Be-e-e-ep!

"It would mean ... that Tillie would end up in the loony bin," Ginnie spat, anger overtaking fear as her need to protect Tillie kicked in. "We can't let that happen!"

Toran grimaced. "Of course not! Let's tell Dad. He'll know what to do."

"Are you kidding me? He'll be devastated!" Ginnie straightened, shaking her head. "It took him over eight years after Mama died to even ask a woman out on a date. Now he's engaged to her. The *same* woman Jasper wants. No way." She stormed toward the family room, shaking her head with determination. "We're erasing the message and telling him that Miss Amanda moved and didn't leave a forwarding address."

Toran blocked her way. "Yeah, lying is always a good plan ... *not!*"

He scowled and pointed at the cake mess. "And how are we going to call him back? You don't know where he is. He doesn't even have a phone—he said he borrowed someone else's."

"It's *not* a lie. Miss Amanda's moving *here*." Ginnie opened the pantry door and pulled out the broom and dustpan. "Jasper doesn't need to know that."

"You're delusional. How do you know when Jasper will call again? What if someone else answers?" Toran reached for the broom. "There are seven people living here, and five of them have phones in their rooms. *We're* the two who don't. Your plan has too many holes and I'm *not* getting busted for sneaking and lying. We're. Telling. Dad."

"No. We're. *Not.*" Ginnie handed her brother the yellow dustpan. "He'll call back. It's summer break. We'll unplug the phones at night. We're not gonna let Jasper hurt Tillie, or Miss Amanda *ever again.*"

Toran swept the red velvet cake mess into the dustpan and then dumped it in the trash.

Ginnie grabbed a washcloth to wipe up the leftover frosting and cake crumbs from the hardwood floor.

Her twin rinsed the dustpan in the sink. He was like their dad—obsessively tidy. "Yes, we *are* telling Dad," Toran retorted, matching Ginnie's determined tone.

"No. We're. *Not.*" She rolled her eyes and marched backward toward the side porch door, keeping her gaze fixed on her brother. "Dad doesn't need to know. We'll figure out a way to make him go away."

Toran's mouth formed a capital "O".

Ginnie stopped abruptly; backing into what she thought was the wall.

"Careful," Dad's voice cautioned at the same time Ginnie stumbled over his feet.

He reached a hand to steady her.

His mouth pulled into a frown. "Just *what* doesn't Dad need to know?"

Sugar beets! This won't be good!

SPEAK UP

*W*ell?" Dad narrowed his royal blue eyes and pointed an aggravated finger at Ginnie. "I'm waiting—which: *hint, hint,* is your cue to start talking."

Ginnie scrambled to come up with a response that would keep her out of trouble.

"Just to be clear ..." Dad folded his arms across his chest and deepened his frown. "Any sentence that has 'Dad doesn't need to know' in it is a very good indication that I *do* need to know. Start talking or you're grounded."

"I didn't do anything wrong," Ginnie protested.

"Then you should have no trouble telling me what I need to hear." Dad raised a finger. "One ..."

"Dad, wait. She really *didn't* do anything wrong." Toran crossed into the family room. "She just wants to protect you."

"Toran, *don't!*" Ginnie yelled. She took a step toward her brother only to be stopped when her dad's arm reached around her middle, keeping her firmly in the kitchen.

The side porch door squeaked open.

"Let go." Ginnie pushed against her dad. "It's not good. I don't want you to get hurt."

"Thanks for your concern, but I'm sure I can handle whatever it is you don't want me to know." He tightened his hold as she bobbed to escape it. "Go ahead, Tor."

"No, *don't*." Ginnie wriggled to face her dad. "You don't understand!"

Uncle Ben walked up behind them from the side porch.

Ginnie struggled to break free of Dad's hold. "He's going to ruin everything!"

"Who's going to ruin what?" Uncle Ben asked, his gray-blue eyes widening in alarm.

Ginnie blinked quickly. "Jasper."

"What about Jasper?" Dad and Uncle Ben asked as one.

Dad dropped his jaw and then his hands.

"Just listen." Toran reached the answering machine and pushed the "play" button. "This will explain it all."

"I'm sorry, Daddy." Ginnie threw her arms around his waist, trying not to hear the voice that would ruin the rest of her life ... and her dad's ... and Toran's ... and Tillie's.

"Uncle Ben? Aw, man. I really wanted to talk to you. Okay, here's the deal ..." Dad shuffled through the kitchen toward the family room, moving Ginnie along with him. "Today's the one-year anniversary of my sobriety. I want to celebrate by coming home. I know I've been an idiot, but I've gotten help."

"Toran, turn it off!" Ginnie pleaded.

"Shh!" Dad hissed.

"Uncle Ben. W—will you help me get my family back? I miss my little girl. I'm ready to keep all the promises I made to Amanda and Tillie, and be the husband and father they deserve."

Dad sucked in a quick breath.

Uncle Ben walked past them to stand next to Toran.

Ginnie tried to blink the burning from her eyes, burying her face in Dad's royal-blue dress shirt. The same one he wore to propose to Miss Amanda, Jasper Taylor's ex-wife, earlier that afternoon.

"I've really changed this time ... *for good*. I'll do right by them, I swear it. This is a borrowed phone, so I can't leave a callback number. Please, Uncle Ben? Will you help me? It would mean ..."

Dad backed up and leaned against the doorway, squishing Ginnie's forearm. "Ow."

He moved forward, but Ginnie could tell he didn't see her.

His eyes latched onto Uncle Ben's, his face draining of color like Toran's had.

Be-e-e-ep!

4

BRUISED AND BROKEN

*T*he horrified expression Dad wore reminded Ginnie of a night in kindergarten when a frantic Miss Amanda had banged on their door, begging for help.

Jasper Taylor had left a bruised cheek on her best friend, and a bloody, swollen lip on Miss Amanda. The look of devastation Tillie sported that night had haunted Ginnie ever since.

She couldn't stand seeing it on her dad as well.

Her mind blanked.

She turned from him, searching out Uncle Ben's eyes, needing her great-uncle to fix her very broken dad.

"Dad, it's okay," Toran mumbled.

"Of course it's okay." Uncle Ben squeezed Toran's shoulder. "That's a big accomplishment for Jasper."

Dad nodded quickly, rubbing Ginnie's arms, and moved forward. "I'm glad Jasper's doing well. It sounds like he's finally getting his life together." He swallowed, acting like he didn't know how to finish his thought "Good for him."

"Are you two nuts?" Ginnie slipped from Dad's grasp, stood in front of him, and planted her hands on her hips. "He wants Tillie and

Miss Amanda ... after he *threw them away.* They're *ours* now! *He ... can't ... have ... them!"*

Her voice pitched higher with each syllable.

"Certainly not," Uncle Ben agreed.

"Well, he wants *your* help." Ginnie's voice vaulted as her disgust mounted. "Are you going to give it to him? Because that means we'll lose them, and I don't want to."

"Virginia Maie, watch your tone." Dad grimaced, raising a finger. "You know better than to speak to Uncle Ben like that."

"Really?" Ginnie took a step backward, incredible fury sizzling. "The same jerk who hurt my best friend ... wants her back ... and you're busting *me* because I'm mad about it?" She blinked hard, trying to figure out where her *real* dad, the guy who asked Tillie to be his daughter just a few hours ago, had gone. "Way to be a great stepdad!"

"That's enough, young lady," Dad scolded, striding closer. "Calm down."

"No, sir." Ginnie backed up and tripped, landing roughly on her rear. She straightened her back defiantly. "You can't give them to him." She wiped her palms on her blue jeans and glared. "I won't let you."

Dad stopped, looking at her like she'd just sprouted a banana from each ear. "I have no intention of doing any such thing." He reached a hand to help her up.

Ginnie folded her arms across her chest, not wanting his help. "Then what *are* you gonna do? He wants them."

"But he doesn't have any right to them," Toran broke in. "Right, Dad?"

Dad shrugged. "Of course he has rights."

Ginnie shook her head like an Etch-A-Sketch. "No, he doesn't. He can't have them."

Even as the words crossed her lips, she couldn't fathom such a reality.

Fuzzy white noise buzzed in her ears, thinning the air around her, making it difficult to breathe.

The look of dismay that crossed Dad's face might have been comical if the situation wasn't so serious.

He squatted next to her. "You think that little of me?"

"What?" Ginnie demanded, confused by this conversation.

"Yes ... I *am* glad Jasper is doing well. *Of course* he has rights." Dad took her chin firmly in his hand. "But there is *no way* in this universe that I am giving up Amanda or Tillie to him ...or anyone *else* for that matter. So get a grip and *calm ... down.*"

5

HMMM

Stunned, Ginnie sat motionless, trying to process her dad's words. His firm grip on her chin focused her thoughts. "You're *not* going to let Jasper take them away?"

"Absolutely not." Dad reached his hand to Ginnie's again. "While I'm glad Jasper loves them enough to want to do better by them—and even himself—that's *his* issue, not theirs." He helped Ginnie to her feet. "You were there. Did I base my proposal on Jasper's approval?"

Ginnie slowly shook her head. "So it doesn't matter?"

"If Jasper approves of me marrying Amanda?"

"Yea ... what if he hates you?" She swallowed, then whispered her worst fear. "Or worse ... what if he hurts them?"

Dad slipped an understanding arm around her shoulder. "After hearing this phone call, I don't imagine he'll be giving me his blessing, Gin, and honestly, I couldn't care less. I love Amanda and she loves me. And even better ..." Dad gave Ginnie's nose a friendly tap. "She loves you and Toran every bit as much as I love Tillie. Amanda wants the five of us to be a family as much as I do."

"But ..."

"No buts." Dad shook his head firmly. "I'm sure Jasper has learned to keep his hands to himself by now. Don't worry about this. *I'll take care of it.*"

As much as Ginnie wanted to believe him, she didn't.

Dad tended to take the path of least resistance and wasn't the type to punch people.

And anybody who could hurt Miss Amanda or Tillie probably needed to be punched.

Then she remembered the very angry dad who stood in her bedroom not long ago, professing his love for her mother and his anger at Mama's father for disowning her for marrying "a farm boy."

After Mama died, her father, Cabot Stratton, tried to get custody of Ginnie and Toran, but Dad wouldn't let him. Maybe the dad who fought to keep his kids *could* protect Miss Amanda and Tillie from the likes of Jasper Taylor.

Ginnie's hopeful eyes met his. "You promise?"

"To what?" He raised a confused eyebrow. "Marry Amanda?" Dad grinned as her name rolled off his lips. "No problem there. What part of 'I love her' didn't you understand? I loved your mother and made a great life with her—in spite of a very irritated father-in-law." He offered a playful wink. "And between you and me, Cabot Stratton is a lot scarier than Jasper Taylor."

"But Dad," Toran objected, "Cabot didn't beat Mama. Jasper *did* hurt Miss Amanda and Tillie. What makes you think he won't do that again?"

"Because I won't let him." Dad shook his blond head. "And Jasper loves them—"

"He has a lousy way of showing it!" Ginnie jerked out of his hold. "He made Miss Amanda bleed. He's awful."

Anxiety lit Dad's face before understanding replaced it. "You're remembering the last time he hurt them?"

"Well, *yeah!* It's kind of hard to forget. Tillie's face was bruised for a long time. She still has nightmares about it." Ginnie folded her arms again, frustrated he wasn't angrier.

"I remember. That was a horrible night." Dad clenched his jaw shut for a few seconds. "But look at it this way—it was also the night

Amanda started to think seriously about divorcing Jasper Taylor. Because of *that* decision, I was able to propose to her earlier this afternoon and your best friend can now be your sister, just like you two schemed. Maybe we should focus on that. I think today was pretty terrific—how about you?"

Toran laughed. "The balloon ride was epic, Dad, even if it was in a giant strawberry." He turned to Ginnie and smiled. "And Uncle Jake took care of Jasper that other night. Remember how Uncle Jake went after him? That's probably why Jasper left and didn't come back. Uncle Jake pounded him good."

Relief washed over Ginnie at the mention of Dad's older brother.

Even though Uncle Jake and Jasper had been friends since high school, once her uncle saw the battered faces of Jasper's family, Uncle Jake had repaid Tillie's father the favor of a beating.

Uncle Jake will take care of Jasper if Dad doesn't.

Ginnie grinned. "Yeah, that was pretty cool of Uncle Jake to give him a taste of his own medicine."

Dad put his hands up in a "whoa" motion and turned on his "lecture" voice. "Letting your temper get the best of you doesn't help anybody. Losing control is what got Jasper into this mess in the first place. And anyway, Jake didn't feel good about beating him up." He nodded at Uncle Ben. "Jasper realized that in addition to hurting his family, he had betrayed Uncle Ben's kindness to him from all the times when *Jasper* was the abused kid."

"Todd ..." Uncle Ben said, looking a little uncomfortable.

"No, sir, it's the truth." Dad pointed at the phone, and then glanced between Ginnie and Toran. "Why do you think Jasper was calling Uncle Ben?" He didn't wait for an answer. "Because Uncle Ben has always been there for him, no matter what, through good and bad. Just like he is for anybody else who needs help." Dad frowned. "And the truth is, Jasper left because he realized he had turned into *his* father, the man Jasper despised more than anyone, and he was too ashamed to face Uncle Ben."

"Todd, that's enough." Uncle Ben cleared his throat. "Jasper has reached out several times since he left."

Ginnie peered at her dad, not used to him being the focus of a scolding.

Usually she or Uncle Jake were on the receiving end.

Dad's gaze volleyed between Ginnie, Toran, and Uncle Ben before he replied in a strained, yet respectful, tone. "True, but he didn't contest the divorce because he was still drinking and hadn't kept his promise to *you* to clean up his act." Dad reached one hand to Ginnie's shoulder and the other to Toran's. "He's had plenty of time to sober up and make things right with Amanda and Tillie. He didn't." Dad gave a firm squeeze. "As much as I want him to stay sober and find peace in his life, he's going to have to figure it out without Amanda. She's spoken for."

The firmness in Dad's tone calmed Ginnie's fears some. "Are you going to tell Miss Amanda he called?"

"Of course I'll tell her. She needs to know so we can figure out how to deal with this." Dad grimaced at the question and released Ginnie's shoulder. "Nothing has changed. I still believe honesty is the best policy ... for me, and most especially for *you*. And I was right—I *did* need to know that Jasper called."

Heat rose to Ginnie's cheeks as she recalled her half-baked plan.

She swallowed hard, hoping this wouldn't turn into a full-blown lecture.

"We know, Dad," Toran quickly interjected. "Ginnie didn't want Jasper to ruin your special day. Until Jasper called, today was completely epic."

"Yeah. Super fun." Ginnie offered a grateful smile to her brother before turning up the dazzle a few notches for her dad. "Miss Amanda told me a few days ago that you were better than Prince Charming, but I didn't believe her."

She laughed at Dad's arched eyebrow and then hugged him before he could keep scolding. "I'm glad I was wrong. A balloon ride and a banner asking Miss Amanda to marry you was w-a-y cool. And the extra banner for Tillie was totally awesome sauce."

"You don't play fair, Virginia West." Dad chuckled and pulled

Toran into their hug. "I'm glad you liked the balloon ride and the banners, though. Maybe I'm not so lame, eh?"

"Well ..." Ginnie teased, burying her face in his shirt.

Dad tsked at her. "And I *will* tell Amanda, though probably not until I see her in person tomorrow. I put a lot of thought into making today good for her, and for you guys as well." He fiddled with Ginnie's braid and sighed. "I need to give some careful thought to how I'm going to tell Tillie about Jasper wanting to come back. She's not going to be happy about it, but he does have a right to see her."

Ginnie froze, her belly plummeting to her knees. "She shouldn't have to see him if she doesn't want to."

"While that may be true in one sense, the law will not agree." Dad sighed, looking pained at Tillie's future upset. "His rights to her will trump her dislike of him. Knowing Jasper, he'll exercise that right."

"That's not fair!" Ginnie and Toran protested together.

"No, but your dad is correct. It's going to happen." Uncle Ben nodded at Dad. "But between us all, we'll figure out how to help her be okay with seeing him and help him deal with this new reality in a way to keep his pride intact so he can still go forward."

Dad's mouth formed a grimace in spite of their uncle's cheery words, all the while nodding his agreement.

Ginnie's belly dropped again ... this time to her toes.

6

AT PIERCE'S HOUSE

*P*ierce Owens sat at his dinner table, jiggling his foot, waiting impatiently for the right time to ask his father to take him to the West farm again. Pierce really wanted to spend time with Hamilton, the runt hog he had bottle-fed into independence while his dad spent time in jail for hurting him.

Even more, he wanted Uncle Ben to work his magic and make Pierce's father more agreeable.

His father was starting to ignore his part of the agreement that Uncle Ben had helped the three of them establish so Pierce and Mom felt safe with Dad at home again.

It had been three days since Pierce had been to the farm, and Dad was becoming short-tempered and mean. Pierce really missed being around Uncle Ben and Toran ... and even Toran's annoying twin sister, Ginnie.

When Pierce could forget about the two times she had knocked him on his rear, he could *almost* like her. Well, *tolerate* her was probably more accurate.

Not that he could ever like her as a girlfriend or anything dumb like that.

Sure, she was pretty in a blonde-haired, blue-eyed, twelve-year-old pop star sort of way, but she was more trouble than she'd ever be worth. Kind of like a rabid cocker spaniel ... cute, but dangerous.

Pierce didn't mind that she wasn't afraid to climb higher than him in a tree, or pick up corn snakes, though snakes of any kind gave him the creeps—not that he'd ever admit that in front of *her*.

She was pigheaded, bossy, and quick to shoot off her mouth ... and there was no reasoning with someone like her. Even so, Pierce would rather spend time with that psycho than walk on eggshells at home with his father.

He glanced at Dad, wishing he was the same nervous father that Uncle Ben and Mom had picked up a week ago from the county jail and brought out to the farm for their reunion. Pierce hadn't been sure what to expect, but he didn't want it to be just his mom and him when he saw his father again.

The West family hadn't disappointed him.

They welcomed his dad to their home, even giving them some space while still hovering nearby so Pierce felt safe. When his father saw Pierce's bruised face in the sunlight—the result of the beating he'd given him for not taking out the trash—Dad's eyes lit with alarm.

His father actually apologized for hurting him. Pierce really wanted to believe his father was sorry, but as the days passed, it was getting more difficult.

Dad played along fine while Pierce showed him around the Wests' farm, acting interested in Hamilton and in Ginnie's horse, Calliope. He did genuinely seem to like Uncle Jake's hunting dogs, Bandit and Rascal, which surprised Pierce—probably because Rascal took a shine to Dad, even licking him and staying nearby.

Unfortunately, Dad wasn't impressed with the baby kittens, shattering Pierce's hopes of talking him into taking one home when it weaned from its mom.

Pierce had gone home with Mom and Dad that day, hopeful Dad would be nicer so they could be a happier family. However, the faster Pierce's face healed, the faster his father's remorse disappeared.

Pierce almost wished the ugly green-and-yellow bruises were

permanently tattooed on his cheeks. He liked that his father censored his words more and acted nicer when he realized what he had done to Pierce—at least physically.

The more the bruises faded, the less his father tried to work things out. He was settling back into his old habits, using crude words, ugly looks, and intimidating gestures to get his way.

On the plus side, his father didn't rant as long as he used to, and when he started getting loud, he sometimes just left and took a walk —something Uncle Ben had suggested.

Mom placed a bowl of homemade strawberry ice cream in front of Dad. "This is the last of the ice cream Pierce made with Uncle Ben." Her voice practically sprouted flowers, trying to make his father stay happy. "We should look into getting an ice cream maker so we can make our own. It sure tastes better than store bought. Maybe you and Pierce could invent a new flavor."

Pierce grinned. There was his "in."

Dad frowned, stopping his spoon before it scooped the straw-berry goodness. "Marsha, I wish you'd stop calling that man 'Uncle Ben.' He *ain't* your uncle." Dad stabbed the spoon in Pierce's direc-tion. "Or yours neither, boy."

A cannonball-sized pit dug into Pierce's middle. His grin disap-peared. "It don't mean nothin', Dad. It's just what people call him. He's not Austin's or Tillie's uncle either and they call him that. So does Austin's folks. He's just a nice guy that people like."

"Well, *I* don't like him much. Always meddling. Makes you think your own dad isn't good enough for you." He stabbed the spoon toward Pierce again. "You could have a worse father, you know, or no dad at all, like I had. Just a bunch of my mom's idiot boyfriends traipsing in and out, acting like they had some kind of right to boss me around."

"Ray, Pierce knows you love him," Mom pandered. "And he loves you, don't you, Pierce?"

Maybe not so much right this minute.

Pierce nodded. "Yeah, Dad. Of course I love you. You're the best at

Quest for Zyndor." Pierce swallowed, hoping the compliment would be enough to open up the possibility of going to the farm again.

"I've always been here for you, Pierce Owens, and don't you ever forget it," his father insisted.

"Sure, Dad." Pierce scrambled to come up with something else nice to say so he could at least avoid an undeserved lecture, even if he couldn't see Hamilton.

And Toran ... or even Toran's dad.

And Uncle Ben.

Pierce really wanted to see Uncle Ben.

Dad's crazy mood swings were getting harder to deal with and Uncle Ben had a way of calming him that seemed to keep him from spiraling completely out of control.

Tillie seemed convinced that Uncle Ben was a miracle worker on her mean, absentee father, and Pierce had seen a little of that firsthand.

Uncle Ben was the only man Pierce could ever remember not cowering to his father's aggressive ways. He had called Dad out on his bad behavior and Dad hadn't even decked him.

But Pierce could tell that his father wanted to.

Yeah, psycho girl or not, if Pierce had his way, he'd be moving out the farm, if only to hide behind Uncle Ben.

7

THIS IS THE LIFE

*a*fter church, Tillie and Mom went to the farm for lunch. Tillie loved Sundays. Uncle Ben and his daughter, Vi, always made the best food and everyone pitched in to help ... unless the adults wanted to chat in private. Then the kids got dispatched to amuse themselves however they wanted.

Today, Mom and DT–which stood for "Daddy Todd"—went for a walk.

Tillie had given him the secret nickname a few years ago after she scraped her knee and he bandaged it, and then sat with her on the front porch swing. That was the day Tillie realized she didn't need Jasper to come home ... ever again. Since that day, she replaced Jasper with DT—in her mind, anyway.

Soon she might even be able to call DT just "Dad."

Ginnie, Toran, and Tillie shucked corn for Uncle Ben, and then played a video game in the family room while the corn-on-the-cob boiled.

Preston, Vi's fiancé, joined them for lunch. Tillie watched the two of them sneak a kiss in the archway between the family room and the kitchen when they thought Uncle Ben wasn't looking.

A conspiratorial giggle bubbled out of Tillie.

When Uncle Ben winked at Tillie over the stockpot of boiling corn cobs, she knew he'd seen them as well.

Now that DT had proposed, Tillie wanted him to kiss Mom even more, loving how her face lit up when they kissed.

Mom's radiant look lessened the icky feelings Tillie tried not to recall from when Mom was married to Jasper. Those feelings were going away.

She fully expected them to disappear for good when Mom and DT tied the knot.

"We're here. Let the eating begin!" Uncle Jake's happy voice boomed as he rounded the corner from the dining room into the kitchen. He carried his seven-and-a-half-year-old daughter piggy-back, tickling her sides as she slid to her sneakered feet on the hard-wood floor.

Mysti giggled loudly. "Daddy, stop!"

"Stop what?" Uncle Jake turned his eyes upward and thrust his hands behind his back while whistling his innocence.

"You know what!" Mysti's tone scolded, but her eyes twinkled, enjoying their game.

The dimple in her left cheek matched her dad's when she smiled.

Her mom, Miss Clarissa, stood behind Mysti, laughing at their antics. Mysti's wavy, dark-honey locks and pretty heart-shaped face matched Miss Clarissa's, but there was no denying that Uncle Jake had contributed his bright blue eyes—complete with teasing glimmer.

It looks like Uncle Jake's forgiven Miss Clarissa for keeping Mysti from him. Good.

Uncle Jake had been pretty shocked to find out he had a daughter a few nights ago, but fortunately had been pretty accepting of Mysti ever since they met her.

Luckily, Mysti didn't seem to care that her parents weren't married—to each other or to anyone else.

"I'm so glad you could join us for lunch," Uncle Ben said, offering a welcoming smile to Miss Clarissa.

"Jake said Sunday dinner was a mandatory meeting for all Wests and their significant others. I—I'm sure that applies to Mysti more than me." Miss Clarissa fiddled with the hem of her turquoise blouse. "I wouldn't want to help her break *that* rule."

"Good plan. I already told you that when you're here, you're family ... and doubly so, since you're Mysti's mom." Uncle Ben gave a friendly wink. "I can see we'll get along just fine." He nodded at Uncle Jake. "You're a good influence on him already."

"You said I wasn't welcome without her. And no way am I missing Vi's fried chicken," Uncle Jake teased as he slipped an arm around Miss Clarissa's shoulder and then tickled Mysti when she wasn't looking.

He pasted another innocent grin on his face.

Mysti let out a loud squeal. "Daddeeeeee!"

Uncle Ben threw Uncle Jake a mock-scolding look. "Some people take a little longer to grow up than others."

Uncle Jake widened his eyes in playful innocence.

Tillie liked him being an overgrown kid. He rocked at video games and aced ghost-in-the-graveyard, as well as flashlight tag and all other varieties of "tag" games.

Best of all, he could easily be talked into an ice cream cone or other treats when they were out.

"Sugar beets!" Ginnie protested, thumbs flying over the game controller as her avatar picked up a basket of scattered jewels.

Toran laughed. "I told you to watch out for the troll."

"You didn't say he'd jump out of a flower! Trolls live under bridges and in caves ... *not* in flowers."

Mysti ran into the family room. "Can I play?"

"Sure." Ginnie handed her the controller as "GAME OVER" flashed across the TV screen. "I'd rather ride Calliope than play video games, anyway."

"Mommy says I can get a horse too." Mysti pointed the controller at the TV. "Then we can ride horses together, huh?"

Ginnie shrugged. "Sure."

Alarm trotted across Tillie's middle. *Mysti can't get a horse before I do.*

Even though Ginnie had told Tillie that DT had refused to consider a horse for Tillie's twelfth birthday earlier in the month, she still held out hope that she or Mom could change his mind after the wedding. Since Ginnie's mom died from a broken neck after being thrown from her horse, asking for a horse was tricky.

"We'll talk about a horse when you're ten," Uncle Jake answered, his tone uncharacteristically firm. "Ginnie was ten when she got hers."

"Um, Uncle Jake ... I was *nine*," Ginnie corrected.

"Trouble ..." Uncle Jake shook his head and frowned, using his pet name for Ginnie. " ... *don't* help."

Mysti's bottom lip jutted out. "But I want a horse *now*."

"Sweetie, don't fuss," Miss Clarissa cajoled.

"But you already said I could get a horse." Mysti's hands flew to her hips. "Ginnie has one. That's not fair."

Miss Clarissa's cheeks pinked as she glanced between Uncle Jake's narrowed eyes and Mysti's pouty lips. "I said we'd *talk* about it, honey."

"You *said* I could get a horse. You lied!" Mysti stomped her foot. "You're being a meany-head!"

Tillie glanced from Mysti to Ginnie, who stood beside her, and mouthed. "Told ya."

Ginnie had bet Tillie the night they met her new cousin that Mysti would have a complete meltdown the first time Uncle Jake told the little girl "no."

Tillie had countered that bet—certain Mysti would like having her own dad so much that she would do whatever he asked.

Mysti's outburst made Tillie rethink her position.

Uncle Jake crossed the room in two steps.

"Jake!" Miss Clarissa followed him, sounding concerned as Uncle Jake knelt in front of Mysti and reached for her upper arms. "What are you going to do?"

He turned toward Miss Clarissa and stared like she had grown a second head.

Tillie's belly churned, hating the rising conflict.

"Be her dad. Isn't that why you *finally* told me about her?"

Hoping the words came out more spiteful than Uncle Jake meant them to, Tillie shot a worried look at Ginnie.

Ginnie seemed equally flummoxed.

Yikes! I guess he's not quite ready to let bygones be bygones.

Unaccustomed to an angry Uncle Jake, Tillie wasn't sure what to do.

"Don't, Jake." Miss Clarissa protested when Uncle Jake pointed a finger at Mysti.

"Don't *what*, Clarissa?" Icicles dripped from Uncle Jake's question as he stood and faced Miss Clarissa. "Tell her that she should treat her mom with more respect and that it's *not* okay to call you names? Because that's what I was going to tell her."

Uncle Ben cleared his throat as Uncle Jake glared.

Miss Clarissa's face flamed.

Tillie wanted to snatch Miss Clarissa away and hide her until Uncle Jake regained his senses and his usual good humor. *So much for a happy family gathering.*

"Ginnie, Toran, and Tillie, please take the food to the table. Your folks'll be in soon." Uncle Ben motioned toward the kitchen while moving into the family room.

Uncle Jake clamped his jaw shut.

Glad to have something to do, Tillie quickly followed her soon-to-be siblings into the kitchen.

Vi pointed to the bowl of mashed potatoes.

Preston lifted the platter of fried chicken and handed it to Toran.

Mysti burst into tears.

Tillie turned in time to see her run into Miss Clarissa's arms and watch Uncle Jake swivel away, all the while clenching and unclenching his fists.

Her belly churned faster.

Uncle Ben nodded for the three kids to continue to the dining room.

The outer side porch door squeaked open.

Tillie stopped at the inner side porch door that led to the kitchen, happy to see DT motioning Mom to go ahead of him into the porch.

"Buzz and Faith are parking, so we thought we'd come back and help with lunch."

Relieved to see DT and Mom, Tillie forced a smile and followed Toran to the dining room.

It only took a couple of minutes to deliver the salad, fried chicken, mashed potatoes, biscuits, green beans, gravy, corn-on-the-cob, and lime-and-carrot gelatin while gathering around the table.

By the time Uncle Ben's son, Buzz, came through the front porch door with his girlfriend, Faith, Uncle Ben had worked his magic on Uncle Jake and Miss Clarissa, smoothing their squabble. *Whew!*

This was Tillie's favorite part of their Sunday lunch ritual— having everybody together, joking, laughing, and eating great food.

DT pulled out a chair for her.

She wouldn't have to pretend much longer that this was her family.

Soon enough, they would be ... *for real.* She had always felt welcome, but today felt even better.

Crowded, but better, all because of the proposal. She and Mom were official—except for the actual exchanging of the "I do's," of course.

All twelve people squeezed around a table designed for ten.

Preston caught Tillie's eye and winked. His contented smile seemed to reflect her inner thoughts.

Soon, he and Vi would be married—and Preston would be an official West as well.

Uncle Ben offered a blessing on the meal.

Once the "amens" were said, bowls and platters passed through the air.

Busy hands scooped food, piling waiting plates.

Smiles and nods were exchanged along with platters.

Murmurs of "smells delicious" and great anticipation were exchanged with the entrees.

Tillie studied each face.

Uncle Jake helped Mysti stick corn handles in her corn cob.

Uncle Ben's gaze marched up and down the table, making sure all was well.

Faith gazed dreamily at Buzz while passing the peas.

Tillie giggled. *Maybe we'll have three weddings soon.*

Ginnie and Toran focused on eating. Mom darted worried eyes between DT and Tillie, causing panic to spike in Tillie's belly in spite of the friendly atmosphere.

Miss Clarissa chewed her bottom lip nervously.

Vi reached over and patted her hand. "Just dig in, Clarissa. We don't stand on ceremony here."

"It all looks so good. I don't know where to start," Miss Clarissa replied.

Tillie thought her hesitation had more to do with feeling out of place than with the food.

Uncle Jake must have thought so too. Or maybe he felt bad about being impatient earlier. He sent her an extra-kind smile. "Start with the chicken. I don't know what they do to it, but it's the best."

Vi shrugged. "It's just flour and seasonings."

"And love," Preston insisted, wiggling his dark eyebrows at Vi. "It's the love that makes it so good."

"Awww." Vi leaned toward him until their lips touched. "I knew there was a reason I wanted to marry you."

Ginnie rolled her eyes at the display of affection.

Tillie grimaced at her friend, wanting the kissing to continue and better yet, to start a chain reaction.

As if on cue, DT acted on her telepathic request and kissed Mom.

A super-jazzed "Yes!" escaped Tillie's lips before she realized she'd spoken.

Good-natured laughter circled the table.

Mom glanced at her plate, cheeks pinking.

DT winked at Tillie. "I'm glad you approve."

Ignoring her warming cheeks, Tillie grinned at him. "Of course. You can kiss her any time you want, *Dad*."

Oops. The name tumbled out of her mouth before she could stop it.

She'd never called him that before. Her cheeks heated more as her heart raced.

Too late now.

She searched his face, hoping to find approval.

Instead, she found alarm.

8

YOU CAN CALL ME ...UMM

illie's cheeks deepened from pink to crimson in the time it took for her mouth to open into a capital "O." Her hand flew to cover the "O" as her eyes clouded over. Feeling Tillie's embarrassment, Ginnie reached for her friend's wrist to reassure her. "It's okay."

Tillie shook her head, face-planting her flaming cheeks into her palms.

Ginnie's gaze flew to Miss Amanda's, whose lips turned to a worried frown.

Dad looked like he'd just witnessed a train wreck.

If he didn't act soon, there would be a "Tillie-wreck" of major proportions.

"Dad, *say* something," Ginnie hissed.

"I ... I ..." Dad gave a quick shake of his blond head, which must have jump-started his brain. "Tillie ... honey."

He tried to reach across the large table, but couldn't reach Tillie. He stood.

Awkward silence pounded the air.

Ginnie nudged her friend, whispering, "It's okay. It was just a misunderstanding."

Tillie hunkered lower in her chair.

"Why's everybody quiet?" Mysti asked.

"Because," Dad said, coming around the table, "Tillie just gave me an amazing gift and I was so stunned by her sweetness that I didn't know what to say." He squatted next to Tillie's chair. "But now I do."

"Oh." Mysti glanced at Uncle Jake and then Dad. "What did she give you, Uncle Todd?"

"Her love."

Mysti scrunched her face in thought.

Uncle Jake raised a finger to his lips.

Ginnie scooted her own chair over to give Dad more room to reach Tillie.

He lifted her chin.

Tillie tried to cover her face again, but she must have heard the kindness in Dad's tone.

She lowered her hands.

"Tillie, Tillie, Tillie." Dad brushed her straight medium brown hair away from Tillie's eyes. "I love you. I'm *honored* that you want to call me 'Dad'. Thank you for extending that honor to me."

Tillie blinked.

Her mouth imitated the back flap of an old-fashioned pair of long johns.

Ginnie sucked in a worried breath and then scanned Tillie for signs of understanding.

It took three seconds longer for her friend's brain to engage and her eyes to broadcast her acknowledgment of what Dad said.

In another split second, Tillie's arms were wrapped around Dad's neck, squeezing him in a combination grateful hug and choke hold.

Ginnie grinned, relieved at Tillie's delight.

Dad held her for a few seconds before loosening her grip. "I chose you."

He wiped a tear from her cheek with his thumb and smiled. "Thank you for choosing me."

"Yay!" Mysti clapped her hands and squealed. "Tillie gets a nice daddy too."

Yeah, she does. Ginnie had never been prouder of her dad than she was right then.

Then she remembered the phone call and shivered.

I hope she gets to keep him.

9

MOVING ON

*I*t felt like forever between the time Tillie called DT "Dad" and he made her realize it was the best mistake she'd ever made. Seeing the sincerity and kindness in his eyes when he released her from their hug was totally worth any embarrassment she had endured.

And for him to *thank* her for choosing him when she'd only been dreaming he'd adopt her for a whole eternity—well, she was speechless.

DT kissed her forehead and stood.

Wait—maybe I can call him "Dad" out loud now instead of "DT" in my mind. Tillie didn't want to ruin the moment by asking, but she wanted to make sure it was really okay before she did it again.

"Okay, so that was just about the sweetest thing I've ever seen," Vi gushed. "Except for Preston's proposal to me, of course. Tell me about the balloon ride and the plane with the banners, Tillie. I haven't had a chance to talk to you since Todd proposed to your mom."

Tillie was happy to oblige her, replaying the story of her dreams coming true as they sailed in a strawberry-shaped hot air balloon over ribbons of highways and backroads that tied together quilt blocks of family farms with red farmhouses, white silos, green tractors, combines, and other farm machinery dotting the landscape like buttons.

"Ginnie was the first to see the plane with the banner that read: *Amanda, I love you to the moon and back. Will you marry me? Love, Todd.*"

"That's pretty romantic, cuz," Vi said to DT, then turned to her brother. "You might wanna take some notes."

Buzz nodded at Faith and kissed her. "Duly noted."

"Oh, it was!" Tillie grinned at DT, who reached an arm around Mom and grinned back. "And then he got down on one knee and said, 'Amanda, will you please do me the incredible honor of becoming my wife?' Mom was a little stunned, so I had to help her out."

"I'll say." Ginnie giggled at the memory. "You guys think *I'm* impatient. Miss Amanda was so surprised, Tillie jumped in and told her to say 'yes'. Daddy told Tillie he'd need an answer from her mom."

Laughter rounded the table, but Tillie didn't care.

"Can't fault a person for keeping a schedule on track," Uncle Ben said, smiling at Tillie.

"The coolest part was when Ginnie and I got to shoot flare guns at the plane and it unfurled *another* banner," Toran added.

"That was *totally* awesome sauce!" Ginnie squealed. "Daddy asked Tillie to be his daughter, and she was even more surprised than Miss Amanda. She looked like she got hit with a stun gun."

Toran laughed. "But that didn't last long."

Ginnie elbowed Tillie's ribs lightly. "She about broke the sound barrier with her 'yes!', huh Toran?"

Toran nodded.

"Because it was so cool that he asked me, *too*." Tillie pointed her fork at Ginnie. "You're the one who said Mom and I were a two-for-one special."

"Because *Daddy* said Toran, me, and him were a *three*-for-one special." Ginnie pointed her own fork at Tillie and then gave a shy smile to Miss Amanda. "That's a good thing, 'cause I like you both."

"Me too," Dad agreed.

Miss Amanda's eyes lit up as she laughed. "You three are the best deal I've ever run across."

"Are you going to take me on a balloon ride and ask me to be *your* daughter, Daddy?" Mysti asked excitedly.

"I don't think so. You're *already* my daughter and I took you on a shopping spree." Uncle Jake narrowed his eyes at DT in mock annoyance and kissed the crown of Mysti's head. "Remember all the princess stuff I bought you? Games, clothes, and cowgirl boots ... oh, my. I even bought you the princess doll you wanted."

The night he met Mysti, Uncle Jake had taken Ginnie and Tillie to Uncle Quincy's, a video game and pizza place. On the way home, they stopped at a shopping center.

He bought Ginnie, Toran, and Tillie each something special to celebrate getting a new cousin, and then overfilled the shopping cart with everything pink, purple, and princess that had caught Mysti's eye.

Uncle Jake had been in heaven.

Mysti thought he hung the moon.

Tillie was excited for them both.

"Oh yeah, but I still want to go on a *balloon* ride. I've never done that. Have you, Mommy?" Mysti asked.

Miss Clarissa shook her head. "No. But you should probably eat your dinner. It's getting cold."

Mysti frowned and took an obligatory bite of carrot gelatin. "We should go on a balloon ride, Daddy, and you can ask Mommy to marry *you*."

Miss Clarissa's cheeks turned as magenta as the banner asking Mom to marry DT.

Uncle Jake didn't look like he thought the idea was as good as Mysti did. "Your mom's right. Dinner's getting cold." Uncle Jake picked up Mysti's fork, speared the gelatin again, and offered it to Mysti. "Eat up."

Forks scraping plates filled the awkward silence.

Uncle Ben lifted the corn-on-the-cob platter and offered the last two cobs. "So, who wants seconds?"

Preston and Buzz each took one.

"Oh, Dad, I forgot," Toran said.

"Forgot what?" DT asked.

"Pierce called earlier and was asking about Hamilton." Toran's voice lowered with concern. "I think he wants to come out and see him, but he sounded nervous."

Alarmed looks shot around the table.

"Who's Pierce?" Miss Clarissa asked.

"He's a kid from school. He used to be a bully, but now he's our friend." Ginnie paused, scrunching her eyebrows in thought. "Well, sorta my friend. He's more Toran and Tillie's. I knocked him down a couple of times when he was picking on them, and he's still mad about it."

Uncle Jake chuckled. "Ginnie's pretty impressive, Clarissa. Pierce is almost twice as big as her and she nailed him in no time flat —twice."

Ginnie grinned at her uncle.

DT cleared his throat. "Which is wonderful in an emergency, but *more* important is how Ginnie, Tillie, and Toran came together and decided to be Pierce's friend to stop the ugliness. They figured out that creative thinking and being kind go a lot farther in trying to change their corner of the world for the better."

Tillie liked being included in the plan to help Pierce deal with his abusive dad, but didn't mind *not* being part of the determined look DT shot Ginnie.

"Yes, sir. I'm *his* friend." Ginnie clarified. "He's just not mine—at least, not all the way."

"He'll come around. At least he doesn't growl at you as much as he used to," Tillie offered.

"True, but Dad ..." Toran stopped, worry crossing his face. "I got the feeling he wants something else. That he's worried or something's wrong, but he wouldn't say."

Tillie's belly clenched.

Pierce's dad scared her, and not just because he reminded her of Jasper at his worst. Pierce's dad was just naturally meaner than a pile of hungry snakes in a room full of mice running around in hamster balls.

Tillie pushed out a troubled breath, feeling a little guilty when DT's gaze met hers and he smiled.

At least Jasper is gone. Poor Pierce has to live with his bad dad.

Tillie smiled back, grateful her own nightmare was ending and her dreams were finally coming true.

10

JUST A GAME ... REALLY?

*H*ey, Boy-o, we got 'em now!" Dad elbowed Pierce as he leaned forward, thumbs flying over the controller.

"We sure do!" Pierce agreed.

Sitting next to Dad on their brown couch playing video games was fun. It was kinda cool being on the same team, working together to defeat the Evil Sorcerer.

"Watch out!" Dad yelled. "Cover the exit, Pierce."

Pierce zoomed his boy wizard to the back of the castle, annihilating all the sorcerer's minions with a steady stream of red lasers. *They don't stand a chance.*

"Yes! All dispatched to the nether lands!" Pierce grinned at his dad. "That'll teach 'em."

The Sorcerer screamed while throwing his hands up. Giant fireballs dropped from the turrets, surrounding Dad's avatar, a centaur quickly running out of magic arrows.

Pierce aimed his wand at the biggest fireball and encased it in an igloo. Before he could duplicate the trick, two ginormous hawks descended with loud shrieks and grabbed the centaur, flying him out of the castle before the boy wizard could help.

"Sorry, Dad." Sucking in a worried breath, Pierce wondered if he'd get blamed for his father's defeat. The phone rang.

Pierce jumped up, glad to have a reason to get out of swinging distance of his father's hand.

Dad shrugged. "It's just a game."

"Right." Pierce forced a smile, remembering a time when making Dad lose the game had cost Pierce a stinging blow across his chest. He picked up the phone. "Hello?"

"Hi, Pierce. This is Todd West. How's it going?"

"Good." Pierce eyed his father, not sure if it was okay to let him know a West was calling.

"Is it for me?" Dad asked.

Pierce shrugged. "Do you want to talk to my dad?"

"Sure."

"Jus 'sec." Pierce handed over the phone, mouthing, "It's Toran's dad, but I don't know what he wants."

Dad's smile faded. He squashed a growl as Pierce handed over the phone. "Hullo."

Pierce cringed.

His dad narrowed his eyes, then nodded. "An hour?"

For what? An uneasy feeling mixed with hope.

"I'll see if we got plans. If not, I guess we can." His father stood and walked to the kitchen.

Pierce moved out of his way.

"Yeah, you too." As his father pushed the "end" button, Pierce swallowed, hoping that whatever had just happened wouldn't ruin Dad's good mood. "Marsha, where are you?"

The master bedroom door opened. "What's going on?"

"We just got invited for some peach cobbler out at the West farm. Wanna go?"

Mom's eyes brightened considerably, but her tone remained cautious. "If *you* want to."

Pierce held his breath. *Say yes.*

Dad eyed each of them.

Pierce concentrated on keeping a straight face while his insides whooped with excitement.

After turning, Dad walked back to the living room and set the phone on the coffee table. "Those Wests are annoying, but they do know their way around a kitchen."

Yes! Pierce glanced at Mom.

She smiled back.

Pierce concentrated on keeping his voice even. "So, we can go?"

"You wanted to see that hog of yours, didn't you?"

"Sure, Dad."

Dad shrugged. "Fine. Ben can see he's got nothing to worry about and back off. That man's more irritating than a yippy Chihuahua." He dropped into his La-Z-Boy.

"Yeah." Pierce didn't mean it, but his father didn't need to know that.

Anything to keep his dad's fists from flying.

11

THE OWENS'

*T*ires crunched down the lane. Toran peeked up from his hiding place near the front porch. *The Owens'. Good, we've got reinforcements.*

He scanned the front yard. His family had taken up posts all over the front and sides of the redbrick farmhouse playing hide-and-seek.

Uncle Jake was backed against the red-slat woodshed while Tillie and Ginnie worked together to keep him cornered. Each formed a separate ray, simulating a "V" that couldn't make up its mind whether it would be wide or narrow. *He'll go toward Tillie, then dodge between them.*

Sure enough, Uncle Jake did just as Toran predicted and escaped them both.

"Sugar beets!" Ginnie swore, dashing after their uncle since she was "It." Uncle Jake headed toward the garden, which sat between the woodshed and the farmhouse, with Ginnie on his heels.

When Tillie saw the Owens' red car driving down the dirt lane, she gave up chasing Uncle Jake and walked over to Faith, hiding behind Vi's purple VW bug. They blended in with the lineup of the six vehicles stretching across the gravel in front of the farmhouse.

Dad appeared out of nowhere, rushing to herd Uncle Jake back Ginnie's way. Dad was the only one faster than Uncle Jake, though Buzz was a close second.

Between them, Uncle Jake was forced to take his chances with Ginnie—who kick-started her sneakers and tagged him. "Gotcha!" she squealed, high-fiving Dad, and then Buzz. "Score!"

"You do know that I'm not the *only* player, right?" Uncle Jake complained as Ginnie backed away.

"True, but you're a bragger and the most fun to catch," Miss Amanda teased from behind the woodshed.

Miss Clarissa and Mysti giggled beside her.

Uncle Jake made a beeline to Miss Amanda.

Ginnie, Dad, and Buzz moved to intercept.

The bug zapper hanging on the side of the woodshed sizzled a loud ZZT! ZZZZZZZT! It flashed neon purple light while frying its newest victim—by the sounds of it, a larger-than-usual mosquito. ZZZZT!

Toran would have helped intercept his uncle, but his ribs were still sore from the last game of hide-n-seek a few days ago, when he slid into the back bumper of Uncle Jake's tricked-out black truck and slam-dunked onto the gravel.

That was also the day most of the family met Mysti and Miss Clarissa for the first time.

Today, Toran stood outside the fray, enjoying almost one hundred-percent accuracy predicting the others' tactics.

Mysti ran straight to Uncle Jake before her mom could stop her. "I'll be on your team, Daddy!"

"No!" Groans and giggles pealed from the other players. They wouldn't be able to go after Uncle Jake as aggressively with Mysti on his team.

The car came closer. Everyone backed away from it.

Uncle Ben motioned Mr. Owens to an empty space at the end of the line of vehicles.

"Sure, Princess." Uncle Jake offered an evil grin around the playing field and swung her into his arms while approaching their company. "Ray, Marsha, Pierce—jump on in, we're just getting this party started. I'm 'It', but I'll give you time to hide."

Mr. Owens didn't seem happy about the invite.

Mysti kicked out of Uncle Jake's arms and ran back to her mom, who moved a little slower than she had earlier in the game. Uncle Jake knew full well that the rest of them would have to modify their tactics so Mysti would stand half-a-chance at winning.

Uncle Jake is slicker than bacon grease on newly waxed linoleum. Toran grinned as he approached Pierce. "Hey, Pierce. Hello, Mr. and Mrs. Owens."

Pierce grinned back, ready to play.

Various family members shouted their greetings and invites as the Owens exchanged looks of debate.

Vi took hold of Mrs. Owens' hand and led her away.

"Okay, I guess I'll play." Mrs. Owens seemed relieved that Vi made the decision for her.

Dad offered a welcoming handshake to Mr. Owens. "The cobbler's cooling and the ice cream is still freezing. Steer clear of Jake —he's sneaky."

Toran chuckled, remembering the night a couple weeks ago when Uncle Jake had threatened to drop Mr. Owens like a sack of oats when he falsely accused Tillie, Ginnie, and Toran of ganging up on Pierce and blacking his eye.

While it was true that Toran had defended himself from Pierce's attack earlier that day, it turned out that Mr. Owens had been the perpetrator of the fading black, green, and yellow eye Pierce now sported—worsened by a second beating, as they later found out.

Toran's lucky pop with his knee probably didn't contribute all that much to Pierce's garish, rainbow-colored face the night that Mr. Owens accused them.

Toran searched Mr. Owens' face, trying to understand how a dad could punch his own kid—multiple times.

Since Pierce's cheek was still bruised, Toran figured it hadn't been a one-time strike.

He forced the sickening feeling away and smiled for Pierce's benefit. "Yeah, Uncle Jake's fast. Watch out for him."

"Yeah, yeah, yeah. Move it or lose it, buster!" Uncle Jake teased.

Toran grinned and backed up.

Pierce did a chicken dance in front of Uncle Jake, who played along and lunged in response. Pierce danced sideways to avoid being tagged, but Toran suspected his uncle missed his friend on purpose.

Mr. Owens didn't act overly happy about his family being drawn into the game, but he didn't seem to know what to do about it. He slipped his hands into his jean pockets and frowned.

Uncle Jake wiggled his eyebrows. "You've been given fair warning, Ray. Whatcha gonna do about it?"

Looking like a bully on the playground, Mr. Owens narrowed his eyes and cracked a smile. "Bring it on."

It didn't take long for Uncle Jake to tag Mr. Owens. Pierce's large dad moved faster than Toran thought he would and tagged Tillie, whom Toran suspected let him so he didn't feel bad.

Tillie was like that, after all.

The game lasted a few more minutes—until Uncle Ben announced the food was ready. Everyone happily abandoned the game to enjoy a bowl of peach cobbler and French vanilla ice cream.

Pierce wolfed his down and asked to see Hamilton. He led the way to the hog shed. "I can't wait to see him. I bet he missed me."

"Of course he did." Toran walked a little faster to stay in step with Pierce, who was a good five inches taller. "How's it going?"

"Okay, I guess. My dad found a new job a couple days ago. He starts tomorrow. We've been playing Quest for Zyndor a lot, and that's been pretty epic."

Pierce's answer seemed a little too cheerful.

"That's good." Toran's doubt radar turned on. "Since you can't come out here as much as you want, I take extra time with Hamilton for you."

"Thanks." A defensive look crossed Pierce's face and entered his tone. "We've been busy—that's why I haven't been out."

Toran felt bad about causing the look. "No problem. I figured you'd come over when you can."

"Now that Dad has a job, I bet Mom and I can come out more." Pierce opened the gate to the hog pen and waited for Toran to go through.

"Sure. Sounds good."

Hamilton rushed over to them, squealing a greeting. Pierce grinned. "Hey, boy. You miss me?"

Pierce bent to pet the hog. Hamilton squealed again and stood still while Pierce patted him. The boy might not be so good with people, but he rocked with hogs. "What's new here? Any more baby animals? And who's the new kid?"

"No new animals. Mysti is Uncle Jake's and Miss Clarissa's daughter. She's my cousin."

"I didn't know he was married."

"He's not." Toran waited as incredulous understanding lit Pierce's eyes.

"Ohhhhhhhhhhh."

Toran decided to share all of their news. "And my dad took us on a hot air balloon ride and proposed to Miss Amanda."

The bigger boy's jaw dropped. "Geez, I miss a few days and your family goes crazy." He whistled. "Cool. I've never been on a hot air balloon ride. How was it?"

"Epic. The whole world below us was like miniature toys. The cars and trucks were the coolest—until the puddle jumper with the banner asking Miss Amanda to marry Dad showed up. I'm going to learn to fly a plane when I'm old enough."

Pierce laughed. "Your dad really hired a plane to propose? Isn't that kinda unoriginal?"

"Miss Amanda didn't think so. She couldn't stop kissing Dad and hugging on us." Toran picked up the hog next to his cowboy boot and grinned, all the while shaking his head at the memory. "The girls squealed like piglets ... and bounced the balloon with all their happy dancing."

Pierce chuckled and lifted Hamilton, stroking his neck in a thoughtful manner. "You're kinda getting overrun with girls, aren't ya? Two sisters and a wicked stepmom?"

Stiffening, Toran paused before answering. He was pretty sure Pierce didn't mean to be insulting, but Toran didn't like anyone dissing his future stepmom. "Miss Amanda is anything but wicked. Her ex-husband might be, but definitely *not* her."

"Don't get all girly on me. I was just joking." Pierce scratched behind Hamilton's ears. "She seems nice enough. My mom likes her."

"She *is* really nice." Toran set his black-and-white British saddle-back hog down in the pasture. It waddled off toward the trough. "Can you see Miss Amanda actually hurting anyone or making Ginnie miss a fancy ball?" Toran chuckled. "If anybody was gonna lock my sister up, it'd be my dad. He says Ginnie's not dating until she's thirty-seven. I don't think he has anything to worry about, though. She thinks most boys are too dumb to bother with."

Pierce frowned.

"Not be *friends* with. Just to date. Ginnie just wants to ride her horse. She couldn't care less about dances and dressing up."

"Speaking of horses, why is she the only one who has one? Don't you want one?"

Toran considered how to answer. He did want a horse, but he had never wanted one bad enough to risk asking his dad for one. Ginnie got Calliope by dumb luck. "You know my mom died after being thrown by her horse, right?"

"Yeah."

"After her funeral, my dad sold Mama's horse. The guy who bought her saw us at the fair a few years ago and offered the filly—Calliope—to Ginnie. Dad refused to accept Calliope for a long time. Ginnie begged and begged, even crying until she threw up—and Ginnie almost never cries. It really tore my dad up, but eventually he agreed."

When an uncomfortable look crossed Pierce's face, Toran hurried to lighten the mood. "Obviously he agreed—she has the horse—but it's hard for him, so I never asked for my own horse. I think he only agreed to Calliope because she's the daughter of Mama's horse, Eternal Love. He tolerates her, you know?"

Shrugging, Pierce set Hamilton on his feet. "Yeah, but it doesn't seem fair to you."

Toran changed the subject. "I may not have a horse, but I can ride the ATV. You want to?"

"Of course. That's cool. Can I drive?"

"Sure."

"Epic." They finished caring for the hogs and then Toran led the way out of the pasture, stopping by the family room to ask his dad if they could ride the ATV.

All the adults were visiting and finishing their cobbler.

Dad glanced at Mr. Owens. "If it's okay with Pierce's dad *and* you both wear helmets."

"Sure, Dad." Toran turned to Mr. Owens.

"Yeah. Be careful," Mr. Owens agreed in a gruff tone. Toran got the feeling that the "be careful" was Mr. Owens's attempt to sound "dad-like."

Pierce smiled and nodded. "Thanks, Dad."

A softer expression crossed his father's face. "Have fun."

This time, the words seemed almost sincere.

Mrs. Owens offered a tentative smile.

A warm feeling crept across Toran as Pierce's smile brightened.
Pierce nodded and gave an awkward wave.

"Race ya," Toran called as they left the house.

"You're on."

They bolted up the hill to the main barn.

12

RIDING CALLIOPE

Once Pierce and Toran escaped to see Hamilton, Ginnie and Tillie made a beeline to Calliope. Neither girl wanted to hang around while all the adults pretended there was nothing awkward about Pierce's abusive dad eating homemade ice cream and making small talk.

"I'm glad Mom and Vi are being good friends to Mrs. Owens, but *Mr.* Owens gives me the creeps," Tillie said as she and Ginnie entered the pasture where Calliope grazed.

"No kidding." Ginnie offered her horse a carrot, resting the fatter end on her open palm so Calliope couldn't mistake her fingers for more carrots while she chewed. "I know Uncle Ben believes that if you want to change the world for the better, you have to start by fixing your own little corner of it, but, man—I wish he'd make an exception for Pierce's dad."

Tillie nodded. "You can say *that* again."

And Jasper. Ginnie clamped her mouth shut to keep from blurting her last thought. She was in no hurry for Dad to tell Tillie about Jasper's phone call, but she was feeling worse all the time about keeping it a secret from her best friend. *If I have my way, Tillie will NEVER find out.*

How Uncle Ben, Dad, and Miss Amanda were going to make Jasper Taylor okay with giving up his family was beyond Ginnie, and frankly, she was tired of thinking about it. *Time for a diversion.* "Tillie, I'm thinking we need to talk Dad into letting you get a horse. What do you think?"

Tillie grinned. "I'm all for it. What's your plan?"

Ginnie unlatched the pasture gate and walked over to Calliope's saddle, which sat on a post. She pulled it down. Tillie grabbed the saddle blanket. "I don't know. But we figured out how to get our folks to date after Dad said he wouldn't." She shrugged and strode toward Calliope. "So getting you a horse should only take a little creative negotiation. Your mom likes horses, and right now my dad's all about making her happy."

"Very true. I like how you think." Tillie put the saddle blanket on Calliope. "Besides, you need a friend, huh, girl?"

Calliope raised and lowered her head twice, pawing the dirt.

"Then it's settled. Calliope agrees." Ginnie set the saddle on her mare's back. "Let's come up with a list of fool-proof arguments to present to Dad. Horses need friends, just like kids do. And if all else fails, we bring your mom on board as our secret weapon."

Having a stepmom was appealing to Ginnie more and more all the time. "Maybe she can even talk my dad into letting me compete in barrel racing."

"Maybe, but let's focus on getting me a horse first." Tillie led Calliope to the wrought iron chairs next to the side porch door. She handed Ginnie a helmet, then put one on her head and fastened it. "Maybe if we both have horses we can *both* compete. Mom'll help. She's always wanted a horse too."

"You know, Tillie, Miss Amanda should tell Dad that *she* wants a horse." Ginnie mounted, then swiveled to offer a hand to her friend. "Because if your mom gets one, Dad's not gonna say *you* can't have one."

"Duh, why didn't we think of that before?" Tillie slapped her forehead, then climbed onto Calliope's back, settled behind the saddle, and wrapped her arms around Ginnie's waist. "Seriously, that's a brilliant plan. It could work."

"Of course. It *is* brilliant." Ginnie tapped Calliope's sides.

Tillie gave an excited squeeze. "Being sisters for real is gonna be so much fun."

"It sure will." Ginnie agreed, forcing her words to sound confident and enthusiastic.

That is, if Jasper doesn't mess everything up.

13

THE ATV

*I*t didn't take long for Toran to show Pierce how to work the brake and throttle on the ATV's handlebars. "Pierce, drive around the open area between the cars and the hay barn where we played hide-n-seek earlier."

Pierce didn't need to be told twice, only stuttering the ATV to a jerky stop once. "Hop on, Toran. I've got this."

Toran swallowed, eying the bigger boy straddled on the red four-wheeled miniature truck. Its bed was just big enough to haul two bales of hay—or Ginnie and himself, when Dad was feeling so inclined.

Pierce wore a huge grin.

Toran didn't want to say no, but he wasn't sure he wanted to be chauffeured by a beginning driver who had a well-established reputation for having a short fuse.

When the grin dimmed, Toran sucked in a breath and made a decision. "Okay. Scoot up a little." Toran slid behind Pierce, bumping his bright blue helmet lightly against Pierce's black one. "Sorry." Toran scooted against the back of the seat and noted that his shoulders were a good three inches shorter than Pierce's and less muscular.

He slid his arms around Pierce's waist, surprised to find how solid it was. Pierce wasn't fat—just bigger all around. Toran felt even scrawnier when he realized Pierce's back completely hid his own body. He pointed toward the quarter-mile lane. "Go that way, but watch out for cars."

"Sure thing." Pierce gunned the ATV's engine. They took off, jostling and rocking.

The wheels found every rut in the gravel lane. "This is epic!" Pierce yelled.

"Sure is!" Toran yelled back, not having as much faith in his words as he tried to project. He gripped his right hand around his left wrist and hung on, doubting that Pierce would be talked into switching places easily.

A couple of minutes later, they arrived at the end of the lane where it met the main road. Pierce turned too sharply, lifting the right wheels.

Toran leaned right to counterbalance. "Careful."

"That was totally epic!" Pierce replied.

"Yeah, but not so fast around corners."

"I got this—nothing to worry about." The words were barely out of Pierce's mouth before Toran was jerked backward. They flew down the lane toward the two-story red brick farmhouse.

Toran grabbed his wrist harder.

Pierce circled the open space between the cars and the hay barn, careful at first, then made his turns sloppier and tighter until they were doing doughnuts.

Although it didn't surprise Toran to see his dad jogging down the front porch steps toward them, he sucked in a worried breath, knowing a lecture about being more careful was inevitable.

Pierce wasn't real good about receiving such lectures.

He slid the ATV to a stop shortly after blowing past Dad.

Please don't go into full-blown worrywart mode.

Dad seemed to understand Toran's silently broadcast concern. "Good job, Pierce, but I'd appreciate it if you took the corners a little slower, okay? I'm always a little nervous when my kids—or their friends—are on anything that moves—ATVs, horses, bikes, snowmobiles. Nothing personal—it's just how I am."

Pierce whipped his body to face Toran. "You guys have snowmobiles?"

"Yeah. You'll have to come over this winter."

"Epic." Pierce turned toward Dad. "I'm getting the hang of it, but I'll be more careful."

Dad smiled. "Thanks."

"Can we go to Austin's?" Toran asked.

"I'd rather you hang out around here."

Disappointed, but not surprised, Toran nodded. "Okay. How about the outskirts of the corn field? We'll stay out of the crop."

Dad's hesitant gaze scanned the farm's layout.

"The dirt is softer than the rocks," Toran reminded him.

"And muddier—I don't want you stuck."

"We won't get stuck, Dad. I promise." Toran offered the brightest smile he could muster; hoping Ginnie's trick would work for him as well as it often did for his twin.

Dad gave a knowing smirk. "Two laps." His finger circled the area where they had been riding. "Then around here so I know you're fine."

"We're not babies," Toran protested.

"Humor me," Dad replied, his tone holding very little of that quality. "Or find something else to do."

Pierce stiffened.

Embarrassed, Toran gave a quick nod, thankful the helmet hid his warming cheeks.

"And if you go down the lane, only start if there are no cars coming, and turn around before the end. I don't want someone turning into the lane and crashing into you guys."

Oh, man. Pierce is gonna think I'm a wimp.

Toran struggled to keep his tone light. "Sure, Dad. Can we go now, *please?*"

"Yes."

Pierce pushed the throttle and edged forward, following the gravel dirt path up toward the main barn.

"Sorry about that," Toran apologized when they were out of earshot.

He waited for Pierce to make a snide remark about his dad's over-protectiveness.

He didn't. Instead, Pierce shrugged. "That could get old, but at least he cares."

Before Toran could respond, Pierce gunned the throttle, jerked Toran backward, and sped toward the corn field.

14

PIERCE'S THOUGHTS

*P*ierce leaned into the breeze, pushing the throttle as hard as he could, hoping to outrun the dark feelings clouding what could have been a perfect day. He had been so relieved when his father had agreed to come out to the farm.

The day had quickly gotten even better.

Hamilton seemed happy to see him, Toran was turning out to be a really good friend, and Ginnie wasn't even bugging him as much as she usually did.

Though he still couldn't figure out how someone as tiny as she was could drop him—twice.

She must be really lucky. Pierce shrugged, certain that luck had to be the reason. *Nothing else makes sense.*

After seeing Toran's dad make too much of a few ATV doughnuts, Pierce realized his own dad probably wouldn't give two brain cells' worth of thought to Pierce getting hurt.

While being ignored sometimes made Pierce's life easier, it was also nice to know Toran's dad actually cared about whether or not Pierce got hurt.

Quit being a girl! Pierce swallowed hard, then stomped on the accelerator. *My dad at least trusts me to run a man's toy. Toran's dad hovers over us like we're babies.*

Even though the last part of the justification didn't seem completely true, Pierce ignored the underlying thought that plagued him—*My dad doesn't care about hurting me. He only cares if he gets caught.*

Scanning the path ahead, Pierce caught movement in the grass on the left.

He jerked right. A sickening thud popped under the left front wheel.

Pierce jerked the vehicle to an abrupt stop. He forced his gaze to where he had seen movement.

A flailing, fluffy tail swung like a frantic pendulum, and then fell straight down.

Swallowing, Pierce did his best to not see the crumpled body of a brown ground squirrel lying lifeless in the wild grass. Horrified realization splashed over him. The straps from the helmet seemed to strangle him.

He unfastened them and dropped the helmet on the ground.

"It's okay, Pierce," a muffled voice reassured him. Toran reached one hand to Pierce's shoulder while the other unfastened his helmet straps. "The squirrels are everywhere. It wasn't your fault."

Toran set his blue helmet next to Pierce's black one.

Pierce stiffened, the deathly "thud" repeating in his mind.

He shuddered, barely aware that Toran was still speaking.

"And they can be a real nuisance in the garden. They eat the young seedlings. You probably saved our strawberries. People think squirrels are harmless, but they can be really big pests."

"It didn't deserve to die," Pierce spat, shrugging off Toran's grip. "It might be nothing *to you,* but it still has a right to live."

A hurt look crossed Toran's face. "True, but you didn't hit it on purpose. I know you feel bad, but if it helps, it died quickly. I doubt it felt any pain."

Maybe not. Pierce whirled away, not knowing how to voice his jumbled feelings.

The swishing tail haunted him.

Pierce didn't want to feel better about running over the squirrel any more than he wanted his dad to be okay with the fading bruises he caused on Pierce's eye and cheek.

Uncle Ben had talked a lot about "doing the right thing" lately when he chatted with Pierce and his folks about owning their behavior, good and bad.

That advice seemed spot on when it came to Pierce's father needing to realize that hitting Pierce and being mean to his mom were wrong. But now that Pierce had killed a squirrel, accident or not, he didn't want to own the nauseated feeling burrowing into his belly.

Toran's right. It was just an accident. Pierce peeked in the squirrel's direction, then wiped a nervous palm down his jean leg. *But I don't need to feel good about killing it.*

Scowling, Pierce adjusted his helmet. *Wow, Pierce Owens, you are turning into a girl.* Disgusted at his wimpy thoughts, he straightened. "Let's ride. My dad didn't want to stay real long—he's probably had enough of Uncle Ben about now."

Toran ignored the slight. "If it makes you feel better, we can bury the squirrel."

"Why would I want to do that?" Pierce asked, wondering all of a sudden if there was a proper order to such things. The roads were littered with dead squirrel bodies this time of year.

Maybe when squirrels die on somebody's property though, they need to be disposed of.

"We don't have to." Toran shrugged, dropping his gaze and his voice. "I thought it might make you feel better. I can bury it later, after you go home."

"Not so fast." Having a squirrel funeral seemed like a better option than going home. "What's the point? It'll just become fertilizer, won't it?'

"Yeah, but I don't want to see it full of bugs and worms. The sun and rain will help it decompose, but it seems more respectful to bury it." Toran's cheeks pinked. He turned toward the ATV truck. "Let's ride."

"Hold on." A few weeks ago at school, Pierce would have made fun of Toran acting so weak.

But here, on the farm, Pierce was beginning to see life differently.

Toran's sensitivity to the squirrel didn't seem so weak. It seemed right. "Let's bury it. But it doesn't need prayers and songs and everything like at a people funeral, right?"

Pierce recalled his grandpa's funeral where his mom had blubbered and his dad had walked out, completely disgusted with her tears. No way did he want anyone crying over a squirrel—even if he did kill it by accident.

"No prayers and songs. Just a hole—and maybe a good-bye." Toran shook his head and smirked. "But if there's any cobbler left, I could go for refreshments."

Pierce laughed. "Yeah, refreshments are a good idea. Especially since we have to dig the hole."

Toran hitched his thumb over his shoulder toward the tool shed. "Let's get a shovel. If we hurry, there might even be some ice cream."

"Good idea." Pierce picked up his helmet.

An image of the fluttering squirrel tail sickened him. "You can drive."

"Nah, go ahead. It was an accident." Toran glanced around the empty field. "Don't worry—it won't happen again."

"I ain't worried. Like you said, it was an accident," Pierce said defensively, not liking the idea that Toran might think he was afraid. "There can't be two suicidal squirrels around."

Toran mustered a smile, but didn't seem to appreciate Pierce's humor.

He picked up his blue helmet.

Pierce climbed onto the ATV, and waited for Toran to slide onto the seat behind him.

Once he felt Toran's arms circle his waist, Pierce gunned the ATV, preferring the roar of the engine to the noise of his conflicting thoughts.

15

PLAYING HOUSE

*T*illie adjusted behind the saddle and sighed in Ginnie's ear. "Do you think that when our folks get married, Uncle Jake will change his mind about marrying Miss Clarissa? He needs to get over being mad. It's not fair to Mysti."

Calliope cantered them smoothly toward the far end of the *Heart of the Wests* farm along a dirt path bordering their back-fence neighbors' spread.

"Who knows?" Ginnie shrugged, then giggled softly, recalling her cousin's tantrum. "I thought he was gonna blow a gasket when Mysti freaked." Her voice turned serious. "And anyway, I'm not sure I want them to get married. He'd have to move out, and I'd miss him."

Uncle Jake wasn't just Ginnie's uncle—he was her buddy.

Uncle Ben always said the two of them were cut from the same cloth—which she liked—because sometimes Uncle Jake understood her when her own dad didn't.

"No problem. When Vi leaves, he can have her room." Tillie shrugged, bumping Ginnie's back with her shoulder. "And anyways, he's gonna have to move when our folks get married so my mom can move in with your dad."

Ginnie started to protest, but realized just in time that Tillie's suggestion made sense.

Even so, it didn't feel right. "I can't see Daddy sharing that room with anyone but Uncle Jake. They've lived there since they were our age."

"Ginnie, he proposed. They're getting married." Tillie's voice filled with exasperation. "You guys can't move into our apartment 'cause there's no place for Toran. Besides ..." Tillie's arm swept the field. "Your dad works here when he's not driving the truck. It's silly to move."

"Well, Mama and Daddy had their own place. We came every day to help with the farm and care for Mama's horse." Panic coursed through Ginnie as that reality hit her. "Surely Daddy won't want to buy another house. I don't want to leave Calliope. That'd be awful!"

"That *would* be awful. Don't worry," Tillie soothed. "He'll want to stay. This has been his home forever."

"What if Uncle Jake *does* want to marry Miss Clarissa?" The warm breeze swished over Ginnie, spiking her panic. "Where would they live? Dad might think it's better for *us* to move. There are five of us and only three of them."

"No problem." Tillie didn't hesitate. "Mysti could move into your room with us and Miss Clarissa would move into Vi's old room with Uncle Jake."

"Hmm. Too bad Mysti's not a boy ... then Toran could share with her." Ginnie turned to Tillie. "I don't mind sharing with you, but she's seven. She has baby toys."

"Yeah, but somehow I think she'd like makeup and doing hair more than you do. You should let me straighten your hair sometime so we can match. Since you hate your curls—which is crazy." Tillie smirked. "Just saying."

"Braided is fine. Maybe I should color it. I hate blonde jokes. Do you think I'd look better with red hair or brown?"

"Brown, like mine. Then we'd look like sisters."

"You and Mysti look like sisters already." Ginnie rolled her eyes. "Both of you look more like my family than *I* do."

"Yeah, that's kinda weird. But kinda cool as well." A large grin played across Tillie's lips. "I wonder what our baby brother or sister will look like?"

Ginnie pulled Calliope to a stop and swiveled in the saddle. "*What* baby brother or sister? Your mom's not pregnant, *is* she?"

"Of course not. They're not married."

"Neither's Uncle Jake ... but he has Mysti."

"Quit being silly." Tillie mimicked Ginnie's eye roll. "But after they get married, I want them to have a baby, and maybe two or three. I *love* babies."

Ginnie's anxiety ratcheted up double-time.

Dad and Miss Amanda getting married was one thing, but having a baby?

That was something else altogether.

16

THE FUNERAL

*O*nce Toran located the shovel, he closed the tool shed door. He set the shovel in the ATV's mini truck bed, and slipped onto the seat behind Pierce. He held the shovel handle with one hand and slid the other around Pierce's waist.

He braced himself for a quick jerk backward as they plunged forward.

Smooth starts didn't seem to be one of Pierce's talents.

Pierce swiveled toward Toran and yelled over the roar of the engine. "Where are we gonna bury the squirrel?"

"Where it is," Toran yelled again.

"Okay." Pierce drove back to the field, circled the area until he found the squirrel, and pulled up next to it.

Toran hopped off the ATV first.

Pierce seemed to avoid actually looking at the squirrel.

Toran didn't blame him, but living on a farm brought the reality of dead animals regularly into his life. Stumbling upon a dead rabbit, chicken, or lamb still startled Toran, but it didn't bother him like it used to.

The circle of life--and death--had a way of making its rounds.

Just two weeks ago, Toran had found a nest of newly hatched

robins. Last week, their pregnant hog delivered a litter of seven piglets.

A dead squirrel today sorta evened things up, in a sad kind of way.

Pierce snatched the shovel from the truck bed and stabbed it into the dirt. "Where should I dig?"

Toran shrugged. "Right there is good."

"Okay." Pierce shoved the spade with his sneaker and brought up a good-sized mound of dirt. He repeated the process several times, making short work of the chore.

Before Toran could offer to help, he heard the sound of rapidly approaching hoofbeats. He turned, watching Calliope carry Ginnie and Tillie closer.

Ginnie stopped her mare next to Pierce.

"What are you guys up to?" Tillie asked.

"Burying a dead squirrel," Pierce replied.

Tillie's face flipped from happy to horrified in a split second.

Toran might have laughed at her quick expression change, but dead animals really freaked her out. Instead, he nodded at the squirrel hidden behind Pierce's frame. "Don't look over there."

Tillie locked her eyes on his, but Ginnie peeked over Pierce's shoulder. "What happened? Did you just find it?"

Pierce dug with more energy.

"Something like that. We want to bury it before it becomes worm food," Toran said quickly, wanting to spare Pierce from having to admit he was the cause of the squirrel's demise.

"Cool." Ginnie swiveled toward Tillie. "We wanted to know if you guys would like to play Tarzan in the hay barn. We won't be able to once Dad and Uncle Ben fill it with alfalfa bales this week."

"What's Tarzan?" Pierce asked.

"Like it sounds." Ginnie pointed to the weathered gray hay barn across from the farmhouse. "We swing across the hay loft on ropes—you know, like tree vines. It's fun."

Since Toran's ribs ached enough just riding with Pierce, he shook his head. "My ribs couldn't take it. But you can go with them if you want, Pierce. I'll finish up."

"Sounds fun." Pierce's eyes darted toward the squirrel, but didn't linger.

"I've got this." Toran reached for the shovel.

Pierce let go of it.

"Tillie, close your eyes." Toran walked over to the squirrel and slid the shovel under the body and picked it up. He jiggled it a little as he separated it from the grass.

Pierce and Tillie averted their eyes while Toran walked quickly to the hole and slid the squirrel gently into the ground.

A quick glance at Pierce, and Toran realized he had peeked.

Pierce's face paled. A greenish hue colored his face, and it wasn't the fading bruises.

Toran scooped the first shovelful of dirt and trickled it over the squirrel's body.

A second shovelful covered every little bit. "You can look now, Tillie."

Toran tried not to smile as relief swept her face.

A similar expression crossed Pierce's face. The green hue of his cheeks turned to light pink. Toran made quick work of transferring the rest of the dirt back into the hole. He tamped down the dirt. "Done." He smiled at Pierce. "No songs or tears, but I think refreshments are in order."

Pierce nodded, returning a friendly smile.

A few weeks ago, Toran would never have believed that he could be friends with the biggest bully in sixth grade.

Today, it was hard to believe that *Pierce* had been the biggest bully in sixth grade.

Seventh grade was certainly looking up.

Toran and Pierce drove the ATV to the front of the farmhouse. They parked underneath the huge maple shade tree. The girls followed on Calliope and tied her to the antique hitching post installed in the 1850s by their eighth great-grandfather, Obadiah West.

Ginnie slipped the reins through the big ring hanging from the shiny black horseheads mouth and patted Calliope's neck. "We'll be back soon, girl."

The four of them trooped through the hallway and dining room, meeting Dad in the kitchen. He poured the last of a two-liter bottle of root beer over ice cream for their guests. He looked at each tween. "Getting too hot outside?"

Toran brushed his shoulder against his cheek, catching dripping sweat with his blue T-shirt. "Yes. We gave a dead squirrel a proper burial, so now it's time for refreshments. Can we have the leftover cobbler?"

"You could *if* we had any leftover cobbler," Dad teased, scuffling his hair. "How about root beer floats instead?"

"Even better," Pierce said.

"Wash your hands." Dad nodded at the kitchen sink. He lifted a platter with six drinks. "I'll help you in a minute."

"That's okay—we can handle it," Ginnie replied.

"Fair enough. Clean up when you're done." Dad headed for the family room, nearly colliding with Mysti as she rushed to join the bigger kids. "Careful, Mysti."

"Sorry, Uncle Todd."

Toran took a second look at Mysti, still not used to his dad being Mysti's uncle. She had a determined look in her eye. *She's definitely related to Ginnie.*

Mysti frowned. "Can I ride Calliope with you, Ginnie? Daddy said I couldn't play outside 'coz you guys were riding Calliope and the ATV." She threw a disgusted look Uncle Jake's way and stomped her foot. "He thinks you'll run over me. You wouldn't do that, would you?"

"Not on purpose." Toran cleared his throat, trying to cover a laugh.

Her insulted look was too funny. She rolled her eyes and struck a diva pose. "I'm seven—*and-a-half*. I *know* how to watch out for cars."

"The problem is that you're kinda little. Cars and ATVs might not see *you*," Tillie said.

"Cars and ATVs don't have eyes. You're being *silly*."

Pierce laughed. "You're right about that."

Tillie grimaced. "That's not what I meant."

Mysti sidled up next to Ginnie and grabbed her hand. "Will you ride me on Calliope?"

"Can she have a 'please' with that?" Uncle Jake asked, appearing in the kitchen doorway. "And you don't need to be rude to Tillie. Please apologize."

"Cars *don't* have eyes." Mysti scrunched her face, peering at her dad with disgust. "That's true."

"I can take her for a quick ride, Uncle Jake," Ginnie offered, then took a second look at her uncle. His frown made her pause. "I mean, if that's okay with you."

"Maybe if she asks nicely and apologizes to Tillie," Uncle Jake bargained. He arched an eyebrow at Mysti, reminding Toran of his own dad going a round with Ginnie.

He peeked at his sister and coughed a laugh into his fist.

Ginnie smirked.

Toran and Ginnie rarely had "twin telepathy" anymore, but right now, there was no denying that she knew what he was thinking.

And she didn't like being compared to their younger cousin one little bit.

"Okay, I'm *sorry,*" Mysti declared in a rude huff, barely glancing Tillie's way before turning determined eyes to Uncle Jake. "*Now* can I ride?"

"I think we need to have a little chat." Uncle Jake swooped her up into his arms, walking quickly toward the side porch door, calling "Back in a bit" over his shoulder.

"Hey!" Mysti protested. She and Uncle Jake disappeared onto the porch and out the second door before anyone could say a word.

Pierce glanced uncomfortably around the room, clearly worried about Mysti.

Toran pulled out the ice cream and set it next to his friend. "Don't worry—he won't hurt her."

Pierce's gaze darted into the family room, where his parents sat with Dad, Miss Amanda, Uncle Ben, and Miss Clarissa, whose expression mirrored Pierce's.

Then Toran remembered Uncle Jake threatening to flatten Mr.

Owens. "Honest, Pierce, Uncle Jake won't hurt her. Wanna scoop the ice cream? I'll get more root beer."

"Okay."

Ginnie handed Pierce an ice cream scoop.

Toran walked to the extra fridge on the side porch where they kept the soda.

Mysti sat in one of the black wrought iron chairs outside the screened window with Uncle Jake squatting at her eye level, talking quietly to her.

The scene made him wish he'd asked Pierce to come with him.

Relief washed over him, proud of his uncle for being so patient.

He hadn't really doubted Uncle Jake's intentions, but seeing the alarm on Pierce's face made Toran appreciate that he never had to fear his family.

He wished Pierce could have the same reassurance.

17

SAY WHAT?

*O*nce the Owens left and the Wests ate a quick supper, Toran got pressed into service as the night's dishwasher while Ginnie and Tillie dried and put away the clean dishes. Tillie reached a plate to the matching stack in the cupboard in front of her.

"Thanks, Tillie." DT said, intercepting the plate with a playful wink. "Will you please join your mom and me in the family room?"

The green plastic bowl Ginnie was drying, slipped, bouncing twice on the hardwood floor before stopping against DT's boot.

He picked it up and passed it to Toran to rewash, joking, "Didn't know we were playing soccer."

"Sorry." Ginnie licked her lips. "I want to come too."

DT shook his head, spiking panic in Tillie's belly. "Help your brother. We won't be long." He motioned for Tillie to go ahead of him into the family room.

She locked her gaze on Ginnie's, wondering if she should be alarmed.

Sadness filled her friend's eyes, causing worry to mingle with the rising panic.

"Miss Amanda, *I* can come too, *right*?" Ginnie stated more than asked.

Mom turned to DT, raising an eyebrow in question.

DT shrugged. "It's up to you."

When Mom nodded, Toran dried his hands. "Me too."

"Since we're going to be a family, I guess we should act like one." DT backed up and swept a hand toward the family room, ushering Tillie through the archway.

Although these were the people Tillie had wanted for her family forever, being the center of their attention—all at once—unnerved her.

Ginnie leaned toward Tillie. "It's okay. You're not in trouble. When he wants to talk to you in the *living* room, *then* you worry."

"Spoken by one with *lots* of experience," Toran teased.

"You're so funny." Ginnie threw him a smirk. "Not!"

The three kids filed to the couch, each twin sitting as a sentinel on either side of Tillie.

Their presence calmed her. She glanced at Mom, whose face bore a mix of pleasure as she eyed all three of them, and then concern when her gaze rested on Tillie.

Taking a note from Ginnie's playbook, Tillie decided to hurry this along and find out what she *really* wanted to know. "Is this about what happened at lunch?"

Puzzled looks crossed both Mom's and DT's faces until DT's lit with understanding. "No, honey." He sighed. "Well, in a way, but not what you think."

"Way to clear that up, Dad," Ginnie joked.

"Just let him talk, Gin." Toran's scolding tone ratcheted up Tillie's anxiety.

He seldom acted impatient.

DT pressed his lips together. "Enough, you two."

When "Yes, sir," echoed on each side of Tillie, her belly flipped. *If I'm not in trouble, then something's gone wrong.*

"You're still getting married, right?"

"Of course." Mom stepped closer to DT. "But there's been a complication."

"Like what?" Tillie asked.

"Like Jasper." Ginnie threw her arms around Tillie, hugging her too tight. "He wants you back." Fuzzy white noise buzzed in Tillie's head. She barely heard Ginnie's next words. "But Dad promised he won't let it happen, so you don't have to worry. Right, Dad?"

"What?" Icicles pierced Tillie's belly. She bolted out of Ginnie's arms and stood. "Are you serious? Tell me she's joking," Tillie demanded, steeling her gaze first on Mom, and then on DT. "Tell me that it's a *bad* joke!"

Frustration, distress, and then sadness crossed DT's face in quick succession.

It's true.

Tillie burst into tears.

Her worst nightmare had come true.

18

THE NIGHTMARE BEGINS

"Tils, honey, don't cry," Miss Amanda said, reaching to draw Tillie into a hug. "It's okay."

"You *knew*? How could you *not* tell me?" Tillie pushed her mom away. She glared at Dad, then pointed an accusing finger at Toran and Ginnie. "And *you* ... and *you*?"

Each "you" stabbed pain deeper into Ginnie's heart.

After all, it was her job to protect her best friend, and now she'd not only pulled the Band-Aid off Tillie's worst sore, she'd poured salt all over it and stomped on it too.

"It's not what you think, Tillie," Toran said.

"Jasper just wants to get to know you." Miss Amanda tried to hug Tillie again. "He's been sober for a year ..."

"Don't you get it? Jasper's *not* a complication!" Tillie said, waving away the hug. "He's a *nightmare*!"

"Tillie, calm *down*." Dad turned on his "lecture" voice, surprising Tillie into silence. "Please hear us out."

Tillie folded her arms and glared at Dad.

Ginnie almost laughed when she realized Tillie seemed to be transforming into a brunette version of herself. When Dad's eyes narrowed, Ginnie realized he'd come to the same conclusion.

Oops. "Tillie, we *just* found out—last night. Daddy didn't want to ruin our great day. Plus, he wanted to tell you in person." Ginnie gulped, realizing her mistake. "Sorry I messed that up."

"I know you meant well." Dad sighed and led Tillie to the couch. He squatted in front of her. "Please let me take it from here, Gin."

Ginnie nodded. "Yes, sir."

Dad cleared his throat. "Part of the reason I didn't respond right away at lunch was that as much as I wanted to tell you yes, you can call me 'Dad', I realized that will complicate things when Jasper shows up."

"H—He's coming *here*?" Tillie stiffened.

Fear flung off her like ice-cold drops from a water gun.

"We don't know for sure." Dad took Tillie's hand in his. "What we *do* know is he wants to get to know you, and to apologize. Maybe even try to make up for the pain he's caused you and your mom."

"That's *not* gonna happen." Tillie snatched her hand back, glaring past Dad's shoulder. "Because I'm *never* seeing him again. *Ever.*"

"Matilda Grace, settle down," Miss Amanda scolded softly, moving closer. "Todd's just trying to help."

"Well, it's all *your* fault anyway," Tillie fumed. "If you'd never married Jasper in the first place, this wouldn't be a problem."

Ginnie's mouth opened like a tent flap in a windstorm. *Okay, now she's going nutburgers.*

"Enough." Dad wagged his finger at Tillie. "I know you're upset, but let's get something straight right here and *now*. All *three* of you."

Here comes the lecture. Ginnie clamped her jaw shut, knowing better than to interrupt.

Toran sucked in a quick breath.

Tillie's cheeks colored pink and then paled.

Dad let out a quick breath, then squatted again to Tillie's eye level and continued using the "scary-quiet" voice that Ginnie hated even more than his "lecture" voice.

"I *never* allowed Ginnie and Toran to be rude to their mom, and I won't allow *any* of you to treat Amanda rudely either." Dad sent a warning look to Ginnie and Toran before resting it on Tillie. "I mean it. You can be angry, but you aren't going to treat your mom badly."

Tillie dropped her gaze.

Dad lifted her chin. "You're welcome to rethink whether or not you still want to call me 'Dad', but you need to understand that I have every intention of marrying your mom, and that means I expect you to live by the same rules as my kids. Understood?"

Tillie blinked and gave a slight nod. "Yes, sir."

"Thank you." Dad lightened his tone. "Let me make something else clear, Tillie. Without Jasper, I couldn't have *you*, and that would make me very sad. So please give your anger a rest and work with me —and him—so we can make this as easy as possible on all of us."

When Miss Amanda looked at Dad with googly eyes, a warm feeling of "right" showered over Ginnie.

19

FOUNTAIN OF SPEWTH

*D*T gave Tillie's knee a friendly squeeze.

Tillie forced a small smile, seething inside.

"My kids?" Just because I don't want to see Jasper, I'm not one of "his kids" anymore? What happened to me being his daughter? I'm still *second-rate?*

Tillie blinked, willing herself not to cry. *How can he just let Jasper walk into my life like nothing's happened? Oh, man. Mom and I are gonna have to talk.*

Toran jostled Tillie. "Are you okay?"

"Yeah." Tillie continued to smile. Until she figured things out, she didn't need him asking a lot of questions.

Toran returned the gesture.

A tingly light feeling pushed away the gloom that was settling. *Wow, he's cute.* She turned away so he couldn't see her thoughts.

"Don't worry—nobody here will let him hurt you. And I'm your brother now as well as your friend, so I'll make *doubly* sure you're fine."

Tillie let his words soothe her, even though they reminded her of the only drawback to "Operation: Secret Sisters"—the scheme she and Ginnie cooked up to get Mom and DT together.

Being brother and sister instead of being able to date when they were older had been the only flaw in the awesome scheme—at least until just now, when DT shared his not-so-brilliant idea about including Jasper as part of their could-have-been-a-happy family.

This new flaw felt more like a giant crack in a sidewalk.

Her belly flopped just thinking about seeing Jasper.

DT adjusted his position in front of Tillie. "Toran, you're forgetting that Jasper is coming back with the intention of making things better. Why don't we give him the benefit of the doubt that he will do that and try not to think the worst of him?"

"Why should we?" Tillie could hardly keep her voice from vaulting up the panic-o-meter. "He doesn't deserve any benefit. I don't need him or want him. He's been gone for *six years*. He should just *stay* gone!"

DT's blond eyebrows knit together as he frowned. "As much as I want to respect your wishes to pretend he doesn't exist, Tillie, Jasper *does* exist. He has a right to see you ..."

"But what about *my* rights?" Hot tears burned her eyes. "He's the one who left. You said Mom and I are a package deal. How come you're giving me away?"

"I'm *not* giving you away." Hurt swept his face. "Honey, I'm trying to make this easiest on everyone."

"Then tell him to stay away." Tillie folded her arms and glared. "You said you love me. Why would you make me see that creep? Or Mom? You saw what he did to her, and that wasn't the worst!" Tillie shut her eyes, hoping to not remember the last time she'd seen Jasper.

"Tillie!" Mom protested.

Shuddering, Tillie popped her eyes open, this present unpleasantness still being better than that memory.

"She's upset, and rightfully so. She needs time to get used to the idea." DT's understanding tone just made Tillie's panic grow. "It'll be okay."

"Seeing him is *not* okay."

He sighed. "Tillie ... honey. If I could make him go away, I would, but I can't."

"Why not?"

"Because that'll just make things worse. Jasper has a legal right to see you ..." He held his hand up to silence the protests ready to stampede out of her mouth. "You don't have to like that he has rights, but a judge will make sure he sees you if that is what he wants to do."

"Why? He left *me*—I didn't leave *him*!"

"Because he's your dad and he loves you."

Tillie put her hands over her ears. "No, he doesn't."

"Dad, let her hear the message." Toran leaned forward, wrapping a protective arm around her shoulders. "If she hears it from Jasper, she might feel better."

Tillie dropped her hands and locked her eyes on Toran's royal blue ones. "*What* message?"

"Jasper called last night." Ginnie tossed Toran a disgusted look. "I wanted to erase it, but Toran wouldn't let me. Then Dad found out and here we are."

"I thought we agreed that *I* would handle things from here?" DT frowned at Ginnie. "And just how were you going to explain Jasper showing up and telling us he'd left a message—and there was no message?"

"I don't know." Ginnie shrugged. "I had planned to tell him never to call back."

"Which wouldn't have worked—even though it was a nice thought." Mom leaned forward and gave Ginnie's shoulder a quick squeeze. "Thanks for looking out for us, but I'd rather know when Jasper's around than be surprised by him."

"Yes'm." Ginnie glanced at Tillie, making her feel a little better. "She's my best friend and I want to protect her. I want Jasper to go away too."

Tillie grabbed Ginnie's hand and squeezed. "Thanks."

At least SHE has my back. Tillie turned to DT, no longer sure how she felt about him.

She'd spent a lot of time since Jasper left thinking about what it would be like to have a nice dad in general, with DT being the dad in particular.

Having pretended a lot of scenarios at the farm—doing chores with Ginnie and Toran, playing ghost-in-the-graveyard with DT and Uncle Jake, and cooking with Uncle Ben and Vi, having DT talk about Jasper's rights felt very, *very* wrong.

She'd even imagined DT and Jasper arguing about her, but in her mind that always looked like DT fighting *for* her, not handing her over to the enemy.

How could I be so wrong about him? Tillie shuddered, gripping Ginnie's hand tighter. Then she remembered just a few days ago being mad enough to slap Ginnie's back when they were riding Calliope together after her friend had called DT "lame." Tillie had been frustrated that Ginnie didn't appreciate having a great dad like DT when Tillie had to claim Jasper.

"Tillie, I get that you're feeling hurt and scared right now, but it's gonna be okay," DT said.

It's really not.

Ginnie had warned her that DT wasn't perfect, but Tillie had refused to believe it. Now she regretted defending him—after all, it was one thing for him not to keep Jasper away from her, but a whole other thing to invite the creep into her future home.

She turned to Ginnie. "Let's go ride Calliope."

DT shook his head. "Not right now. I know you're in shock, but running away and hiding from the truth isn't going to change it any."

But it'll make me feel better, since YOU obviously don't care. Tillie clenched her jaw shut so the words couldn't escape, her sense of self-preservation kicking in.

One glance at Mom, and Tillie saw that her mother still loved him. *Not* marrying Tillie's new enemy wasn't going to be an option right away. That would take some time.

"Dad, can I turn on the answering machine? I think it'll help," Toran asked again.

DT nodded. "We might as well put all the cards on the table." He offered Tillie a hopeful smile. "We can figure this out together. I promise."

Tillie's heart thudded in her ears.

Toran crossed the room and pushed the "play" button.

It took a few seconds to start. Tillie concentrated on not caring about what she was about to hear.

"U—Uncle Ben? Hey, it's Jasper." Tillie sucked in a breath, wanting to scream, "Turn it off!"

She couldn't. Fear paralyzed her vocal chords.

"Uncle Ben? Aw, man. I really wanted to talk to you. Okay, here's the deal ... today's the one-year anniversary of my sobriety. I want to celebrate by coming home. I know I've been an idiot, but I've gotten help."

Idiot's an understatement. You're a creepy nightmare that I NEVER want to see again.

"Uncle Ben. W—will you help me get my family back? I miss my little girl."

"I'm *NOT his little girl!*" Tillie shouted, panic seizing her heart.

Nausea bounced in her middle, burning its way up her esophagus.

Her arms and legs shook.

DT reached for her.

She only resisted for a second before letting him pull her into a tight hug.

Mom gasped.

Tillie searched for her mother, tears blurring her vision.

"I've really changed this time ... *for good*. I'll do right by them, I swear it ..."

"No, no, no!" Tillie pushed against DT's chest, needing to flee.

Be-e-e-ep!

Her head spun.

The nausea whirled faster.

Tillie clamped her hand tighter over her mouth as she flew toward the bathroom, her supper threatening to beat her to the toilet. She stopped at the kitchen sink and let it spew.

Again and again she heaved, barely feeling Mom pulling her hair out of the way and turning on the faucet to make the puke and bad feelings swirl down the drain into the garbage disposal.

Hot tears mingled with the horror spewing out of her.

Deep, hurtful sobs complicated the business of throwing up.

Supper, and disgust at the idea of Jasper actually becoming a part of her life again, twisted inside, forcing their reality against her need to thrust them back where they belonged—deep inside her where no one could see them—where she could pretend they didn't exist.

"Sweetie, it's okay. Jasper won't hurt you," Mom soothed, smoothing her hair with one hand and rubbing Tillie's back with the other. "It's okay."

Tillie heaved until she couldn't anymore.

The vile smell from the sink burned her nostrils.

"Excuse me." Tillie barely recognized D.T.'s tight voice as he jostled her a little while adjusting the faucet and lowering a cup under the water stream to fill. "Take a sip and rinse your mouth. Then take another sip and swallow."

"I told you it was a bad idea to keep that recording," Ginnie said, disgust staining her words.

"Not now, Gin," DT scolded. "Tillie, breathe slower."

Tillie obeyed before remembering DT couldn't be trusted anymore.

She willed Ginnie to voice her concerns while alternating between breathing and puking.

Ginnie didn't disappoint her. "Now that you all see this is a bad idea, we can forget about Jasper coming, *right*?"

"I said 'not now', Virginia," DT snapped. "I mean it."

Tillie shuddered, not used to hearing him sound cross.

"Todd, Ginnie's just trying to help," Mom quietly pointed out, rubbing Tillie's back faster.

"Maybe, but it's *not* helpful." His voice softened. "Tillie, do you want some more water?"

Unable to speak, Tillie shook her head and blinked away the last of her tears while searching for Ginnie.

Her friend stood just behind DT, gripping the antique blue kitchen bar stool so hard, her knuckles turned white. Ginnie would obey her dad for the moment, but Tillie could tell from the look in her eye that this conversation was far from over.

That gave Tillie the courage she needed.

She took a breath and calmed some.

At least her BFF wouldn't abandon her to the nightmare named Jasper Erasmus Taylor—unlike her mom and future stepdad.

20

THAT NIGHT

The rest of the evening just got worse. The puking stopped, but the fear and anxiety didn't. Tillie spoke as little as possible. Ginnie gave her dad the silent treatment while Toran tried to reassure Tillie that her world wouldn't blow up or end suddenly.

Mom decided it was time to head for home. She took a step toward DT in the dining room and motioned for Tillie to follow. "I have to finish up a project for work."

Although the farm didn't hold its usual soothing magic, Tillie stiffened, not wanting to leave.

DT took Mom in his arms.

She seemed to melt against his chest.

After a couple of minutes, Mom sighed, straightened, and then pulled away.

Before they could separate fully, DT slipped his arms around her again and they lingered over a long kiss.

Joy radiated through Tillie, bubbling out in a big grin before she remembered she was still angry with DT for not kicking Jasper to the curb and making him stay gone.

He caught her eye and winked.

In spite of her frustration, Tillie found herself returning his friendly smile, just like old times.

DT might not be the perfect dream dad anymore, but she couldn't shake how good he made her feel ... or how safe. She turned to say good-bye to Ginnie and Toran.

The five of them trooped from the dining room toward the front door.

DT motioned Mom ahead of him and then followed, holding the door for all of them.

Tillie came next. As she passed through the red screen doorway, panic gripped her belly.

She froze.

Somebody plowed into her.

"Hey, Til, Sorry," Toran said. "I didn't mean to bump you. Are you okay?"

She shook her head. "No."

Paralyzing fear made the word come out in a hoarse whisper.

Mom reached a hand to Tillie's forehead. "What's wrong, honey?"

"I want to stay here." *D.T. may not be so perfect anymore, but he's still better than Jasper—way better.*

Toran and Ginnie came out onto the porch as well.

Uncle Ben joined them from the hallway. "You'll be back in the morning."

Tillie swallowed, forcing herself to confess her fear. "I don't want to go to the apartment. Jasper might show up."

"No, he won't," Mom said, gently squeezing her shoulder. "He'll come to the farm first."

Tillie's anxiety increased. "You don't know that."

Mom frowned. "Tils, Jasper doesn't want to hurt us."

"But he wants you back ... and you're engaged. That's gonna make him mad." Tillie shivered, the nausea from earlier storming back. "He's awful when he's mad."

Ginnie reached an arm around Tillie. "They can stay here until we find out what Jasper wants, right, Dad?"

"We'll be fine," Mom interrupted, shaking her head. "He doesn't know I'm engaged, and if he does show up *there*, we'll call *here*." Mom smoothed Tillie's hair with her fingers, then took Tillie's chin firmly in her hand. "Uncle Ben and Todd can be right over, and I don't think Jasper can get here in a day. Last I heard, he was in California."

"He can fly from California in a day. People do it all the time," Tillie protested.

"You're forgetting that he called asking for Uncle Ben's help." Mom nodded at him. "Jasper wants to make sure he has support before he comes back. We'll be fine."

Panic squeezed Tillie's belly. "No!" DT cleared his throat. "I mean, no, ma'am."

"Your mom is right. Jasper will come here first." DT reached an arm to Tillie. She let him hug her tight. "But if it makes you feel better, you're both welcome to stay. Right, Uncle Ben? The living room couch pulls out, Amanda, and Tillie practically lives in Ginnie's room already."

Uncle Ben nodded. "Certainly. This is your home too. You're always welcome."

"See?" Ginnie grabbed Tillie's hand excitedly and squeezed. "Told ya that you didn't need to worry."

The panic ebbed. "Please, Mom?" Tillie begged.

"*You* can stay if you want. I have to go back to the apartment for my work and clothes." Mom leaned forward to give her a hug. "I'll see you tomorrow after work."

Tillie's heart raced as her voice vaulted. "You have to stay *too*! He might go to the apartment. I don't want him to hurt you."

"He won't." Mom's voice turned firm. "I refuse to live my life afraid of him. I did that for too long. You heard him say he wants us back— he isn't going to mess that up by being ugly. We'll be okay. *Believe that.*"

"I can't. He always hurt you more." Hot tears burned Tillie's eyes. "Just. Stay. *Here.*"

Mom shook her head. "I have spreadsheets all over the place. It would take too long to set it all up here. Besides, I *really* don't think he's going to show tonight."

"Are you sure, hon?" DT nodded at Tillie and took Mom in his arms, wiggling his eyebrows. "I can hang out at your place until you're done and then bring you back."

"That's sweet of you, but no. I need to finish, and you'll just distract me." Mom's firm tone turned to amusement, like she thought such a distraction might be a good idea after all. "This project could mean a raise, but I have you on speed dial. I'll call if I need you." She locked her eyes on Tillie. "But I *won't* need him. Don't worry." She kissed DT and then quickly hugged Tillie, Toran, and Ginnie.

"Dad!" Ginnie protested.

"Miss Amanda should stay," Toran added.

DT glanced at each of them and then followed Mom. "I'll be back after a bit."

"Todd, I'll be fine," Mom insisted.

Tillie glanced at DT, gratitude showering over her.

He shrugged. "I'll just make sure. Uncle Ben, are you okay with keeping the kids?"

"Certainly. Amanda, you're welcome to stay any time," Uncle Ben said.

"Thank you." She gave him a hug. "Maybe another time. Honestly, I'm really not worried about Jasper."

DT offered his arm.

She grimaced and then took it before smiling. "I'm fine, Todd."

"Just making sure."

Tillie blew out a relieved breath, happy Mom wouldn't be going alone.

The familiar joy she felt when seeing Mom and DT together rose within her.

She grinned at Ginnie.

Her friend smiled, then looked past Tillie and frowned.

Tillie followed Ginnie's gaze.

DT gave Mom a quick kiss and waited for her to get in the driver's seat of her car, shut the door, and then headed toward his own.

Frustration and panic battled each other while Tillie struggled to voice a protest.

Too late.

Each of them backed up, turned, and headed down the lane ... in separate cars.

No! The joy surged into panic.

By the time Tillie freed her feet from fear, each car had turned down the lane.

21

GOOD NIGHT ... NOT SO MUCH

illie waited impatiently for her mom and D.T. to return, ignoring Uncle Ben's reassurance that Mom would be fine. Nobody understood that it was Tillie's job to keep Mom safe.

After all, it was her fault Jasper had left in the first place. Of course, Tillie didn't say that out loud. Uncle Ben would just deny it and try to convince her she was wrong, but that didn't make it less true.

Toran, Ginnie, and Uncle Ben kept Tillie busy with board games until bedtime came. Since *both* DT and Mom were gone, Tillie tried not to worry and found herself actually enjoying Sorry! and Chinese checkers.

After Toran and Tillie each won a game of checkers, Uncle Ben suggested they prepare for bed. All three kids grumbled good-naturedly, but put the games away and headed upstairs.

Usually, Tillie liked getting ready for bed at the farm because it meant giggling and whispering with Ginnie under the covers and pretending that she was already part of the family ... for real.

But tonight, an uneasy feeling hung like a shadow over Tillie as she changed into her pajamas, brushed her teeth, and slipped between the satiny emerald-green sheets on Ginnie's full-sized bed.

She enjoyed the initial cool feel of the sheets, knowing it wouldn't last.

The humidity was finally lifting, but the heat of the day still drifted around the second story.

Ginnie and Tillie chatted about Pierce and how to help him.

They discussed Mysti and her situation, and Vi's upcoming wedding. Anything except Jasper and his possible appearance.

Frogs croaked outside.

Tillie heard Bandit and Rascal give chase to something, probably a rabbit. She tried not to think about what would happen if they actually caught it.

Her belly shifted, remembering the dead squirrel and its funeral. She pushed away the icky feeling and listened harder for the front screen door to open and close, hoping to hear Mom's voice. If anybody could convince her mom to change her mind, it would be DT.

When Ginnie's clock read ten-thirty and she still hadn't heard the door open, Tillie's anxiety doubled. *Maybe I just didn't hear them come in.*

She crept out of bed to check.

Ginnie rolled over, but stayed asleep.

Tillie tiptoed to Ginnie's door and stopped.

Years ago, Ginnie and Toran's rooms had been Uncle Ben and Aunt Sadie's master bedroom, but were now two rooms with a wall down the middle to separate them. Ginnie's door opened into Toran's room. Tillie listened until she heard his quiet breathing. *He's asleep.*

She glanced back at Ginnie and then strode ahead, feeling a little weird about being in Toran's room without him actually being aware.

He's your brother now. It's okay.

Tillie swallowed her uneasiness.

She needed to see if Mom and DT had come home.

With Ginnie's room nestled away in Toran's, it was quite possible she didn't hear the squeak of the front door.

When she got to the hallway, she turned left and walked to the window at the end of the hall that faced the lane.

Uncle Ben's white pickup, Uncle Jake's black truck, and Vi's purple VW bug sat in their parking spaces. DT's hunter-green sedan and Buzz's metallic-blue lo-rider truck were still missing.

Tillie spun to face the opposite wall, where Vi's door stood directly across from her at the top of the stairs.

Panic surged as she recalled her kindergarten year when Mom shared Vi's room for two weeks after Jasper hurt them.

She glanced at the door to her left—DT's and Uncle Jake's door.

Tillie smiled, thinking how it would soon be Mom and DT's room.

DT's with Mom. She's fine.

Then she frowned, remembering DT's plan to welcome Jasper into their family, ruining any possibility of Tillie ever being truly happy again. She listened at the door, hoping to hear Uncle Jake moving about. Maybe he could talk some sense into her stepdad-to-be.

Nothing. He must be asleep.

Swiveling, Tillie peeked out the window, not sure if she was happy that DT's car was still missing or if she should be concerned that he stayed late. He and Mom were both morning people—it wasn't like them to still be up.

Maybe Jasper did come and they're talking, or worse ... fighting. Uneasiness turned to fear. *Maybe I should ask Uncle Ben to make sure they're okay.*

Tillie crept as quietly as she could while forming an excuse for being up at this late hour. As she stepped onto the entryway floor and turned toward the dining room, she heard Vi giggle.

Tillie paused, heart pumping loudly, and glanced at the study door to her right. It was slightly ajar.

"Preston's such a great guy, Dad! He scored us tickets to the Land-slide's sold-out concert! He had all of his staff call on their cell phones at the same time and offered anyone who got through a two-hundred-dollar bonus if they would give us the tickets! He actually got through on his own phone, but he was so happy, he told them lunch was on him! He's so amazing!"

Uncle Ben chuckled. "Since I'm allowing him to marry my one and only daughter, I'm happy he's living up to my expectations."

"Dad, sometimes you set your expectations too high," Vi scolded. "But in Preston's case, I'm glad. He's wonderful."

"I think he was worth the wait. I'm sure your mama agrees. Besides, I only want the best for my little girl."

My little girl. The way Uncle Ben said those words showered a sweet warmth over Tillie.

Then she realized no one would ever say that about *her* in the same way. *Ginnie is D.T.'s little girl, and I hate Jasper. I don't care what he says. I'll NEVER be HIS little girl.*

Tillie sighed. *I'll just be D.T.'s second choice instead—that'll have to be good enough.* Shuddering, Tillie fled to the kitchen.

22

UNCLE JAKE

*illie slowed as she rounded the refrigerator, coming to an instant stop when she heard the voice that haunted her.

"—Please, Uncle Ben? Will you help me? It would mean ..." Be-e-e-e-p!

"Stellar timing as usual, Jet!" Something crashed next to the doorway, making Tillie squeal.

She clamped her hand over her mouth and froze, hoping she hadn't been heard.

"Sorry, Turtle." Uncle Jake's body filled the archway to the family room. "Didn't know you were here."

"I—I just got here."

Uncle Jake smiled. "I should start calling you 'Mouse' instead of Turtle—you're too quiet. Though, turtles aren't very loud either."

Tillie concentrated on breathing normally. "Who's Jet?"

"Your dad ... Jasper."

Fury pumped her heart as she snapped her automatic retort to that statement. "He's *not* my dad. Real dads don't hurt their kids. And they don't leave them, either."

"Turtle, stop." Uncle Jake frowned, shaking his head. "I know you think Jasper's the worst man in the world, but he's not." He crossed

91

the kitchen to stand next to her. "That honor should go to his father —who really *was* an evil monster. Jasper may have been a messed-up kid, but he was a pretty decent man."

"No, he wasn't!"

"Yes, he was. I'm conflicted about him too, but he's still coming." Uncle Jake set his hand on her shoulder. "I realize that'll put a clog in the buttermilk, but we need to figure out how to deal with it."

"Easy-cheesy. Make him go away."

"Not so easy. He wants to make things right. You can't kick a man when he's trying to do the right thing."

Tillie smirked. "Let's make an exception."

"Wow, I see Trouble's rubbing off on you." He returned the smirk. "Good for you. I like to see your fighting spirit. But before you continue, figure out what you really want."

"What's that supposed to mean?"

"What I said. Part of you wants Jasper to apologize and try to fix things with you and your mom."

"No way! I *NEVER* want to see him again, *ever!*"

"Maybe, but you still *need* him to fix this."

Hot tears welled in her eyes. "My life was finally getting good. Why does he get to mess it up again? He needs to stay gone."

"Sorry honey, but he's not staying away, so you're going to have to figure out how to deal with him."

Hurt and angry, Tillie swiveled away from him.

He took hold of her wrist, forcing her to stay.

She pulled her forearm. "Let go."

He held tight. "Jasper's not the only one who deals with his problems by running away."

"I'm *not* running away!" Tillie scrunched her nose. "And anyway, this is different."

"Of course it is." Uncle Jake frowned. "He left to protect you from himself. You just don't want to hear anything good about him."

Tillie jerked her arm from his grasp. "That's not true!"

"Yes. It. Is." Uncle Jake gave a firm nod. "As long as you can convince yourself he's a monster, you don't have to deal with the fact that he's just a person who's made mistakes—ones he wants to fix."

"He left me!" Tillie yelled.

"To protect you," Uncle Jake countered.

"Whatever. He shouldn't have hurt us in the first place."

"No, he shouldn't have. But you need to give him credit for all the good things he *did* do for you."

"Like what? He's a loser."

"You don't remember *anything* good about him?" Uncle Jake's eyes widened in surprise. "There was a time when you were very much a daddy's girl. You adored him as much as he adored you."

"That's not true! I *hate* him!"

"Stop saying that!" Uncle Jake insisted, then softened his tone. "I get that you're angry he left, and you're angry he's coming back, but Turtle, you don't really hate him."

"Don't tell me how to feel!"

He blew out a frustrated breath. "You don't have what it takes to truly hate anybody—and I admire that about you."

"You don't .... Wait ..." Tillie stopped, not sure how to protest his compliment. "I never want to see him again."

"Unfortunately, that won't be an option." He winked at her and motioned to the couch. Tillie shook her head. Uncle Jake sighed. "Trust me, I've considered stealing you away to help you out, but it's not really practical."

"Really?" *Now that sounds like a good plan. If Jasper does come back, I don't have to stay.*

"Yeah, but it won't work." He shrugged. "I have to think about my own little girl now. Clarissa has all the legal rights to Mysti. It bites that even though I'm her dad, I can only see Mysti if I keep her mom happy." He rolled his eyes. "On a side note, get married *before* you have a baby ... it makes things easier."

Tillie giggled in spite of herself. "I'll try to remember that. But I'm good with going away with you."

"You're gonna make me regret telling you that, aren't you?" Uncle Jake hugged her. "I told you I was conflicted. Jasper was my friend, practically my brother. Amanda *is* my friend and engaged to my *real* brother. For the first time in years, Todd is truly happy." He lowered his voice. "Queenie's death did a number on him."

"But he seemed happy before he proposed."

"He was, Tillie. He loves being a dad and that was enough to fill the hole Queenie left. But he still missed the companionship of Ginnie's mom."

Tillie bristled. "He's friends with *my* mom!"

"I know, Turtle. Todd's good at being married. It was a huge part of him, and why he resisted dating until you and Ginnie nudged him along." He laughed as he shook his head. "Shoot, *I* told him to date Amanda a long time ago, but he'd made up his mind not to date anybody until Ginnie and Toran were grown."

"Why?"

"He wanted them to be mothered by someone who truly loved them. Like our mom and Aunt Sadie did for the two of us after we were orphaned." Uncle Jake swept his hand toward the last family portrait he'd taken with his parents above the mantle. "My mom and Aunt Sadie rocked the 'mom' thing, and Todd wanted that for his kids. Queenie was also a great mom. He didn't think she could be replaced—not that Amanda's trying to replace her. He shrugged. "It's complicated."

"I'm sorry she died," Tillie said, straightening protectively. "But *my* mom's cool and she's a good mom—even though Ginnie doesn't really want a new mom."

"I agree. Amanda's great. Ginnie loves her, Turtle. She's fine with them getting married." He shook his head quickly, like he was hoping the right words would somehow pop out his mouth. "You have the opposite issue. You want a decent dad, and Todd has stepped up for you. But now your real dad is staking a claim ..."

Tillie stiffened.

"Like I said, it's complicated. Unfortunately, my brother has fallen in love with the same woman my used-to-be-best-friend still loves. More complications. You know Todd loves you very much, don't you?"

Tillie shrugged, happy to hear it even though she wouldn't let herself believe it. "It'd show better if he would Jasper disappear for good."

"Could you change the music, Turtle? I swear you're starting to sound like Jasper."

"I'm *nothing* like him!" Tillie spun around and headed for the kitchen, done with this conversation.

Uncle Jake caught up and blocked her way to the dining room.

Tillie leaned both ways to look around him.

He followed her movements, scolding. "Could you please quit feeling sorry for yourself and hear me out?"

Deeply offended, Tillie crossed her arms and glared.

The screen door creaked open. *Mom. She'll make Uncle Jake back off.*

The study door swung open. "Welcome home, cuz," Vi greeted in a teasing tone. "It's a little late to be coming in from a date, isn't it, Todd Benjamin? People might talk."

"Let them. Amanda and I are engaged," DT retorted playfully. "And I *really* like saying that. Amanda is wonderful."

I really like hearing it. Tillie glanced at Uncle Jake. *You can move now.*

"Where's Amanda?" Uncle Ben asked.

"She insisted she'd be all right. She got her presentation done and was heading to bed when I left."

"I'm sure she'll be fine," Uncle Ben agreed.

Tillie pushed past Uncle Jake and ran to the hallway.

"You just *left* her? You're supposed to keep her safe." Tillie glared at DT, burst into tears, and bolted for the front door. "I can't trust *anybody* anymore."

23

NOT SO FAST ...

old up!" DT reached an arm around Tillie's middle as she tried to rush past him. "What's going on?"

"If you aren't going to keep my mom safe, I don't want you to marry her," Tillie insisted, trying unsuccessfully to wriggle free of his grasp. "I want to go home."

"Hang on," DT insisted. "First of all, why are you still up?"

"I was waiting for you to bring my mom back, *but you just left her.*" Tillie wiped at her cheeks defiantly. "You said you love her."

"I *do* love her. She's fine."

"How do you know?" Tillie waved her hand at the door. "You just left her—all by herself!"

"*After* listening for her to dead-bolt the front door and *after* I made sure her back door and all of her windows were locked. I even checked your closet."

"Oh." Warmth spread across Tillie's cheeks.

"I drove down the streets by her house and made sure there were no unfamiliar cars. I circled back and walked around the apartment building, checking the bushes in case Jasper was lurking around. He's *not.* I feel pretty confident about that or I would've stayed."

As DT's list of protective measures lengthened, Tillie's anxieties ebbed. "Double-oh. Sorry."

He loosened his grip. "Are you okay?"

"I don't know. Mom shouldn't be alone."

"I love her, honey. I promise I'll keep her safe." DT lifted Tillie's chin and looked her in the eye. "I told her if we don't hear from Jasper soon, I'd like you two to move in until we do. She protested, but she *agreed*, okay?"

Tillie nodded. "Okay."

"*Sweet!* Slumber party time," Vi teased, squeezing Tillie into a hug. "Twenty-four-seven G.N.O."

Uncle Jake rolled his eyes. "Girls!"

"Gotta love 'em." DT winked at Tillie.

She smiled at him and then turned to Vi. "We can still have 'Girls Night Out'? Even when you get married?"

"Of course, girlfriend." Vi swished her finger at each man. "These three can play with Preston, Toran, and Buzz, while you, Ginnie, Amanda, and I can G-N-O."

"Cool." That was good news. Since they were best friends, Mom and Vi always planned a fun night at least once a month and took Ginnie and Tillie out with them.

Uncle Jake elbowed DT and joked. "At least we're not outnumbered ... *and* we get a cool new playmate."

"You're forgetting about Miss Clarissa and Mysti." Tillie pointed out. "We're even. Six boys, six girls."

"Yes! The West women have *never* outnumbered the West men before. We're almost there." Vi hi-fived Tillie. "Score!"

"Hey, not so fast. Clarissa and I aren't getting married—at least, not any time soon," Uncle Jake protested. "Besides, she's a Lawson, so she doesn't count."

"Potatoes, pa-*tah*-toes." Vi waved away his protest. "Buzz and Faith are getting serious, so we *may* actually *outnumber* you soon."

"Since when did dating become a competition?" Uncle Jake asked, swiveling to Uncle Ben. "And now that she mentioned it, where is young Buzz? What happened to being in by eleven?"

"He's twenty-one. He gets till midnight."

"That's not what you said when *I* was twenty-one."

"*You* were incorrigible and in the Army," Uncle Ben reminded him with a grin. "Besides, Buzz is hanging out with Faith and her folks. They're in good hands."

Uncle Jake smirked. "You're getting soft in your old age. You just won't admit it."

"Hey, watch your mouth." DT backhanded his brother's chest lightly. "You're being a bad influence on my kid. Speaking of which, Tillie, you should be in bed."

Tillie giggled at the exchange and nodded. "Yes, sir."

She didn't even mind being "his kid" again.

She walked into his open arms and let him hug her tight.

"Your mom's fine. I promise."

Tillie really wanted to believe him.

He kissed the top of her head. "I'll walk you up if you want. I like to know my kids are safe in their beds before I go to bed myself."

"Okay." She gave a quick hug to Vi, Uncle Ben, and Uncle Jake before starting up the runner on the stairs.

"Night, guys. See you in the morning." DT waved and followed. "You can call your mom first thing in the morning. She wanted me to tell you good night for her—not that I expected to see you awake again tonight."

"Thanks. When do you think Jasper will be here?"

"I don't know." He slipped an arm around her shoulders. "It depends on what travel arrangements he's made, and that will depend on how much money he has. He's not big on planes, so I suspect he'll drive or take a bus. So that's at least two or three days."

Tillie stopped outside the door and faced her future stepdad. "Are you really going to make me see him?"

He sighed and lowered himself to her eye level. "I'd rather not *make* you do anything. I think seeing Jasper again will go better if you could be more open to the idea."

"But do I *have* to?" She searched his face for a "no".

For the second time that day, he disappointed her deeply. He nodded. "If you don't meet with him willingly, he can get a court order. A judge will force us to take you to neutral ground—probably in the Children and Family Services building. I *really* think both of you would do better here at the farm. Uncle Ben has a way with Jasper. He's the dad Jasper wished he'd had, but didn't."

Tillie understood that. Until this afternoon that's how she felt about DT, and she knew Mom considered Uncle Ben a bonus dad for herself.

"If you insist on *not* seeing him, we can try to reason with him. Just don't be surprised if it gets ugly quick. Once he finds out your mom and I are engaged, he'll either back off or dig in ... and I doubt he'll back off."

"Yeah, me too." Tillie shuddered as she imagined being as close to Jasper as she stood to DT. "Do you think Uncle Ben could talk him into leaving me alone?"

He shook his head. "He's good, but he's not a miracle worker."

"Can't *you* make him stay away?"

"I'm going to be the last person he listens to when he finds out I intend to marry your mom. He loved her very much. You too. He can't force her to love him, but he *can* insist on visitation with you."

Tillie's knees wobbled. "He can't get custody of me, can he?"

"Not custody." DT tilted her chin up. "I called the lawyer I used to fight my father-in-law for custody of my kids. He says if Jasper can prove he's made great strides in becoming sober and responsible, he has a good shot of getting at least supervised visitation."

Knowing he talked to a lawyer for her, made her feel better. Then she remembered how long he had been gone. "But he hasn't seen me in almost six years," Tillie protested. "That's not very responsible."

"No, but he's been pretty consistent about sending child support since he left. He hasn't missed many months, he's paid it straight for almost two years, and extra for the last year. If he can prove he's been sober for a year like he says, that will also work in his favor. And even though he hasn't seen you, he's kept in touch, at least sporadically with your mom and Uncle Ben and Jake."

"Why is it all about him?" Tillie backed away from DT's words, bumping into the doorframe. "I shouldn't have to see him if I don't want to. He hurt me, *remember*?"

"Yes, I do." He brushed her hair out of her face. "I also remember him searching high and low for a special baby doll you loved that got left at a picnic spot. He drove almost an hour to find it because he knew how much you loved it. And how you'd sing along with him to preschool songs and you'd both laugh at a silly frog sound he'd make. You would giggle until tears rolled down your cheeks." He stroked her cheek gently with his thumb. "He loves you, Tillie, and I think part of you still loves him."

"Not anymore," Tillie whispered, shaking her head. "He could've come back years ago. Why didn't he?"

"You'll have to ask *him* that."

A solution to the whole mess crystalized.

"What if you and Mom got married tomorrow and you adopted me? Then I could see him and I wouldn't worry so much. He couldn't mess up our new family."

"Oh, sweetie." DT hugged her tight for a minute before looking her in the eye. "I *could* marry your mom tomorrow, but I can't adopt you without Jasper's permission. Even if he were to say yes, adoptions take months to finalize."

"Oh." She dropped her gaze to his knees.

He lifted her chin. "You know, Tillie, I keep thinking that if you'll give Jasper half-a-chance, he might surprise you—in a good way. Jasper has overcome a lot of horrible things in his life, things nobody should ever have to go through. He made some mistakes, but he's really not a horrible guy."

Tillie shrugged away his compassion. "The last thing he did before he left was throw a vase at my mom." Tears welled. "I couldn't stop him. I wanted to, but I couldn't. I was too afraid of him."

His eyes widened as her tears overflowed.

"You were *five*. It wasn't your job to make him behave. He knows that." DT wiped the tears with his thumb. "Maybe we should see what Jasper's made of himself before judging him for the past. If he has gotten the help he said he did, you may be worrying for nothing."

"But what if he hasn't?"

"Then we'll take legal steps to protect you in addition to never leaving you alone with him. But I really think it would be better if he visits with you here—Uncle Ben, Jake, your mom, me—we all love you and want what's best for both of you."

"But I don't want *him*."

"That's what you say tonight. If he's changed for the better, you may feel differently. He really was a decent guy most of the time."

Tillie shook her head. "That's not what I remember."

"I know. But I remember he wanted to be a good dad to you." DT hugged her tight. "He and I talked about that several times before he left. His message mentions he wants to be a good dad. If that's his priority, and it sounds like it is--his coming back could be a good thing. If it's not, we'll make sure you are safe."

Tillie hiccupped, torn between compassion at his reasoning and anger at her memories. "*You* wouldn't have hurt us in the first place."

"No, but I think he's punished himself quite a bit by staying away from two of the greatest people I know and love—you and your mom. I couldn't have done that."

Tillie shrugged, unsure how to respond.

"I keep remembering him telling me that the best decision he ever made was marrying your mom. Since that's a decision I've made as well, I feel for him because I know he was right."

He slid up the other door frame and straightened. "I love your mom, and I love *you*. Think about this—Jasper has worked for six years to get to a place in his life that he feels worthy enough to take a chance on asking for your mom and your forgiveness so he can put his family back together." He sighed. "Part of me wants to let him."

Tillie swallowed hard, panic piercing her heart.

"The bigger, *selfish* part of me wants you and Amanda—no matter what."

"That's not selfish." Tillie locked her eyes on his. "That's what *we* want."

"It *feels* selfish." He paused, and then his voice took on a hard edge. "Jasper never had *anything*. His dad was an atrocious excuse for a human being and his mom wasn't much better." DT clamped his mouth shut.

Tillie sucked in a concerned breath.

"Honey." DT's voice and expression softened.

He motioned her toward Ginnie's door and followed her to the full-sized bed. "My folks died, but I got to live with Uncle Ben and Aunt Sadie, who took really good care of Jake and me. Jasper used to wish his folks would die so he could stay at the farm. That's pretty sad."

"They were *that* bad?" Tillie shuddered, trying to consider how awful Mom would have to be to wish her away like that. Tillie couldn't even imagine such a thought.

He nodded. "I think we owe him a little compassion. He's losing you guys to somebody who's supposed to be his friend—and more than that. At one time, we were like brothers." DT lifted the comforter and waited for Tillie to slide in. "And believe it or not, Jasper was less annoying than Jake can be at times.

Although his voice had a teasing tone, Tillie got the feeling that DT meant what he said.

He must really like Jasper. Or at least he used to. Not knowing how to respond, Tillie adjusted on the pillow.

The soft, cool sheets welcomed her as DT laid the covers over her. He kissed her forehead. "Good night, Tillie. Pleasant dreams."

"Night. You too."

He walked around the bed, adjusted Ginnie's covers, and kissed her forehead as well, whispering, "Pleasant dreams, Gin." He straightened. "See you in the morning, girls."

Tillie waited for him to cross the room and close the door before she let the many thoughts tumbling around in her head free fall where they may.

She tried to picture the kind Jasper that DT described, but drifted to the most familiar and often-played memory she had of him, the one she always tried to forget.

Tillie was almost six and stood in the hallway, out of Jasper's line of vision, while he and Mom argued in their bedroom.

"Jasper, calm down. I've got a job. We'll manage."

Jasper shook his fist. "It's not supposed to be like this."

The anger in his voice made Tillie's belly tremble. She put her hands over her ears to muffle the words, but she couldn't take her eyes off her mom. *Please don't hurt her.*

Mom had reached a comforting hand to Jasper, but he raised his own and pushed hers away. The tremble in Tillie's belly radiated over her whole body.

"Jasper, let me help," Mom begged.

He turned back to her, hand raised.

Tillie ran forward. "Don't hurt Mommy!"

"I'm ..." Jasper stopped and glared.

Tillie grabbed Mom's leg and buried her face in Mom's jeans. She'd done it now. He would hurt *both* of them. Jasper jerked her away from Mom. "Tilda, look at me."

Tillie scrunched her eyes closed and tried to move her shoulder to protect her face.

"Tillie, I didn't hurt her. *Look* at me."

But she couldn't look at him. She just couldn't.

"Daddy wasn't going to hurt me." Mom's quiet voice said. "He promised to stop. It's okay."

Tillie shook her head and scrunched her eyes shut harder. He'd promised to stop hurting Mom many times, but he never kept that promise.

"My own kid doesn't ..." Jasper grabbed Tillie's arms. He squeezed her arms and shook her once.

"Jasper, don't!"

He let go. Tillie stumbled backward.

"Jasper, she didn't mean ..."

Tillie opened her eyes in time to see Jasper pick up a vase and throw it against the wall behind Mom.

Tillie screamed as it crashed into a million pieces.

He pointed a finger at Tillie and then opened his mouth.

No words came out.

He grabbed his jacket off the bed and shook his head. "I'm done."

Tillie latched onto Mom's leg as he rushed past them.

Mom tried to follow him.

Tillie grabbed harder and burst into tears.

"Tils, it's okay. Jasper! Come back."

The front door slammed so hard, it bounced back open.

Tillie shivered, glanced around Ginnie's room, and rubbed her arms to smooth the goose bumps dotting them.

24

AUNT RONI RETURNS

 nock, knock," a cheery voice called out from below.

Ginnie rounded the banister of the second floor and jogged down the stairway. Her riding boots tapped the red runner down the middle of the wooden steps in quick succession.

Glancing straight ahead, she took a closer look at the guest standing on the other side of the front screen door. Curly platinum-blonde hair framed a familiar face. *Mama!* Ginnie's heart pounded. *No, wait.* She hastened her steps as a grin crossed her face. "Aunt Roni!"

"Hi, sugar." Her aunt's soft Southern accent dripped over Ginnie like warm pancake syrup.

Aunt Roni backed up.

Ginnie blasted through the screen door. "I thought you wouldn't be back until Vi's wedding!" She wrapped her arms around her mom's identical twin, enjoying the floral scent of her perfume. "Mmm, you smell nice."

"Why thank you, sugar." Aunt Roni pulled Ginnie into a tighter hug. "I couldn't stay away. My husband and daughters are stuck in England for a few more days." She tickled Ginnie's forehead with a kiss. "You and Toran are the miracle tonic I've been praying for! Your granddaddy looked at the pictures I took of you two when I was here last and started getting better immediately. I put them in a digital frame. He stares at it constantly."

That news creeped Ginnie out a little. She hadn't resolved her conflicting feelings about Cabot Stratton.

Granted, she didn't know very much about her mother's father, but what she *did* know, she didn't like.

Cabot Stratton had disowned Mama after she married Dad and spent over four years refusing to make amends—even after she and Toran had been born.

Finally, Cabot and Mama had called a truce and made plans for Mama, Daddy, Toran, and herself to make a trip to South Carolina. Mama had wanted to introduce her children to the father she loved fiercely, even though he was too pigheaded to realize that Daddy had been the perfect husband for his daughter.

Unfortunately, Mama died three days before the trip and Cabot Stratton had to come to Ohio for Mama's funeral instead.

That hadn't turned out so well.

So fast forward eight-and-a-half years to today. Daddy had no use for Cabot Stratton, Aunt Roni still adored him, and Ginnie tried not to think about him.

"You two look so much like Widget that even my dad's breath caught when he saw the picture of you on Calliope—sitting in the saddle he'd had custom made for your mama's fourteenth birthday." Aunt Roni squeezed her tighter. "You have her same impish smile."

Ginnie frowned.

She didn't want to be the salve for the man who had caused her parents so much unnecessary pain.

"After he realized he wasn't seeing the ghost of my sister, something happened to him." Aunt Roni lowered her voice. "I don't know how to describe it. He saw your picture and I think he realized how much he'd truly lost over the last eight years. He started crying."

Ginnie locked her gaze on her aunt's face. "No way."

To hear Dad tell it, Cabot Stratton was made of unbending steel and void of all kindness. Well, maybe not void—but definitely lacking.

For whatever reason, though, Cabot's twin daughters were willing to go to great lengths to please him. Ginnie remembered just in time that for all of her grandfather's faults, Mama and Aunt Roni loved him very much. She softened her look of disbelief.

"I haven't seen him cry so broken-heartedly since your mama passed. Only this time, when his sad tears stopped, healing tears started flowing. He just kept staring at your picture." Aunt Roni loosened her grip. "Seeing you look so much like the Ginnie he lost ... well, he regrets even more deeply that he cut off my sister and her family. He'd like to apologize to you, your daddy, and your brother, and build a few bridges ... if you'd allow him. He would've come with me, but he's too weak to travel."

Conflicting emotions clogged Ginnie's airway, stifling her protests. She wasn't sure she ever wanted to meet the grandfather who disowned her mother. Because Cabot Stratton made her dad feel so angry and vulnerable, Dad took away Mama's journals after Ginnie found them a month ago.

Dad didn't want Ginnie to ask him about her mother's family.

"He has *you*, and you have to look more like Mama than I do. After all, you two were identical twins." Ginnie was still getting used to the knowledge that Mama had been a twin *and* had also been called "Ginnie" all her life—that is, until Dad had nicknamed her "Queenie" while they dated. Dad said it was because she'd been a nationally ranked beauty queen who owned hundreds of sashes imprinted with assorted titles of "queen" on them.

Ginnie suspected Mama allowed the nickname to stick because Daddy had also called her mother the "queen of my heart." Mama had teased about Daddy being a bit "corny, but a sweet, romantic at heart" in the baby journal where she had recorded Ginnie's first year of life.

That was the only journal Dad had let her keep.

Aunt Roni shook her head. "Our parents, some of the ranch hands, and a couple of our teachers could tell us apart without much effort, but most people couldn't. Your dad was also an exception to that rule. We didn't look alike to him." She sighed before brightening her voice and her smile. "We looked as much alike to *our* dad as you and Toran look to *your* dad. But *you* are the spitting image of her."

That makes no sense. Ginnie scrunched her nose, trying to figure out how she could possibly look more like her mom than Aunt Roni.

"You have Ginnie's .... I mean, *Widget's* personality— as well as her looks. It shines through in your pictures." Aunt Roni offered an awkward laugh. "I'm still getting used to her being 'Queenie' to all of you. When your dad got a court order for us to break off contact with you, I went back to thinking of her as 'Ginnie' or 'Widget'."

Ginnie sucked in a defensive breath for her dad, then realized that Aunt Roni was stating a fact, not making an accusation. "That's okay. I'm still getting used to you even existing. And you and Mama looked just alike in that album you showed me of when you two were little."

"I understand. It's like when a cat gives birth to a litter of solid black kittens. They all look alike to people who don't interact with them. But if you pay attention, their individual quirks and personalities distinguish them from one another. Otherwise, they're just look-alike kittens."

That made sense.

"I think it was 'Opposite Day' in heaven when Toran and I got paired up." Ginnie grinned at her aunt. "*He* says it was 'Be Your Sister's Keeper Day,' but that's because he helps me out when I get in trouble."

Aunt Roni laughed. "I think you're *both* right. Your mama and I may have looked alike, but personality-wise, we were polar opposites. I helped her into—and out of—a lot of trouble. She helped me as well."

"Do you think we'll ever stop missing her?"

The twinkle in her aunt's eye faded with sadness.

"No," Aunt Roni whispered, hugging Ginnie tighter. "But reconnecting with you and Toran has certainly made it easier." Her aunt slid her hands onto Ginnie's cheeks and squeezed, mustering a pleasant smile. "Where's your dad? I should let him know I'm here."

"He's baling hay with Uncle Ben, Uncle Jake, and Buzz. Vi will be home until lunch time, and Mysti just got here."

"Sounds busy. I guess that's to be expected, living on a farm." Chuckling, Aunt Roni looked around. "So tell me what's going on in *your* life. I know you guys are busy, but a nice benefit about country living is that there isn't so much drama."

"Wanna bet?" Ginnie straightened, toggling her head in a teasing manner. "Daddy took us on a hot air balloon ride and asked Miss Amanda to marry him."

"Already?"

Brightening her smile, Ginnie nodded. "That was cool and all, but after he proposed, Tillie's birth dad called Uncle Ben and told him that he has gotten sober—and that he wants to get Tillie and her mom back. Like I'd let *that* happen." Ginnie made air quotes with her fingers. "Tillie was so upset at the news that she puked."

Aunt Roni's eyes grew as big as jumbo-sized eggs.

"And Pierce—the biggest bully in seventh grade—wants to move in, 'cause his dad's a bigger jerk than Tillie's." Ginnie gave an exaggerated eye roll and grimaced. "So you're right. *No* drama."

Aunt Roni took in a startled breath. "Oh, my land! Sounds like y'all got more trouble here than a long-tailed cat in a room full of rocking chairs!"

"You can say that again."

25

LASER TAG

*P*ierce could scarcely contain his excitement as he and his mom drove down the crunchy dirt-and-gravel lane leading to the West farm. His dad started his new job that morning and Pierce was staying at the farm while his mom ran errands.

His dad had even suggested that they might get to play laser tag when he got his first paycheck. Pierce was planning to ask Toran and his dad if they wanted to go.

Maybe Uncle Jake and Ginnie would be fun opponents as well. Now that he and Ginnie were "friends," he couldn't very well knock her down, but it wouldn't be wrong to annihilate her a few times with a laser gun.

They parked in front of the farmhouse.

Toran sat with Mysti and Tillie in the shade of the toolshed, playing with the kittens.

Pierce opened the door before his mother could turn off the ignition switch. "See ya, Mom."

"Hold on. Remember that Uncle Ben and the rest of the men are in the field, so be nice to Vi. I'll be back soon. I love you, Pierce."

"I want to play with the animals. Don't hurry."

Mom laughed. "I'll try not to."

Pierce took a second look at her, happy to hear her laugh. "You know what I mean." He smiled at her and slammed the car door, halfway to the kittens before he heard, "I love you, Pierce."

"You too." He dropped onto the grass next to Toran.

Tillie handed him Cinnamon--the orange, black, and white calico kitten that Pierce wanted to talk his dad into taking home. "Thanks."

"You're welcome." Tillie's kind smile sent a warm pulse through him. He buried his face in the kitten's side.

Cinnamon meowed. "Don't squish her, Pierce," Mysti squealed.

"I'm not, Pipsqueak. She's just really soft." Pierce exchanged amused looks with Toran.

"I'm not a peepsqueak." Mysti rolled her eyes, pointing her own calico kitten, Sushi, at him. "It's not nice to call names."

"That's *pip*squeak, and he meant it as a term of endearment," Toran said.

"Huh?" Mysti's face scrunched in confusion. "What's a deer got to do with it?"

"Ya know." Pierce leaned back to let Cinnamon crawl up his red T-shirt. "You *do* talk like a dictionary sometimes."

"I'm good at English. So sue me. Speaking of suing, did you know my mom was studying to be a lawyer?" Toran turned to Mysti. "Endearment is a *good* thing."

It was Pierce's turn to be confused. "I thought your mom was a beauty queen."

"She was. Turns out she was smart as well as beautiful."

"Impressive." Pierce rolled his eyes, unimpressed. He pulled Cinnamon off his shoulder and put her back on her belly. The side porch door slammed. Pierce turned toward the sound of giggles.

Ginnie, Vi, and some woman with long, blonde, curly hair stood laughing with his mom by the black wrought iron chairs.

"Wow! Who's that hot lady?" Pierce whistled, swiveling toward Toran expectantly. "She's gorgeous!"

"My mom's identical twin sister," Toran replied with a smirk. "Put your eyes back in your head."

"For real?" Pierce backhanded Toran's chest lightly. "You've been holding out on me."

"Like I'm gonna set you up with my aunt." Toran returned the backhand. "Get real. You're a kid."

"You said identical twin?"

"Yeah, so?"

"That's what your mom would look like?"

Toran nodded. "And she was *smart*, too."

"Wow." Pierce sat back, thinking.

Ginnie looks an awful lot like her aunt already. Maybe I'll have to rethink annihilating her at laser tag.

26

BATTLE SHIP

G ood girl, Calliope!" Ginnie whispered, stroking her mare's neck. "She did it perfect that time, huh, Aunt Roni? Wasn't she awesome?"

Calliope had been responding well to the "quiet hand" and leg pressure cues Aunt Roni had shown them.

"She was, because she has a wonderful rider. She knows you love her." Aunt Roni patted Ginnie's denimed shin and then stroked Calliope's neck. "I think the two of you make a great team. You're both naturals."

"You *are* looking good, though, Gin, you need to straighten your lower back a little," Dad's voice agreed.

Ginnie jerked her head toward his voice. He came around the chicken coop and walked to the middle of the pasture, where he joined Aunt Roni, Tillie, and herself.

She grinned at him until she saw him narrow his eyes at her aunt. "Ginnie's not allowed to compete. Why are you teaching her the ins and outs of western pleasure riding?"

Disappointment shuddered through Ginnie.

She had planned to show off Calliope's new skills on her own timeline, not her dad's.

Tillie's mouth opened to a worried "O".

Aunt Roni shrugged. "It's called a 'discipline' for a reason. Ginnie doesn't have to compete to benefit. How many people take years of martial arts because they are planning to fight a ninja?" The easy confidence in her tone brightened Ginnie's spirits.

Dad looked like he wanted to argue, but the soft, Southern-accented reply seemed to turn away his anger.

Ginnie exchanged hopeful glances with Tillie.

"Most people learn a skill for the challenge of mastering themselves as well as the skill. Our Ginnie is a natural horsewoman. She already loves her horse. It seemed like a natural extension to use that love in a way that will benefit them both. As you know, a large part of training a horse is training yourself."

"*Our* Ginnie is *my* daughter. Natural horsewoman or not, she won't be competing and I'm *not* arguing about it." Dad shot Ginnie a warning look to keep quiet before he stepped in front of Aunt Roni.

Ginnie sucked in a quick breath.

"And just so we're clear, she may *look* like you and her mom, but she isn't either one of you." Dad crossed his arms, daring Aunt Roni to argue. "*I* am her dad and I don't have to justify my decisions concerning her to you—or anyone else."

"Of course you don't. You're her daddy. I respect that." Aunt Roni calmly stroked Calliope's satiny neck.

I don't! Ginnie wanted to scream.

Aunt Roni shook her head at Ginnie's open mouth. "I'm just encouraging her to use self-control in a positive way. If she's not allowed to compete, then so be it."

"Hey!" Ginnie glanced at Tillie, hoping for backup, but Tillie just stood behind Dad with her eyes wide.

Aunt Roni raised her hand to Ginnie in a "stop" motion and frowned before giving Dad her full attention. "She did tell me she's not allowed to trick ride. I told her I thought that riding strictly for pleasure has its advantages. Sometimes it's too much pressure to always perform."

Ginnie bristled, barely able to contain her frustration.

Aunt Roni was sinking her battleship before Ginnie even got her battle plan together for Dad.

Dad arched a blond eyebrow her way and then threw Aunt Roni a suspicious smile.

Her aunt seemed not to notice and offered Dad a conspiratorial smile in return. "As you well know, Widget and I spent many hours daily at Ginnie's age practicing on our horses. Sometimes I honestly would have preferred to ride for pleasure or do something else entirely. Riding isn't as much fun if you *have* to do it."

"Don't tell him that! He'll agree with you. I *love* to ride. I wish I could do it even more," Ginnie objected, done with Aunt Roni's meddling.

"If you had to practice for hours every day to perfect a program, you might think differently." Aunt Roni glanced from Dad to Ginnie before nodding at Tillie. "And you have a horse, Ginnie, which is more than Tillie does. So as my mama, your Grandmama Serafina, would say—no pun intended—it'd be best not to look a gift horse in the mouth."

Whose side are you on? You're ruining everything! Ginnie clamped her jaw shut to corral the angry protest.

"Okay, Roni. You have my attention." Dad lowered his arms and hung a thumb from his front jean pocket. "What's your *real* angle? And before you answer, you should know that Ginnie and I have an agreement concerning Calliope, and I'm *not* entertaining arguments to change it."

"It's not really an agreement!" Ginnie folded her arms and glared, fully expecting Aunt Roni to be sympathetic to her cause. "You said if I do tricks on Calliope, you'll *sell* her. There wasn't much of a discussion."

Dad tightened his jaw and swiveled toward Ginnie. "Do you still have Calliope?"

"Yeah, but ..."

"Then apparently we *do* have an agreement, because the first time I see you do tricks on her, she'll find a new home. You made me a promise and I expect you to keep it." He lifted a warning finger to Ginnie and gave a slight smirk to Aunt Roni.

"And since we're being 'punny,' let's go with, there's no need to beat a dead horse. Obey the rule or don't." Dad gave a dismissive shrug. "What happens to Calliope is entirely up to you."

He lifted a second finger just before crossing his arms again.

Ginnie squelched the urge to roll her eyes, but couldn't cork her complaint. "But there's nothing wrong with western pleasure. It's safe. Why are you—?"

"Because he's your *daddy*." Aunt Roni took a step closer and laid a firm hand on Ginnie's thigh while giving a disapproving shake of her head. "It's his right to make decisions for you. Given the circumstances of your mama's passing, I understand his concerns. It didn't stop me from riding, but it did give me pause to consider whether or not I would allow my daughters to ride."

Really? Ginnie stared at her aunt, completely floored by this turn of events. *You're on HIS side?*

"But that's not fair!" Ginnie jerked the reins as she raised her hands in objection.

Calliope snorted her disapproval.

"Sorry, girl." Ginnie patted her mare's shoulder with one hand and planted her free hand on her hip. "Mama didn't die from competing. It was an *accident*."

"And it involved a horse. *Enough said*." Aunt Roni drew herself to her tallest height, which seemed much taller at the moment than her five-foot-nine-inch frame. "You have a horse. You're allowed to ride."

"But ..."

"Be grateful for the blessings you've been given." Aunt Roni pressed her hand firmly on Ginnie's shin. "I won't go against your dad. If he says 'no' to me teaching you horse-related things, then the answer is 'no.' Understood?"

Ginnie's jaw dropped.

So did Dad's. But *he* recovered more quickly and cleared his throat. "Virginia Maie, your aunt asked you a question. I suggest you answer her."

U-N-B-E-L-I-E-V-A-B-L-E! Ginnie threw Tillie a silent plea for support.

Instead of help, Ginnie got a slight shake of Tillie's head and then a quick wave of her hand.

Sugar beets! Some sister YOU are!

"Yes, sir." Ginnie clenched her fists. She had to take a quick breath before she could answer without screaming. "Sorry, Aunt Roni."

"An apology doesn't really answer her question," Dad replied, wiggling a third finger.

Ginnie battled her rage.

A third straightened finger would not be good.

Seriously? One peek at Dad's scowl and Ginnie knew better than to voice her question.

She swallowed hard and forced her tone to be civil. "Yes, ma'am. Understood."

A quick glance to Dad got her a slight nod of approval.

He turned, but not fast enough to hide an amused smile.

Great! Aunt Roni's got a new ally and I've got nothing!

27

BOILING

*T*illie felt the pressure rising in Ginnie until she could almost see steam rolling out of her friend's ears.

Aunt Roni seemed to be doing a good job of calming DT while infuriating Ginnie at the exact same time.

Personally, Tillie agreed with Aunt Roni. *Ginnie has a horse. So what if she can't compete?*

DT didn't say anything about Tillie getting a horse, and she really wished he would.

DT glanced at his watch and then Ginnie. "Slide off and I'll take care of her saddle while you take her to the horse rack. We had a little change in lunch plans. Jake and I came home to check on Mysti and Toran. His ribs are still bothering him. We're bringing lunch back to the others."

Ginnie gave a sharp nod and dismounted, her jaw tightening all the while. She moved a little further from her dad than she needed to and crossed her arms.

Yikes, she's mad.

DT didn't act like he noticed. He uncinched the saddle.

Aunt Roni's expression switched quickly from stern to surprise, and then regret. She moved behind DT to touch Ginnie's arms in apology.

Ginnie shook her aunt's hand off and backed up a step.

Tillie found her voice. "I'll help Ginnie with Calliope."

What she really meant was that she'd try to calm Ginnie down before they got to the farmhouse for lunch. If things didn't change soon, Ginnie would be exploding like a mouthful of Pop Rocks.

Aunt Roni seemed to get Tillie's message and sent a grateful smile.

DT lifted the saddle and blanket from Calliope's back and winked at the girls before heading toward the pasture gate. "See you ladies soon. Roni, let's chat a minute."

Ginnie turned her back to him and Aunt Roni in response.

She reached for Calliope's lead.

Aunt Roni nodded at DT then mouthed an, "I'm sorry," at Ginnie's back before following him.

Tillie ran ahead and opened the pasture gate while Ginnie led Calliope out of the pasture. Tillie closed the gate and matched Ginnie's step.

"Can you believe that? They totally ganged up on me!" Ginnie clicked at Calliope and glared at Tillie. "I thought Aunt Roni was gonna help me and she completely ratted me out. I wish she'd never come."

"No, you don't." Tillie grimaced; surprised that Ginnie would say such a thing. "You love her. If you didn't, you wouldn't be so mad."

"Stop talking like Uncle Ben. I'm so mad I could—I could—" Ginnie stomped her boot.

Calliope shook her head and snorted, shying away a step before throwing Ginnie a look that suggested she get a grip.

"You better calm down," Tillie advised. "You don't want your dad to see you like this."

"That reminds me. Thanks for the backup with him. *Not*." Ginnie whirled to face Tillie. "Why didn't *you* help me out? Dad listens to you."

"I—I was surprised how mad he was at Aunt Roni, and how it

didn't bother her. Everything I thought to say would have made one of them madder, so I didn't say anything."

"Is this how it's gonna be?" Ginnie stopped Calliope. Hurt and anger crossed her face. "If I can't count on you to help me out, Tillie, then maybe I don't want you to be my sister."

Ginnie might as well have punched her.

All the air sucked out of Tillie's body as "I don't want you to be my sister" repeated over and over in Tillie's mind like a bad feedback loop.

28

SISTERS? MAYBE NOT

Ginnie watched as Tillie struggled to comprehend the fallout of her anger. Still feeling betrayed, Ginnie tried not to care as the expressions on her friend's face churned through disbelief, betrayal, guilt, and hurt.

Hurt was the hardest.

Ginnie had spent the last six years trying to make Tillie feel better about everything, and now, right when she'd needed Tillie the most, her so-called "friend" had completely bailed on her.

Why can't she see why I need to ride? I went along with her scheme to get our folks together, didn't I?

Tears shone in Tillie's eyes.

Ginnie turned away. "I'll finish Calliope. Go have lunch." She led Calliope to the side of the farmhouse.

"No! I didn't do anything wrong." Tillie hurried in front of Ginnie and blocked her way. "You're being selfish. You know your dad won't let you compete. Why are you so surprised that he said no ... *again*?"

"*I'm* selfish?" Ginnie couldn't believe her ears. "You say you want to be my sister when you really just want my dad. *That's* selfish."

"That's not true." Tillie waved away Ginnie's protest. "You've got a horse and you're whining because you can't do stuff on your horse like your mom did ... that got her killed. Your dad just wants to keep you safe and you hate him for it. Any time you want to trade, you can have Jasper!"

"Seriously? My aunt just betrayed me, and now my so-called sister? Thanks a lot!" Ginnie clicked at Calliope. "Go tell my dad I hurt your feelings. He likes you better than me anyway."

"That's not true. Why are you being so mean?"

"I'm telling the truth." Ginnie didn't budge. "If you'd stood up for me, Daddy might've changed his mind."

"You're crazy." Tillie raised her hands. "Why can't you just be happy you have a horse? Like your dad said, you're *not* your mom or Aunt Roni. You don't have to be in a horse competition to be loved by your family." Tillie's voice quivered. "You just have to be born in it."

"What's that supposed to mean?"

"Uncle Jake finds out about Mysti one day and boom, the next day she's a full-fledged West. Everyone just accepts her." Tillie's hands flew to her hips. "You *do* know my mom has parents and a sister, *right?*"

Ginnie shrugged, not remembering whether Miss Amanda had a family or not.

And she didn't know why it even mattered right now. Miss Amanda and Tillie were always part of the West family's celebrations because they'd been family forever.

"Do we see them? No. They don't care that I even exist. And I'm the only grandchild. You don't know how lucky you are. Your family cares more about Mom and me than her blood family. And Jasper's?" Tillie pushed her straight hair angrily out of her face. "Never mind—we're not discussing Jasper's. They're mostly all dead and that's okay with me."

"Well, if *my* mom wasn't dead, then *your* mom couldn't marry my dad, now could she?"

"Hey, now!" The side porch door screeched open.

A shudder vibrated through Ginnie.

She swiveled to find Uncle Jake rushing toward them. "Virginia

Maie, tell me, *right this minute*, that I didn't just hear you say something so incredibly spiteful to your best friend."

Ginnie glared at him. "Let me guess ... you *didn't* just hear Tillie say something spiteful about Mysti?"

His eyes popped open, along with his mouth.

No words came out as he glanced between them.

That figures. Of course he didn't. Even so, Ginnie didn't like hearing her accusation echo through her mind.

She liked Miss Amanda being around.

But *I can do without Dad and Tillie right now.*

Tillie glared at her. "I did not."

"You did too."

"Enough." Uncle Jake raised a hand to stop the bickering. "You have two seconds to tell me what you're squabbling about or I'll let your dad sort it out. One ..."

Ginnie clenched her jaw.

Tillie dropped hers.

Uncle Jake wagged a warning finger between them. "Fine. I'll get Todd." He turned toward the house.

"No." Ginnie grabbed his arm. "He'll take Tillie's side. And Aunt Roni just stabbed me in the back."

"No, she didn't," Tillie protested.

"Yes. She. *Did.*" Ginnie pointed an accusing finger at Tillie. "And *you* let her."

"I said 'enough'." Uncle Jake disconnected Ginnie's other hand from his arm and held her wrist firmly. "I came to get juice from the extra fridge, not get involved in girl drama. You two are best friends ... *act* like it."

"Why are you taking her side?" Ginnie asked.

"I'm not taking *anybody's* side. I just can't believe what I'm hearing. Since when do you two fight?"

"Since everybody in my family turned on me." Ginnie jerked her wrist from her uncle's grasp. "Including my *'sister'*. Not that *you* really care either."

"Wow, someone's having a pity party." Uncle Jake arched an eyebrow. "When did *I* spit in your soup?"

Ginnie rolled her eyes. "Everybody else thinks Tillie's perfect. Why not you?"

"I'll admit I'm partial to Tillie. So sue me. I'm also partial to *you*. What's got you at each other's throats?"

"Aunt Roni was showing me how to teach Calliope to respond to leg pressure cues, and Dad went nuts." Ginnie toggled her head defiantly. "Then Aunt Roni went even crazier and said that if Dad didn't want her teaching me horse stuff, she wouldn't. When I tried to tell my side, they both shut me down and Tillie didn't even try to help me."

"She smarted off to Aunt Roni and her dad got mad. What was I supposed to do to fix it?" Tillie protested.

"That's *not* what happened." Ginnie threw Tillie a "what-planet-did-you-come-from?" look. "Now they're both mad at me."

"Somehow I doubt that." Uncle Jake shook his head. "The two of them went into the study to finish a private conversation, about the benefits of western pleasure riding. Since they were both smiling, I think you crossed a signal." He motioned up the hill to the main barn. "Lunch is getting cold. Put your squabble to rest and your horse in her stall. And Gin ..."

"Yeah?"

"I find it highly unlikely that Roni would not share her love of horses with you. Besides being a grand champion horse woman in her own right, she's your mom's sister. I really think you got your wires crossed."

"Really?"

He grimaced. "When have I ever lied to you?"

"But they were both mad."

"They aren't right now. Hug your sister and behave, or I'm grounding you both."

"You can't do that!" Ginnie protested.

"Wanna bet?" Uncle Jake narrowed his eyes.

Um. Not really.

"Fine." She turned to find Tillie standing next to her with an uncomfortable smile and nervous eyes.

Ginnie swallowed hard and reluctantly initiated a hug.

She forced a friendlier smile than she felt.

Uncle Jake better be right or the truce is off.

29

WESTERN PLEASURE

*B*y the time Ginnie finished with Calliope and got to the dining room, lunch was pretty much over. Uncle Jake sat with Mysti reading a book on the family room couch. Dad and Aunt Roni were still in the study while Toran and Tillie finished their lunch.

Ginnie waited impatiently for Dad and Aunt Roni so she could see if Uncle Jake might be right about her being wrong about what happened.

Vi knocked on the study door and told Dad lunch was packed for the guys in the field and ready to go. When Dad opened the door, Ginnie glanced from the dining room to the hallway. Vi handed him a plate of roast, potatoes and gravy, and green beans. They walked together with Aunt Roni to the dining room.

"Thanks, Vi." Dad sniffed the steam rising from the roast. "This smells delicious. You're the best."

"Remember that. You're helping me move out in a couple weeks." Vi patted his cheek. "Preston says to call him about finalizing a date for the bachelor party by tomorrow night."

"Will do. Toran, how are your ribs?" Dad asked before taking a bite of potatoes.

"I'm fine."

"Good. Let me know if that changes." Dad took another bite. He glanced between Ginnie and Tillie as he swallowed his mouthful. "Girls, as long as Toran is doing fine, Aunt Roni wants to take the three of you and Amanda out for dinner tonight. Since Vi's not going to be here and the rest of us will be in the field, I told her that would be okay."

"Really?" Excitement overcame Ginnie's frustration.

"As long as you do the afternoon chores and are back here before we are." He threw Aunt Roni a cautionary look before turning to Ginnie. "If she tries to kidnap you, you have my permission to do whatever it takes to *not* go with her." His tone hovered between teasing and serious. "In fact, I *insist* on it." He took another bite of his lunch.

Toran laughed. "Wow, Aunt Roni, that's like giving a coyote a come-and-get-'em invite to the chicken coop."

"You're so funny," Ginnie said, then smirked. "*Not.*"

"But he's right." Dad's tone was definitely serious this time. "Aunt Roni asked me to trust her ... and I am. I'm just making it crystal clear to everyone involved that I expect my kids to be *here* tonight." He pointed straight down. "Taking a detour to South Carolina is *not* acceptable."

"Thanks for the vote of confidence there," Aunt Roni teased. "Here I thought we'd made some real progress."

"I said 'yes' to going out, didn't I?" Dad said pleasantly. He finished his lunch quickly and set his plate on the table. "That's progress."

"And on that note, we're outta here." Uncle Jake carried Mysti into the dining room, kissed the top of her head, set her on her feet, and motioned toward the hallway.

Dad swept his finger around the room from Toran, to Tillie, to Ginnie. "I love you guys. Be good. Have fun with Aunt Roni, but be *here* when I get back."

Ginnie squelched the urge to roll her eyes. "Got it."

"Yes, sir," Tillie and Toran chorused.

Tillie stood to hug him good-bye.

Ginnie followed.

Dad bent toward her ear and whispered, "We'll talk about riding western pleasure later, okay?"

"For *real?*" She couldn't keep the doubt from her tone. "We can talk and you might actually say 'yes'?"

It was almost too much to hope that he'd let her participate.

He winked, "For real. I'm not making any promises, but I'll consider it. See you tonight."

Ginnie hugged him again and watched him leave.

A happy, tingly sensation coursed through her.

She glanced at Aunt Roni.

Ginnie was pretty sure that even though she couldn't see her, Mama stood, smiling, next to her twin sister.

30

BIT O' HONEY

*A*s soon as Vi's purple VW bug and Uncle Jake's tricked-out black truck headed down the lane, Ginnie turned from the front porch screen door and rushed back to the dining room. She grabbed Aunt Roni's hands. "What did you say to my dad to get him to change his mind?"

Aunt Roni laughed. "Have you ever heard the saying, 'You catch more flies with honey than vinegar'?"

"Yeah, but what does that have to do with my dad?"

"Sugar, let me tell you the secret about your daddy and most people." Aunt Roni glanced at Tillie and Toran to see if they were listening. They were. "Most people just want to be treated like they matter. Figure out what their 'honey' is, and they'll come around."

"I guess there's something to that strategy," Toran said.

"So what's Dad's honey?" Ginnie asked.

"Respect. More specifically, from me, Todd needs to know that *I* know he's the boss where you are concerned. Since I believe he has the right to make decisions for you, we're two peas in a pod on that issue."

Ginnie frowned.

"Which is why I stood up for him outside." An apologetic look crossed her face. "I didn't mean to hurt your feelings--but Todd needs to know that as much as I want you and I to get to know each other better, I won't betray his trust in me." She let out a soft sigh. "Little that there is at the moment."

"But he doesn't get why I want to be like Mama." Disappointment stained Ginnie's words. She didn't need another person on Dad's side —he had enough. "If he'd try to understand, we wouldn't fight so much."

Aunt Roni traced her thumb along Ginnie's cheek before holding her chin firmly. "He understands *very* well. But there are two sides to that coin, Ginnie. Todd wants you to be happy, but he also wants you to be safe. Your mama was thrown many times in her life. She'd get up, brush herself off, and try again ... until the day that she didn't."

Ginnie paused before pushing away her aunt's words. "But that could happen to me just riding around the farm. Or I could get hit by a car or lots of things. Mama rode a lot, and it was only a problem once."

"And that once was plenty." Aunt Roni squeezed Ginnie's chin firmly. "It isn't just about that one time. When you compete in more strenuous competitions, you *do* increase the chances of being thrown. Even if you get up ninety-nine out of a hundred times, Todd knows now—better than anyone should ever know—that the one time you don't may be the one time you *never* do. He's not willing to take that chance with you."

"But—"

"No buts." She shook her head. "Take a minute to let that sink in." She let go of Ginnie's chin and glanced at Tillie and Toran. "Vi said she left snickerdoodles for dessert. Let me grab a bite of lunch and then let's have some dessert. Where's Mysti?"

Tillie pointed toward the kitchen doorway. "She went into the family room."

"I'll check on her while I fix a plate." Aunt Roni glanced at the table and then Ginnie. "Did you eat yet?"

"No, I just finished with Calliope."

"Then I'll make you one too."

Ginnie nodded and then blurted the question that was practically burning a hole in her brain. "Do you think Daddy will let me do western pleasure, at least?"

Aunt Roni shrugged. "He's open to it. But Gin?"

"Yeah?"

"Don't make competing more important than your dad. I know better than most why you need to ride." She gave Ginnie's shoulder a squeeze. "I also know it *feels* more important than it really is. Trust me on this."

Ginnie weighed Aunt Roni's words, knowing her aunt could be a little right about her concerns, but even so, competing with Calliope was still *very* important.

Once Ginnie figured out how to make Dad understand, things would be better all around.

31

BFFS

illie replayed the argument with Ginnie in her head, cringing when she recalled her BFF saying she didn't want to be sisters anymore. Even so, Tillie was glad she didn't budge her point with Ginnie and stood up for herself.

She played with Mysti while Ginnie ate lunch. Mysti's impulsive, busy nature was both entertaining and distracting. She kept Tillie from overthinking Ginnie's mean words.

When Aunt Roni passed out the snicker doodles, Tillie reminded Ginnie that they had promised Vi they'd keep up with the laundry. Ginnie followed her out to the side porch.

Tillie pulled the clothes from the dryer. Ginnie moved the wet ones from the washer, filled the dryer and then started it. Tillie folded the warm T-shirts while Ginnie loaded the washing machine.

Once Ginnie joined her folding clothes, Tillie gathered her courage and decided to ask what was on her mind. "Do you really not want to be sisters anymore?"

Ginnie dropped the blue T-shirt she was folding and looked at Tillie. "What are you talking about?"

Tillie pointed outside. "You said you don't want me to be your sister. Did you mean that?"

Understanding lit Ginnie's face. "Of course not. Sorry. You just made me mad." She rolled her eyes impatiently. "Of course I still want you to be my sister, but you've got to help me out with Dad when he's being unreasonable. That's what *real* sisters do."

"It's not unreasonable that he wants to keep you safe."

"Tillie, you're being ridiculous. Nobody can possibly get hurt doing western pleasure or even barrel racing." She picked up the shirt. "My mom loved competing. She was awesome at it—a grand champion. I could be too, *if* my dad would just let me try."

"Why do you need to be like your mom? Your dad doesn't expect you to be her. He wants you to be *you*."

"It's not about being *her*—it's about being *me*." Ginnie shook the shirt at her. "I want to trick ride and compete. I know why she liked it and I want to do it too. He won't let me *be* me. That's just wrong."

"Why do you need to compete to be yourself? It's not like you've ever competed anyway. It's just something you've *thought* about doing."

"You don't understand." Ginnie snapped the blue T-shirt smooth. "I'm not going to get hurt. And even if I did, I'd have a lot of fun and good memories as well. I don't want to spend my life afraid of doing stuff just because I *might* get hurt. That's lame."

"No, it's not."

"Yes. It. Is." Ginnie folded the T-shirt and set it on a pile. "Toran wants to be a pilot. Planes crash. He could get killed flying a plane."

"That's different."

"How?" Ginnie's jaw dropped for a few seconds before she continued. "People get killed in car accidents all the time—you don't see Dad not driving just because his folks died in a car crash, do you? He even drives a truck for work, plus tractors, balers, and other farm vehicles."

"That's different, too."

"No, it's not." Ginnie picked up another shirt. "My mom died from falling off a horse. I've ridden Calliope for three years and only fell off once. Aunt Roni has been riding longer than my mom—and she's still here."

"Well ..." Tillie stopped, unable to complete her argument.

"Well, *what*? *Your* mom isn't hiding from Jasper—and he used to be a big problem for her. She doesn't want to be afraid of living her life either." Ginnie rolled her eyes again. "Life goes on. You and Daddy need to quit being afraid of what *might* happen and *live* your life. I'm sure going to."

"You're going to start trick riding too?" Tillie shook her head, not liking where this was going.

"Not right away." Ginnie grimaced. "You heard him—Daddy'll sell Calliope if I do. His name is on her pedigree." She set the folded shirt on the stack. "After I get good at western pleasure, he'll let me try other stuff. I'm willing to compromise. I just refuse to be afraid of living my life like he is."

"I don't think he's afraid. He cares about you."

"I know, but he cares so much, he smothers me." She shook her head and picked up another shirt. "I love my dad, but I get to make my own decisions." Ginnie smirked. "Besides, Mama married *him* even though her dad said she couldn't—and that turned out pretty good. Daddy wouldn't even have had Mama—or Toran and me—if Mama had listened to *her* dad."

"Yeah, but ..."

"But what?"

"Um." Tillie blinked. "I forgot the question."

Ginnie chuckled. "If my mom hadn't defied *her* dad, I wouldn't be here, and we wouldn't get to be sisters." Ginnie locked her gaze on Tillie's. "I'm not gonna blow my dad off, but I will figure how to get him to work with me. Just like I'm gonna figure out how to get him to let *you* have a horse."

"Do you really think you can?"

"I don't see why not." She shrugged. "It'll take some doing, but we'll get it done."

Her easy confidence bubbled joy inside Tillie.

She reached across the pile of T-shirts to hug her friend, knocking it over in her hurry.

They giggled, hugged quickly, then picked up the pile. "You're the best sister *ever*, Ginnie West."

"I know." Ginnie buffed her fingernails against her shirt and wiggled her eyebrows. "You're not so bad yourself."

32

GERTRUDE THE GOAT

$\mathcal{T}$oran stood outside the mini red-and-white goat barn and clicked at Gertrude, their nanny goat. "Come on, girl." He let a handful of grain drip into the feed bucket at the front of the milking platform, hoping to entice the brown-and-black goat to poke her head through the stanchion so he could milk her safely.

Gertrude eyeballed the grain and made a beeline to it.

"Well, looky there. She must trust you," Aunt Roni said.

Torn between wanting to engage his aunt in happy banter and confronting her with the questions that had been simmering to a slow boil for days, Toran finally did neither.

He adjusted the stanchion so Gertrude couldn't back up off the feeding platform. "Uncle Ben doesn't need to use the platform, but the rest of us do. Gertrude cooperates with me, but she doesn't like Ginnie or Uncle Jake at all."

Aunt Roni giggled. "That would explain why Ginnie volunteered so quickly to milk Trixie. She must get along better with cows. What's Gertrude's issue with them?"

"No idea. They just don't like each other." Toran picked up the bucket with warm water and a washcloth, then set it next to

Gertrude. He wiped her udder and let it air dry, trying to decide if he would ask his aunt the one thing he really wanted to know.

"I've never milked a goat before," Aunt Roni confessed nervously, sliding her hand down Gertrude's side. "Mind if I try? She doesn't seem to have an issue with me."

"Sure. It's not hard." Toran set the milk pail under Gertrude, in front of her udder. "I'll start her off." He aimed the first squeeze into the waiting mouth of his silver-gray cat, Princess.

"Nice shot. She must be used to the routine."

"She is." Toran wiped the sweat from his cheek with his shoulder. "The first couple of squirts can contain bacteria or dirt. We don't want that in the milk. No sense wasting the milk. Princess is happy to protect us from such evils."

"Such a sacrifice to make," Aunt Roni teased, nodding her approval. "Good job, Princess."

Toran smiled at his aunt and reached for her right hand.

She let him take it.

He compared his own hand to hers and then extended it like in a handshake, wiggling first his middle finger, then his ring finger, and lastly, his pinky finger in quick succession. "Your hand is about the same size as mine. You'll need to use these three fingers, in order. My dad and Uncle Ben only use two because their hands are bigger."

"That's good to know. I don't just pull and squeeze?"

Toran chuckled in spite of his vow to remain distant. "Only if you want her to kick you. Pulling her teats straight down hurts her." Toran backed up and showed Aunt Roni where to place her fingers on the teat closest to them. "It's kind of a massaging motion. Do one teat, then change to another so the first one can refill."

"That's an interesting image." Aunt Roni flashed him a dazzling smile. "Like a continuous dripping faucet."

"Something like that." He kept his voice even. "Squeeze your middle finger, then your ring finger, and then your pinky in a smooth motion." He waited for his aunt to try.

Aunt Roni did, squealing when milk shot into the bucket.

She tried again, jerking so that the first part of the spray made a tinkling sound in the bucket, and then managed to squirt the rest of the stream onto Toran's jean leg.

"Thanks, but I already had a shower." He guided her hand into position to keep the milk in the bucket.

"Sorry." Aunt Roni tried again. "Gertrude is a beautiful animal. I can see why Uncle Ben loves her."

"She's okay. I think he keeps her to remember Aunt Sadie by—she loved goats, and violets." Toran adjusted the bucket a little. "Though, even if there weren't all kinds of goat and violet trinkets, figurines, and tole-painted knickknacks all over the house, I don't think he could actually forget Aunt Sadie. Vi says they're her mom's 'heavenly touches' to remind us that Aunt Sadie is still watching over us. Maybe she is." Toran dropped his gaze to the ground. "I don't remember her exactly, but every time someone says Aunt Sadie's name, a good feeling comes over me."

"That's sweet." Aunt Roni placed an understanding hand on Toran's wrist. "I met Aunt Sadie a couple of times. She was a very lovely woman. I am sure your heart remembers that, even if your mind doesn't."

Toran shrugged, his frustration mounting in spite of feeling a connection with his aunt. "We should finish milking Gertrude before her feed is gone."

"Did I say something wrong, sugar?" Aunt Roni glanced at his face. "Should I not mention Aunt Sadie? I've heard Uncle Ben and your dad talk openly about her, so I didn't think her name was taboo."

He turned away. "You can talk about her."

"But?"

Toran stepped off the platform. "But nothing."

"Toran West, I know a fidget when I see one. What is it that you want to say to me?"

"Nothing."

"You've acted uncomfortable ever since I got here this morning. Have I done something to offend you?"

Toran studied the face that looked too much like his dead mother's and swallowed hard. "Fine."

He didn't like conflict nor did he like causing pain, but he had questions that needed answering.

"I want to know why you stayed away after our mom died. Why did you wait until *now* to see Ginnie and me? And what do you *really* want?"

33

YOU GOTTA DO WHAT YOU GOTTA DO

*A*unt Roni's eyes widened as Toran's questions seemed to circle through her mind. Sadness, concern, then a calm understanding crossed her face. She reached her hand to Toran's and grasped it in a quick squeeze, rubbing her thumb against the back of it in a comforting motion. "Thanks for not beating around the bush."

Toran's cheeks warmed. A smile lit his lips in spite of his embarrassment when his aunt's teasing smile perked his. "Sorry, Aunt Roni, but you asked."

"I know. And I had a feeling you would ask me something like that." She squeezed his hand again. "When I left here a few days ago, I asked myself the very same thing."

"And what did you answer yourself?"

She rolled her eyes and offered a fun smirk at his teasing question before she became serious. "There were a lot of reasons. First and foremost, once your dad got a restraining order against my father and me, we couldn't see you two without his permission. Since you guys were only three-and-a-half and always with him or Uncle Ben or Vi, we didn't have a lot of options. We moved to England and started a new business there."

"That seems a little extreme."

140

"It kept us busy and sane." She shrugged. "At the time, I told myself I would connect with you and Ginnie when you were old enough to see me away from your dad."

Toran bristled, not liking the deception that action would have entailed. He clamped his mouth shut, trying to figure out how to respond.

Gertrude pawed impatiently.

Toran checked her feed bucket. It was empty. "Maybe I should finish milking her."

Aunt Roni nodded and stood.

Toran took her place, happy to have something to focus on. The pinging and tinkling of the milk streams made a nice distraction when his aunt resumed talking, sadness taking over her voice.

"In the meantime, I married and had two daughters of my own. I realized that I wouldn't want some stranger from my past going around me, so I decided to talk to your dad face-to-face and hope he would know I meant no harm to you or Ginnie—or even to him."

Toran relaxed a little as her sentiments echoed his.

Then he recalled the ugly scene a few days before when he and Dad had come home from the emergency room after he hurt his ribs to discover Aunt Roni in the family room.

Normally, his dad was pretty easygoing, but seeing Aunt Roni lit a rage in his dad that Toran would have never believed if he hadn't witnessed it himself. Dad had demanded that Aunt Roni leave the premises immediately.

Ginnie had offered a desperate plea for him to allow Aunt Roni to stay. She wanted to get to know their mom through her twin sister. Dad had reluctantly agreed.

Until that day, Toran had never heard about Aunt Roni or her father. His dad had only recently become open about Mama—and then only because Ginnie found her journals.

Dad had taken the journals away from Ginnie the night he found out she had them, knowing that once Ginnie read about Aunt Roni, she would demand answers to questions Dad didn't want her to ask because he didn't have answers for her. Dad had cut off Aunt Roni and her dad and didn't want to reconnect with Mama's family. But Aunt Roni showed up on her own and kind of forced the issue.

Dad still hadn't returned the journals. Toran was becoming as impatient to have them as Ginnie.

The day Aunt Roni showed up turned their whole world upside down. Since she was here and open to talking, now seemed like a good time to get the information Toran wanted. He glanced up from milking. "I was surprised he let you stay. He didn't really want to see you."

"I know." She sighed. "I was afraid if I called, he would tell me never to call back and just hang up on me."

"Which he would have," Toran assured her with a smile.

"I know." Aunt Roni giggled conspiratorially. "This is better. Todd and I had our little 'come-to-Jesus-meeting', as my mama would say. He let off steam about the past and made his expectations about the future crystal clear. Since I plan to honor his wishes, I can see a bright future for us—provided you can ever come to trust me."

Toran started to protest that statement, then realized he didn't really trust her—not completely. He shrugged instead. "This is a good start."

"Very pragmatic of you. You are your mother's son—and your father's." She tilted her head to the side and studied him. "That's a *good* thing. I think my sister would be very pleased with how you and Ginnie have turned out."

Toran continued to milk Gertrude, concentrating on the swishes that now replaced the tinkling. The bucket was half full. "I wish she were here."

"Me too, sugar." Aunt Roni sighed. "Me too."

Toran couldn't let his frustration go. "Why didn't you try to see us back then?"

"I did try. But once my dad involved the courts, Uncle Ben and his brothers 'circled the wagons', so to speak, and made it very clear that we were no longer welcome." Her voice trailed off. "I couldn't blame them, given how things happened, but I do wish it had been different."

Knowing how protective his four great-uncles were, Toran had no trouble believing they would discourage further communication if that's what his dad wanted.

Ever since Dad and Uncle Jake were orphaned, Uncle Ben and his three surviving brothers had looked out for them. They had become even more protective since Mama died.

"Why did you come back *now*?"

A stream of milk followed his gaze to his aunt.

"My turn for a second shower?" she teased.

"Sorry." Toran adjusted his aim.

"No problem, sugar. Milk is good for the skin." Her lighthearted response made him laugh. Then her friendly eyes dimmed. "The truth? Lots of reasons. I miss your mom. I missed you and your sister. Mostly, though, it's been eight-and-a-half years and it's time."

She strengthened her tone. "Family is important. My girls know about you, but you don't know about them. They wanted to meet you."

Toran let her words repeat in his mind while he milked Gertrude. "I guess that makes sense. How do you feel about Miss Amanda? Dad asked her to marry him, you know."

"Ginnie told me." Aunt Roni smiled. "I think Amanda is lovely. I hope she and I can be friends."

Like that won't be awkward. Toran tried each teat one last time before answering. Three of them were empty. He massaged the last one and watched it drip. "Did you try to see us before?" He glanced at his aunt.

She shook her head. "Well, not through official channels. I went to your school one day when you guys were in second grade, shortly before your birthday."

"Did we see you?" Toran searched his memories for such a meeting.

"No. I watched you at recess on the playground, but you didn't see me. I decided to test the waters and sent presents for each of you here to the farm, hoping Todd would let me see you." She tucked a curl behind her ear. "No such luck. They were returned, unopened, with 'do not contact' written across the bottom. He had his lawyer renew the restraining order."

Toran felt his eyes widen.

Aunt Roni sighed. "I lost my nerve and decided to wait until you guys were teens so that if you *did* want to see me, I'd have half a chance of success."

"Wow. Dad isn't one to hold grudges." Toran met her gaze. "You must have really pulled his chain."

Aunt Roni grimaced. "I like to think it was more my father than myself, but Todd painted us both with the same brush of distrust."

Toran didn't feel overly sympathetic. "Can you really blame him?"

"No, but that doesn't mean he was right to cut me off. I didn't have anything to do with the custody battle. I begged my dad to stop it. I was on Todd's side."

"Except that you took Cabot's."

"I didn't, Toran. I took your dad's."

"Well, he must not have gotten the memo. He always listens to us when *we* have something to say."

"Sugar, there was a lot of not listening at the time. *My* dad wasn't happy about it either." Her anxious eyes sought out Toran's. "Until the accident, Todd and I got along fine. When my dad took leave of his senses, Todd and Uncle Ben cut us *both* off. I was devastated."

Toran scanned her designer jeans, perfectly tailored periwinkle blouse, and beautifully applied makeup to find signs of devastation. Something in her sapphire-blue eyes mirrored the desperate look Ginnie had the day Aunt Roni came into their lives. The hurt he saw made him believe her story—at least some. "I guess your timing got better."

"Yes, but only because Ginnie wanted to see me as much as I wanted to see the two of you. If she hadn't, Todd would've given me the boot—again."

Toran knew that was true.

She leaned forward. "What did you think when you saw me? I know you were shocked, but I honestly never imagined I would be such a surprise to ya'll."

Shrugging, Toran tried to put his feelings into words.

"Your dad told me at your mama's funeral that he would keep my sister's memory alive for you. I never imagined he wouldn't mention her very own twin."

"Was that before Cabot tried to take us away?"

She nodded.

"There's your answer. Well, sorta." Toran thought back to a conversation he'd had with his dad in first grade. He had made a family tree and didn't know when his mom's birthday was or much of anything about her. Dad had spent a long time answering his questions about her, but they really hadn't talked about her a whole lot since—at least not until a few weeks ago, when Ginnie found her journals.

"Sorta?" Aunt Roni probed.

"This isn't the home where my mom lived. Aunt Sadie's stuff is all around, but not Mama's. Dad only talked about her when Ginnie and I did—and we didn't very much."

"Why not?"

Toran shrugged. He'd asked himself that question a million times since Aunt Roni left. He wasn't sure he could make her understand. "My dad's a private guy. He doesn't complain about stuff, but when he talked about her, you could tell he missed her and it made him sad."

Aunt Roni gave a sympathetic nod.

Toran concentrated on gathering his thoughts. "Nobody in our family has a mother—Mama and Aunt Sadie died when we were babies. Dad's mom and dad died when he was eleven. Tillie's dad left six years ago. Having only one parent is kinda normal for us."

"That is just about the saddest thing I've ever heard." She hugged him. "You poor babies."

"You said your mom died when you were sixteen," Toran pointed out, stiffening. "If we *had* asked him about Mama's family, he woulda told us. He doesn't lie to us."

"Sugar, I didn't mean to imply that he does. He's always been honest—sometimes to a fault—with me." She moved her sunglasses to the top of her head. "I've spent the last eight years worried about what he'd tell you about your granddaddy and me. I was a little afraid you'd hate me when I met you, but I never imagined he had erased us. I'm still getting used to *that* idea."

Toran stood and moved the milk bucket out from under Gertrude. "He didn't erase you. He just never brought you up." He set the bucket down next to his aunt. "Dad has what he calls the 'Thumper rule'. You know—'If you can't say something nice, don't say anything at all.' He probably used that a lot when he thought about your father."

"I guess that's better than talking badly about us, but still, I'll never forget the look on your face when you first saw me." Aunt Roni gave him an apologetic smile. "You looked like you'd seen a ghost."

"You're my mom's *identical* twin sister." Toran released the stanchion, still defensive. Gertrude popped her head out. "I didn't know about you. What was I supposed to think?"

"I understand your distress, sugar. The real problem was that I hadn't imagined you didn't know about me."

"Well, now I do." Toran led Gertrude off the platform. "If Dad's okay with that, I can be."

"And if he stops being okay with it?"

"Then I'll have to make a decision, won't I?" Toran didn't want to be rude, but he wasn't ready to commit to his aunt over his dad, either. "Come on, Gertrude."

He clicked at the goat and led her into the pasture.

34

CELL PHONES

*A*fter Miss Clarissa picked up Mysti, Aunt Roni hurried Tillie, Ginnie, and Toran to her Mercedes Benz. "Toran, you sit up front." He happily slid in before Ginnie could protest. He'd never been in such a nice car, and this was One. Bodacious. Ride.

"We're going to meet Amanda at the steak house near the mall. We'll have just enough time to make a quick stop on the way. Buckle up." She didn't need to tell them twice.

They made light conversation around the GPS voice calling out directions.

Before long, Aunt Roni pulled up in front of a cell phone store.

"Why are we stopping here?" Tillie asked.

"Because I want to be able to get a hold of you."

Sweet! Toran had wanted a cell phone forever. Even more since Austin got one for his birthday. *Finally.*

"Daddy won't let us keep them," Ginnie warned.

Aw man! She's right. Disappointment swept over Toran. *Get a grip. You didn't even look at a phone, let alone get one.*

"Let me worry about him. You just find a phone you like." Aunt Roni motioned them out of the car. "You too, Tillie and Toran."

It can't hurt to look. Toran opened his door. "Thanks."

Tillie grinned. "Really?"

"Of course. I can't very well leave you out. Todd considers you his daughter, so that makes you Ginnie's sister, and since she's my niece, you are too. Now scoot."

Even though Aunt Roni's logic was a little convoluted, Toran liked it.

He remembered his initial distrust of his aunt and felt bad.

Tillie's bright smile made him feel better.

"Yes, ma'am." Ginnie and Tillie fist-bumped, then followed Aunt Roni and Toran into the store.

Toran was in heaven. He stopped at the main display featuring the newest iPhone. It was too much to hope that he could actually own one, but it couldn't hurt to admire it before finding a more reasonably priced one.

Aunt Roni came up behind him and gave him a hug. "Good choice, Toran. I love mine."

"I—I'm not asking for it. It costs too much." He felt his cheeks heat. "But I do like looking at it."

"Do you want one?"

"Well, yeah, but ..."

"No buts. It's my treat." She waved the store worker over. "My nephew would like this iPhone. Will you please hook him up?"

"Certainly."

"Thank you."

Before Toran could protest, Aunt Roni approached the girls. "Have you found anything you want?"

Ginnie shrugged. "I like this emerald-green one."

"It *is* pretty. But it's a basic model. Do you want a smartphone instead? We can get an emerald-green case for it so you can tell it apart from Toran's."

Tillie's eyes widened.

Ginnie shook her head.

Toran's jaw dropped.

Aunt Roni laughed. "What's your favorite color, Tillie?"

"Purple."

"Mine too. Cases come in purple as well."

Ginnie shook her head. "Aunt Roni, thanks, but I'm serious. Daddy won't let us keep them, will he, Tor?"

"Probably not," Toran agreed, wishing it weren't so. "He wouldn't even let Uncle Jake buy us cell phones for our birthdays."

"Well, I'm not buying them for *him*. I'm buying them purely out of selfishness, for my own convenience." Aunt Roni grinned conspiratorially. "I want to be able to talk with you every once in a while, and I want you to be able to call me whenever you like. However, it probably won't do to buy you better phones than your dad." She swiveled toward the clerk. "Seven iPhones, please."

"Seven?" Toran's eyes grew wide as he multiplied the cost of seven Androids in his head.

Aunt Roni shrugged. "You did say Uncle Ben doesn't have a cell phone either, sugar. Yes?"

"Yes. I mean, no, he doesn't. Well, not a smart phone. He has a flip phone." Ginnie laughed. "You're confusing me."

"No worries. Todd, Amanda, Tillie, Toran, Ginnie, Jake, and Uncle Ben." Aunt Roni ticked each name off on her fingers. "Vi and Buzz already have cell phones, correct?"

"My dad and Uncle Jake have work cell phones--which they use-- but they are older," Ginnie said.

"My mom has a cell phone too," Tillie pointed out.

"The adults in your family should have the same quality as the kids." Aunt Roni flashed the clerk a beautiful smile. "I think we are all set."

Excitement and dread mingled together. Toran had wanted an iPhone forever, but Dad was not going to be happy about Aunt Roni's shopping spree. *On the other hand, Aunt Roni's an adult, and Dad expects us to obey adults. If she wants to buy us a phone, the polite thing to do is accept it graciously.*

Toran knew he was just fooling himself, but a few hours with an iPhone was better than no time at all.

"Seven iPhones it is." The clerk sported a very happy grin. He motioned them to follow him to the counter.

"Oh, wait. Jake has Mysti." Aunt Roni frowned, then glanced at each tween. "Do you think he wants her to have a phone? Or will he think she's too young?" Before anybody could respond, Aunt Roni hurried to a decision. "My Genna-Maie has a phone, and she's the same age as Mysti. Eight, please. If Jake doesn't want her to have one, he can give it to Clarissa."

"Wow, Aunt Roni. Are you sure?" Tillie asked, her look akin to someone watching a train wreck where boxcars full of candy bars and jelly beans littered the tracks.

"Of course, sugar. You three go pick out some cases and I'll pay for these." She peeked at her watch, an amethyst-studded Rolex. "We need to hurry, though. Amanda will be at the steak house soon."

Toran could hardly believe how close he was to owning the latest iPhone. *I sure hope Aunt Roni can talk Dad into letting us keep them. These are suh-weet!*

They found two black cases, three red ones, and a blue one. Aunt Roni added one of each to her growing stack of purchases. "Please add three $100 gift cards. No, wait. Make that four. You three and Amanda can pick out your cases online once we get your phones activated."

All three shook their heads. Toran voiced their communal thought, even though he wanted very much to play along in his aunt's happy bubble world. "Aunt Roni, that's too much. Dad'll never let us keep them."

For the first time ever, she looked almost fierce.

Then she smiled her dazzling beauty-queen smile. "Sugar, I said *I'll* worry about your daddy. I figure I owe you for at least eight birthdays. Now please, just let me do this. If Todd has an issue, he can take it up with *me*." She wagged a finger at each of them in turn. "*Your* job is to enjoy the phones and call me once in a while to make up for all the time we've lost. Understood?"

Somehow, Toran got the feeling she was channeling their mother, recognizing the determined look Ginnie often had when she went toe-to-toe with their dad.

He swallowed hard, then chorused, "Yes, ma'am," along with his sisters.

Tillie still had the dazed candy-train-wreck look, but Ginnie shrugged, a look of admiration and respect crossing her face.

One thing was for sure—she wasn't going to argue with Aunt Roni either.

35

MISS AMANDA

Once the phones were finally activated, Aunt Roni rushed Tillie, Ginnie, and Toran to the car. "Toran, please call each of your sisters' phones and mine. Girls, save his number and then each of you call the others. Please start with Amanda's." She handed Toran her phone.

"Thanks, Aunt Roni. You're the coolest."

"Why, thank you, sugar. But truly, I just want to be able to contact you easily."

"I hope Daddy lets us keep them, but don't hold your breath," Ginnie cautioned. "He doesn't care for cell phones much. He thinks we're too young for them."

Aunt Roni tsked. "Stop being a negative Nelly. I'll deal with my brother-in-law. You just call the phones." She passed each girl an extra phone and handed two to Toran. "Tor, you be in charge of who calls what phone. You seem to have a handle on how these work."

Toran's face lit up.

Tillie laughed. She liked the idea of having a cell phone, but she knew Toran was absolutely in love with technology and such an instruction put him in hog heaven—or rather, cell-phone heaven.

While Aunt Roni drove to the restaurant, Ginnie, Toran, and

Tillie took turns calling and saving each other's numbers to each phone.

Tillie was enjoying the feeling of truly belonging again. *Things are definitely looking up.*

They weren't quite finished when they arrived at the restaurant.

"No worries—as long as Amanda's is done. You can do the others on the way home," Aunt Roni assured them. "There's Amanda now."

Toran handed over Mom's phone while Tillie finished typing her name in Uncle Ben's. Tillie followed her new aunt's pointer finger to Mom's silver-blue car. Seeing her mom safe caused a happy flutter inside. Ginnie must have felt it too because her grin grew wider.

Ginnie pocketed her phone, picked up Uncle Jake's, and slid it into his bag. Toran met her at the trunk with the other phones. They put them in different places to keep them from getting mixed up.

"Hands back, please. No squished fingers allowed." Aunt Roni instructed.

She closed the trunk and swiveled to greet Mom.

Tillie ran over to hug her.

They exchanged pleasantries. Mom zeroed in on Tillie's phone. "Where did you get that?"

"Aunt Roni."

"That's nice of Aunt Roni to let you play with it. Be careful though, okay?" Mom reached for Ginnie and Toran and hugged them together.

"Sure, but it's mine. Aunt Roni gave it to me."

Mom threw Aunt Roni a puzzled look. "No, she didn't."

Aunt Roni nodded shyly and then brightened her smile. "I did, Amanda. I missed the kids terribly when I left, and no offense—but with everyone coming and going at the farm and with chores, it's too difficult to get a hold of them." She handed Mom a bag from the cell phone store. "Of course, you should have an equally nice phone, so I picked one up for you as well."

Mom shook her head. "Roni, you can't be serious. These cost a small fortune." She pushed the bag gently. "Thanks for the thought, but I can't possibly accept."

"Of course you can. The cell phone plan barely scratches my monthly shoe allowance. I have plenty of shoes. I'd rather talk with the kids, and I want them to be able to talk to me whenever they want."

"But ..." Mom lowered her voice. "Even Tillie?"

Tillie fought the feeling of being second best ... again.

"Of course." Aunt Roni slipped her arms around Tillie's shoulders and squeezed. "I love Tillie already, and Todd, Ginnie, and Toran do as well. If there's one thing I've learned from Queenie and Uncle Ben, it's that family can be who you want it to be, not just who you were born to."

"I know, but ..."

"Mom, please let her talk," Tillie implored, liking that Aunt Roni was including her, like she honestly cared.

Aunt Roni turned to Mom. "My sister gave up our family years ago for Todd's. Of course that hurt, but after we mended fences when Ginnie and Toran were babies, I understood why she wanted to be a West."

"Roni ..." Mom protested.

"Please let me finish." Aunt Roni put her hand up in a "stop" motion. "For a while, I was on equal footing as well. Uncle Ben welcomed me with open arms for the two years before my sister's death. If Widget hadn't passed, she and our daddy would have reconciled, and all the other ugliness wouldn't have happened."

"But it *did* happen, Roni. We can't change that," Mom protested, refusing the bag again. "I don't think Todd would like me accepting the phone—or the kids, either."

"If I can get him to agree, will you?" Aunt Roni asked.

"I doubt he will." Mom shook her head. "Your family is a sensitive subject for him, and so is Queenie."

The anxiety Tillie tried to avoid burrowed deep into her. She felt sorry for both her mom and Aunt Roni.

A quick peek at Ginnie and Toran confirmed they were equally uncomfortable.

"I don't want to dwell on the past, Amanda. I just want to make up for the time we lost." Aunt Roni's voice took on a firm, yet compassionate tone. "I know this is going to sound strange, but even through the ugliness of the last few years, I still consider Todd my brother-in-law."

Mom pinched her lips together, eyeing each of them.

Aunt Roni nodded at Ginnie and Toran, then hugged Tillie tighter. "I only want to be a part of Ginnie and Toran's lives ... and Tillie's ... if you'd be so kind."

"Roni ..."

"I can't lose the kids again. I know very well that you and Todd have all the decision-making power, but I'd like to think you and I can at least be friends." Aunt Roni offered her best smile and the bag with Mom's cell phone. "Please at least think about it. We can put whatever limits on phone use that you'd like. I just want to know that when I leave, I can still be a part of their lives."

"Please, Mom?" Tillie asked as Ginnie and Toran chorused, "Please, Miss Amanda?"

"Really? Four against one? How fair is that?" Mom laughed, and then accepted the bag. "No promises, Roni. Todd is pretty anti-cell phones for kids, but I can see your point."

"Yay!" Ginnie hollered.

"Not so fast," Mom scolded, eyeing each of them.

"Sorry, Miss Amanda," Ginnie apologized.

"There's another matter I want to discuss—with you two in particular." Mom wiggled her pointer finger between Ginnie and Toran. They exchanged puzzled looks and then glanced at Tillie like they were hoping for a clue as to what they were supposed to be discussing.

Tillie shrugged, just as confused as her friends.

"Yes, Miss Amanda?" Toran finally asked.

Mom put her hands on her hips and replied in a stern voice. "That."

"That?" Ginnie arched a confused eyebrow. "That ...? That *what*, Miss Amanda?"

"Yeah, Mom, what?" Tillie echoed.

"That." Mom pointed at Toran and smiled. "Calling me 'Miss Amanda', that's what."

All three tweens glanced at Mom like she had sprouted green hair. "I'll see what I can do about persuading your dad to let you keep the phones *if* you promise to call me just 'Amanda' from now on." She glanced at Aunt Roni and added, "I'm not trying to take Queenie's place. You don't have to call me 'mom,' I just don't want to be 'Miss' anymore. Just Amanda is fine, or Aunt Amanda, like Mysti calls me, or just about anything else."

Ginnie giggled. "You two sure know how to bug my dad. He likes us to use titles. He says it's polite." She peered at Aunt Roni. "And we told you he already vetoed Uncle Jake buying us cell phones for our birthday."

"Not to make this more awkward, Amanda, but 'Miss' is very southern, and their mother would agree with Todd," Aunt Roni added quietly. "I doubt he'll let that go easily."

"Well, 'Miss' was fine when we were dating, but we're engaged now, and I want to move on to being a happy family." Mom slipped her purse strap onto her shoulder.

"Of course." Aunt Roni gave a quick nod. "My apologies, Amanda. That makes perfect sense."

"No problem." Mom motioned toward the restaurant. "I'm starved. I bypassed lunch once we decided to eat here, so let's get going."

"Sure, Miss—*I mean*—sure, *Amanda*." Mom's name didn't fall off Ginnie's tongue very smoothly, but Mom's grateful smile showed she was happy that Ginnie had at least tried.

36

BRIBE, ANYONE?

*W*hile dinner out with Aunt Roni and Amanda had been fun, the real entertainment started when they arrived home. Dad, freshly showered and changed into slacks and a dressy blue shirt with orange and red flames leaping around the bottom, jogged down the front porch steps and met them at Aunt Roni's car.

Uncle Jake followed right behind.

Aunt Roni favored them with her best beauty-queen smile and the two bags of take-out dinners she had ordered before they left the steak house. "Just in time, Todd. Is Uncle Ben home as well?"

"That's him now." Dad nodded toward the end of the lane where a tractor pulled a loaded wagon of light green alfalfa hay bales. "I thought we agreed you'd be here before I was."

"And we would have been if *you* hadn't come in early. It's only eight-thirty, and I brought you hot New York strips—just the way I remember you lovin' them. Medium rare."

He took the bags. "Thanks, except I prefer medium."

"Then you're in luck, because I was just teasing you. Yours *is* medium." She returned his smirk. "I wasn't as sure about the others, so we brought a variety—New York strips, a couple of rib-eyes, and even a filet mignon. Assorted sides as well—deep-fried corn, okra,

157

salads, baked potatoes, and all the fixings. Ginnie, be a doll and grab the pies."

"Yes, *ma'am*." Ginnie happily snatched up the bag and offered her dad a glance. "See, your favorite pie—key lime."

"Looks delicious." He flashed Aunt Roni *his* best smile. "So, what is this scrumptious meal gonna cost me? Or rather, what do you want from me?"

"Not a thang." Aunt Roni fluttered her eyelids and proclaimed in her best Southern accent, "I do decla-eh, Todd West—my, how suspicious you've become."

"Not meaning to pick a fight, but that would be thanks to you and yours." He handed the bags to Uncle Jake, crossed his arms, and offered a cheesy grin. "Whenever you and Queenie go full-blown southern belle on me, it comes with a price. So do me a favor. Make this easy on all of us, and just tell me what you want."

"Now, honey. Be nice." Miss Amanda slid her arm behind his back and waited for him to draw her close.

"Great. She's gotten to you, too." Dad kissed the top of her head and teased, "I should have known better than to let you two become friends."

"Roni hasn't asked a thing from me, Todd. As a matter of fact, she treated the kids and me to a wonderful dinner and a delightful time. Didn't she, guys?"

"She sure did, Dad." Toran nodded. "She's the best."

"Mm-hmmm. I'll bet." He arched an unimpressed eyebrow. "She can afford it."

"Daddy!" Ginnie scolded. The rest of her words were drowned out in the loud blast of the diesel horn Uncle Ben honked in greeting.

She shuddered at the loud noise.

Uncle Jake raised the take-out bags, shaking them. "Hurry back, Uncle Ben. I can't promise we'll wait for you."

Uncle Ben tipped his dark green John Deere cap.

Buzz drove up behind the tractor in Uncle Ben's work truck.

"Why do I get the feeling I'm being softened up for something,

Veronica?" Dad pulled Miss Amanda closer and eyeballed each kid. "And no, you can't have my firstborn—or his sisters."

Aunt Roni rolled her eyes. "You're hilarious."

Toran, Ginnie, and Tillie giggled at the exchange.

Ginnie wanted to deny his accusation, but slipped her hand around her cell phone, squeezed it, and kept quiet.

"The dinner is simply dinner. You have to eat, don't you?" Aunt Roni asked, shooing the kids toward the house.

"Yah, and so do they—but they're happy with drive-through burgers and fries. New York strips, rib-eyes, and filet mignon? That's bribing food."

"Todd, it's not like you to think the worst of people." Miss Amanda frowned at him, then nodded at Aunt Roni. "I know you two have had some rough times, but she seems sincere in wanting to make amends."

"Hon, you're right. I'm not being fair." Dad offered a contrite bow to Aunt Roni, spiking uneasy suspicion in Ginnie. "And I'll be happy to offer an apology if this dinner truly is a 'no-strings attached' deal. Give me your word, Roni, and I'll apologize. I'll even buy the pies."

Toran, Tillie, and Ginnie paused, swiveling as one toward their aunt. *Oh, man, there go our phones.*

"The dinner truly was intended to be a token of my appreciation for you allowing me to reconnect with Ginnie and Toran, and getting to know sweet Tillie here ..."

"But?" Dad asked, eyes twinkling in triumph.

"But ..." Aunt Roni began carefully, eyeing each tween. "At this juncture in our conversation, if I fail to mention that I made a purchase for each of your family members, I fear you will feel deceived—and that will ruin all of the progress we have made. I most certainly cannot allow that."

Dad didn't hesitate. "Then we're on the same page."

"You're going to be a tough nut about this, aren't you?" Aunt Roni's tone wavered between amused and annoyed.

"No, ma'am. That would be ungentlemanly of me. My uncle frowns on such behavior, and I like to stay on his good side." He winked at Aunt Roni and then nodded as Uncle Ben approached. "I trusted you with my children this evening. I just need to know it wasn't misplaced."

Ouch. Ginnie cringed. *Yeah, the phones are history.*

"Touché. Just understand that I miss them, and I want them to stay in touch." Aunt Roni pushed a button on her key fob to open the trunk. "Go ahead and show him, kiddos."

After glancing at one another and exchanging reluctant shrugs, Ginnie, Toran, and Tillie pulled their phones out of their pockets at the same time.

"Aren't they epic, Dad?" Toran asked.

Uncle Jake laughed, backhanding Dad's chest. "Good luck telling them they can't keep them."

"Please, Daddy! Let us keep them?" Ginnie begged.

"Cell phones? Really?" Dad shook his head and glanced with frustration at Miss Amanda. "Did you know?"

"Not until *after* she bought them. Her heart's in the right place, Todd. She just wants to keep in touch with the kids."

"They can use the home phone." He wagged his finger between Ginnie and Toran. "Give. Them. Back."

"But Dad!" they chorused.

"No buts." He pointed his finger at Tillie. "You too."

"I told you he'd say no," Ginnie groused.

"Well at least you aren't surprised that they're not keeping them," Dad said to Aunt Roni, then turned to Ginnie. "You told her that I think you're too young for cell phones?"

"Yes, sir. But she has a point." Ginnie frowned. "You should hear her out."

"No thanks." Dad pointed at Tillie.

Tillie tried to hand it over, but Aunt Roni shook her head. "Can we at least discuss this?" Aunt Roni passed a cell phone bag to Uncle Jake, one to Uncle Ben, and the last one to Dad.

"What's this?" Uncle Ben asked.

"A bribe so the kids can keep the phones," Dad replied, his tone irritated.

Aunt Roni shook her head. "Not so. I bought you matching iPhones so the kids wouldn't have superior technology to the adults in their family."

"You bought iPhones?" A huge grin crossed Uncle Jake's face. "Wow, you really understand the logic behind 'go big or go home'. But why one for me?"

Aunt Roni smiled. "Just because you don't have one-a personal one."

"Miss, I mean, *Amanda* has one too," Ginnie said.

Dad shot her a puzzled look.

"We'll deal with that another time." Miss Amanda slid her arms around Dad's neck and kissed his cheek. "My cell phone plan is almost up, and Roni gave me such a gracious and generous spiel that I told her I would discuss this with you instead of telling her no outright."

"Mmm-hmmm. So now *I* get to be the bad guy. Thanks for that. Ginnie, Toran, Tillie, you heard me. Give. Them. Back."

"But we already put everybody's numbers in them," Ginnie protested. "They're used. She can't return them."

"Dad, think of the phones as back-to-school tools—it has a calculator, and the Internet can be used as an encyclopedia and a research guide. It's basically a pocket-sized computer," Toran offered.

"Which you already own," Dad reminded him.

"But Ginnie and Tillie don't."

"So, what you're saying is, *you* are willing to let your sisters keep their phones, and you'll give yours up?"

"I didn't say *that*, Dad. Be reasonable." Toran shook his head. "There are lots of benefits to us having cell phones."

Dad smirked. "Name three."

Toran grinned. "Research for school, safety if there's an emergency, alarm clocks to help us get up or remind us if we have to be somewhere or do something. We can download a day planner app so we can be organized, and plotting tools for projects. It has a GPS, we can keep track of our ..."

"I said *three*," Dad reminded him, grimacing.

"You can get ahold of us whenever you want—even when I'm riding Calliope," Ginnie chimed in.

"It also has a camera." Tillie waved her phone at her mom. "We can take pictures and movies at your wedding."

Aunt Roni's eyes brightened all the while she kept her expression even. Uncle Jake didn't offer any sympathy for his brother—and even though Uncle Ben sent Uncle Jake a discouraging nod, he couldn't keep from smiling either.

"Let's enjoy dinner while it's hot," Dad said, shooting a warning look around the group.

Ginnie clenched the cell phone tighter in her fist and slid her arms around her dad's waist. "You're the best."

"I didn't say you could keep the phones," he reminded her, squeezing her into a hug.

"I know." Ginnie shot him her best grin. "But you will."

He smirked again. "What makes you so sure?"

"Because it's okay to change your mind about stuff. Remember how you weren't going to date and now you're marrying Miss Amanda? That's a good thing." She hugged him again. "I love her."

"Hmm." He shook his head at Aunt Roni and raised a non-committal eyebrow at Miss Amanda, slipping his hand around her back. "I'll give some thought to your reasoning. But let's eat first. No sense wasting good steak. I will say this, Veronica. You do have impeccable taste."

She curtsied. "Why, thank you, kind sir."

He offered a teasing bow. "You're welcome." He pulled Miss Amanda closer.

Everybody moved toward the farmhouse. Tillie grabbed Ginnie's hand. "Do you think he'll change his mind?"

Leaning forward, Ginnie buffed her fingernails against her green "I ♥ Horses" T-shirt. "He already has."

Tillie giggled. "That was easier than I thought." She caught the screen door.

Ginnie adjusted the bag of pies in her hand. "I told you that your mom was the key to getting you a horse. She seems to be the key to a lot of things." She cackled an evil laugh. "Mwahwhaha, we should use that power wisely."

Nodding, Tillie stifled a giggle. "Of course."

They put the pies in the extra fridge before joining the rest of the family for a blessing on the dinner in the dining room. Once the "Amens" were said, Uncle Ben, Uncle Jake, Buzz, and Dad happily cut into their steak dinners.

Toran and Aunt Roni chatted about Gertrude, making Uncle Ben laugh.

"Let's play with our phones upstairs," Tillie whispered.

Ginnie nodded and followed her into the hallway.

Footsteps on the porch made them look out the screen door.

A man Ginnie didn't recognize stared at them.

"Hi, there." Ginnie smiled at him. "Can we help you?"

He stared intensely at Tillie. "Tilda?"

Tillie froze with her jaw dropped open.

The terror on her friend's face jump-started Ginnie's brain as recognition burned her memory.

The stranger before them was none other than Jasper Taylor.

37

WE HAVE COMPANY

*T*illie stood immobile, not wanting to believe her eyes. Her heart stopped momentarily, then sped up. Blood coursed loudly through her ears. Her throat constricted as she stared at the man she had feared for so long.

He had the same straight mouse-brown hair she had—only he wore his in a stylish man's cut. He had the rotten nerve to smile. "You *are* Tilda, aren't you?"

Her lungs screamed, reminding her that they were oxygen-deprived. Tillie sucked in a breath.

"Um, UNCLE BEN!" Ginnie called loudly. "We've got COMPANY!"

The man glanced at Ginnie. "You must be Ginnie—Todd's little girl, right?"

Ginnie moved in front of Tillie and stopped. "Yes, sir. I'm Ginnie. This is my best friend, Til-*LEE.*"

He chuckled nervously. "Oh, yeah. Her mom calls her that. I always called her Tilda or Angel."

"Gin, invite him in."

Tillie registered Uncle Ben's approaching footsteps at the same time that she recognized his welcoming voice. "Ginnie, this is our good friend, Jasper Taylor. Come on in, Jasper—it's been too long."

Ginnie opened the door. Tillie moved back, giving Uncle Ben plenty of room to reach her worst nightmare and serve as a human shield between them.

Jasper's smile deepened as relief swept his face.

He was barely through the door before Uncle Ben caught him in a welcoming bear hug.

Tillie turned away, belly clenching.

Ginnie grabbed Tillie's hand and pulled her down the hallway.

Tillie stumbled along a few feet, then hunched against the wall beneath a row of West family portraits.

Mom stood next to DT in the doorway leading to the dining room. He offered her his hand, but Mom shook her head. Tillie swiveled back to see Jasper clutch onto Uncle Ben like a drowning man would a raft.

"Oh, man, Uncle Ben. I've missed you so much!" Jasper said, his voice cracking. "I'm so sorry I had to leave. I'm not that guy anymore —I—I promise."

Tillie's gaze locked on Jasper's face, surprised to see tears forming in his eyes.

Bewildered, Tillie glanced at her mom, whose eyes also shone.

When Mom held up her hand to stop DT from embracing her, Aunt Roni hugged Mom instead.

"Jasper, you're always welcome." Uncle Ben hugged him again. "There's time to talk about the past later. Right now, I'm just very happy to see you."

The sincerity in Uncle Ben's words panicked Tillie.

Jasper clung on to Uncle Ben for several seconds longer than Tillie expected him to before letting go.

Uncle Ben took a step back. "Let me look at you."

Jasper ducked his head and wiped his eyes, not quite meeting Tillie's gaze before standing straight and tall. His yellow polo shirt shone against his tanned arms.

"The California sun looks good on you, son. Mighty good." Uncle Ben smiled. "Still working as a brick layer?"

"Yes, sir. And jack-of-all-trades. My boss was so impressed with my work—he asked me if I'd move to Kentucky to start a new subdivision he just bought. It's only two hours from here, so I jumped on the chance to come closer to home. I wanted to see my little girl."

I'm NOT YOUR little girl! The scream froze in Tillie's throat, choking her. Jasper glanced her way. Tillie dropped her gaze to the red-and-blue braided throw rug. *At least he's not gonna live HERE.*

"Amanda?" The surprise in Jasper's voice caused Tillie to look up in time to see him lock his eyes on Mom. "I—I didn't expect to see you tonight." He took a step toward her, pausing when Tillie stiffened. "Wow, you're even more beautiful than I remembered. I—I'm sorry it took me so long to get my life together. I hope you'll give me a chance to apologize and start over."

"Thank you, Jasper. You look well," Mom said.

"Thinking about you and Tilda is what kept me going these last few months—but I did what you and Uncle Ben asked. I didn't come back until I was sober for a whole year. I even brought documentation."

He offered a shy smile and sidled closer.

Straightening, Tillie stepped away from the wall to block his path to Mom.

"Tilda." Jasper stopped. "I can see that I've surprised you, but I've missed you so much." He reached his arms toward her. "I'll make it up to you."

"No!" Tillie jumped back, away from him, toward Mom.

"Tilda, I won't hurt you." A crushed expression colored his face. "Please believe me. I'm not that guy anymore. Give me a chance to prove it to you, honey. *Please.*"

Shaking her head, Tillie backed up even more.

Mom enveloped her in a hug. Tillie blinked back burning tears, unprepared for the hurt in Jasper's eyes.

DT nodded at her, mouthing, "It's okay."

It's NOT okay.

"I'm *not* your little girl." She choked out the words, fleeing toward DT, and then stopped, not wanting Jasper to know that DT was engaged to her mom.

Spinning, she fled around Jasper to Uncle Ben. "I don't want to be *his* little girl. Make him stay away."

"Tillie, he wants to make amends." Uncle Ben pulled her into a hug. "Let him. There's nothing to be afraid of." He brushed his thumb across her cheek. "We're all here."

She darted a quick look to Jasper.

His mouth hung open, stunned.

Her heartbeat quickened. "I can't. He's going to ruin everything. Don't make me see him."

Toran appeared out of nowhere, in front of her, with Ginnie by his side.

"Jet, dude. Good to see you." Uncle Jake frowned at Tillie, but she didn't care.

Uncle Jake shook Jasper's hand, pulling him into a quick hug. "It's about time the prodigal son returned." He lowered his voice, but Tillie still heard his words. "She's surprised—give her a little time. She'll come around." His voice became louder, welcoming. "How ya been? By the way, there's a new-fangled invention called a cell phone. You oughta get one. I just did, thanks to my sister-out-law."

Jasper took in Aunt Roni, apparently seeing her for the first time since he arrived. "Queenie? H—How can that be? I was at your funeral."

"That's sister-*out*-law, not sister-*in*-law." Uncle Jake joked. "This is Roni Stratton, Queenie's twin."

"Oh ... yeah." Jasper slid his hand down his black jeans. "I forgot about that. We met at her funeral."

"I do believe I had the pleasure of making your acquaintance at that time." Aunt Roni extended her hand. "So nice to see you again."

Jasper took the offered hand. "And you as well."

Tillie was surprised at how friendly he sounded.

Jasper smiled and turned to Uncle Jake. "Wing, I did have a cell—"

at least until it landed in a puddle." He gave a nervous laugh. "You got my message, didn't you?"

"Yep. I was a little surprised you didn't call back."

"I lost my nerve." Jasper glanced at Tillie. She looked away. "I didn't expect an open-armed reception—well, only as a best-case scenario—but I'll admit, being rejected outright by my one and only child is a little bit unnerving."

Tillie swallowed, hugging Uncle Ben harder.

Ginnie and Toran backed up as one, closer to her.

"You must be Toran. You're like a Todd clone. I met your dad the first time when he was about your age."

When Toran nodded, Jasper swiveled to DT. "Man, Boy Scout, your kids sure look like you and Queenie. Of course, my girl looks like her mother. Good thing, too. Amanda is gorgeous and a great mom. I see Angel fits right in here." He shot a peek at Tillie, and then DT. "I knew you'd take good care of them when I couldn't. Thanks for that."

Good. Then you won't mind making it permanent. Tillie relaxed a little, but tightened her grip on Uncle Ben.

"Our pleasure," DT said, extending his hand and pulling Jasper into a hug like Uncle Jake had.

Alarmed, Tillie searched his face for signs of betrayal, unprepared for her future stepdad to be so friendly to her lousy-excuse-for-a-birth-father.

DT brightened his smile. "Ginnie and Tillie are best friends and consider themselves sisters. They're very close. It's been a true pleasure having them grow up together."

An expression—maybe relief—battled hurt when Jasper darted his eyes from DT to Tillie. "Well, I always wished I could've been a West. I'm glad my kid can be one." He sighed.

Tillie refused to feel sorry for him.

"I loved being an honorary West, Tilda. All my best memories as a kid are here on the farm—Oma's strawberry bread, Aunt Sadie's hugs, doing chores with Jake. Even getting busted by Uncle Ben when he caught Jake and me ditching school." He laughed. "Playing tag with Vi—she'd always squeal when I caught her." He glanced around. "Where is Vi? And Buzz?"

"Vi's out with her fiancé. Buzz is over there." Uncle Ben motioned to Buzz, who moved past Mom, offering an outstretched hand.

"You're not a kid anymore," Jasper said, seeming surprised.

"I'll be twenty-two in December," Buzz agreed.

"Wow. Time marches on. My baby girl is a young woman." He shot a nervous glance her way. Tillie avoided his look. "Little Vi is getting married?" Jasper turned to Uncle Jake. "She finally found someone who didn't run when you put him through the wringer?"

"Hey, I take my job as a big brother seriously." Uncle Jake winked at him, and then nodded at Mom.

Jasper rubbed his jaw and smirked. "I remember."

For the first time since Jasper came, Tillie felt like giggling.

She didn't, but remembering that Uncle Jake had beat up Jasper the last time he had hurt her and Mom made her feel better about how nice the Wests were being to him.

Uncle Ben gave Tillie's shoulder a reassuring squeeze. "We were just sitting down for a steak dinner. Come join us."

"I'm not really hungry, but I'll let you twist my arm." Jasper arched a questioning eyebrow at Tillie while smiling at Uncle Ben. "Your steaks are the best."

"They aren't his, but they are delicious," Ginnie said, wrapping her arm around Tillie's shoulders.

They all walked toward the dining room.

Uncle Jake invited Jasper to sit next to him.

"Thanks, Wing. I can't tell you how many times I pretended just about every dining room I've eaten in was this one. So many good memories here." He smiled shyly at Tillie before looking at Uncle Ben. "Especially with Aunt Sadie's cooking. Everything that woman touched was good ... the people, too."

Tillie sat across the table from Jasper, between Mom and Ginnie, as far from him as she could. "Why do you call Uncle Jake 'Wing'?" The question popped out before Tillie could stop it.

"I'm glad he's still 'Uncle' to you." Jasper pulled out his chair and sat. "Do you know what a wingman is?"

Tillie swallowed, wishing she'd kept quiet.

She'd rather he think she was invisible.

She shook her head.

He focused on Tillie's eyes, making her cringe. "A wingman is a good friend who has your back and helps keep you safe. He can often see dangers you can't."

Aunt Roni placed an extra dinner with a fork and steak knife crossed on top of the plate in front of Jasper.

"Thank you, Roni."

"You're mighty welcome."

"It's nice to hear a Southern accent again. Not many of those in California." Jasper said to Aunt Roni before catching Tillie's eye again. "Sorry, Tilda. To finish answering your question, I was cursed with the name Jasper Erasmus Taylor. Jake used the initials, J-E-T, or Jet, to make it cool. There's an awesome wingman in the movie *Top Gun* who kept the lead pilot safe. The pilot could be an idiot, but his wingman never failed him. Jake has always been my wingman, even when I made it tough for him." He elbowed Uncle Jake. "I sure appreciate that, brother."

Uncle Jake winked at Tillie. "You're welcome, brother."

Tillie nodded, determined to keep her distance.

"Tils, why don't we go cut and serve the pie while the men eat and catch up?" Mom asked.

When Tillie hesitated, Ginnie piped up. "I'll help."

"Thanks, honey." Mom slid her chair in. "Tils?"

DT cleared his throat.

"Yes'm." Tillie stood, happy to see Ginnie already standing.

"Back in a minute with pie," Mom said brightly, shooing Ginnie and Tillie in front of her.

Aunt Roni followed after them.

38

EXPECTATIONS

*T*oran watched as Jasper kept his eyes glued on Tillie and Miss Amanda until they rounded the doorway leading into the kitchen, then took a quick left turn into the side porch.

The door squeaked closed.

"So, is this where Amanda tells our daughter that she doesn't need to be afraid of me? Or is this where they escape out the side door and disappear until I leave?" Jasper asked, trying to hide his hurt with a teasing tone.

"Don't read too much into Tillie's reluctance," Uncle Ben advised. "You caught them by surprise."

"I didn't even plan to see them tonight, Uncle Ben. I just wanted to see *you* guys, and feel things out." He set his fork down. "I didn't mean to freak them out."

"I don't think they're freaked—just a little surprised." Toran offered. "Especially Tillie."

"If Amanda would ever let me talk to her, she wouldn't be so surprised." This time he didn't hide his frustration. "She's my daughter, too. I *love* her."

"We know you do." Uncle Ben gestured toward his plate. "Eat up. You'll feel better. I'm sure they'll be back with the pie soon."

"Please don't take this wrong, Uncle Ben, but I don't want steak or pie. I want my family." He pushed his chair back a little. "I *never* did to her what Oscar did to me. Most of the time, I was a very good dad to her."

"You *were* a good dad," Dad agreed, cutting a piece of steak. "Tillie and I talked about that last night."

"Is that what *she* remembers?" Jasper picked up his knife and fork. "Because I'm not feeling the love."

Toran shot an expectant look at his dad, waiting for him to catch Jasper up on the engagement.

"I reminded her about that time you drove to Lake Henry to find her baby doll."

"Oh, yeah." Jasper poked his fork into his steak and smiled. "I was her hero that day. She took one look at her baby doll and was my best friend for the rest of that night and the next day. Too bad she was only three. I bet *she* didn't remember."

"She didn't, but she liked that you cared enough to find her doll." Dad's tone offered understanding. "I also reminded her about your singing jam sessions, and that frog sound you made and she'd laugh, remember?"

He chuckled. "Now that you mention it." He searched each man's face around the table. "I had my moments as a good dad. I even made Amanda happy at times." His expression turned serious. "So ... do you think I have a chance with them?"

Toran coughed into his fist.

"I think Tillie needs a little time to get used to the idea of seeing you again." Dad handed Toran a glass of water and a warning look. "It has been *six* years."

"It's not like Amanda ever remarried. She could've." Jasper took a drink of lemonade. "I keep hoping that means part of her wants us to be a family again. We were good together for a long time. If I hadn't started drinking after I lost my construction job, we'd still be together. I *know* it."

"But you *did* start drinking, and there's been a lot of history since then, bro." Uncle Jake drummed his fingers on the table. "*Bad history.*"

"I've been sober most of the last three years, Jake. And solid for the last twelve months." He darted a look around the table like he was daring any of them to argue with him. "Amanda said she'd consider giving me a chance if I could stay sober for a year. I did that." He pointed his fork at Uncle Ben. "I'm *still* doing it and I'll *keep* doing it—you have my word, Uncle Ben. I'm solid on this."

Uncle Ben nodded. "I believe you."

"About Amanda, Jet," Uncle Jake said, not quite meeting Jasper's gaze. "We need to talk."

"About what? She has a boyfriend?" Jasper steeled his gaze on Uncle Jake, puncturing the air with his fork. "She didn't when I talked with her five or six weeks ago—at least not one she mentioned."

"She wasn't dating six weeks ago, but—" Dad started.

"But what?" Jasper's hand and fork froze in midair.

"She did start dating *four* weeks ago."

"Who?" The one-word question held several layers of frustration and warning.

"Me."

"You? You can't be serious." Jasper laughed and then stopped abruptly. "Wait—you're serious?"

"Yes, I'm serious." Dad straightened in his chair.

"Really, Todd? Some boy scout you turned out to be. What happened to being loyal and trustworthy?"

Dad ignored the slight. "I asked her to marry me on Saturday. She said yes."

"So *un*ask her." Jasper stabbed his fork at Dad. "She's *my* wife."

A feeling like a lead ball sunk into Toran's gut.

"She's your *ex*-wife, and I can't. I love her too much."

The lead ball lightened a little.

"Welcome to my world." Jasper grimaced, then shook his head sharply. "Sorry, Todd. You can't have her. I've worked too hard and too long to get my family back."

"Jasper—" Dad protested.

. "No!" Jasper held up his hand. "When we break ground in the new development, I'm going to build Amanda her dream home. I've got it all figured out. It'll take a few months to build the house, which will give me time to fix things between us." He pushed his chair back farther and stood, facing Uncle Ben. "You promised if I stayed sober for a year, kept a good job, and could prove I was a changed man, you'd help me get my family back. I did that. I'm. *Not*. Giving. Them. Up."

"It's not just about you wanting them." Toran stood, swallowing hard. "Tillie and Miss Amanda want *us*. Dad, Ginnie, and I want *them*. We want to be a family too."

"Sorry, kid. Amanda was my wife first, and Tilda will *always* be my daughter." He gave a sharp nod. "The three of us are *already* a family."

Dad pointed toward the kitchen and stood. "Toran, please go help the girls with the pie."

Jasper clenched his fist. "I'm not gonna deck him, Todd. You don't have anything to worry about."

"I didn't say you were." Dad motioned Toran to the kitchen again. Toran took two steps and stopped. "This conversation has made a sharp turn from friendly to adult, and I don't want my son to be a part of it."

"Look, I didn't come to cause trouble. Please try to see this from *my* point of view." He pulled out his wallet, opened it, and showed them a family picture of Miss Amanda, Tillie as a toddler, and himself. "See our smiles? They were real. This was the best time of my life. My wife and daughter loved me, I was a great husband and father, and my good-for-nothing parents were dead. I had a great job. Amanda, Tilda, and I were truly happy."

"Jasper, I know this is hard to hear—" Dad began.

"No, Todd. I *can't* hear *that*." Jasper swiveled to Uncle Ben, thrusting the photo toward his face. "This picture and the thought that we could be like this again is what has sustained me in my darkest hours. I'm *this* man again." He flashed the picture to Dad and

Toran. "I just need to prove that to Amanda, and my life can be good again."

Even though part of Toran felt sorry for Jasper, he remembered Tillie puking at the thought of seeing him and couldn't stay quiet. "But Miss Amanda isn't *that* woman and Tillie isn't *that* child anymore. They want *us*. And *we* want *them*."

"You know, Toran, I was wrong. You should do what your dad said and go to a different room." He clamped his jaw shut, adding a menacing hardness to his dark features.

"Okay, everybody, take a breath." Uncle Ben placed a firm hand on Jasper's shoulder. "The important thing is that you know that we're happy you're back. Obviously you have expectations we hadn't fully considered, and we have news you didn't know about. We'll sort it out."

Jasper shook his head. "How's that gonna happen? I'm not sharing my wife with *anybody*—" He glared at Dad. "Brother or no brother."

Ouch. Toran turned to his dad, curious to see how he'd respond.

Dad opened his mouth, then closed it before he said a word.

Thumper prevails.

Uncle Ben stood straighter, shooting Toran and Dad warning looks as he made his voice more soothing. "We'll all need to make adjustments, but now isn't the time to bang out the details." He gave Jasper's shoulder a gentle squeeze. "Tillie and Amanda will be back any minute, and Jasper, you need to concentrate on making them comfortable with you being here—especially Tillie. She hasn't seen or talked to you in a long time. Be patient. Her way of looking at your return is a bit different than yours."

"That's not my fault." Jasper bristled. "Amanda refused to let me talk to her ..."

"We'll sort that out later as well. Right now, try to move past your hurt feelings so you can put your best foot forward with your daughter. Your ultimate goal should be repairing your relationship with her. I'll hear you out on the rest of it after Amanda and Tillie go home for the night."

As if on cue, the side porch door opened.

Jasper grimaced at Uncle Ben and gave a quick nod.

39

STEEL MAGNOLIAS

illie trembled as she followed Mom and Ginnie onto the side porch. Mom motioned for Aunt Roni to shut the door.

"Tils, it's gonna be okay." Mom tucked her long hair behind her ear and touched their foreheads together. "Honey, you can't be so defensive around your dad if we're going to make this work."

"Jasper's not my dad—not anymore. We picked a new one, *remember?*" Tillie swallowed hard and channeled Ginnie. "Just make him go away."

"Tillie, he doesn't seem so scary in person—not like I remember from before." Ginnie tried to hug her. Tillie pushed her friend away. "Your mom's right. My dad and uncles aren't going to let him hurt you. You don't have to hug him or anything. Since you already told him off, he'll leave you alone." Ginnie smiled. "You surprised me, but good for you."

"I'm staying *here.*" Tillie swiveled as everyone crowded around. "I don't care what any of you say. When a guy disappears for six years, he should have to cut up his 'father' card. *Your* dad would never do that."

"No, but my dad is crazy the other way." Ginnie rolled her eyes. "He's smothering."

"Trade ya!"

"Tils, that's not fair." Mom frowned. "Jasper has made an effort to change, and he's been very good about sending child support and alimony these last couple of years."

"Why are you taking his side? He was always worse to you than to me." Tillie crossed her arms. "Why are you being nice to him?"

"Because he's done everything I asked him to do," Mom said, leaning against the extra fridge.

The too-familiar sickening feeling trembled in Tillie's belly. "What does *that* mean?"

Mom sighed. "I didn't really expect him to do it."

"Do what?" Tillie demanded.

"Stay sober long enough to come back."

The tremble worsened.

Mom grimaced, like she was sucking a lemon. "He does well for a while—then loses his job or something crazy happens and things tank. I told him I couldn't keep riding his emotional roller coaster."

Ginnie shook her head, looking puzzled.

Mom tried to explain. "Jasper always has good intentions. I just got tired of hoping he could consistently be who we both wanted him to be." Mom reached a hand to Tillie's shoulder and one to Ginnie's. She glanced at Aunt Roni. "It was too hard on Tillie when he'd get his life together only to have it fall apart soon after."

Ginnie let Mom hug her.

Tillie stiffened.

Mom straightened and rubbed Tillie's upper arm. "I stopped letting him talk to you. Since I hadn't dated in a while and Jasper wanted so much to get back together, I told him that when he could stay sober and keep a good job for at least a year, we could reassess things at that point." She glanced at Aunt Roni. "He's never made it this far before—at least, since he left. I don't want to be the reason he fails—*if* he fails again."

"I can understand that." Aunt Roni offered a sympathetic smile. "I sincerely admire you, Amanda. We have a name for women like you down South. We call them steel magnolias. Beautiful, feminine, and strong."

"I'm not feeling so strong right now. I want to keep what I have with Todd and hope Jasper can deal with it without falling apart."

Aunt Roni nodded. "Well I suspect you're feeling like a grasshopper in a hen house about now. But if you bounce high and quick enough, you'll be alright. We'll help."

Mom gave a hopeful smile. "Jasper really does love Tillie and me. I know that. So, it's hard to just kick him to the curb like Tillie wants me to."

"Now there's a good plan!" Tillie said.

"Yeah," Ginnie agreed.

"No, it's not." Mom got her sour-lemon look back. "Part of me still loves him—just like your dad will always love *your* mom, Ginnie."

"But my dad never hit my mom—and he'd never hurt *you,* either," Ginnie protested.

"Your dad wasn't raised by evil people. *Jasper was.*" Mom straightened, steeling her gaze on Tillie. "Jasper and I have a child together— you—and we both love you very much. Jasper has a right to be a part of your life, as long as he behaves like the decent man I know he can be."

"Mom!"

"I *don't* want to be married to him, Matilda Grace. *I love Todd*. I want to make a life with the five of us—but I *do* want Jasper to stay sober and be happy. He deserves that much."

"He can do that in Kentucky," Tillie snapped.

"Tils, *stop*. It's not like you to be so hard-hearted." Mom shook her finger. "I don't like this side of you."

Tillie blinked in disbelief. She crossed her arms and glared. "I don't want him back."

"I'm not asking him back. But he was a good dad to you more than he wasn't."

"That's not what *I* remember."

"I know—the last few months before he left were the hardest on all of us." She turned to Ginnie. "You used to like him too. Your dad, Jake, and Jasper spent many days at parks playing with you three kids after we moved back."

"Didn't you always live here?" Ginnie asked.

Mom shook her head. "We moved away soon after Aunt Sadie died. That was the worst decision we ever made."

Tillie tried to remember not living nearby and vaguely recalled a strange apartment. "Why'd we move?"

"Jasper got a new job, but it didn't work out." She sighed. "He went from job to job, made bad friends, and started drinking. Things got pretty ugly. After a couple years of that, I ran into Jake on one of his truck runs and asked him to help."

"Was that when we started kindergarten?" Ginnie asked. "I don't remember meeting Tillie before then."

"Yes." Mom nodded. "We moved back just after school started. Jake and Todd got Jasper hired on with them at Seb's Trucking. Things turned around for a while, but then other things happened."

Ginnie frowned. "I don't remember much, but once he hurt Tillie, I didn't want anything to do with him."

"I understand. Uncle Ben told him that if he couldn't keep his hands to himself, he had better leave. Jake was even more blunt." Mom smiled at Ginnie. "I was surprised at how supportive your family was to me, since they were Jasper's friends first. But Uncle Ben doesn't hold with violence against anyone—*especially* women and children."

"I'm sure," Aunt Roni said, looking uncharacteristically fierce. "I imagine Uncle Ben gave Jasper quite the earful at their 'come-to-Jesus' meeting. I'd be disappointed in Uncle Ben if he hadn't."

In spite of her anger, Tillie giggled at the image.

"He did, but what made it harder for both of them is that Uncle Ben had championed Jasper against *his* father when Jasper was a kid. Oscar Taylor brings a whole new level to the term 'child abuse'." Mom shook her head, shuddering. "When Uncle Ben found out that Jasper had hurt me a few times, Uncle Ben told Jasper to straighten up in no uncertain terms. For a short while, things were a lot better. Then things tanked and Jasper felt desperate--but he left before hurting us again."

A knowing smile crossed Tillie's lips. "Pierce said Uncle Ben had the same kind of talk with his dad when he got out of jail."

"The difference is that Ray Owens doesn't like Uncle Ben at all." Mom sighed. "On the other hand, Jasper loves and admires Uncle Ben to a fault. He needs Uncle Ben's approval even more than he needs mine."

Recalling Jasper's desperate hug, Tillie cringed.

Mom seemed to force a smile to her lips. "At any rate, having Uncle Ben on my side has kept Jasper trying to fix things. Which has been good—until now."

"It does make things more complicated in some ways, doesn't it?" Aunt Roni gave Mom's hand a friendly squeeze. "Trying to find the best in someone when they've lost their way can be very wearying."

"True, Roni. Jasper has a good heart, but his parents were so vicious that he gets short-tempered and defensive and makes things worse than they need to be." Mom's tone softened, making Tillie cringe. "However, when things are going well, he can be every bit as charming as Todd or Jake or Uncle Ben."

"Mom, you can't think like that." Tillie scrunched her face in concern. "We. Don't. Want. Him. Back. *Ever*."

"I told you I don't want to marry him again, Matilda Grace. I *also* don't wish him any harm." Mom lowered her voice, speaking firmly. "You don't have to be alone with him, but I *expect* you to be polite. He needs a little time to adjust to me marrying again—especially since it's not to him."

"But Mom—"

"No, Tillie." Mom furrowed her brow. "I haven't let him talk to you since Christmas because it upset you so much. You can return the favor by being pleasant tonight so that he can keep his pride intact. He's handled you rejecting him very well. Please don't push him."

Tillie opened her mouth to protest.

Ginnie nodded at Mom. "She's right, Tillie. He could have blown his top when you ran to Uncle Ben, but instead, he made a joke. Unless he tries to hit you, it can't hurt to be polite."

"Seriously?" Tillie couldn't believe her ears. "Some sister *you* are. You're supposed to be on *my* side."

Ginnie arched an offended eyebrow. "Hmmm."

Recalling similar words spoken to her earlier and how they made her feel, Tillie glanced at her BFF. "Sorry."

"You gather more flies with honey than vinegar," Ginnie said evenly before brightening her voice into a teasing tone. "Or weren't you paying attention at lunch?"

Aunt Roni smiled.

Tillie smirked. "That's different."

"How so?" Ginnie narrowed her eyes. "I don't like Jasper any more than you do, but he hasn't said anything mean. Your mom already said you don't have to be alone with him." Ginnie walked over the fridge and opened the door. "Let's have some pie and see how things go."

"Can we just go home, Mom?" Tillie whirled to the screen door. "We can come back later when Jasper leaves." She grinned at Aunt Roni. "We have cell phones now. Ginnie can call us when the coast is clear."

"Not!" Ginnie shook her head. "If I have to see him, *you* have to see him." She handed Tillie a box of pie, kept one, and closed the refrigerator door. "I'll be right next to you, so quit being a worrywart. Nothing's gonna happen."

"She's right, sugar." Aunt Roni brushed a soft thumb against Tillie's cheek. "And if something did, there are plenty of people to help you. Listen to your sister." Aunt Roni smiled at Mom, who nodded. "Your mama needs you to cooperate so she can stay strong. This is just as difficult for her, and maybe more so. Steel magnolias need to stick together. I know you to be very brave, sugar."

I'm not brave. I want to hide until he leaves.

Something in Aunt Roni's eyes and her words made Tillie shake away her thoughts. "Okay, but I'm *not* hugging him."

"Fair enough, Tils." Mom motioned to the door.

Aunt Roni opened it.

Ginnie snaked her arm through Tillie's, adjusting the pie box and whispered. "We'll be steel magnolias together."

"Deal." Tillie sucked in a breath and tried to feel brave.

Mom gave her a quick hug and made a circle with her finger to include all four of them. "We'll *all* be steel magnolias ... *together.*"

The trembling eased.

Tillie let out her breath and forced her feet to move forward.

40

UNCLE JASPER

oran watched as Aunt Roni stepped into the doorway of the dining room and offered her friendliest hostess smile. "We hope you've been enjoying your meal, fellas. Give us two shakes, and we'll have the pie served and ready to deliver."

Tillie faced straight ahead and rushed into the kitchen.

Ginnie smiled awkwardly and kept pace with Tillie.

"Be right back," Miss Amanda called, following them.

"I guess that answers your question," Uncle Jake teased quietly, elbowing Jasper. "They stayed."

Jasper elbowed him back. "You know, Jake, I'm not sure I missed your snarky mouth, not even a little bit."

Toran chuckled, more out of relief of seeing the girls than in response to Jasper's comment. "And bonus, they're bringing pie."

Aunt Roni walked over to the rectangular cherry wood dining table. "May I freshen your drinks, fellas?"

"I'm fine, thanks," Jasper replied, his eyes glued on her.

He had the same look all of them did, when Aunt Roni first came, like he was seeing a ghost.

"Wonderful." She smiled, then walked around the table and reached between Toran and Dad. She picked up Dad's glass. "More lemonade, Todd?"

He nodded. "Yes, please."

Aunt Roni whispered, "She'll be fine," then picked up Toran's glass. "More lemonade, Toran?"

"Yes, please." Toran stood. "Buzz, your drink's empty. I'll get a refill for you." He picked up his cousin's glass and eyed Jasper's almost empty one. "Mr. Taylor, you sure you don't want a refill?"

Uncomfortable silence pounded in the air.

"No, thanks." Jasper glanced at the empty space behind him, then turned toward Dad and lowered his voice, not bothering to mask his frustrated look or tone. "Jake's 'uncle' to my kid, but I'm 'mister' to yours? Thanks for that ... *brother*." He swiveled to Toran, seeming to force a smile. "No offense, Toran. I don't blame you. I know how big your family is on good manners."

The hurt look on Jasper's face made Toran's gut clench.

He opened his mouth, then clamped his jaw shut, then shook his head. "It's just that you and Ginnie used to call me 'Uncle Jasper.' I didn't realize I'd been demoted." He turned to Dad, shaking his head. "Please don't tell me that Angel calls you 'Dad' or 'Daddy'. I don't think I could stand it."

Remembering yesterday's awkward lunch, Toran's gaze searched his dad's pinking cheeks, trying to figure out how to help them all out. "Tillie doesn't usually call my dad anything. But she calls the rest of our family whatever Ginnie and I do—Uncle Ben, Oma, Opa, Uncle Jake, Aunt Roni, Vi, Buzz."

Buzz straightened in his chair. "That's true, Jasper. Tillie usually doesn't address Todd as anything. She goes to him and talks to him instead of calling him from a distance to get his attention."

"Because he's her secret 'perfect' dad, right?" Jasper put the 'perfect' in air quotes. "Believe it or not, I understand *that*." He studied Uncle Ben for an uncomfortable minute before continuing. "I understand it, but I don't want to hear about it."

He took a quick gulp of lemonade. "I don't have to be in Kentucky until Thursday. I had hoped to come home and recharge my batteries tonight and deal with whatever fallout I needed to tomorrow with Amanda and Angel."

Dad set his fork down. "Jasper, honest, Tillie really doesn't call me anything, but if it makes you feel better, Ginnie doesn't think I'm anywhere near perfect." He smirked, raising his fingers to air quote. "I'm too 'lame' for her tastes and I 'ruin all her fun.' If you'd been here earlier today, you would have witnessed that yourself."

"That's true, Uncle Jasper." Toran nodded, chuckling. "I haven't seen you in so long that I just forgot what to call you. Sorry about that."

"Nice save, Toran. Thanks." Jasper flashed a suspicious smirk at Dad, but seemed to relax when he saw Aunt Roni offer a sympathetic smile. "How are Oma and Opa? Still living with Uncle Eli and Aunt Daniele?"

"They're doing well." Uncle Ben speared his okra. "I mentioned to Mama and Daddy that you might be back soon. Daddy told me to make sure you give him a call when you get to town and Mama said she'd make you a loaf of strawberry bread."

"Yum, I've been craving her strawberry bread. I'll call them tomorrow—first thing." Jasper laughed. "I love how you still call Opa 'Daddy'. That would be weird in California, but it sounds so right here on The Heart." His tone turned serious. "Good riddance to California though. They can have it—I'd rather be here."

He straightened and pointed a finger at Dad. "Todd, as much as thinking about you and Amanda being together is making my blood boil, I can't leave again just yet. I'm not giving Amanda up without a fight, either. Just so you know. I. Just. *Can't.*"

The uncomfortable silence got louder.

"Jasper," Dad said.

"I mean that metaphorically, of course." Jasper blew out a frustrated breath. "You haven't married her yet, right?"

"I intend to."

"But you *haven't* married her, so I'd appreciate it if you'd let me have tonight, before *all* my dreams are shattered." He lowered his voice. "I've been gone a long time. Please let me have tonight."

"Fair enough." Dad searched out Uncle Jasper's eyes. "For what it's worth, I *am* glad you're back and I want you to feel welcome here."

Toran stopped the protest he was forming when he caught a slight shake of his dad's head.

Jasper nodded at a plaque decorated with violets hanging in the hallway spelling out one of Uncle Ben's favorite greetings:
Welcome to Our Home: When You're Here, You're Family.

"Thank you." Jasper gave Dad a sharp nod and turned to Uncle Ben. "That sign's been burned into my brain ever since Oscar beat me with that telephone wire and tore up my back." He pointed to the plaque. "I must have read that saying a hundred times straddled on one of these chairs, trying not to cry while you patched me up."

Toran sucked in a horrified breath, his belly clenching tighter as the image of a hurt kid shifted through his mind. "Sorry, Uncle Jasper. That sounds awful."

"It was." He glanced at Dad. "I'm sorry. I wasn't thinking about Toran being here. Honest, no offense."

"None taken. That was a horrible night," Dad said, cringing some. "I'm sorry it happened. Seeing your back like that gave me nightmares. You didn't deserve that. Nobody does."

"No kidding. Just remembering Oscar coming at me *still* gives me nightmares ..." Jasper shuddered. "Anyway, the iodine stung so bad that concentrating on that sign made me feel better—well, that and Oma's strawberry bread." He glanced at Toran. "They still lived here then."

Jasper attempted a laugh, but it came out sounding more like a kitten being strangled.

He blinked a couple of times, clearing his throat to hide the break in his voice. "That sign comes to mind every now and again when I start feeling sorry for myself. You guys were friends to me when I couldn't find any other good in my life. I really need to feel that again."

"You poor dear. I can't even imagine." Aunt Roni's sickened expression mirrored Toran's queasy belly. "The monster! I hope he spent years in jail for hurting you."

Jasper shrugged. "Not even close. Nobody cared about kids like me back then." He swiped at his cheeks and locked his eyes on Uncle Ben. "Except you and Aunt Sadie. Thanks for being the exception to the rule. I try to remember how much *you* cared, rather than how much my own father *didn't*."

"We still do, Jasper." Uncle Ben strengthened his tone. "I meant it when I said I'm glad you're home."

"I'm glad to be here—and thank you. I sure needed to hear it." Jasper drained his glass and held it out to Toran. "I've changed my mind, if you'd be so kind."

He imitated Aunt Roni's Southern accent, lightening the mood.

"Yes, sir." Toran took it. "Refill coming up, Uncle Jasper."

"Thanks, Toran, but no need to 'sir' me." He gave Toran's wrist a gentle squeeze. "Though the 'Uncle Jasper' part sounded pretty good."

"Yes, si—um. Sure, Uncle Jasper." Toran smiled and headed for the kitchen, glad to have a reason to leave.

41

BRAVE

*G*innie froze in the kitchen doorway, watching Tillie's face churn through a kaleidoscope of emotions. Sympathy and anger seemed to battle her features most fiercely.

Listening to Jasper describe himself as a hurt, desperate kid, clinging to Uncle Ben's and Aunt Sadie's compassion and kindness challenged most of the other images Ginnie always recalled of him. She could tell Tillie struggled with the same issue.

Toran approached them with glasses to be refilled. He nodded for Ginnie to back up.

She did. Ginnie gripped the two dessert plates tighter.

"Did you hear him talk about calling him 'Uncle Jasper'?" Toran whispered.

Ginnie nodded.

"You should do that."

"Okay." Ginnie tried out "Uncle Jasper" in her mind. It didn't come naturally, but felt more right than wrong. She glanced at Tillie.

Her friend shrugged. "I'm *not* calling him 'Dad'. But I'll bring him pie."

Ginnie smiled at Tillie's newfound feistiness and led the way to the dining room. She walked around the table and gave a piece of key lime pie each to Dad and Buzz.

Tillie stopped next to Uncle Jake and glanced quickly at Jasper, setting the dessert plate on the table in front of him instead of into his outstretched hand. "Thanks, Tilda."

"Welcome." Tillie rushed the word out, handed Uncle Jake his pie, and fled back to the kitchen.

"She's a little shy, Uncle Jasper," Ginnie said, coming back around the table. "Enjoy your pie."

"I will. Thank you." His hesitant smile widened, even though his eyes scrunched with uncertainty.

Ginnie felt his gaze on her back as she escaped to the kitchen.

Aunt Roni snatched her into a hug. "I am so proud of you two."

Miss Amanda held Tillie in her arms. "Breathe, Tils. It's okay."

Giggling nervously, Ginnie shook her head. "I just delivered some pie. It's really no big deal." Even so, she returned her aunt's hug, enjoying being fussed over.

Aunt Roni squeezed her again. "It's a very big deal to Jasper, I can assure you."

"Tillie's the true hero. I'm not really afraid of him." Ginnie shrugged. "He never hurt me."

"He never hurt me like *that*." Tillie grimaced, sucking spit through her teeth. "But he still gave me nightmares."

Toran filled the glasses. "Are you guys going to join us for pie? I almost feel like eating again."

Ginnie considered his words. She had been too full when they arrived home to eat another bite. Witnessing "Uncle Jasper's" arrival and Tillie's bad reaction made dessert even more unappetizing.

However, the yellow-green pie dotted with a dollop of whipped topping and a sliver of fresh lime became more tempting. Ginnie picked up two plates. "I'm in. Tillie?"

Tillie's cheek color mimicked the key lime pie. She swallowed hard and searched each face in the kitchen. "Okay, but I'm not sitting next to him."

"That's my girl." Miss Amanda rubbed Tillie's upper arm and smiled. "Steel magnolias—*unite*."

Toran wrinkled his eyebrows, puzzled.

Ginnie laughed. "It's a girl thing, Tor. Come on, Tillie."

Tillie straightened her shoulders and motioned toward the door with the dessert plate of pie. "After you."

"Fine." Ginnie rolled her eyes and led the way.

42

WHAT MAKES A DAD?

illie followed Ginnie and Toran into the dining room, purposely avoiding Jasper's gaze. *I may have to be here, but I don't have to make it easy for him to talk to me.* She walked around the table and sat next to Uncle Ben, then placed her pie on the table. Picking at it would keep her busy while she played nice to make her mom happy.

Aunt Roni gave Uncle Ben a piece of pie and sat next to Jasper.

Mom sat on the other end directly across from Uncle Ben, with Uncle Jake between her and Jasper.

When Tillie refused to make eye contact, Jasper's gaze bounced between Ginnie to Aunt Roni. "Man, she looks like Queenie—they both do, like 'then' and 'now' photos. No offense, but it's blowing my mind a little."

"I know the feeling." DT tapped his fork on his plate nervously, then grinned at Uncle Jake. "Why don't you share your good news before she shows up in the morning?"

"What news?" Uncle Jake and Jasper asked together.

Tillie squelched a giggle, but Ginnie didn't.

"Um, Uncle Jake, I think he means Mysti—bacon hater extraordinaire," Toran said, smiling.

"No way! You're finally getting married?" Jasper elbowed Uncle Jake, laughing. "But if she hates bacon, how is that gonna work? You know, some things just can't be compromised. And by the way, thanks for putting me on to peanut butter-bacon shakes. Delicious."

"You're welcome." Uncle Jake rolled his eyes. "Mysti isn't my fiancée—she's my daughter. But every time I think of her anti-bacon stance, I have to wonder."

"Daughter?" Jasper's eyebrows knitted together. A strange look crossed his face. "Wing, I know I've had my flaky moments, but we talk every few weeks and I'm pretty sure I would remember you mentioning a wife and daughter. When did you get married?"

"I didn't and I'm not." Uncle Jake's cheeks flamed red. "Mysti's seven-and-a-half *years*. The 'half' is a big deal to her." He picked up his glass of lemonade. "And since you're gonna find out, I only met her last week. So, make your jokes now so I don't have to field them in front of her."

"Wow. Seven *years*?" Jasper's teasing laugh grated on Tillie's nerves. "Last week? Really? Sounds like I'm not the only one who has some catching up to do."

Good-natured laughter circled the table.

Tillie clamped her jaw shut.

Uncle Jake drained his lemonade. "Not funny."

Ginnie giggled again and got a warning shake of DT's head for a response.

Jasper winked at Ginnie and toned down his smile.

Ginnie winked back.

Traitor. Tillie glared, not liking the comparison between her situation and Mysti's. *Uncle Jake didn't know about Mysti. You LEFT ME.* She put a bite of pie in her mouth, refusing to let the tangy sweetness make her feel better.

"No jokes. I'm just a little shocked." Jasper raised his hands in mock surrender. "Remember that uncomfortable discussion Uncle Ben had with us before we went on our first dates? Maybe you shoulda paid more attention."

Buzz, Toran, and Ginnie laughed louder. Even Uncle Ben, Mom, Aunt Roni, and DT chuckled a little.

Tillie clenched her jaw harder. Not having a dad wasn't anything to joke about.

Nobody knew that better than her.

"Sorry. I couldn't resist." Jasper swallowed a bite of pie and smiled. "Who's her mom?"

"Clarissa Lawson, the girl I was going to propose to the day Aunt Sadie died."

"Oh, yeah. That was lousy timing." Jasper sobered his tone. "Then you tried again a year later, only Queenie ..." He stopped abruptly, glancing at Aunt Roni.

"Yeah, my timing with Clarissa has a long history of lousy." Uncle Jake finished for him. "Let's just say she and I lingered our good-byes the night before I went on terminal leave. I came home, she stayed there. Fast-forward eight years, and I have a daughter."

"Wow. Sorry, Wing. I mean—not for having a kid. I'm sure you love her. A little girl?" He glanced at Tillie, a sad kindness in his eyes. Tillie looked away. "That's really cool, man. Little girls are great."

"Thanks. I love being a dad, but it's more complicated than it needs to be because Clarissa and I aren't married." Uncle Jake glanced around the table, catching Toran, Tillie, and Ginnie's gaze in turn. "I missed out on most of her life because I did something without thinking. But you guys can see that and can make better choices as you get older." He brightened his voice. "Mysti's a cutie."

"Mysti is a trip. Pure Jake in pigtails," Mom joked.

"There's a great image. I'm looking forward to meeting her," Jasper teased, seeming relieved at Mom's joke. "And Clarissa? Is she just in town to introduce you two? I'd love to meet her before I have to leave."

Uncle Jake shook his head angrily. "She moved here. I'm still irritated that it took her eight years to figure out that I might have something to offer my own daughter. You know, dads are pretty important—"

"Yeah, Wing, I know," Jasper muttered, avoiding Tillie's gaze.

His flaming cheeks soothed Tillie's anger.

She was happy to see him squirming like a worm on a hook.

You should be ashamed. You're a lousy excuse for a father.

"Umm, Jet. That rant was for me—not you." Uncle Jake mouthed "Sorry" to Tillie and face-planted into his palm. "I'm still getting used to having a kid. I'm having even more symptoms of 'foot-in-mouth' disease than usual."

The uncomfortable silence returned.

Tillie stabbed at her pie, ready to be done with this "family reunion."

43

PINBALL, ANYONE?

*A*fter what seemed like F-O-R-E-V-E-R, Uncle Ben pushed his chair back. "Jasper, why don't you and I go for a walk and catch up? It's been too long since you've seen the sun set here on The Heart. It's breathtaking."

"Yes, sir. I'd like that," Jasper replied.

Oh, good! Relief pulsed through Tillie. *He's leaving.*

Jasper scooted his chair back and stood when Uncle Ben did. "By the way, Uncle Ben, I think your great-great-great-however-many-grandfathers ago was inspired to name the farm 'Heart of the Wests'." He glanced around the table. "It seems to be the heart of a few Taylors as well."

Yeah ... no. Tillie caught her mom's eye. *We're NOT Taylors—well, not for much longer.*

She swallowed the disgust rising in her. *Well, Mom's not, but ...* Tillie gulped, remembering last night's conversation about adoption with DT. *Aw nuts ... I am.*

"'Heart of the Wests' has been heart and home to a number of families over the years." Uncle Ben rubbed Tillie's upper arms as he passed behind her. "The door is open to whoever needs it. That's always been my daddy's motto, and I've never seen a need to change it."

Uncle Ben's light touch restored the peaceful feeling Tillie had been missing ever since Jasper showed up. She braved a peek at the man she'd dreaded seeing for so long.

He nodded along with Uncle Ben's words, seeming to cling to them with a desperate hope that they would always be true.

Jasper's eyes met hers.

Tillie tried to turn away, but couldn't … for a full breath.

She recognized the same anxiety coursing through him that way too often coursed through her.

Shaking her head, Tillie tried to disrupt the connection between them. *Be a steel magnolia. He left. You don't need him anymore.* Tillie blinked. *I don't even want him—why would I need him? Get a grip.*

"Um, Tilda … Amanda." Jasper cleared his throat.

Mom glanced at DT, then at Jasper. "Yes?"

Tillie turned her face toward his, keeping her eyes locked on his yellow polo collar.

"Um, I hadn't planned to see you until tomorrow, but I can't pretend that I'm not seeing you right now." He took a quick breath and let it out. "Look, I knew this was going to be awkward for all of us, but there's something I gotta tell you. Maybe it'll make this better."

His gaze darted around the room, landing on Tillie. "But maybe not."

The sickening tremble burrowed into her belly.

"Um …" Jasper motioned to the hall. He swallowed. "Tilda, Amanda, can you come with us—for a few minutes? I have something to show you —and tell you. Please?" His eyes met Tillie's. She turned and stared at the table. "Uncle Ben can be there. I just didn't rehearse this with a crowd."

Tillie shook her head.

Uncle Ben laid his hands on her shoulders and gave a gentle squeeze. "I'll stay with you."

"Tilda … *please?*" Jasper's vulnerable plea shot into her.

The same vulnerability had bounced around inside her ever since she heard his phone message, like a steel marble in a classic pinball game, only now it plugged her throat.

"Amanda? Please help me with her. I won't hurt her—or you. Angel, is that what you're afraid of?" Jasper walked around the table, coming too close. "Tilda, I'm still your dad. I love you. Give me a chance to prove how much I love you. Please?"

Tillie grabbed Uncle Ben's hands and squeezed her eyes closed. She tried to swallow the pinball, but couldn't. She managed to choke out, "I don't want to." She tried to cover her face with her shoulder, but jerked forward instead, moving her hands to hide her face.

"Hey! What the—?" Jasper's surprised tone pushed Tillie farther forward. "Tilda, I'm *not* going to hurt you."

Tillie gulped.

"Uncle Ben! What do I do?" Jasper's stunned question made Tillie pop her eyelids open.

Ginnie was trying to pass DT as he rounded the table. He put his hand in front of her, corralling Ginnie while calling out, "Tillie, it's okay." He stopped behind Jasper.

Stunned, shocked faces met Tillie's gaze.

Mom's mouth formed a capital "O"—as did Jasper's.

Aunt Roni's hand covered hers.

Toran and Buzz exchanged alarmed looks.

"I'm not going to hurt you," Jasper repeated, standing in front of her, pointing a finger frozen in midair. "Matilda Grace Taylor, give me a chance to prove that."

His scolding tone popped the steel pinball from her throat. "I don't want to be a Taylor anymore—and I don't want *you* to be my dad. I picked a *new* one."

The back of Jasper's hand flinched toward her.

Tillie ducked as Uncle Ben's voice commanded, "Don't!"

Tillie squeezed her eyes shut, bracing for the blow.

44

DON'T TOUCH

asper, stop!" Uncle Ben's stern tone made Tillie shiver.
"Back up."

Two seconds passed.

Tillie's heart raced.

No blow.

"No, sir. I can't." Jasper's voice sounded further away. "It isn't supposed to be like this. I don't know why she's afraid of me. I NEVER treated her like Oscar treated me—*ever*! I swear it!"

Tillie squinted through the cracks of intertwined fingers.

"I don't deserve this." Jasper stood by the hallway, swiveling to go forward—out the front door.

Blinking, Tillie tried to make sense of this scene.

Mom shook her head, frowning at Tillie.

"Mom ..."

"Jasper—stop." Uncle Ben strode closer to him. "This is fixable. Just take a breath and simmer down."

"My kid hates me. She didn't used to." His voice cracked. "She *used* to talk to me. Now she won't even look at me." He swiveled to Mom. "Amanda, you said you didn't badmouth me to her—and I was foolish enough to believe you!" Jasper moved forward.

"Calm down, Jasper." DT stepped between them, motioning for Ginnie and Toran to head to the kitchen. They didn't. They stepped toward Tillie. "No need to yell."

"Says *you*! She thinks you're perfect. I'm such an idiot!" Jasper smacked his forehead, then fisted his hand, glaring at Mom. "Look at our daughter! She's terrified. What did you say to her?"

DT slipped his arm around Mom's shoulder, guiding her a little behind him. DT faced Jasper straight on.

"Jasper. I told her that you love her. Todd, it's fine." Mom moved out of DT's hold and reached for Jasper's hand. "I also told her she should give you a chance. Didn't I, Tils?"

All eyes focused on Tillie.

She shrugged.

Jasper shook his head. "You wouldn't let me talk to her for the last several months—"

"To protect *you* as much as Tillie."

"That's crazy." He pulled his hand out of hers.

"No, it's not." Mom sighed. "I still care about you."

"Great way to show it." He hitched a thumb at Tillie. "You made our daughter *hate* me."

"I don't hate you." The words surprised Tillie as much as they did those around her.

Jasper didn't seem convinced.

Tillie swallowed, moved forward, then stopped behind DT, and tried again. "I want Ginnie to be my sister and Toran to be my brother. I want to *really* belong here." She remembered the words Jasper said shortly after arriving and repeated them, enunciating each word. "I want to Be. A. West."

"We talked about this, Tillie." Ginnie moved past DT to grab Tillie's hand. "You're *already* a West." She rolled her eyes and grinned. "Remember? You're a *double* West."

Jasper knitted his eyebrows. "How do you figure?"

Ginnie smiled. "Uncle Ben and Aunt Sadie chose you a long time ago, Uncle Jasper—so you're a West. You and Miss Amanda had

Tillie." Ginnie hitched her thumb behind her at DT. "We chose Miss Amanda and Tillie *again*, so that makes Tillie a *double* West."

"It's convoluted, but it works," Toran added, taking up a post on Tillie's other side.

A happy giggle bubbled out of Tillie.

Ginnie squeezed her hand.

Tillie squeezed back and grabbed Toran's as well.

DT chuckled and hugged all three of them together.

"I agree with Ginnie and Toran." Uncle Ben slid his hand onto Jasper's shoulder and squeezed. "I've told you for years that family is as much who you choose to be with as it is about whom you are born to. Maybe we should take that walk and discuss this?"

"Yes, sir." He arched a questioning eyebrow at Tillie.

A calm feeling soothed her panic. She nodded.

"Can I hug you?" Jasper whispered.

Be a steel magnolia. Tillie took a step forward, nodding again.

She tried not to stiffen as he slid his arms around her.

Surprisingly, she didn't feel all that awkward.

She reached her arms around his waist and gave a half-hearted squeeze.

He tightened his hold on her.

Tears burned Tillie's eyes as she leaned against his chest.

He pulled her in even tighter.

Somebody sobbed behind her.

Pushing away from Jasper a little, Tillie squinted through tears and saw Mom wipe her eyes, smiling big.

Ginnie blinked, nodding as she swiped at her cheeks.

DT winked at Tillie, making her feel better about their conversation last night.

Maybe being a LITTLE open to Jasper would be okay.

Tillie winked back at DT and then let Jasper envelop her again.

45

MORE SECRETS, ANYONE?

Ginnie swiped at her eyes, trying to hide her worried tears.

Although part of her was happy that Tillie didn't seem afraid of Jasper anymore, watching him cling to her best friend set off a series of new alarms.

Happier tears rolled down Miss Amanda's cheeks. She smiled at Dad, but shook her head when he held out his hand to her.

More alarms blared.

Miss Amanda moved closer to Jasper and Tillie.

The longer the hug lasted, the more anxiety Ginnie felt. When a strangled kitten sound came from Jasper's direction, Ginnie looked at him, dismayed to see tears tracking down his cheeks.

He seemed to hug Tillie even tighter, like he would never let her go.

Dad's eyes shone. He blinked, then tapped Ginnie's and Toran's arms. "Why don't we give them a minute?" he said quietly, nodding toward the kitchen.

Jasper wiped his eyes and slid his palm down his black jeans. "Sorry. I've just been waiting so long to see my little girl." He hugged Tillie again. "I didn't want to come back until I knew I would never have to leave you again."

His words were kind, but not the least bit comforting to Ginnie's ears.

She forced a smile at Jasper, then buried her face in her dad's shirt.

Panic pulsed through her.

She squeezed her eyelids closed for a second to stem the tide of burning tears behind them.

Dad rubbed her back.

"Why don't we go for that walk now?" Jasper asked Tillie, his voice barely audible.

Ginnie opened her eyes, willing her friend to refuse the request.

Tillie nodded.

Miss Amanda patted Ginnie's back and smiled.

Ginnie tried to return the smile, but was pretty sure she failed.

Dad nodded at Miss Amanda and mouthed, "It's okay. Go ahead."

No, it's not! Ginnie clamped her mouth shut only long enough for Uncle Ben, Miss Amanda, Tillie and "Uncle" Jasper to go down the front porch stairs. *Go after them, Daddy!*

When Dad ignored her telepathic plea, Ginnie stopped trying to hold back her tears.

They burst out, along with the most devastating thought she'd ever had. "You said you wouldn't give them to him—or anybody else. But You. Just. *Did*."

She pushed away from her dad and turned, blinded by a flood of tears. Stumbling forward, she bumped into a chair instead of leaving the room as she intended. "Ow." She rubbed her knee, preparing to flee.

"Sugar, be careful," Aunt Roni called.

"Are you okay?" Buzz asked at the same time Dad took hold of her arm.

Clenching her teeth, she whirled to correct her path, jerking against her dad's hold.

"Ginnie, I'm *not* giving them away."

"You're not stopping them from leaving!" The words burned her throat as they left her lips. The truth of them made her tears fall faster, burning her eyes and cheeks as well. "Why aren't you stopping them?"

"Honey, I can't stop them. That wouldn't be fair."

"To who? They're *our* family now. He left them. He shouldn't get them back." Ginnie swiveled toward her aunt, reaching for her.

"Hey! Stop a minute and *listen* to me." Dad pulled her close. Ginnie resisted. He kept a firm hold. "I know this is hard for you. It's hard for me too, but it needs to happen."

"What?"

"This process."

"*What* process?"

"Letting them reunite. Honey, it's not up to you or me or Jasper any more. The only people who can decide Amanda and Tillie's future is *them*. Our job is to support their choice."

"No way!" Ginnie shook her head. "They chose *us*—in the hot air balloon. They said 'yes' to us being a family." She caught Toran's gaze. "There's no take-backs. Right?"

He shrugged. "Things have changed, Ginnie. Jasper wasn't a part of the deal then. Now, he is."

"Whose side are you on?" Ginnie jerked out of Dad's grasp and faced her twin. "Family sticks together." She swiveled to her dad. "That's what you always say."

Dad nodded. "And I stand by that."

"So why aren't you telling Miss Amanda that she can't change her mind?"

"Because ..." He sighed, fidgeting with Ginnie's braid. "She's allowed to change her mind if she wants to."

Ginnie shook her head. "No, she's not."

"Yes, Gin ... she *is*." Dad's reply had to repeat in her mind before she really heard it.

"No." She shook her head defiantly. "*She* promised and *you* promised." She wiped her eyes, willing the tears to stop. "*NO take-backs.*"

"Trouble, Jasper just got back, and he's gonna leave in a couple of days." Uncle Jake reached a hand to her. "There's a lot of time between now and then to let the dust settle."

Ginnie pushed his hand away. "No. We're gonna be sisters. He. Can't. Have. Her." She glared at the three men towering over her, determined to make her point.

Aunt Roni appeared behind Buzz.

Ginnie ducked between Buzz and Uncle Jake to reach her aunt.

"Sugar, it's gonna be okay." Aunt Roni swept her into a hug. "It will work itself out the way it needs to. Remember how Amanda told you and Tillie just a little while ago that she still plans to marry your daddy?"

"She did?" Dad asked, relief washing his tone.

"Of course, Todd. She cares about Jasper just like the rest of you. She knows her engagement to you is going to be hard for him. She doesn't want it to be the reason he loses all the progress he's made." She brushed the hair from Ginnie's eyes. "Sugar, she'll be walking a tightrope to keep everybody happy the next few days. Your daddy is right. Our job is to support her. Can you do that?"

Ginnie shrugged. "How do we make sure she doesn't choose *him*?"

"Just trust that it will work out the way it should." Dad gently wiped her cheek with his thumb. "Tillie needs you to let her feel whatever she needs to feel. Try not to pressure her. She'll be even more confused than you are."

"Yeah, Gin. Remember how Tillie was so jealous and upset when Aunt Roni showed up?" Toran said.

"She was?" Aunt Roni asked, surprise coloring her tone.

"Yes." Toran blinked, then plunged on. "Tillie didn't want you here because she thought Ginnie would see you looking like *our* mom and that Dad might not want *her* mom. But she worried for nothing. Since Tillie knows Dad still wants to marry Miss Amanda, she's fine with you."

"Did *you* think I wouldn't want to marry Amanda because Roni's here?" Dad wiped Ginnie's cheeks again. "Or you, Toran?"

Toran shrugged, smiling. "Nah, I know you two are pretty tight. Girls just like drama."

"Not true." Ginnie rolled her eyes at Toran and turned to Dad. "I just want you to be nice to Aunt Roni. We know she's not our mom. And since she's the reason you took Mama's journals, how's about you giving them back now?"

The question came out more like a thinly veiled demand, but Ginnie didn't care. Enough was enough. If she might lose Tillie and Miss Amanda, she should at least get to have what she could of her very own mom.

"I was hoping to get a couple read before you started asking again." Dad chucked her under the chin. "With Toran getting hurt, me proposing to Amanda, and Mysti, Roni, and Jasper showing up, things have been a bit crazy lately. Give me a few days and I'll hook you up."

Instant elation surged through Ginnie, popping out in a happy squeal. "For real?"

"Yes, for real."

"Awesome sauce!" For the first time since he took the journals a month ago, she had a real return date. At least one she could live with. She spun from Aunt Roni and hugged him. "Thank you!"

He laughed. "You're welcome."

"What about me?" Toran asked.

"I'll give you each one." Dad pulled him close, squeezing Ginnie into the middle of a hug sandwich. "I feel like we might need more pie. Any takers?"

"I'm in," Buzz said.

"I need to finish my steak first." Uncle Jake grinned at Aunt Roni. "Thanks for the scrumptious dinner. Maybe we can finish it now. I think the dinner show is over."

Dad chuckled. "Or at least it's at intermission."

"I hope it's done. There's only so much drama a guy can take," Toran teased. "Do we have any other mystery family members who'll show up?"

"Yeah, Daddy. Do we?" Ginnie echoed.

"Not that I know of. First wife's identical twin sister—check." Dad smiled at Aunt Roni. "Second wife-to-be's ex-husband—check. Three kids between us—check. No more secret family for me. How about you, Jake?"

"I see where you're going with that and I'm insulted." Uncle Jake smirked at Dad. "Unless Clarissa had twins, I know with certainty that I only have one kid—and you've all met her. Check. The real mystery would be young Buzz here. What have you and Miss Faith been up to?"

"Some of us learn from other people's experiences." Buzz teased, hitching his thumb at Uncle Jake. "Faith and I are just enjoying the 'wooing and pursuing' phase. I do love wooing her, but that's all I'm saying on the issue." He pulled out his chair. "Pie's getting hot and steaks are getting cold—we should fix that."

Uncle Jake groaned. "You're hilarious."

Ginnie giggled. "Sounds like a plan to me."

46

FAMILY REUNION

Once outside, Jasper led Tillie, Mom, and Uncle Ben to the front of his black sports car.

"I see you finally got that GTO you've always wanted," Mom remarked. "Good for you."

"Thanks. I feel like I've finally earned it." Jasper patted the hood. "About five months ago, I got a great deal on it and bought it to celebrate hitting my seven-month sobriety mark. I've done seven months before, but this time was different. I knew without question that I'd get to a year and beyond."

Mom gave his hand a firm squeeze. "I've always known you could do that."

Tillie got the feeling that they'd had this conversation before.

"Thanks." He shrugged. "Every time I drive this car, I realize I can achieve my goals and dreams. It helps me stay focused on what I really want ... my family back."

"Jasper ..." Mom let go of his hand.

He glanced at Mom and then looked just past her. He cleared his throat. "Todd already told me." He put his palm up in a "stop" motion. "I can't hear it from you too—at least not tonight." He shook his head. "Maybe tomorrow. Tonight, I have something important to tell you."

"Jasper, I'm sor—"

"Please don't apologize. It may only be a fantasy now, but I've been practicing what I'd say to you for the last two thousand miles. Please just let me get it out."

Alarm lit Mom's eyes, but she pressed her lips together and nodded.

"I'll leave out the 'will you consider remarrying me' part for now, okay?" Jasper's gaze bore into Mom, like a rock-climbing bolt anchored into a cliff so he'd have something secure to cling to while plunging into his speech. He probably meant to sound like he was teasing, but hurt and disappointment stained his words.

Uneasiness rumbled in Tillie's belly.

"Okay," Mom quietly agreed.

Tillie couldn't tell if Mom was also disappointed, but she looked like she wanted to say something else.

Jasper glanced at each of them and then focused on Tillie. "I've admitted this many times, but it's most difficult for me to admit this to *you*. Angel ... I'm an alcoholic."

Tillie didn't know how to respond. Jasper being an alcoholic was old news to her ... and not happy news.

"You'll always be my little girl—at least to me." He gave a quick glance behind her to the farmhouse.

Tillie blinked, remembering her outburst in the hallway. She didn't regret it, but she also didn't want him blowing up at her. Having Uncle Ben here increased the odds that he would use his self-control, but didn't guarantee he wouldn't seek revenge later if she irritated him too much.

"The hardest part about admitting that I'm an alcoholic is that I've had to realize how much I've failed you and your mom—the two people I love most in this world."

"I understand," Tillie replied more to be polite than comforting.

"You can't possibly understand. I mean—" He pointed to himself. "*I* don't understand it. But I need you to know that I've never stopped loving you or wanting to be a good dad to you." He offered a shy smile, and nodded at Uncle Ben. "But since I couldn't be here for you, I did try to leave you in the care of the best dad I know—as well as your mom, of course."

Uncle Ben put a gentle hand on Jasper's shoulder while slipping the other around Tillie's. "A lot has happened since she's seen you last," Uncle Ben said in a calm voice. "There have been a lot of promises made ...."

"And too many of them broken," Jasper finished, exchanging a long look with Uncle Ben.

Tillie could almost see the strength flow from Uncle Ben to Jasper.

She waited while Jasper siphoned enough courage to speak again, this time with more confidence. "That's why I asked them out here. I want to show them both that I can keep my promises to them." He pulled his keys out of his pocket and pushed the trunk button. It made a slight "pop."

Curious, Tillie exchanged intrigued glances with Mom.

"Excuse me." Jasper walked to the back of his car, pulled the lid open, and lifted two medium-sized boxes wrapped in pink princess paper, tied with fancy gold ribbons and topped with huge gold bows, and brought them over to Tillie. "I know these are late, but happy birthday."

Surprised joy surged through her. She pushed away the ugly thoughts she'd had when he hadn't called or sent something for her birthday a couple weeks ago—even though she didn't want anything to do with him.

"Thanks." The paper was a little juvenile, but so pretty that Tillie didn't want to tear it.

Mom waved excitedly at the gifts. "Go ahead, open them."

Tillie set the packages on the hood of the car and slid the ribbons and bows off, excitement pulsing as she tried to guess what they were —quickly determining it wasn't clothes, video games, or a horse.

She checked to see if Jasper was watching her.

He was ... with a happy grin firmly in place.

Hmmm, he wants to make me happy. Maybe Jasper can be 'Plan B' if DT says 'no' to a horse. Hey, Ginnie's rubbing off on me. Liking the confidence of her BFF's influence, Tillie carefully peeled the tape from the top box and decided to see where this gift took them, feeling-wise.

"It's okay if you rip it," Jasper said, chuckling.

His happy grin encouraged hers.

"Okay." Tillie tore the paper. Excitement quickly turned to bewilderment when she discovered an Easy-Bake Oven box. Thinking it must be holding her real gift, she checked each end for signs of re-taping.

The box was brand new.

Disappointment flooded her. *Why would he buy me an Easy-Bake Oven?* Puzzled, she glanced at him.

His happy smile dive-bombed into open-mouthed awkwardness. "You don't remember?"

Shaking her head, Tillie struggled to make sense of this gift.

Uncle Ben bore an equally confused expression.

Then a light bulb seemed to appear over Mom's head. "I get it, Jasper. That's so sweet, but ..."

"She's twelve—not six." He shook his head, then smiled apologetically. "Tilda, I know you aren't six anymore. But the Easy-Bake Oven is less about the gift itself than the promise I made to get it for you."

Tillie blinked, uncomfortable with this "mending fences" moment. She wasn't ready to exchange years of betrayal and fear for a plastic toy she didn't want anymore.

"Buying the oven was the last big promise I made to you face-to-face." He tilted his head and waited for Tillie to acknowledge him. She gave a reluctant nod. "Tilda, I want you to know that you can count on me from here on out."

Sorry, that's what I have DT and Uncle Ben for. YOU tore up your trust card a long time ago. Tillie pasted on what she hoped was a pleasant, yet non-committal smile.

"I got you this oven because it's one of the few un-kept promises that I've made to you."

That can't be right. The reality of too many tear-filled nights hunkering beneath her comforter, full of uncertainty and fear, sifted through her mind to challenge his statement.

But she couldn't find the words to protest Jasper's claim.

Irritated at being reduced to a to-do list that needed to be checked off, Tillie searched Mom's face for guidance. *She's no help. She's actually buying his pity party.*

Uncle Ben's expression mirrored Mom's.

Frustration started to build in Tillie.

She must have waited too long to respond because Jasper gave a nervous laugh.

"You don't have to keep it. It's a symbol of my intentions more than anything. I know I took too long to keep this promise, but the important thing is that I *did* keep it. That's what I want you to get from this." He shrugged, brightening his tone with visible effort. "You can give it to Jake's little girl. Maybe she'll like it."

"I—I don't hate it." Just because Tillie thought it was a lame gift didn't mean she wanted to give it away. "I'm just a little surprised." She searched her memory back when Jasper first left and recalled a tangle of conflicting feelings over the Easy-Bake Oven.

Mom had bought her a garage-sale Easy-Bake Oven for that birthday, but it didn't have all of the accessories and no cake or cookie mixes. Tillie grew to hate it and tossed it in the back of her closet until the day she realized Jasper was never coming back.

He had thrown Tillie away, so Tillie threw the Easy-Bake Oven away.

"That's a great start to building bridges." Mom slid gentle hands onto Tillie's cheeks, her not-so-subtle suggestion that Tillie should be gracious and take the high road. "It's what you wanted most for your sixth birthday."

Jasper must have gotten hope from Mom's response as well. "You were so happy when I told you I would get one for you ... that you made me feel like Superman."

Conflict over.

No way was Jasper ever going to be "Superman" to her.

DT had earned that role, not her lousy-excuse-for-a-birth-father.

She stood straighter, channeling some of Uncle Ben's quiet strength for herself.

If he thinks he's Superman, then I'll be his kryptonite.

Tillie locked her gaze on Jasper, years of hurt and anger building to a tempest inside her. "My sixth birthday was the lousiest birthday *ever*—and that was All. *Your*. Fault."

47

KRYPTONITE

*T*illie!" Mom scolded.

"What?" Tillie glared at her mom and then Jasper. "Dads who beat you, and who beat your mom, and then throw you away are *not* Supermen. They're garbage."

Jasper's eyes widened at her verbal assault.

Tillie wanted to laugh an evil, maniacal laugh, but plunged ahead, spewing kryptonite as fast as she could. "My sixth birthday was horrible. You said I was going to have a wonderful princess party and instead you called drunk, telling me you were a lousy excuse for a dad and wanting me to feel sorry for you."

"Tillie," Uncle Ben warned, frowning.

She ignored him. "But you were right about that. You *were* a lousy excuse for a father and I stopped wanting you." Tillie straightened as he backed away, fury and spite growing and unleashing as hurtful words came together and flowed out as payback for all the pain and anxiety he'd caused her over the years. She leaned forward, stabbing her finger at him. "I don't want you *now*, and I'll *never* need you again. Ginnie's dad is the one who's been here for me. He gets to be my Superman—*Not. You!*"

Jasper's hands twitched. He fisted them and shoved them straight down at his sides.

Uncle Ben squeezed Tillie's shoulders in warning. "That's enough, Matilda Grace."

"I'm not apologizing!" Tillie whirled to face Uncle Ben. "Everything I said was true! I. Don't. Need. *Him.*"

"Enough!" Uncle Ben's gray-blue eyes flashed. "I know you're angry, but you're crossing the line to hateful and destructive. You need to give him a chance to respond."

"Why? You let *him* talk," Tillie spat. "And he's lying."

"Matilda Grace," both Mom and Jasper scolded.

Tillie looked their way, not liking that Jasper thought he had a right to be her parent.

Mom shook her head at Jasper and stepped in front of Tillie. "Don't use that tone with Uncle Ben. You know better." Mom slipped her hands firmly onto Tillie's cheeks in warning and leaned close. "You can tell Jasper whatever you need to tell him, but I agree with Uncle Ben—you don't need to be hateful. Take a breath and calm down."

"But ..."

Mom pressed her lips together and gave a slight shake of her head.

Tillie knew she meant business. Her gaze landed on Jasper, who looked like he would defend Mom's position. Resenting that, Tillie swiveled slowly to Uncle Ben. "I'm sorry for being rude ... *to you.*"

"Thank you." Uncle Ben's eyes narrowed at her, then softened as he searched her face. "Honey, you have a chance here that many people don't ever get. Jasper is willing to make things as right as he can with you. He knows he hurt you, and he wants to fix it, but being spiteful won't help."

"He's going to ruin everything." Tillie glanced between Jasper and Mom, then focused on Uncle Ben, knowing she would have to get her concerns out now or never. "He thinks he gets to be my dad, and he doesn't. I picked a new one because *he ... left ... me.*"

Tillie turned to Jasper, determined to make him understand the hurt and anger she suffered because of him. "Do you know what it feels like to have your dad, the one guy who's supposed to keep you safe and take care of you, *throw* you away so he can be a drunk who-knows-where for years instead of being a good part of his family?"

"I do." Jasper gave a firm nod and took a step toward her. "I also know what it's like to hide in my closet and hope he won't find me because he's in a drunken rage."

Tillie swallowed, suddenly remembering all the horrible things she'd heard about Jasper's father, regretting asking her question as soon as Jasper stopped in front of her.

His features hardened. He narrowed his blue eyes to slits, his jaw clenched tight.

Uncle Ben put up a warning hand. "Count to ten if you need to. Tillie's not Oscar and neither are you. Help her understand why you left."

Jasper seemed to siphon more courage and softened his look.

Tillie held her breath.

He continued speaking in a calm, almost emotionless voice. "I also know what it's like to be locked in a car trunk for almost two days because my dad threw me in it and slept off his drunken stupor. I nearly starved to death because he forgot what he did, and my mom didn't realize I was missing. She only cared about scoring her next high."

Tillie sucked in a horrified breath.

"It could've been worse." He shrugged like that experience was no big deal. "Thankfully, it was early spring—otherwise I would've died of heat stroke or hypothermia." He reached for Tillie's hand.

She dropped it out of his reach.

Uncle Ben frowned. "That's not what I meant. You're scaring her. We're talking about you, not Oscar. Help her see the good, compassionate man I know you to be."

"Sorry, Tilda." Jasper hung his thumb from his jean pocket. "I didn't tell you that to scare you or one-up you. You asked me if I knew how it felt to have a dad who'd rather live in a bottle than be there for his family. I understand it *very* well. I lived it—and I hated it."

"If you hated it so much, why did you do that to us?"

"I *didn't* do that to you." Jasper stood straight and speared Tillie with a determined look.

Cringing, Tillie concentrated on the gravel at their feet.

Jasper lifted her chin and waited for her to meet his gaze. "I've never struck *you* with anything besides my hand and I didn't do that but a very few times. There were only a couple times I punished you in anger. But when I saw I was scaring you, I stopped. *My* dad didn't care. *My* dad would beat me with anything handy—belts, sticks, two-by-fours, even telephone wire. And he wasn't particular about where he hit."

Horrified by those images, Tillie tried to jerk her chin out of his hand, but he held tight. He steeled his eyes on hers. "I wished him away more times than I can count. I wanted better for you."

Tillie squeezed her eyes shut, not wanting to see his hurt expression.

She tried to replace it with an image of DT.

"Please look at me." Jasper loosened his grasp, but still held her chin. "I won't hurt you, but I need you to understand something."

Reluctantly, Tillie opened her eyes.

His face transformed from firm to almost vulnerable.

He let go of her chin and pointed his finger too close to her nose. "I made you a promise as a newborn baby in my arms that I would never hurt you like my father hurt me. I've kept that promise, Matilda Grace Taylor. If I've done nothing else, I've kept *that* promise."

Conflicting images of him slapping her so hard she fell and of her giggling as she rode on his shoulders zipped through Tillie's mind.

"I get that I haven't earned the Father-of-the-Year Award, but I'm back—*for good*—like it or not. I'm still your dad." He stabbed his finger at her. "And you don't get to fire me. *Understood*?"

In spite of swallowing so hard that she heard her ears pop, Tillie wanted to protest his stern tone. When his features hardened again, she went with the safest response that crossed her mind. "Yes, sir. Understood."

48

DON'T ASK,

AND I WON'T TELL

Once Tillie responded, Jasper took a step back from her. "Thank you." He nodded at the other pink gift. "I had to go to five different stores to fill that with Easy-Bake Oven mixes for you, but you don't have to keep it." He sighed. "I guess Uncle Ben is right —you and I have a huge difference of opinion on how the last six years have played out."

Fuming that he wanted to be her dad, Tillie ignored the other gift, glancing at Mom and Uncle Ben for back-up. Neither acted interested in protesting on her behalf.

She took a slow breath to calm down. "What do you mean?"

"I expected this reunion to be a little awkward. That maybe you'd even be angry. I was—and still am—prepared to give you some space to get used to me again. But I didn't expect you to be afraid of me or replace me with anybody—especially since your mom didn't remarry."

"But she's going to—" Tillie stopped talking when his eyes narrowed again.

"Maybe, maybe *not*. But even if she does marry Todd, you're still *my* kid and I'm *not* giving up my rights to you." He made a point of making eye contact with Uncle Ben and then Mom before resting his gaze on Tillie. "So it would be in everybody's best interest to get used to the idea that I'm back in town and here to stay—at least on the weekends."

"But why do you want me?" Tillie's belly clenched as his words whirled through her mind. "You don't even know me."

"I know and that's gonna change, Tilda." He lifted two fingers. "The two things I know I've done right were to pick your mom for my wife and us having you. I love you more than you'll probably ever believe. But it doesn't change the fact that I do." He motioned toward Mom. "I may have been an absentee dad, but I've never been a dead-beat one. Have I, Amanda?"

Mom smoothed her dismayed look into a more pleasant one. "You've always been good about providing for us."

He nodded. "I have. Maybe that isn't a big deal to you, Tilda, but it's a huge deal *to me*. I was gone for too long, but I left to wrestle my demons so they wouldn't be a problem for you. It's cost me too many years of your life that neither of us will get back."

I'm okay with that. Tillie blinked, wishing she could voice her discomfort and anxiety about his return.

"But I *am* back, ready to be a good dad to you. In my mind, that puts me leaps and bounds above *my* dad, so I don't get why you're so afraid of me. Would you care to shed some light on that for me?"

Are you kidding? Images of Jasper throwing the vase at Mom and him backhanding Tillie across her cheek blazed across her memory.

Her hand flew to her cheek, feeling the memory of the bruise he had left there many years ago.

Understanding lit his eyes while she struggled to put the incidents into words. "You're remembering the last time I got drunk—before I left, aren't you?"

"I don't know when—but I remember you hurting my mom .. and me," She glanced at him to see if she dared continue.

"I was hoping you'd forgotten that." Jasper sighed. "I guess that was just wishful thinking on my part. What else are you holding against me?"

Her gaze flew to Mom for a clue how to answer him. If Jasper was going to insist on being her dad, she didn't want to give him a reason to punish her. He might be right about never hitting her with an object, but she remembered his hands leaving an awful sting.

"Jasper, maybe you can rephrase that?" Uncle Ben suggested gently. "I don't think Tillie is holding anything against you as much as she has concerns she doesn't know how to express. Like you said, you two have different perspectives of how these last few years have played out."

"Is that true?" Jasper seemed to consider his words. "Please look at me."

Tillie forced herself to look into his eyes while still trying to muster an answer. The same blue eyes that stared at her in the bathroom mirror every morning stared back at her now.

She looked away when she didn't see her fear or his anger, just concern. She nodded.

He lowered his voice. "The night I bruised your cheek was the last time I raised a hand to you. I'm not going to hurt you. What can I do to help you not be afraid of me?"

She swallowed hard. "I don't know."

"Would it help if I apologized? I apologized at the time, but maybe you don't remember that."

Not sure that she would believe any apology he offered, Tillie shrugged. "I guess."

"That night is the biggest regret I have, next to allowing your mom to divorce me." Jasper weaved his thumb into a belt loop. "The only thing that makes that night better is knowing I hurt you on accident."

What? Stunned, she shook her head. "No, it wasn't."

"No, *what* wasn't?"

"It wasn't an accident. You hurt me *on purpose*."

"That's not true. It was an accident."

"No way." She might have to deal with him, but she didn't have to let him rewrite history. "I tried to be invisible, but when you hit my mom, I screamed. You turned around and smacked me in the face. I fell down."

A shocked expression crossed his face. "I didn't hit you on purpose."

Too angry to be afraid of him, Tillie jutted out her chin. "How do you 'accidentally' hit someone so hard you leave your handprint on their cheek?"

Pierce's bruised face leaped into her mind. That was no accident either. She crossed her arms and glared.

Jasper's mouth dropped open, but no words came out.

"*I'll tell you how*—You. Hit. *Me.*" She toggled her head and whirled toward Uncle Ben. "He did."

"I don't hear him denying that, Tillie." Uncle Ben motioned her closer. She took a step into his open arms. "But maybe you should simmer down and hear him out."

She frowned, wanting more sympathy from Uncle Ben now that she'd spilled her darkest memory. "He's lying."

"No, I'm not." Jasper stuffed his hands into his jean pockets. "I may be an alcoholic, but I'm *not* a liar. I don't even make promises that I don't intend to keep."

"You've broken plenty of promises." Tillie squelched the urge to roll her eyes. "It's the *same* as lying."

"No, it's not." Jasper nodded at Uncle Ben. "Ask *him*. Uncle Ben is a human lie detector. He's always in the back of my head telling me to own my behavior. I'll admit I've done some pretty despicable things, but I don't lie about it." His tone dared her to argue. "That's the truth."

Uncle Ben nodded. "I can attest that Jasper's admitted some pretty ugly truths to me over the years, Tillie."

"See? I won't insult you by lying or making excuses. My dad did that. I refuse to be like him." Jasper cleared his throat. "I was wrong that night, plain and simple. I *did* hurt you—but I didn't mean to. I thought you were in bed. Your scream startled me. I turned fast to see where you were and caught your cheek with my hand and knocked you down." He shuddered. "The sound of your head cracking against the sofa still makes me sick."

Shaking her head, Tillie looked at Mom for back-up.

"No, honey, he didn't hurt you on purpose. But it happened pretty fast. I can see why you'd think that. Not that it should've happened at all ..." Mom sent a stern grimace Jasper's way.

"Your mom's right. It shouldn't have happened at all. You didn't deserve that." Jasper nodded. "Either of you."

"I know we didn't." Mom agreed sharply, then softened her tone. "As soon as Jasper realized what happened, he apologized over and over. I screamed at him to leave and he did. Since he left on foot, I put you in the car and drove here to the farm. Tils, he did hit you on accident."

Tillie let her mom's words run through her mind again, hearing something she hadn't the first time.

[pShe glanced at Jasper and decided to test his theory on truth telling. "So, you're saying that you didn't hit me on purpose?"

"Yes." He gave a confident nod. "I'm very sorry you got hurt, but I swear to you, it was an accident."

She looked him in the eye and backed closer to Uncle Ben. "And you promise to tell me the truth?"

"Of course."

When Mom gave an encouraging nod, Tillie licked her lips and plunged ahead, hoping she was wrong. "Maybe hurting *me* was an accident, but you hit *my mom* on purpose, didn't you?"

After glancing between Mom and Uncle Ben, Jasper took a sudden interest in his shoes and gave a reluctant nod. "I wish I could say that was an accident, but it wasn't."

The bug zapper caught a bug, barbecuing it with a sickening zzzzzzt-zzzzzt-zzzzzzzzzt sound. It flashed a cheerful neon purple while performing its grisly duty.

White noise filled the air.

The oxygen disappeared from Tillie's lungs.

Hearing Jasper admit that he had intended to hurt her mom changed things somehow.

And not in a good way.

49

NOT-SO-HAPPY

BUBBLE WORLD

*Z*zzzzzt-zzzzzt-zzzzzzzzzzzt.

While the bug zapper seared a new victim, Tillie tried to breathe through her rising nausea. She'd known for years that Jasper had hurt Mom on purpose, but hearing him admit it, sickened her.

"I don't have a reason for hurting your mom that night." Jasper sought her gaze. Tillie refused to engage it. "Just a bad excuse."

Her belly flip-flopped while she sorted through her jumbled feelings.

"I had been given bad information and acted on it in the worst way possible." Jasper swallowed. "I won't try to justify it, because I was totally wrong. Your mom didn't deserve to be treated like that, and I can only offer my sincerest apologies to her for doing that and to you for witnessing my bad behavior."

Bad behavior? You didn't blow your nose with somebody else's napkin —you backhanded my mom as hard as you could.

Tillie shook her head, needing to erase the image of her mom's split lip dripping blood down her chin. She backed up against Uncle

Ben, offering a telepathic plea to him to make this crazy person go away.

"Tils, that was a long time ago. I'm fine." Mom tried to envelop Tillie in a hug. Tillie squirmed out of her hold. "Some good things happened after we worked that out."

Like him infecting you with his craziness?

"I don't want to hear it." Tillie turned to Uncle Ben, tired of both of her parents. "Can I please leave?"

Uncle Ben arched a questioning eyebrow at Mom.

"No, Tils, you can't. Please listen to me." Mom glanced at Jasper and sighed. "He and I worked that out a long time ago. I don't want you to get stuck on that incident."

Channeling Ginnie, Tillie shook her head and tried to sound like the reasonable adults her parents should be. "I get it. He hit you, you divorced him. We're good. Can I go now? *Please?*"

Jasper cleared his throat. "What did your mom say?"

Really? Home for an hour after being gone for six years and you think you get to boss me around?

Upon closer inspection of his furrowed brows, Tillie realized that he *did* feel entitled to boss her around. Deciding it would be in her best interest not to voice her thoughts, she concentrated on the unopened gift.

"Tilda, I asked you a question," Jasper said.

And I'm ignoring you.

Uncle Ben frowned at her.

"Matilda Grace." Jasper took a step and stopped in front of her, too close for her comfort. He seemed to force a smile. "I'm pretty sure you already know this, but just in case you don't, the polite thing to do when an adult is speaking to you is to respond, not ignore them, okay?"

While his voice held a teasing quality, Tillie didn't miss the underlying command to obey. Resenting his presumed authority, Tillie shot a quick glance at each adult, quickly tallying a three-to-one vote for obedience.

Uncle Ben cleared his throat. "Tillie, I'm sure you're just trying to figure out how to respond to Jasper's admission, but it would be better if you at least acknowledge you've been spoken to."

Leave it to Uncle Ben to interfere. She grimaced. *If I sass him, Mom and Jasper will both come down on me.* Then she realized, just in time, that Uncle Ben was giving both her *and* Jasper a way out of the situation.

"Yes, sir. Sorry. I don't know what to say." Tillie threw a quick glance Jasper's way before looking past his shoulder. "I knew you hurt my mom on purpose. I just don't know *how* you could do that. I love her." She dropped her gaze to his shoes. "You were supposed to love her too."

"I know I did a horrible thing, Tilda." He came closer. She tried not to cringe. "I love your mom very much. It's part of why I left. I didn't want to be the kind of person who could hurt *anybody*, let alone someone as wonderful as Amanda."

While squelching the urge to roll her eyes, Tillie forced her voice to stay even. "You just shouldn't hit people, *especially* my mom. That would solve the whole problem."

"I agree, but it wasn't that easy." He shook his head and grimaced. "I had a lot of anger and some very real fears to deal with. They came out in ways I didn't want. I know I was wrong to hurt your mom ... and you. I'm not trying to justify it, just acknowledge that it happened."

"That doesn't make it better."

"I think it does. At least I'm willing to admit I was wrong." He stood straighter and pointed a finger. "Your grandfather would have flattened you several times during this conversation." The matter-of-fact way he spoke burrowed a chill into Tillie's middle. "I can guarantee if you spoke to him the way you've spoken to me, that not only would that bruised cheek *not* be an accident, your other one would have matched it."

Tillie shuddered as she made the family connection between Oscar Taylor and herself.

Mom has to marry DT. I can't be a Taylor anymore.

Uncle Ben grimaced. "I don't think that's helping."

"Maybe not, but if she's going to hold grudges, she should understand that her life could have been a lot worse than it was and is. Compared to Oscar, *I* was a saint."

Tillie cringed at the truth of his insight.

"Again, we should focus on you and Tillie. She doesn't remember Oscar," Uncle Ben reminded him. "Tillie needs to know what she can expect from *you* from now on."

"Overcoming what he did to me is a big reason I've been gone for the last six years," Jasper insisted to Uncle Ben before turning to Tillie. "I didn't want my demons to affect you. I was a way better dad to you than Oscar Taylor was to me. I *won't* let you take that from me. Or you either, Uncle Ben." Jasper placed a hand on Tillie's shoulder. She resisted the urge to shake it off. "I protected her the best way I knew how. In my mind, leaving—instead of hurting my child—proved that."

Tillie sucked in an uncomfortable breath as the challenge passed between the two men.

"I know Oscar's treatment of you affected the way you dealt with Amanda and Tillie, but it doesn't *excuse* it, Jasper," Uncle Ben scolded, then softened his tone. "Oscar was vicious and brutal. Even if you didn't do to Tillie what he did to you, it is apparent that you and Tillie have a few things to resolve. She's got a very real fear of you, like you did of Oscar, and that needs to be addressed."

Jasper stared at Uncle Ben open-mouthed a few seconds.

His eyes narrowed angrily before his gaze focused on Tillie.

She stepped closer to Uncle Ben, swallowing hard.

Surprise lit Jasper's face.

Then understanding.

"I'm sorry, Angel. He's right. Since I wasn't here to be a problem for you, it didn't occur to me that your memories would turn to the bad ones instead of the good ones I tried to replace them with." He glanced at Uncle Ben and Mom then settled his gaze on Tillie. "I knew Uncle Ben would look out for you. It's what I wanted for myself —to be away from Oscar and have Uncle Ben be my dad."

He glanced at Uncle Ben quickly before setting his gaze on Tillie. "I never intended to stay away this long, and I have *always* planned to come back. I just wanted to make sure that when I came back, I would never have to leave again to keep you safe from my demons."

"I—I didn't know that." Tillie let his words roll around in her mind, trying to hear them with the kind tone he was using rather than the automatic anxiety she was used to. "I just remember you throwing the vase at my mom. You scared me. I didn't want you to hurt her again."

A puzzled look crossed his face. "I didn't."

"Yes, you did."

"No, I didn't."

"I was there." Tillie toggled her head. "It hit the wall instead of Mom and smashed into a million pieces. You grabbed me. Mom told you not to hurt me. You squeezed my arms and then pushed me away from you. Then you said 'I'm done' and ran away."

He blinked. "That's how you remember that night?"

"Yeah—because that's what happened. I still have nightmares about it." Tillie mimicked his stance, done with being Miss "Trying-To-Make-Amends-With-Her-Loser-Dad." She planted her hands on her hips and let Miss "I'm-Done-Being-Afraid-Of-You" roar into town. "You were gonna hurt us both."

Jasper took a step back, eyes wide, giving Tillie courage.

Good, it's your turn to be afraid!

50

TURNABOUT IS FAIR PLAY

*T*he bug zapper barbequed a new victim.

ZZZZZT-ZZZZZZZZZZZT-ZZZZT

Her confidence building, Tillie tried not to smile as she watched Jasper process her words.

Jasper shook his head. "The night that I *did* hurt you both changed everything for me. I didn't leave until a month after that. And the night I left, I was *not* going to hurt your mom. We had some really good times between those two nights. You don't remember *any* of them?"

"No, because that didn't happen," Tillie protested.

"Yes, it did. Ask your mom." Jasper threw Mom an incredulous look. "Amanda, why didn't you remind her? We put a lot of effort into making good memories of the three of us before I left."

Mom frowned at him. "I didn't know I needed to. Whenever she acted afraid of you coming back, I told her you left to get help because you loved her. I didn't know she'd forgotten about the good times. I was trying to help her not to remember the bad times."

"I don't remember any good times," Tillie said.

Jasper shoved his hand in his pocket and clamped his jaw shut.

Tillie swallowed hard.

"Honey, we had a lot of them," Mom said, putting up a hand in an "I've got this" motion to Jasper. "Tils, remember when we went to Carriage Hill Farm and made caramel apples? You rolled yours in marshmallows and chocolate chips. Or when the three of us played at the park and got caught in the rain?"

Tillie shook her head.

"You and Jasper had a 'biggest splash' contest in the puddles on the way to the car. You talked about how much fun that was for weeks. After he left, you asked why he didn't come back and play with you again."

A faint memory of jumping in puddles and shivering as a cool breeze hit her soaking wet shorts and T-shirt surfaced. She tried to shake away the memory of Jasper scooping her up in his arms and making her giggle, before he slid her over his shoulders to give her a piggyback ride.

"What about when I took you and your mom to that roadside carnival? You and I had a cotton-candy-eating contest. You realized if you squished it into a ball, you could stuff it in your mouth all at once. You won, remember?" His eyes begged her to recall that day.

Instead of pushing away that memory, Tillie let it dance around the edge of her mind a minute. "I had pink, you had blue, because boys should have blue cotton candy and girls should have pink."

His smile grew wide.

Tillie took a step back.

"You remember." He grinned even bigger. "That's what you said that night. Then I let you try some of the blue and you liked it better than the pink. So we had a contest and the winner got to pick the next ride."

Tillie giggled, in spite of her desire to remain distant. "I picked the carousel, and you wanted the potato sack slide."

"Because we'd already ridden the carousel three times."

Tillie shrugged, smiling shyly. "I liked the pink-and-gold horse. It was so pretty."

He offered a playful wink. "You wanted me to ask the operator if we could ride it home like on Mary Poppins. I had to buy you a huge lollipop to distract you when you figured out that it wasn't a magical carousel." He caught her gaze. "Tilda, I really wish it could have been. If I could have made that happen for you, I would have."

Something about the way he said that made her believe him, but Tillie just couldn't shake her fear of him.

"Look. The night I hurt you guys, I was drunk. Someone told me something about your mom that was wrong—but for whatever reason, I believed him, and I acted horribly. After I saw that I hurt you, but that you'd be okay, I left. Jake found me later that night and literally pounded some sense into me and then stayed with me until I was sober."

"He told me," Tillie said.

"I figured." Jasper grimaced. "The next day, Uncle Ben lit into me something fierce and made his expectations crystal clear about how I was to treat you and your mom or he'd see to it that I'd never see either of you again. He doesn't make threats lightly. I knew he meant it ... and it scared me."

Tillie glanced at Uncle Ben and smiled. "Really?"

He nodded. "But I knew Jasper would do right by you."

"And I tried, Tilda." He slid his palm nervously down his black jeans. "For the next two weeks, you and your mom stayed here at the farm. She and I dated—"

"Wait, weren't you already married?" Tillie asked.

"Yes, but Uncle Ben pointed out that if I was so disconnected from your mom that I would believe a virtual stranger and treat her so badly, I needed to reconnect with her. So, after the three of us set some ground rules, your mom agreed to date me for a probation period and see how things went." He wiggled his eyebrows at Mom, grinning. "That was fun—except leaving you two here and going back to the apartment alone." Jasper nodded at Uncle Ben. "You were right. Leaving my family here every night made me think differently about them." He looked at Tillie. "Not only did I want you more, but I wanted more *for* you."

Uncle Ben returned the nod. "Which was the point."

"Yes, sir." Jasper nodded. "I got it—loud and clear." He winked at

Tillie. "I dated my wife. I made good memories with my kid—or so I thought. We helped Todd throw a great treasure hunt party for Ginnie and Toran's sixth birthday and made plans for a princess one for you."

"I remember that." Tillie blinked away her disappointment. "But you left before my birthday."

"I know." He steadied his gaze on the unopened gift. "We were going to rent a castle bounce house and set it up over there." He pointed at the huge maple that shaded the corner of the farmhouse. "But I got fired."

"That wasn't your fault," Mom said.

He shrugged. "It didn't change the fact that we wouldn't be able to pay our rent, let alone pay for a pink-and-gold princess bounce house. You don't know how badly I wanted to make that happen, Tilda. I was so angry at how unfair life was." He pointed between Mom and Tillie. "You two had just moved back into the apartment and then I got fired. I just wanted to vent."

"I should have let you," Mom said.

Jasper turned to Tillie. "Your mom tried to calm me down, but I wasn't hearing her. The night I left, you acted so afraid of me. Since I'd just spent a month trying to show you both I wanted to be a good husband and dad, I got frustrated. I threw the vase and got a grip ... until I saw the look on your face."

Tillie took a quick breath in.

"That look reminded me of myself—as a scared little kid just before my dad would hurt me or *my* mom."

Not knowing what to say, Tillie closely inspected the back tire of his car.

"You closed your eyes and wouldn't let me explain—just like you did a little while ago inside." He pointed behind him at the front porch. "I wasn't going to hit you then, either. Was I, Uncle Ben?"

Tillie looked at Uncle Ben for confirmation.

He shook his head. "He wasn't, Tillie. He backed up as soon as you closed your eyes."

"I—I ..." Tillie swallowed, not sure how to continue. She glanced at Jasper's face, then at the pewter dragon on his belt buckle. "Sorry. I thought you were."

"I know, but I wasn't." He let out a breath, then plunged ahead. "The night I left, you acted like I was going to hurt you no matter what, so I considered spanking you."

Old fears spiked through Tillie, trembling in her belly.

"Then I realized that's what my dad would do." Jasper gently lifted her chin. She blinked, anxiety dancing up and down in her middle. "I didn't want to be my dad, so I grabbed my coat and left." His voice softened and strengthened at the same time. "I wanted to be the dad that I had promised *you* that I'd be."

Swallowing, Tillie forced herself to look at him.

His blue eyes bore uncomfortably into her, but not in a threatening way.

She recognized the desperation to be accepted that she often felt.

Her throat thickened as she whispered, "What kind of dad is that?"

He brushed her cheek gently with his finger. "The kind of dad a little girl can depend on and not be afraid of." He let out a slow, pained breath. "Only my little girl isn't so little anymore."

"But she still needs her daddy," Uncle Ben suggested. "That never changes. Even Vi still needs me."

Jasper nodded, offering a shy smile. He arched an inquiring eyebrow at Tillie, but didn't voice the question his eyes broadcast. Part of Tillie wanted to offer him a second chance, but she just couldn't make the words come together. She glanced at her mom, hoping she could help.

Mom gave her a non-committal shrug and a friendly smile, but Tillie knew this decision would be left up to her. Mom wouldn't make promises for Tillie to keep.

Swearing she heard a game show count-down buzzer, Tillie tried harder to figure out just how much trust she could give this man she'd written off so long ago.

She didn't want to make a mistake or be forced into something she couldn't get out of. When her heart threatened to leap out of her chest, Tillie opened her mouth, not sure what was going to pop out.

Mom squeezed her hand. "It's okay. Take your time."

Relief slowed the pounding in her chest a little. "I want a dad like that, but ..."

"But?" Jasper whispered.

Tillie took a quick glance at each adult. "But ... um." She swallowed. "I want to trust you, but I don't know if I can. I don't want to hurt your feelings, but ..."

Quiet seconds passed like pudding through a strainer.

Jasper sighed, then gave a resolute nod. "You've already replaced me with Todd?"

Spinning toward Uncle Ben, Tillie gave a quick nod and slipped her arms around Uncle Ben's waist, hot tears burning her eyes. "I'm sorry." Tears slid down her cheeks. "I didn't know you wanted to be a *good* dad."

Uncle Ben rubbed her back.

"It's okay, Tilda. This is my fault. I should have been back a long time ago." Jasper blew out a slow breath. "You know, I had considered that maybe Jake and your mom might get together if I didn't come back, but I don't think I ever thought about Todd being any competition."

Anxiety burrowed into Tillie again. "Ginnie's like my sister."

"Don't worry. I know Todd's a good dad. Ginnie could be quite a handful at times, but he seldom got rattled with her. I admired that about him." Jasper wiped her tears again with a gentle finger. He chuckled. "It also made me grateful that *you* were *my* kid. I guess I can see why you'd like him. We'll figure this out."

She had an idea. "Maybe ..."

"Maybe what?" Jasper asked gently.

"Maybe we could ..." Tillie glanced at Uncle Ben. He nodded, giving an encouraging smile. "Ginnie's dad and Uncle Jake take Ginnie and me on dates sometimes—together. We have fun. Maybe you and me and Ginnie and her dad could do that? Until we get to know each other again? Like you did with Mom?"

"Sure." He looked as relieved as she felt. "That's a great idea. As long as you're willing to give me a chance, I'm willing to do whatever it takes to make it easy on you."

Hopeful, Tillie returned his smile and slid her arms around his waist, brushing the pink gift with the side of her arm as she hugged him.

Strangely, Tillie wanted to open it, her interest in the oven from long ago re-surfacing.

Before she could act on her thought, Jasper returned her hug and then straightened. "Hey, wait. I have something else for you." He walked to the trunk again and came back with a small gift wrapped in bright purple paper, decorated with a silver bow and ribbon. "The oven represented an old promise. I'd like this to represent a new one." He held it out to her and grinned. "This one should be more to your liking."

"Thank you." Excitement bubbled inside her as she eagerly ripped open the paper, pleasantly surprised to find a brand new iPhone. "Awesome sauce!"

"My boss's daughter said I couldn't go wrong with an iPhone. She's fourteen." His eyes danced nervously while he searched her face. "Do you like it?"

A surge of happiness swelled inside.

She nodded. "I do."

His hesitant smile morphed into a confident one. "Good. I had to replace mine and a second phone came with my plan. You're practically a teen now. You need a phone." He grimaced at Mom. "I want to be able to talk to you after I leave for Kentucky on Thursday."

His words echoed a recent sentiment Tillie couldn't place right away.

Mom sucked in a quick breath as her gaze met Tillie's.

The happy bubble burst.

Then Tillie remembered the sentiment ... and the iPhone ... in her front jean pocket.

51

BARIWON

*P*ierce sat on his living room couch, fingers flying over the remote as his linebacker-sized avatar, Bariwon, battled a small army of ogres. He'd lost count of how many games he'd played that day, but for the second time this evening, Bariwon's ragtag group of cohorts were soundly defeating the green-skinned bullies, in spite of their huge size.

"Take that!" he shouted, pummeling an ogre with a wooden club.

A tall, skinny blond sidekick named Twigg covered Bariwon's back as another ogre leaped from behind. Bariwon clobbered the first ogre, then turned to help Twigg. Twigg always seemed to be around when Bariwon needed him. *Just like Toran.*

Pierce hadn't really expected Toran to keep being his friend after school let out, but Uncle Ben had said "Wests don't do friendships halfway" the night Pierce's father was arrested for hurting him. Toran had stayed true. Pierce leaned forward and clubbed a new ogre making a beeline to Twigg. *Neither do I.*

Together they vanquished two more ogres while the only girl member of their band of renegades, a feisty redhead, annihilated a fifth ogre with her bow and arrow.

Pierce called her Trouble, like Uncle Jake did Ginnie. The two of them had a lot in common.

A smaller, quiet cohort named Squirrely reminded Pierce of Tillie. Every time Pierce discounted him as useless, Squirrely came through for him.

Tillie had always been quiet at school, so Pierce had never really noticed her until he and Ginnie got into a fight at the movie theater and Pierce had threatened to wipe Ginnie's hard drive.

Tillie had tried to keep Ginnie from fighting Pierce, but when Pierce told Tillie to bug off and grabbed her arm to make her leave, Ginnie had gone all kinds of Hulk on him.

A fifth member of the renegade troop, Alec, reminded Pierce of Austin, Toran's best friend.

Austin invited Pierce and Toran over to ride horses a few days ago.

The three of them had fun together. Pierce didn't feel like an intruder, even though he knew Toran and Austin had been friends since they were babies.

Alec didn't say a lot, but he made a good scout. He'd get the drop on the bad guys and let the rest of the renegades know to be prepared. Austin reminded Pierce of an easy-going river—just flowing along, making room for Pierce when Toran asked him to.

Thumbs pressing quickly over the controls, Pierce made Bariwon hurriedly climb a tree and dive spread-eagle to take out two ogres sneaking up on Alec. Trouble aimed her arrow at a third ogre and let it fly, making it bull's-eye into the ogre's.

Squirrelly dived behind the speared ogre, causing him to fall backward and bump his head on a large boulder, knocking him out of his misery.

The front door squeaked open.

Pierce's dad walked through.

His narrowed eyes and pinched lips spiked panic in Pierce's middle.

"H—hi, Dad!" Pierce greeted, mustering a friendly tone.

"Hi," his father replied stiffly.

Each glanced at the TV just as an ogre punched Bariwon in the face. His dad sucked in a breath, then shook his head as the ogre lifted Bariwon and tossed him into a bush.

"Turn it off. I'm sure you can do something else for a while. I'll bet you've probably been playing for hours."

Bariwon gave a moan as Pierce fumbled with the remote to close the game.

He turned the power off, wishing the renegades—or his new friends could materialize as his dad crossed the room.

"Marsha! What's for dinner? I'm starved."

"Taco casserole." Mom appeared in the kitchen doorway. "It'll be ready in a few minutes. How was work?"

"My supervisor is an idiotic, snot-nosed kid barely out of high school." His father geared up his rant, pumping his fist. "I'm late because that punk kid doesn't know his head from a hole in the wall."

Pierce held his breath and stood.

"I'm sure it will get better," Mom soothed. "I have brownies for dessert."

Pierce watched his father for a few seconds to see if he needed to worry about his mom's safety.

At the mention of brownies, his father dangled his fingers, leaving enough room between himself and Mom that Pierce decided he could disappear into his room.

52

PRANK WARS

*A*fter finishing the pie, Ginnie helped Dad and Toran wash, dry, and put away the dishes. Aunt Roni, Buzz, and Uncle Jake cleaned up the dining room and put the extra food away. "Anybody want to watch a movie?" Dad asked, pointing to the family room.

"No, thanks." Ginnie shook her head. "I want to show Aunt Roni something in the journal Mama wrote for me." She turned to her aunt. "Would you like to look?"

"Sure, sugar. I'd love to see what Widget had to say." Aunt Roni nodded at Ginnie and Toran. "One of these days, I'll bring you two some of the journals our mama wrote to her when she was a child, if that's alright with you, Todd."

A playful grin lit Dad's lips. "It'd be fun to see what Miss Serafina wrote about my wife as a little girl. To hear Queenie tell it, you two kept her pretty busy."

"Just being the mother of twins did that." Aunt Roni offered a teasing laugh. "She complicated things by putting us in pageants and insisting on us being genteel. Miss Letitia's Charm School was something else."

Dad's grin grew wider. "Was that the one where Queenie got on the wrong side of the instructor and super-glued all of the lady's dishes and eating utensils to the table as payback for having to practice her walk a hundred and fifty times?"

"No way!" Toran protested as Ginnie giggled.

"No, that was Miss Bettina's School for Proper Young Ladies." Aunt Roni giggled with Ginnie. "She put a goldfish in Miss Leticia's teacup. Miss Letitia was almost seventy years old—it nearly gave her a heart attack."

"How old was Mama?" Ginnie asked, wide-eyed.

"Five. Widget didn't like the tea Miss Letitia served, so she decided that if Miss Letitia wouldn't let her add more than one cube of sugar to hers, she'd add a fish to Miss Letitia's. Our mama was absolutely mortified she'd do such a thing."

Ginnie and Toran laughed harder.

"I'm just gonna say it. I am *very* thankful Queenie was my wife and not my child. Those situations are funnier when they involve somebody else's kid." Dad chuckled, shaking his head at Ginnie. "Don't get any ideas, or I may have to rethink letting you read your mom's journals. She didn't always make the most appropriate choices as a child."

"That's okay, Daddy. She chose you." Ginnie tried to keep a straight face as she slipped her arms around her dad's waist. "That was the best choice she ever made."

Uncle Jake roared with laughter.

"And there's a classic 'Queenie' move," Buzz said, smiling. "In the nature-versus-nurture argument, we always say that Ginnie is the winner for nature while Toran is a shoo-in for nurture."

Ginnie stopped laughing. "What does that mean?"

"It means they think Mama influenced you just by being your mother—even though you didn't get to be with her very long," Toran explained.

"Oh." Ginnie shrugged, contemplating his answer. "Well, that's a good thing. Right, Daddy?"

"For the most part." He gave a quick nod. "We're not doing so badly—you've been in school for seven years and I've only been called to the principal's office twice because of you." He glanced at Aunt Roni. "How many classes was her mother asked to leave by the time she was five?"

Aunt Roni shrugged, laughing. "To be fair, only two—and she was closer to Ginnie and Toran's age. However, she was put on probation at several places."

"Yeah." Dad grimaced, taking note of Ginnie's great interest in this conversation. "Don't be filling Ginnie in on the details, please." He backhanded Uncle Jake's chest lightly. "*His* influence is bad enough."

"You should talk." Uncle Jake feigned an offended expression. "And who was it that put the dead bird in Howie Bryant's desk?"

Toran laughed. "Yeah, Dad, who?"

"Hey, I spent days gathering seeds and leaves from twenty different trees and plants to make the most awesome ecology poster. Howie ripped it up in like ten seconds flat." Dad pointed a finger at Uncle Jake. "The bird was *your* idea ... *you* brought it to me. I just put it where it could be easily found and properly disposed of."

"Keep telling yourself that. Howie squealed like a pig, and you know you enjoyed freaking all the girls out—including your teacher." Uncle Jake pointed at Dad. "He's not as innocent as he'd like you to believe."

Dad shook his head. "*You* started the trouble with Howie. He took it out on me because I had the misfortune of being your younger brother."

"Whatever." Uncle Jake leaned against the kitchen counter, folding his arms. "I took care of him for you."

"Except *I* got detention," Dad reminded him. "Not you."

"Really?" Ginnie asked.

Her dad was a stickler for rules. Thinking he would get busted at school amused Ginnie ... very much.

"Teachers frown on dead animals in desks." Dad said, shrugging innocently. "Who knew?"

Ginnie giggled. "Um ... *everybody*?"

"Big deal. I got busted by Uncle Ben." Uncle Jake lifted his hands to air quote. "I'll take detention over his 'creative consequences' any day." He rolled his eyes at Aunt Roni. "Our uncle wasn't big on 'punishment', but he had nothing against 'creative consequences' for bad behavior. He had a knack for making them hard, or gross, or worse yet, *both*."

"Even worse, Daddy gets ideas from him." Ginnie stopped laughing and speared her dad with a look of disgust. She swiveled to Aunt Roni. "He made me paint the fence along the lane when I knocked Pierce on his rear—even though it was to protect Toran."

"Don't even start," Toran protested. "I could've handled Pierce. You're just a busybody."

"It coulda been worse," Dad said, tugging her braid lightly. "I could've tanned your hide."

"Nope, that would've been better," Ginnie argued.

"Really?" Aunt Roni asked, surprise coloring her tone.

"Yeah, no contest." Ginnie rolled her eyes. "It took me two days to finish—*with help*. My arms hurt for a week. I would've gladly traded for a few swats on the rear."

"Stop rolling your eyes. It's rude," Dad scolded, wagging an annoyed finger at her. "*That* attitude is exactly why being creative with consequences works for you. You'll think twice before starting a fight at school or you'll be painting it *again*."

Ginnie groaned. "I didn't start the fight—Pierce did. I just finished it." She smirked at her dad. "But Daddy ended up apologizing for making me paint the fence."

"I apologized for not handling the fights better—not so much for having you paint the fence." Dad turned to Aunt Roni and frowned. "The day after she finished the fence, her school suspension was lifted. That day, she got into *another* fight with Pierce and then hid it. I admitted to her that I realized too late that I was so angry about *what* they'd done that I hadn't taken the time to figure out *why* they did it. Then they snuck out and pranked Pierce's house—or tried to."

Ginnie held up her arm. "I wanted to pay Pierce back for twisting my wrist. Before we could do anything, I saw Pierce's dad knock him flat and kick him."

"Oh, my heavens!" Aunt Roni's hand flew to her mouth.

A sick feeling churned as Ginnie remembered several fierce kicks into Pierce's leg. "It was awful."

Aunt Roni's eyes grew wider. "Did his father see you?"

"Only after I banged on the door and screamed at him to stop hurting Pierce—I didn't really think that part through. I just wanted him to stop hurting Pierce."

"Austin and I had no idea what was happening," Toran added, moving closer to Aunt Roni. "We were waiting for her to let us know the coast was clear and she started banging on the door." He smiled. "Sometimes I forget she's a little psycho. You'd think I'd remember that after all these years."

"You're hilarious," Ginnie snapped.

Aunt Roni frowned. "It sounds like she was very brave. Pierce is a big boy. I imagine he takes after his daddy that way."

"Brave ... foolish ... sometimes one looks like the other." Dad teased, moving his palms up and down, imitating a scale. "However, by doing something foolish like pranking, they helped Pierce when he needed it most." He shook his head. "How do you discipline your kids when their wrong thinking ends up helping someone who needed it?"

"What did you do?" Aunt Roni glanced from Dad to Toran, a shocked expression covering her features.

"I called 9-1-1," Toran said, shrugging. "Then we came home and confessed to Dad."

"Yeah, I was still freaked out—then Uncle Ben said we had to go back to the Owens' and tell the police." Ginnie shivered as goose bumps formed. "That was really wild."

"It worked out. Ray was arrested before we got there." Dad let out a quick breath. "Pierce, Toran, and Ginnie—as you would say—had a little 'come-to-Jesus' meeting. Pierce was furious. I realized that night that Pierce was a bigger danger to Ginnie than I had previously thought—which is why I apologized for punishing her when she defended her brother with her fists instead of her words."

"She didn't need to use either. She should have let me handle

Pierce," Toran interjected. "He came after *me*. If she had let me deal with him, the rest of it wouldn't have happened."

"But if we didn't prank his house, Pierce's dad would still be hurting him," Ginnie protested.

Dad gave Ginnie's shoulder a gentle squeeze. "I didn't realize he was so much bigger than my kids. After the dust settled, we invited Pierce and his mom over for a BBQ the next day and went out for chocolate malts that night. The kids have become friends and Pierce's dad has gotten some help."

Ginnie grinned. "Getting chocolate malts was fun—it was late, so we had a pajama party and took Tillie and Miss Amanda with us. Tillie freaked out when she found out Mr. Owens got arrested, but the next day, she told Pierce about what 'Uncle' Jasper had done to *her*, so Pierce stopped feeling so weird around us."

"What *did* Jasper do to her?" Aunt Roni whispered, looking like she didn't really want to know.

"You saw the bruise on Pierce's face? Uncle Jasper did that to Tillie—and Miss Amanda too—only he gave Miss Amanda a big, fat lip." Ginnie shuddered at the memory.

"Yeah, that was pretty ugly," Buzz agreed.

"Jasper swears hurting Tillie was an accident," Uncle Jake insisted, standing a little straighter. "He turned so fast, not knowing she was there, and caught her with his hand. She was tiny and quiet —it could happen."

"But it shouldn't have!" Ginnie declared.

"Absolutely! And if he hurt Amanda on purpose, then that's terrible." Aunt Roni gave Dad's wrist a squeeze. "I felt bad hearing Jasper talk about his father, but if he could hurt Amanda and Tillie, they're definitely better off with you."

"Thanks," Dad said in a teasing voice. "I think."

Ginnie giggled as Aunt Roni's cheeks pinked.

Aunt Roni pursed her lips. "You know what I mean."

"Speaking of Tillie, she might need me. I should go find out." Ginnie turned toward the dining room.

"Freeze." Dad stepped in front of her, blocking her way. "She has her mom and Uncle Ben. She's fine." His voice didn't sound as confident as his words, but his narrowed eyes meant business.

"Can't I at least see?" Ginnie asked.

He shook his head. "Give Jasper a little space. He's going to be overly sensitive to anything you or I do."

Disappointed, Ginnie grimaced. "Can I still show Aunt Roni the journal?"

"Yes." He motioned at the dining room. "Stay inside."

"Yes, sir." Irritated with him, Ginnie glanced at her aunt and hurried to the front of the house. She stopped by the screen door. The front porch light lit up the car area. Tillie stood close to Uncle Ben. Ginnie couldn't see her face, but she had a bad feeling about how their chat was going.

"She's fine. Uncle Ben is right there," Aunt Roni said.

"*I* should be there." Ginnie watched Jasper backup a step. She could swear Tillie frowned.

Ginnie considered bolting out the door.

Aunt Roni touched her elbow. "She'll be okay. I'm sure each of them has things that need to be said, even if they don't want to hear them. And Uncle Ben is there. He'll keep her safe. "

Uneasiness bubbled in Ginnie. "But Tillie gets freaked out easily. She can't always say what she wants to. That's why I should be there —to help her."

Tillie toggled her head and leaned forward with a determined look. She spoke words Ginnie couldn't hear.

"It looks like she's handling herself very well, sugar. Trust her. She can do this."

Ginnie shook her head, wanting very much to be at Tillie's side. "She needs me."

"Your mama used to speak for me." Aunt Roni sighed. "I don't think I ever found my own voice until our father forced her to choose between us and your dad. I was so lost without her. I think this may be Tillie's time to find her voice. She knows you're with her in spirit."

"I should be there in *person*. That's what friends—and sisters— do." The uneasiness surged in Ginnie as Jasper advanced a step and

Tillie backed up against Uncle Ben. He placed his hands on Tillie's shoulders.

"This is hard for her. Look."

Then Tillie crossed her arms and jutted out her chin, relieving a little of Ginnie's anxiety. *Go, Tillie.*

"Some journeys are difficult, but have to be taken." Aunt Roni slipped her arm around Ginnie and swept her toward the stairs. "She knows you're here for her."

Ginnie stopped on the third step and locked her gaze on Aunt Roni's. "He'd better not hurt her. We're sisters. *No dad* is getting between us—hers or anybody else's."

Her words sounded harsher than she meant, but gave Ginnie the courage to climb the stairs without her very best friend.

53

GIRLS JUST

WANNA HAVE FUN

*G*innie sat down next to Aunt Roni on her emerald-green comforter with her bright pink journal and flipped it open toward the back. "I've always needed to ride horses, see?"

April 10

Dear Gins,

I took you riding on Eternal Love with me this morning and you loved it! Ten months old and already a real cowgirl! I let you ride by yourself (walking beside you with my hand on you while your daddy led Love around the pasture). I don't think you really needed me, though. You adjusted as Love walked and stayed glued in the saddle—like you'd been riding your whole life.

(Well, you have, but usually you're in a baby sling.)

You cried when Daddy tried to take you off.

So he let you ride longer and teased about how we'd have to get you your own horse soon. You must've understood what he said, because you lit up like a Christmas tree. 😊

I can't believe you and Toran turn one in 6 weeks. The time has flown by. Aunt Sadie can't get enough of you two. She bribed you with a graham cracker to get you off Love today, but you didn't trade out easily. No question about it, you're definitely my girl. I guess we'll dress you up as a cowgirl and bring your stuffed rocking horse to the next pageant for outfit of choice. You'll really "rock" that show. 😊 *Get it?*

Groaning at her mom's joke, Ginnie turned to Aunt Roni and let Mama's words soothe her. She was glad she and Mama could have a conversation of sorts.

"I brought you a miniature horse during a pageant when you were three. You owned that performance," Aunt Roni said, eyes bright. "You rode in singing, slid out of the saddle, did a little dance, and had the horse literally eating out of your hand. The judges loved it. You won 'queen supreme' for your age division."

Hazy images of fancy dresses and colorful costumes paraded quickly through Ginnie's mind. Dad had told her once that he was never fully comfortable with her participating in pageants, but allowed it to keep Mama happy. After Mama died, he packed up everything to do with Ginnie's pageant days and hid it away.

"I don't remember. Daddy said they were going to buy us horses for our fourth birthday, but since Mama died a few months before then, it didn't happen."

Aunt Roni nodded. "He was pretty done with horses by the funeral ... and done with your granddaddy and me by the time your birthday rolled around. We were in England by then."

Ginnie pushed away her conflicting feelings about Cabot and patted her pocket. "Thanks again for the phone. I think Daddy's gonna let us keep them."

"You're welcome. But they come with a condition." Aunt Roni

fixed a serious expression on her face. "Well ... make that *two* conditions."

"Great." Ginnie hammed a tortured look and groaned, asking in a mock serious tone, "What are they?"

"You are so-o-o-o my sister's child." Aunt Roni tousled Ginnie's hair. "But I think you can handle them."

"Fine. Lay them on me."

"One—don't do anything your dad would disapprove of on it--and I'm very serious about that--I don't want you giving him any excuse to take them." Aunt Roni took a firm hold of her chin. "... and two—you have to call me at least twice a week."

"Hmmm." Ginnie rubbed her chin, putting on a show of considering her aunt's words, before offering an exaggerated sigh. "If I must."

"You most definitely must, young lady," Aunt Roni teased, wagging a reproving finger. "Or I'll be on you like a honeybee to a field of buttercups."

"Which means what, exactly?" Ginnie teased back.

"Which means, you'd better call or you won't want to find out 'what,' young lady. That's *what*."

"Yes, ma'am. Thanks for making that as cle-ah as mud," Ginnie joked, imitating her aunt's Southern accent.

"You'd best stifle your sass or I just might talk your daddy into sending *you* to Miss Bettina's School for Proper Young Ladies." Aunt Roni arched a scolding eyebrow over a twinkling eye. "My sister met her match in Miss Bettina. She's one steel magnolia who never lets sassy young ladies get the best of her. Trust me on this."

"What did she do to my mom?"

"Let's just say Widget learned the hard way that there are a few people even more determined than she was." Aunt Roni gave Ginnie's knee a firm squeeze and stood. "Enough about that. When will Vi be home?"

"Who knows?" Ginnie shrugged. "She's never home anymore. Even before she and Preston got engaged, she's always with *him*."

"Do I detect a hint of jealousy?"

"Not really. But until Dad started dating Miss Amanda, Vi was the closest thing I had to a living mom."

"And now she's getting married and moving out," Aunt Roni surmised. "I can see why that would be upsetting."

"Yeah, I miss her already." Ginnie brushed a loose hair out of her face and stood. "But it's okay, as long as Vi comes and visits. She'll be over on Sundays and she said we can do sleepovers at her new house and she'll help us make yummy treats."

"Sounds like fun."

"It will be. Tillie loves to bake and so does Vi. Which reminds me —I want to check on Tillie and make sure she's okay."

Before Aunt Roni could object, Ginnie hurried to the upstairs window facing the lane and peeked out.

Because she had to look over the front porch roof, it took a few seconds to locate all four people.

Ginnie made out Uncle Ben, Miss Amanda, and Jasper fairly quickly, but couldn't find a fourth distinct head. She leaned closer, watching Jasper sway a little.

Ginnie sucked in a quick breath.

Jasper hugged Tillie tight in his arms.

Panic surged.

She swiveled away from the window, nearly crashing into Aunt Roni.

54

WINDING ROADS

'll be in soon," Mom said to Tillie, squeezing her into a quick hug. "We need to head home before too long."

Tillie nodded, looking again at Jasper.

The looming shadows from dusk hid his brown hair some, but she made out a satisfied sparkle in his eyes.

It brightened a dark and forgotten space within her.

"Night, Angel girl. Thanks for talking with me."

"You're welcome." She returned his smile, trying to sort her conflicted feelings about him. "Thanks for the phone and the Easy-Bake Oven." Tillie reached for the oven.

"Here, let me help you." Jasper took the phone box out of her hand, set it on the oven, and then set both on the unopened gift. He lifted all three and nodded at the porch. "I can take this inside for you."

"No, thanks. I got it." She reached for the stack.

"If you're sure." He reluctantly handed her the boxes.

The kindness in his tone felt good, like when DT talked to her. "Thank you."

"Any time." They walked a few steps together. He took an extra-long stride. "I'll get the door."

As if on cue, Ginnie opened the screen door.

"I guess she's got it." Tillie stared at Jasper, feeling a little awkward.

Part of her wanted to hug him again, and the other part wanted to hurry to Ginnie.

"I see that." Jasper glanced at Ginnie and seemed to force a smile. "See you tomorrow?"

Tillie shrugged. "I guess so."

Jasper locked his eyes on Tillie's, searching her face for a few seconds.

The screen door squeaked.

Tillie blinked, turning toward her friend. "Thanks again."

"You're welcome. Sweet dreams."

"You too." Tillie hurried to the farmhouse.

Ginnie raised questioning brows at the Easy-Bake Oven box and swung the red wooden door open wider.

"I'll tell you later," Tillie whispered, passed through the archway and stopped, surprised to see Toran in the hallway. DT and Aunt Roni stood behind him.

Ginnie gasped.

Tillie swiveled, following her friend's gaze to Mom and Jasper, whose foreheads touched.

Jasper moved slightly forward and stopped for half a second before sweeping Mom into a tight hug.

Mom seemed to melt into his arms.

A mixture of panic and warmth showered over Tillie.

"What's wrong?" Toran asked.

Shrugging, Tillie glanced behind him, taking in the cascading figures—tallest to shortest—of DT, Aunt Roni, and Toran. She saw both DT and Aunt Roni reflected in Toran's features, making the three of them seem like they were posing for a family portrait.

One that Tillie wanted to be a part of, but felt out of place in.

Familiar anxiety burrowed into her middle.

She spun toward the front porch.

Ginnie's dropped jaw twisted the anxiety into a loose, but winding knot.

Mom took a step back from Jasper, exchanging a warm smile with him.

The knot tightened.

55

TORAN'S CHAPTER

Toran rushed forward, wanting to see what made Ginnie gasp and Tillie look like she was gonna puke.

Miss Amanda smiled at Uncle Jasper, and then gave him a quick hug, sliding her palms down his arms, and squeezing his hands in a friendly manner.

Ginnie's eyes narrowed angrily.

Color returned to Tillie's face.

Concern wriggled inside Toran for as long as it took him to come up with reassuring words for his sisters. "Miss Amanda is just being a good friend. She wants to make Uncle Jasper feel welcome."

Ginnie glared. "She can do that without touching him."

At the mention of Miss Amanda's name, Toran felt strong hands on his shoulders, moving him to the side as his dad's voice spoke near his left ear. "Of course. He's been gone a long time. It will be easier to work out visitation and whatnot if Jasper isn't on the defensive."

Pretty sure Dad's words were to convince himself as well as the rest of them, Toran nodded. "She's like that. She wouldn't want anyone to feel awkward, and this has to be as weird for them as it is for us."

Jasper turned toward them, sporting an amused look, followed by an annoyed one.

A more pleasant expression crossed his features when Miss Amanda said something no one else could hear.

She smiled, wiggling her fingers their way.

Dad lifted his hands from Toran's shoulders. "Come on. This isn't a 'you got punked' YouTube video."

Toran didn't have to look at his dad to know his cheeks were pinking.

Dad's voice conveyed his discomfort.

Ginnie followed them into the house. She reached for Tillie's wrist. "Fine. We have girltalk to catch up on."

"Not so fast." Dad plucked the iPhone box off the stack of boxes Tillie carried. "Nice phone."

"Late birthday gift," Tillie said, adjusting the other two boxes she carried. "A couple weeks late on that one, and six years late on these."

"Want some help?" Dad set the phone back on top and reached for the stack. "They're almost as tall as you."

Tillie let him take the stack. "Is it okay if I keep the phone?"

"If Jasper gave you that phone, I'm not going to tell you that you can't keep it. He *is* your dad."

Tillie's hopeful smile turned to an anxious frown.

"Can we keep *ours*?" Toran and Ginnie asked together.

"I'm still thinking about that." Dad grimaced at them, then glanced at Tillie. "What does Jasper think about you having two phones?"

Shrugging, Tillie threw an apologetic look at Aunt Roni. "I didn't tell him. Mom sent me in before I could."

"I guess Amanda and I'll be talking about that later, then." Dad glanced at Aunt Roni, who offered a quick nod, before setting his gaze on Tillie. "Do you want to take these to the apartment, or leave them here?"

"Leave them here. I thought Mysti might like to play it with me tomorrow."

"She probably would. I'll set it on the dining room table for you, then. Do you want the phone?"

"Sure she does." Toran said, swiping it off the stack. "I'll help her set it up. Come on, girls."

Glad to have an excuse to follow them upstairs, Toran motioned toward the steps, knowing Ginnie would pump Tillie for information on her meeting with Jasper.

For once, he would get the news firsthand.

56

PUMPING FOR INFO

Ginnie and Tillie dropped as one on Ginnie's emerald-green comforter. Toran sat on the floor in front of them. Ginnie didn't waste any time. "Okay, Til. *Spill.*"

Tillie glanced at Toran. He straightened. "Unless there's something you don't want to tell us."

"There's nothing you can't hear." Tillie made a circular motion with her pointer finger on the satin comforter.

"Well?" Ginnie asked, trying to be patient, but losing the battle. She needed to find out if anything had changed during Tillie's little chat with "Uncle Jasper" or if they could go forward with their plans to be sisters.

"There's not a whole lot to say." Tillie shrugged. "Jasper says I can't fire him as my dad, and he wants to be involved in my life. He gave me the phone so we can keep in touch when he's working in Kentucky."

Ginnie scrunched her face. "What about your mom? Does he want *her* back?" The thought of losing Vi and Miss Amanda both gnawed at her something awful.

She felt like termites were feasting on her insides.

"He wants her," Tillie said.

Ginnie sucked in a quick breath.

"I don't know if she wants him, though." Tillie shrugged again. "He was nice and all, but we didn't talk about it. He wanted to propose to her, but he said he wouldn't tonight."

The termites doubled in size and number.

"Gin, don't panic. Miss Amanda loves Dad. One conversation won't change that," Toran said. "And just because Uncle Jasper wants her doesn't mean Miss Amanda has to take him. Nobody gets to force her to do anything she doesn't want to do."

"They better not ... except Dad," Ginnie insisted.

"Even Dad, Gin." Toran frowned at her. "You heard him say that what happens now is up to Miss Amanda and Tillie."

Eyes wide, Tillie turned to Ginnie. "Your dad doesn't want us anymore?" Anxiety strained her tone.

"Of course he does. He just said he won't pressure your mom." Toran sent a stern look Ginnie's way. "Dad will support whatever your mom wants to do."

"She'd better still want him," Ginnie and Tillie said together.

Their unexpected echo lightened their worry some.

Happy that Tillie hadn't changed sides, Ginnie waved her hand impatiently. "So, what happened?"

After taking a quick breath, Tillie told them about being very angry about Jasper thinking he could just show up and boss Tillie around after six years of being gone.

"He has some nerve!" Ginnie spat.

"Shhh!" Toran hissed.

Then Tillie told how she spouted off at Jasper about him hurting Miss Amanda, and she called him out about making her a lot of promises that he didn't keep.

"Good for you!" Ginnie and Toran exclaimed together.

Tillie shrugged. "He wants to keep all of them now."

"Wow, Tillie! You really stood up for yourself." Ginnie hugged her friend; glad Tillie hadn't been as helpless as she had thought she would be. "I bet Jasper won't be as bossy since he knows how you really feel." Ginnie squeezed her again, giggling with relief.

"Yeah, I started getting nervous. But then he made me mad, so I thought about what you would say and the next thing I knew, your words were popping out of my mouth."

Toran shook his head and smiled. "That's what I need—identical personality twin sisters."

Ginnie smirked. "Feel free to leave my room."

Laughing, Tillie leaned forward. "I need you guys to help with something, though."

"Anything," Toran said.

Ginnie nodded. "Yeah."

"Jasper wants to get to know me better, but I don't want to be alone with him."

"That could be a problem," Ginnie agreed.

"Well, I think I figured out a solution." Tillie grinned. "I asked him to let you and your dad go out with us until I get to know him better. He said he was fine with that. So now we gotta think up some fun places to go—like what we did when we set up your dad and my mom."

"I want to go, too." Toran drummed his fingers on his denim-clad knees. "Laser tag would be epic, or go-karts again."

"Yeah." Ginnie mulled over those suggestions. "Either would keep him out of your personal bubble and you could still have fun with him. And more importantly ... you can have fun with us, if he turns out to be lame. Also, paintball could be fun."

"I don't think he'll be lame. We talked about stuff we did together before he left—and I remembered we actually had fun."

Ginnie wanted to protest Tillie's softening position on Jasper.

Then she realized it wouldn't do any good to make Tillie feel bad about spending time with her birth dad, especially when they couldn't keep it from happening.

Instead, Ginnie racked her brain for more activities. "Putt-putt golf? The swimming pool? The fair?"

She relaxed as Tillie and Toran cracked jokes and came up with more ideas. Each of them startled when they heard a knock on Ginnie's bedroom door.

Miss Amanda appeared. "It's nice to hear you guys laughing and having fun together. Sorry to break up the good time, but Tillie and I need to go home."

"Can't I spend the night? It's getting late," Tillie said.

Miss Amanda shook her head firmly. "We need to talk."

The termite colony in Ginnie's belly tripled.

57

THE DRIVE HOME

Tillie waved at DT, then slid into the front seat of her mom's car and buckled up, dread and curiosity taking turns twisting inside as she wondered what was on Mom's mind.

Mom kissed DT good-bye.

DT opened her door, waited for Mom to slide in, then closed the door. "See you in the morning, Todd."

"Sure thing." He leaned into Mom's window, smiling at each of them. "Pleasant dreams, Tillie."

"You too." She returned his smile, searching his face for signs that he had changed his mind about marrying her mom. As far as she could tell, he hadn't.

He pulled back a little and glanced at Mom. "I love you, Amanda. We'll make this work." His tone didn't project as much confidence as Tillie would have liked.

"I love you, too." Mom shrugged, seeming to force a brighter smile. "Pleasant dreams."

Bumblebees rumbled in Tillie's belly.

Mom pressed her lips together, backed out of the parking spot, and turned the car. She put it in gear and drove silently down the lane.

Something is definitely wrong.

Tillie played out different scenarios in her head, trying to make Mom's determined look not mean she was considering breaking off her engagement and taking Jasper back.

The longer her mom remained quiet, the louder the bumblebees buzzed. "Mom? What's wrong?"

Her mom didn't answer right away, pulling to a stop where the gravel lane met the main road. "I'm not sure how to say something I want to say to you."

The bees rumbled faster. "Is it bad?" *They're gonna break up. How can she want Jasper more than DT?*

Mom sighed and waited for the traffic to clear. She started to go forward, then tapped the brake, put the car in park, and stared intently at Tillie. "I'm trying to figure out why you are so afraid of everything."

"What do you mean? I'm not afraid."

"You about jumped out of your skin when Jasper approached you in the farmhouse. I know he hurt you the last time he got drunk, but that was a long time ago and *not* the last time you saw him."

"Why wouldn't I be afraid? I saw him bust your lip."

"We worked through that. *With* you. He shouldn't have done it, but the man he was that night isn't the only person he is. He made a lot of good changes after that for you." Mom pursed her lips into a frown. "And that happened over six years ago. I've made sure nobody has hurt you since."

Tillie shrugged, unable to voice the fear that always seemed to envelop her like a scratchy, ill-fitting sweater.

"Why didn't you remember any of the good things we did to replace the bad memories?" Mom leaned closer. "I'm trying to figure out why you clung to the bad times."

"I didn't exactly cling to them." Tillie backed away. "Do you think I liked being afraid of my own father? I used to hide under my covers when you two would fight and try to make myself invisible so he wouldn't find me. I hated when he would yell at you. Sometimes he'd grab my arms and squeeze." Tillie moved forward, locking her eyes on her mom's. "It hurt. And even when it didn't, I was always afraid he would hurt us. He hurt you a lot. I *hated* that."

"It wasn't a lot," Mom whispered.

Tillie folded her arms and glared. "It shouldn't have been at all. Ginnie's dad would never hurt you."

"We can't all have good dads like Todd and Uncle Ben." Mom glared back. "It would be nice, but it's not reality for a lot of people. Todd and Uncle Ben aren't perfect, either."

"They're perfect enough," Tillie snapped.

"You didn't think so last night when Todd didn't do what you wanted. And that's the point, Tillie. *Nobody* is perfect. My dad was worse than Jasper ever was to me and not near the monster Oscar Taylor was. Jasper did things he shouldn't have, but he had a lousy example to follow."

"That doesn't make it right!"

"Of course it doesn't. But he didn't *keep* doing it."

"Why are you making excuses for him? People shouldn't hit people—especially adults. You tell us kids to 'use our words'—why doesn't that apply to adults?"

"It does apply to adults."

"This is what you wanted to talk to me about?" Tillie slumped back in her seat. "Not hitting people? I already know that."

"No, of course not." Mom sat back herself and blew out a frustrated breath. "It's complicated."

"What's complicated? You married a bad guy and then divorced him." Tillie shrugged. "You made a mistake and then fixed it. It's okay. You always say that if I learn from my mistakes, I won't repeat them. Marrying Ginnie's dad is *not* repeating that mistake, but marrying Jasper *would* be."

"I'm glad you have it all figured out."

Surprised at the sarcasm in Mom's words, Tillie searched her mom's face.

Mom stared straight ahead, lips pressed together, keeping more frustrated words corralled up tight. After a long moment, she looked at Tillie. "I didn't marry a bad guy. I married a dream that turned into a nightmare ... and I don't mean Jasper."

"What does that mean? He *gave* me nightmares."

"I don't know how to explain it to you." She blew out a breath. "Jasper and I came from similar backgrounds. We both wanted better for each other and for you. We tried ... and we failed." Mom blinked as emotion choked her throat. "Then we tried again and—again— and *still* failed. I didn't want you to be afraid of your dad—like I was growing up. But I've failed you, and I don't know how to fix it."

"What are you talking about? You *didn't fail me.*" Tillie reached for her mom's hand. "Jasper went away and we stayed here, on the farm. Even Jasper knew that was a good thing."

As the words crossed her lips, Tillie realized there was a lot more truth to the idea that Jasper actually cared about her more than she had ever considered.

The thought brightened the dark place within her even more.

Jasper's words from earlier repeated in her mind. *"Tilda, I'm still your dad. I love you. Give me a chance to prove it."* This time she heard truth in them.

"I did fail you. I swore my kids would never have to be afraid in their own home, and I didn't keep that promise. I should have left the first time he acted aggressively toward me, but I didn't."

"Why not?"

"I was pregnant with you. He didn't know I was pregnant. He apologized for hurting me and promised it wouldn't happen again. I asked him how he would treat our children. We talked a lot about being better parents to a future baby than our parents were to us. I wish I had known then that most men who hurt their wives will keep doing it."

"But you did leave him eventually."

Mom gave a slight nod and shrugged. "Things were good for a long while after we married. We had some great times. Jasper promised that he wouldn't hurt our baby and he kept that promise. Uncle Ben and Todd were great role models for how husbands should behave--and Jasper paid attention. But he had a harder time finding and keeping a good job than Todd did. When Todd and Queenie announced their pregnancy, Jasper paid even closer attention.

"Really?"

"Yes. Aunt Sadie and Uncle Ben were equally excited for us and them. None of you are their grandkids by birth, but that didn't matter. All three of you were special to them. Aunt Sadie called you three her triplets. She even made you guys matching outfits a couple times."

"That sounds nice." Tillie tried to picture Aunt Sadie, but could only recall pictures she'd seen of Uncle Ben's late wife. "I wish I could remember her."

"I wish she was still here. While she was, Jasper was a great husband and father. When she died, something broke inside him. And none of us were able to fix it." Mom's voice cracked. "Jasper was so lost. And then we moved to get a fresh start. Things were good for awhile. But it got worse after Queenie died. She was my age, and of course, you, Ginnie, and Toran are only 11 days apart. When she died, it freaked us all out, but *especially* Jasper. "

Mom patted Tillie's leg. "We came back for the funeral--but the farm felt different to Jasper--it didn't bring him comfort. Todd was devastated and heartbroken, and while Uncle Ben had mostly adjusted to Aunt Sadie dying--Queenie's death made the wound of losing Aunt Sadie fresher--for everybody. Jasper withdrew into himself and that was the beginning of the end for our family of three." Her voice broke as she wiped at her eyes. "I tried, Tillie, but I couldn't fix our family again. We were never the same. "

Tillie let her mom's words repeat in her mind. The regret in Mom's voice made her blink back hot tears. "But you did fix it. He left and you divorced him. He seems better now. That's the important thing."

"I stayed too long in Columbus. That's where he hurt me the most." She shook her head. "I should have insisted we come back. Or left him when he wouldn't come back."

"Why didn't you tell Uncle Ben? He would've helped."

Mom paused, looking embarrassed. "Pride. Neither of us wanted

Uncle Ben to know that Jasper hurt me, and more often than not, he'd be really nice for quite a while afterward." Mom offered an apologetic smile. "At the time, I thought I was doing the best for you. Back then, you adored him, and he adored you. It took a while to figure out that I wasn't doing you any favors by allowing him to treat me badly."

"So why did you?"

Mom shrugged. "It's what I knew, except for when Aunt Sadie was alive. My mom put up with it and Jasper was better than my dad, so I felt like I'd upgraded at least."

"That's pathetic," Tillie said, regretting the harsh judgment as soon as it left her mouth.

"It *was* pathetic. And I didn't want *you* thinking it was okay. That's why I quit waiting for him to get better and divorced him four years ago. I needed to be strong for you, even when I couldn't do it for myself."

"I'm glad you did." Tillie flashed her mom the most grateful smile she could muster. "It musta been hard to be a steel magnolia all by yourself."

"Not really." Mom returned the smile. "Since we're a two-for-one special, we've always been steel magnolias together. I wouldn't have that any other way."

"Me either."

After Tillie hugged her mom good night, she changed for bed and thought about the crazy day she'd had.

Aunt Roni coming again so soon had been a great surprise. Fighting with Ginnie was rough, but Tillie felt good about standing up for herself and knowing Ginnie would still be her friend.

She smiled big when she pulled not one, but two, cell phones from her pockets to charge on her dresser for the night. Tillie knew she'd at least be keeping the one Jasper gave her, but nobody had said she had to give up Aunt Roni's. Until they did, she would enjoy having two.

She slipped between her deep-purple sheets, thinking about the Jasper she had met tonight. In some ways, he was the same Jasper she had feared all her life, but more importantly, he was also somebody she might learn to like or even love again.

Not that she wanted Mom to remarry him, but the thought of spending time with the Jasper who said he wanted to be a good dad to her didn't scare her as much as it might have.

"That's how you remember the night I left?" Jasper's question haunted Tillie as she drifted off to sleep.

She replayed the night he left.

This time, while almost six-year-old Tillie stood in the hallway, she heard her parents' voices a little differently.

Mom was less scared and more confident. "Jasper, calm down. I've got a job. We'll manage."

Jasper shook his fist. "It's not supposed to be like this."

Although the anger in his voice sounded more like frustration, it still made Tillie's belly tremble.

"Jasper, let me help," Mom begged.

He turned back to her, hand raised. This time, though, his hand moved slowly and reached for Mom's hand.

Tillie still ran forward. "Don't hurt Mommy!"

"I'm not ..." Jasper stopped. His look was more surprised than angry.

Tillie grabbed Mom's leg and buried her face in Mom's jeans.

Jasper pulled her to him. "Tilda, look at me."

Tillie scrunched her eyes closed and tried to move her shoulder to protect her face.

"Tilda, I didn't hurt her. *Look* at me." His voice still sounded frustrated, but not as angry as usual.

Even so, she still couldn't look at him.

"Daddy wasn't going to hurt me," Mom's quiet voice said. Tillie could hear reassurance rather than fear this time. "He promised to stop. It's okay."

Tillie still scrunched her eyes shut harder.

"My own kid doesn't ..." Jasper grabbed Tillie's arms. He squeezed and shook her once.

"Jasper, don't!"

He let go.

Tillie stumbled backward.

"Jasper, she didn't mean ..." Tillie opened her eyes in time to see Jasper pick up a vase and throw it against the wall behind her mom. Tillie screamed, but this time the vase seemed farther from Mom.

Jasper pointed a finger at Tillie and then opened his mouth. No words came out. He grabbed his jacket off the bed and shook his head. "I'm done."

This time, Tillie heard defeat rather than anger.

She watched him leave, wanting to call out for him to return.

For the first time in years, present-day Tillie really felt the loss of Jasper Taylor that long-ago day.

Sighing, she blinked back tears for the umpteenth time.

58

GOOD MORNING...

NOT SO MUCH

W hen Dad woke Ginnie the next day to do morning chores, she was surprised to not find her best friend next to her. "Where's Tillie?"

"She went home with her mom last night, remember?. Amanda wanted to make sure Tillie was okay with Jasper being here." Dad lifted her covers, smiling when Ginnie groaned. "Don't worry—they'll be here soon. Uncle Ben had me invite them for breakfast. He's making strawberry pecan waffles. Let's hurry."

"Mmm. I love his strawberry pecan waffles." Ginnie sat up and slid off the bed. "Is everything okay between you two?"

His grin grew. "You heard me tell Roni I try to stay on Uncle Ben's good side. Life is just better that way."

"Very funny. That's not what I meant, and you know it."

"I know." He nodded, his tone more serious. "Amanda and I are fine. Jasper and I talked last night."

The termites returned. "About what?"

"He said if I would agree not to flaunt the engagement around him, he would try to get used to the idea. I agreed, okay?" Dad gave her a quick hug. "So—no need to worry."

"Okay." Ginnie hugged him back, relieved. "Dad, should we call Jasper 'uncle'? It feels weird."

"I'm fine with him being your uncle. We're still friends--though admittedly, it's more awkward now." He shrugged. "It might make the rest of this easier if you do."

"Tillie doesn't even call him 'Dad.' It seems a little weird for us to call him 'Uncle Jasper'."

"I think that will change. He *is* her dad and he wants to be a part of her life. Please get dressed so we can enjoy breakfast before we have to finish baling the alfalfa."

"Yes, sir." She followed him toward the door, stopping at her dresser. "I'll be right down."

"Thanks. Save the eggs for Mysti. She'll be over this morning and will want to gather them."

"Sure." After changing, Ginnie called Tillie, excited to use her new phone, and repeated Dad and Jasper's agreement.

"Oh, good. Mom's acting a little strange."

Ginnie sat on her bed. "What do you mean by strange?"

"I can't explain it. She's mostly good. Just a little weirded out because Jasper came back, I guess."

"Can't blame her for that. I have to do my chores. Uncle Ben's making strawberry pecan waffles, so hurry up and get here."

"Yum. Ask Vi if we can have that strawberry syrup we helped her can. It's delicious."

"I will. See you soon. Bye." Motivated by Uncle Ben's waffles dripping with homemade strawberry syrup, Ginnie flew through Toran's room on the way to the hallway. She shoved the phone into her pocket as a shadow crossed her path. "Sorry, Uncle Jake."

"Wrong uncle ... but no problem, Gin. People used to mix us up all the time." Startled that Uncle Jake's voice didn't match his body, Ginnie looked at his face, realizing that the man standing before her wasn't Uncle Jake at all, but Jasper Taylor.

"Where did you come from?"

"Jake's room. Your dad gave me his bed last night so I could chat with Wing, like old times." His smile made the termites wriggle inside Ginnie. "He took the couch. I guess he figured that's the least he could do, since he intends to take my wife and kid as well."

Ginnie blinked at the hurt in his voice, even though he tried to cover it with a brighter smile. "Sorry, that came out of my mouth sounding worse than it did in my head."

Swallowing hard, Ginnie nodded. "No problem. I gotta do my chores."

She turned and fled downstairs, ignoring him when he called out her name and another apology.

59
========

STRAWBERRY SYRUP

*G*innie finished feeding and watering the chickens and nearly ran into Tillie on her way out of the chicken coop.

"You're done already?" Tillie asked.

Ginnie shrugged. "I didn't have to gather the eggs. Mysti likes to do that and she's coming over today."

"She's already here. I told her we'd play with the Easy-Bake Oven later."

"I'll bet she'll be your best friend all day." Ginnie said, then grimaced. "Jasper's here as well. Apparently Uncle Jake had a sleep-over." Remembering her run-in with "Uncle" Jasper, she tried to figure out how to tell Tillie that her birth dad gave her the creeps.

"Really?" Tillie glanced around. "Where is he?"

The excitement in Tillie's voice surprised Ginnie. "I dunno. I had to do my chores."

"Well, cool. I've been thinking about him a lot. I've decided to give him a chance to be the dad he said he wants to be." She grinned conspiratorially at Ginnie. "And who knows, maybe he'll even buy me a horse."

Stunned at her friend's thought process, Ginnie took a step back. "Wow, Til, way to be a go-getter."

272

Tillie grinned. "I spend a lot of time with you and Toran. What can I say? I learn from the best."

Not sure that was as complimentary as it sounded; Ginnie took a closer look at her friend. She seemed truly happy about her decision, which complicated Ginnie's desire to warn her about Jasper.

Before she could figure out what to say, Tillie grabbed her hand and pulled her toward the farmhouse. "Look, there he is!"

Uncle Jake and "Uncle" Jasper walked down the hill from the main barn.

They carried a full milk can between them. Uncle Jasper waved with his empty hand and called out, "Good morning, Angel. Morning, Ginnie."

"Morning!" they called together, Tillie more happily than Ginnie.

She pulled Ginnie along with her up the hill.

"Gee, Turtle, keep moving like that and I'm gonna have to change your nickname," Uncle Jake teased.

"Maybe not. Turtles have been known to move pretty fast when they are properly motivated. I like that she seems happy to see me," Jasper commented. "By the way, Turtle is an okay nickname, but I think Angel is a better fit for my little girl."

Uncle Jake shrugged. "These two are always together, like twins. The names Turtle and Trouble go together like ice cream and hot fudge sauce."

Tillie giggled. "Mom said last night that Aunt Sadie called us and Toran her triplets. That's cool, huh?"

At the mention of Aunt Sadie's name, a reverent look graced Jasper's face, surprising Ginnie.

"Yeah, she had a huge heart. Amanda reminds me of her." Uncle Jasper glanced from Tillie to Ginnie and back again. "Aunt Sadie really loved children. You two couldn't have asked for a better grandma, girls. I wish she was still here."

"She was pretty special," Uncle Jake agreed, then caught Ginnie's eye. "Of course, so was my mom."

"I didn't mean anything against your mom, Jake. I never met her." Uncle Jake set the milk bucket on the grass. "Since there was no way I was exposing Tilda to *my* mom, I was really grateful Aunt Sadie embraced Angel as her grandchild. Kids *should* have loving grandparents. Not that I would know about that firsthand—except for Oma and Opa."

"Agreed. No offense taken. I just wanted Ginnie to realize her West grandparents would have loved her—and even Tillie—as much as Uncle Ben and Aunt Sadie did. Mama and Aunt Sadie were two peas in a pod that way." Uncle Jake frowned. "Not that Turtle isn't equally lovable. See? Foot-in-mouth disease."

"Yeah, I had some of that myself this morning." Uncle Jasper gave a quick glance over Ginnie's way before settling on Tillie. "Sometimes my mouth outruns my brain. No offense meant earlier, Ginnie. I was just trying to sort things out."

He sounded sincere enough, but his explanation didn't completely erase Ginnie's bad feelings about him.

"If anybody understands that, it's Trouble," Uncle Jake declared too lightly for Ginnie's taste. "She and I suffer from that very ailment as well, don't we?"

Not knowing what to say, Ginnie gave a reluctant nod.

Her narrowed eyes seemed to surprise Uncle Jake. He arched an eyebrow.

Ginnie turned away from them both.

Tillie squeezed Ginnie's hand. "She may say things without thinking, but over-thinking things can be even worse."

Ginnie swiveled to her friend, wondering what she meant. Before she could ask, the side porch door slammed shut and Toran appeared. "Good, you're all together. Uncle Ben wants to know how much longer you'll be."

"We're heading in now," Uncle Jake said. He motioned toward the door. "After you, ladies."

Tillie's smile grew as quickly as Ginnie's irritation with her "uncles."

Ginnie followed her brother inside.

The dining room buzzed with activity, more crowded than usual for breakfast.

Miss Amanda and Vi brought in plates of waffles while Miss Clarissa fixed Mysti's plate.

The doorbell rang. "Come on in, Roni!" Buzz called from the doorway, hands full with a plate of sausage.

Hearing her aunt's name lifted Ginnie's inexplicable gloom.

She rushed toward Aunt Roni's outstretched arms, happy to be squeezed into a hug.

"My, my, my. The West farmhouse must be the new party central." They walked to the table. "Y'all seem about as busy as a stick of butter in a kitchen full of frying pans."

"And you're just in time for breakfast. Pull up a chair," Uncle Ben greeted, setting a pitcher of milk on the table.

"Yes, sir. Don't mind if I do." She reached for Tillie and Toran, squeezing them into a double hug. Mysti burrowed her way into the embrace. "Hi, sugar. My, isn't your hair pretty this morning. I do love French braids on little girls."

"It is," Mysti said, nodding. "Uncle Todd did it."

"Really?" Aunt Roni threw Dad an impressed look. "You've been trained well."

Dad shrugged. "That happens when you marry a beauty queen and have a little girl. It kinda comes with the job."

"Sterling would disagree." Aunt Roni shook her head. "You'll have to talk with my husband, Todd, and show him that real men *can* do their daughter's hair. He most definitely is not a modern thinker in that arena. He says since I'm the beauty queen, *I* should style their hair."

"Where is he?" Miss Clarissa asked.

"Across the pond—in England. The day after we arrived there, my daddy fell ill here. So my mother-in-law insisted that I should tend to my dad, and she'd entertain my girls while Sterling worked. I suspect he has wrangled her into being their hair stylist. Once Daddy was fine, I decided it was the perfect time to reconnect with my sister's family."

"I'm so glad you did!" Ginnie said.

"Me too, sugar. Me too." Aunt Roni pulled out a chair. "The day before my family was to return, my youngest came down with a raging double ear infection. She couldn't fly. She's on the mend now, so they'll be stateside soon."

"I want to meet them. We need more cousins my age." Mysti threw Tillie, Toran, and Ginnie disgusted looks. "You guys don't let me do all the cool stuff."

"They will as you get bigger." Uncle Jake swung her into his arms and glanced around the dining room. "Speaking of bigger, I'm thinking we need a bigger table."

Uncle Ben nodded. "For now, though, Ginnie and Toran, why don't you bring the chairs down from your rooms and we'll squeeze in around this table and make it do."

"Yes, sir," they replied together and turned to leave.

Mysti squealed loudly, causing Ginnie to see why. Uncle Jake tickled her again. "Daddy—stop!"

He rolled his eyes innocently upward. "Stop what?"

"You know what." She threw her head back and caught sight of Uncle Jasper. "Who are you?"

"Oh, right. You snuck in while I was outside." Uncle Jake set her upright. "This is my friend, Jasper Taylor. You can call him Uncle Jasper. He's Tillie's daddy."

Uncle Jasper smiled. "Hi, Mysti. It's nice to meet you."

Mysti scrunched her face, eyeing him like a bug under a magnifying glass. "Hmmm." She glanced at Tillie, then pursed her lips. "He doesn't look like a big meany-head."

Tillie's cheeks flamed as bright as the strawberry syrup waiting to be poured on the waffles.

Uncle Jasper's jaw dropped, then he clamped his mouth shut, and swiveled toward Tillie, a hurt expression lighting his eyes. "Thanks, Tilda."

Ginnie actually felt sorry for him ... until he took a step toward her friend.

Tillie froze.

Ginnie grabbed her hand and pulled her along. "You should help us get the chairs."

Dad stepped into the doorway, blocking Uncle Jasper from following. "You're in for a treat, Jasper. Uncle Ben cooked up a mess of bacon as well as sausages. There might even be enough for both you *and* Jake."

Ginnie led Tillie toward the stairs as Dad maneuvered Jasper into a chair.

Oh, boy—this is gonna be a l-o-n-g day.

60

DECISIONS, DECISIONS

$\mathscr{B}$reakfast went better than Tillie expected. Once Jasper mouthed, "Don't worry, no hard feelings," Tillie relaxed and sat across the table from him.

After Buzz offered a blessing on the meal, platters of food were passed and served. A happy rumble of forks scraping plates and mumbled gratitude for the delicious breakfast erupted.

All thirteen people made quick work of breakfast.

When plates were emptied, people started leaving for work.

Uncle Ben, Buzz, Aunt Roni, and Vi went in and out of the kitchen and dining room, putting away the extra food and clearing dishes.

Miss Clarissa hugged Mysti good-bye and asked Uncle Jake to walk her to her car.

Mom and DT followed.

Jasper stood when Mom said good-bye, plastering a pleasant smile on his face, only turning his attention to Tillie when Mom left the room. He sat back down. "What are you doing today, Angel?"

She shrugged, liking his nickname for her more and more. "I promised Mysti I'd play Easy-Bake Oven with her. I opened the other box. Thanks for all the great mixes."

"I'm glad you liked the oven after all." Jasper revved up his grin. "Maybe I can be your official taste tester?"

His grin put her at ease. "Sure thing."

"Did you show Ginnie the other gift I got you?"

"The iPhone?" Toran asked. "It's epic, Uncle Jasper. I helped her set it up last night."

"So you're the technology expert around here?" Jasper picked up a piece of bacon. "Good to know. I'm having trouble with my playlist. Maybe you can help me out."

Toran nodded. "I'd be happy to."

"I want a cell phone," Mysti said.

"Maybe your dad will let you have the one I bought for Tillie." Aunt Roni reached for Mysti's empty glass. "No sense wasting it. Do you want more juice?"

Jasper stiffened. "You bought Tilda a cell phone?"

"Of course. I couldn't get one for Ginnie and Toran and exclude Tillie. Since you bought her one as well, I imagine she'll want to keep yours rather than mine."

Hey, I want them both. Tillie swallowed the milk in her mouth, and then clamped her jaw shut when she realized how selfish wanting to keep both phones would sound. She took a second drink.

Aunt Roni pointed to Jasper's glass. "Are you finished, or would you like some more milk?"

"No, thanks. Why would you buy everyone phones?" He shook his head. "Did you turn into the cell phone fairy?"

She offered a friendly smile. "I thought giving them all cell phones was the most efficient way to stay connected with the kids when I go back to South Carolina."

"That's why I bought Tilda one." He made a point of catching Tillie's gaze. "I'm hoping these next couple of days go well so she'll want to keep in touch when I have to work in Kentucky. I'll see her most weekends, though. I'm done being an absentee dad. I've missed too much of her life."

His declaration offered peace to the part of Tillie that wanted to believe he cared about her, but mounted nervous anxiety in the bigger part of her that still wanted Mom to marry DT so she could be a *real* West.

"I didn't realize how opposed Todd would be to the kids having phones," Aunt Roni said, pouring Ginnie more milk. "Has he given a definitive answer about them yet?"

Ginnie shook her head.

"Todd doesn't want them to have phones?" Jasper asked, locking his gaze on Tillie. "Did he take yours?"

Tillie's cheeks heated. She shook her head and cut the last of her strawberry pecan waffle into bite-sized portions while trying to figure out how to diffuse his frustrated tone. "He said I could keep yours. He didn't mention Aunt Roni's."

"He'd *better* let you keep it." Jasper stabbed at his last two squares of waffle with his fork and pointed it at Tillie. "You may see Todd more, but *I'm* still your dad. I can buy you a phone if I want to."

"He knows." The fierceness in his tone made Tillie's belly tremble. "He said he wouldn't tell me I can't have the phone you gave me. He's not mean."

"Good. Then we're on the same page."

Tillie didn't know how to respond to his defensiveness.

She wanted to be open to Jasper, but felt more loyal to DT.

"My dad will probably let us keep them," Ginnie replied, turning to Jasper. "He knows you're Tillie's dad. He just wants us all to get along. But Tillie's like our sister, so Aunt Roni treats her the same as Toran and me."

Jasper glanced between each kid. "To be fair, Todd told me last night he wants to make this work. I'm still getting used to the idea that he has so much influence in my kid's life. I mean, I expected Uncle Ben to have a say, because he runs things around here. I just don't like being number three on the dad totem pole. I *am* her real dad."

Tillie swallowed hard, uncomfortable with that reality.

Uncle Ben cleared his throat. "I think everyone respects that. Just like we talked about last night, it's going to take some time and patience to figure out everyone's exact roles. But at the end of the day, we are family, by choice if not by birth. That means we *will* make this work."

A chorus of "yes, sirs" circled the table.

"Amen," Aunt Roni added with a smile.

"Yes, sir. Understood," Jasper said. "I don't want to sound ungrateful. You've looked out for Amanda and Tilda for me and I do appreciate that."

"Believe it or not, I'm looking out for *you* as well." Uncle Ben reached for his empty plate.

Jasper handed it over. "And I know Todd's a decent guy, but that doesn't mean I like the idea of him being Amanda's husband or Tilda's dad." Jasper paused while he seemed to wrestle with what he wanted to say. "In my mind, those are *my* roles. I've spent a lot of time and effort trying to shackle my demons and make myself better for Amanda and Tilda."

Tillie blinked at the hurt in his voice and focused on finishing her waffle so she didn't have to meet his gaze. She hadn't really thought about how he'd feel about her and Mom wanting to move on without him. Juggling both dads was going to be a lot harder than she thought. *Hopefully DT will be better with the drama.*

"Can I have your other phone, Tillie?" Mysti asked.

Tillie swallowed the last of her bacon. She liked the idea of having the same phone as everyone else in the family—as well as keeping the one Jasper gave her.

"You need to ask your daddy," Aunt Roni replied.

"But you already bought Mysti one, remember? The extra one?" Tillie said.

"You did?" Mysti squealed.

Tillie nodded as Aunt Roni frowned. "That's up to Jake. He may give it to Clarissa."

"How many phones did you buy?" Jasper asked, eyes wide.

"Eight," Ginnie answered.

"iPhones?" Jasper's eyes grew wider.

The front porch door squeaked open and shut.

"They're awesome," Toran added, and then saw Uncle Ben give a shake of his head. "I mean, I'm happy to have a phone at all. Dad didn't want us to have any."

Footsteps sounded in the hallway.

"Dad doesn't want you to have what?" DT asked, walking in the dining room.

"Cell phones," Toran replied sheepishly.

Ginnie grinned.

Tillie knew it was because Toran—and not her BFF—was on the hot seat for once.

Tillie grinned back.

Mysti leaped out of her chair and ran to Uncle Jake. "Can I have my phone, Daddy? Aunt Roni says I can."

"I said you need to ask your daddy," Aunt Roni corrected gently. "Please don't put words in my mouth. I think I'm in enough trouble without any more help."

"About those." DT pulled out his chair and sat next to Tillie. "I talked with Amanda, and we've decided that since Tillie has one, Ginnie and Toran can keep theirs."

"I have two," Tillie mumbled, still wanting to keep both.

"You only need one," Jasper and DT said together, DT's tone was a little more understanding than Jasper's.

"But I want them *both*." Tillie bit her lip, glancing at each man. "They were given to *me*. I should get a say."

DT and Jasper exchanged puzzled looks.

Apparently, Jasper decided he got to be her dad. "Okay. We're listening. You don't want the one I gave you because it's different from everyone else's, right? And you don't want to upset me by giving it back?"

"I want them *both*," Tillie repeated firmly, staring straight at him. "I want the phone *you* gave me because you gave it to me. I also want the other one, because *Aunt Roni* gave it to me. I know it sounds selfish, but I don't care." Tillie glanced at each face in the room. "I always feel like the outsider here, because I'm a Taylor and not a real West. For once, I really like being both a Taylor *and* a West. And since Aunt Roni isn't even my real aunt, it's even better."

Silence blanketed the room as the adults exchanged questioning looks.

Uncle Ben shrugged, nodding at Jasper and then DT.

Finally, Jasper spoke. "I understand that sentiment very well. I know exactly what she means."

"You do?" Tillie asked, surprised he wasn't angry.

He nodded. "My dad left me a lousy legacy. I've been trying to elevate our name for you. But Angel, lately I've realized a couple things."

"What?" Tillie whispered, not sure she wanted to hear what he would say.

"One—my choices affect you." Jasper straightened in his chair as he caught her gaze. "And two—my choices don't have to be bad."

"That's true," Uncle Ben said.

"I do pay attention when you talk," Jasper teased before looking at Tillie again, sobering his tone some. "I'm sorry, Tilda. I should have helped you understand my reasons for leaving so you knew why I stayed away. Since Taylor is our real name, I want it to be a name you can be proud of."

Tillie swallowed, doubting she would ever share that sentiment.

Jasper seemed to zero in on her hesitance.

"You don't have to change your name to be a good person, Angel. You just have to live your life in such a way that your name means something good. You already do that. I've been doing it better. Being a Taylor is a good thing now because we *choose* it to be."

"I'll try." She tried to sound more confident than she felt for Jasper's sake, but she'd still rather be a West.

"That's all I ask. As far as the phones go, I think you only need one. You pick which phone you like better and we'll put it on my plan. I'm paying for two no matter what, so we'll save Roni or whoever some money on their plan."

Nodding at his compromise, Tillie considered what she should do. She glanced at Aunt Roni. "Will it hurt your feelings if I keep his? I really like yours and all, but ..."

"Of course not, sugar." Aunt Roni flashed her warmest beauty-queen smile. "You should keep the phone your daddy gave you. Don't give it another thought."

"Thanks." Tillie pulled Aunt Roni's phone out of her pocket, handing it over as *"You should keep the phone your daddy gave you"* repeated in her mind.

For once, acknowledging Jasper as her dad didn't bother Tillie much.

The look of gratitude on Jasper's face made her happy that she chose his gift.

61

GREENER PASTURES

Ginnie leaned forward, synching her body with Calliope's. She patted her mare's strong neck, enjoying the rhythmic clopping of hooves while trying to clear her mind. Unsure what to say or do about Tillie's acceptance of Uncle Jasper, Ginnie decided that for once, she'd keep her mouth shut until she figured it out.

Horse and rider rounded the edge of the cut hay field. Ginnie squinted slightly while seeking the outline of the tractor and baler at the far end of the field. The huge farm vehicles looked like toys from this distance.

After riding a few acres closer, Ginnie turned Calliope toward the creek that flowed in the middle of the farm. She liked knowing Uncle Ben and Uncle Jake were close by, but didn't want to interact with anybody.

Instead, she welcomed the breeze humming beside each ear, blinking when she lifted her face into the oncoming gust. Humidity mingled with the sun's amplifying heat, filling her nostrils with the comforting smell of rich soil and growing hay. She welcomed these scents of summer; breathing them in at the same time she tried to exhale her worries.

Tapping Calliope's sides firmly with her riding boots, Ginnie urged her mare to run faster as if she could outrun her concerns about how "Uncle" Jasper's presence was going to impact the rest of her life and Tillie's. She couldn't figure out if she liked the man or not, but knew she didn't trust him.

He represented too much drama for Ginnie to be as open to him as Uncle Ben was.

Slowing Calliope, Ginnie had her walk the rest of the way to the creek. She swung out of the saddle and led her horse down a small path so Calliope could drink easily.

A honey bee buzzed near some purple clover.

Ginnie squatted next to her horse. She scooped up the chilled water and let it slip through her fingers a couple of times before she patted her face, enjoying the refreshing coolness.

Calliope rolled her eyes as the water dripped back into the creek with a slight splash.

"What, you don't want to play?" Ginnie teased.

Her mare snorted, then continued drinking.

"You're still young. Quit acting like a snobby old nag." Ginnie drizzled water onto a flat rock, splattering her jeans and the white of Calliope's forelock. "You might get to have a baby soon, so you gotta be more fun than that. Even my dad can be a lot of fun to play with ... and he's lame."

Calliope snorted again, this time shaking her head as well. Her black mane cascaded down her neck, shimmering in the morning sun.

Laughing, Ginnie mimicked the shaking motion, sending her braids flying around her head. "Seriously, lighten up. Life is too short to be a stick-in-the-mud."

Just as Ginnie leaned forward to scoop more water, Calliope lifted her head.

Ginnie felt a quick nudge.

Her horse's nose pushed her off balance and into the chilled, rushing water of the creek.

"Hey!" Ginnie protested, unable to stop her body's forward motion when her palm slipped off the slimy moss growing on the rock she had hoped would stop her fall.

Instead, the right side of her body crashed into the frigid creek, stealing her breath as she gulped in humid air and water spray. "No fair!"

Swearing her horse was laughing at her, Ginnie grimaced. "Not funny, Calliope." She splashed a wave in her mare's direction, but Calliope backed up, snorting her amusement at getting the best of her rider.

"Fine. See if I give you an apple today." Ginnie stood, shivering as a breeze caught her wet clothes.

Calliope snorted, nodding her head up and down three times.

Ginnie gave in and laughed along with her horse. "Okay, I'll admit it, you got me."

Lifting the leather reins over Calliope's head, Ginnie put her left foot in the stirrup and arched her right leg above her horse's back, settling smoothly into the saddle. "But you get to help me dry off."

After whinnying what seemed like her agreement, Calliope eased into a comfortable canter. The two of them skirted the back pasture around the barn and followed the gravel path down to the farmhouse.

Toran and Mysti played with the baby kittens in the shade of the woodshed.

Mysti jumped to her feet. "Can I ride with you?"

"Stop!" Toran lurched after Mysti, catching her arm. "Don't run straight at Calliope—you'll startle her." Toran took a closer look at Ginnie. "How come you are all wet?"

Ginnie smirked. "Because Calliope thought we should go swimming in the creek, only she decided not to join me after she pushed me in."

Chuckling, Toran let go of their little cousin. "I see."

"How did she push you?" Mysti glanced between Ginnie and Toran. "Calliope doesn't have any hands."

"She doesn't need them, with that big snout of hers," Toran teased.

"You'd better watch what you say. You'll be next," Ginnie warned, sliding her hand down her mare's neck.

"Somehow I doubt that." Toran shook his head and smiled at the horse. "She likes me, don't you, girl?"

"She *loves* me." Tires crunched behind Ginnie. She swiveled toward the gravel-and-dirt lane.

Pierce's mom drove more quickly than she should to the farmhouse.

Mrs. Owens turned the corner and drove past all five family cars and slid to a stop in the open space next to Uncle Jasper's black sports car. She dropped her face into her hands. Her shoulders shook. Pierce reached across the car to pat his mom's arm, and then opened his door.

Ginnie clicked at Calliope and guided her closer.

Toran took Mysti's hand in his and followed.

"Hey Pierce, what's up?" Ginnie called out.

His head rose above the far side of the car. A red smear ran from his nose around his lips and down his chin. Dried blood.

The termites from last night gnawed at her belly.

She lowered her gaze, catching Mrs. Owens wiping her eyes. *Oh, man. This can't be good.*

"Mysti, go get my dad," Toran told their cousin as he opened Mrs. Owens door. "Are you okay?"

Mrs. Owens shook her head and then nodded.

Mysti stomped her foot. "Why? I wanna ride Calliope!"

"Go." Ginnie pointed at the farmhouse. Just then she heard more gravel crunching. She turned in time to see Mr. Owens' beater car flying down the lane. "Go! You too, Mrs. Owens."

Mrs. Owens hurried out of her car.

"But I wanna ride!" Mysti protested.

"Later!" Ginnie nudged the little girl with her foot. "Get my dad —*now!*"

"Hey!" Mysti started to pout.

Toran slammed Mrs. Owens' door, then grabbed Mysti's hand. "Now, Mysti!"

"Come on, Mom!" Pierce yelled. He slammed his door and rounded the car quickly.

Toran pulled at Mrs. Owens, hurrying her and Mysti to the front of the farmhouse.

Ginnie turned Calliope in time to see Mr. Owens' car spit gravel in slow motion as it slid to a stop perpendicular to all the parked cars.

She sucked in a breath.

Mr. Owens roughly pushed open his door. His giant form oozed out of the car.

The front porch door slammed closed, echoing a hollow place inside Ginnie.

Realizing she was now alone, Ginnie swallowed hard and watched as Mr. Owens rose to a taller stature than Ginnie would have liked.

He wasn't as tall as Dad or Uncle Jake, but his bad attitude more than made up for his lack of height.

Ginnie knew from experience that the man moved quicker than she expected.

"I came to get my family. I have my rights." His dark eyes narrowed menacingly as his tone dared her not to interfere.

Calliope shied backward.

"So do we." Ginnie stroked her horse's satiny neck. "This is private property. We don't want trouble."

He glared at Ginnie. "If your uncle keeps interfering with my family, you'll have plenty of it."

Remembering that Uncle Ben and Uncle Jake were in the field— and not here to help—burrowed panic into Ginnie's belly and the termites happily feasted on it.

Mr. Owens ignored her and strode with determined steps to the farmhouse.

"Hey!" Ginnie clicked at Calliope and rode in front of Mr. Owens, wheeling Calliope around and stopping him in his tracks. "You should leave. Get a grip and come back when you've calmed down. They'll still be here."

"No, they won't, girly." The snarl on his face froze Ginnie in her saddle. "I'll make it so this is the last place they ever come." He shook his fist and then slashed his hand through the air, pointing an angry finger at her. "You and your family have meddled enough."

Ginnie clicked at Calliope to back up.

"That's right. Be a good little girly and go play with your dollies." His sarcasm grated on Ginnie's nerves, lighting an anger that overcame her fear of him.

I can call Uncle Ben. She slid her cell phone out of her front pocket. She straightened in the saddle and glared back at him. "You should leave ... before someone gets hurt."

"As soon as I get my family." His hands sliced through the air as he moved forward. "Out of my way."

"*Now* would be better." Ginnie swallowed, trying to figure out if he was drunk or just angry.

His words weren't slurry, but his movements weren't steady. She glanced at the phone. A black screen with a huge crack stared back at her. Ginnie tried to power the phone on. No luck.

A humid breeze chilled Ginnie, reminding her of her earlier dip in the creek. *Aw, man! It's broke and waterlogged!* She urged Calliope to match Mr. Owens' footsteps, staying between him and the farmhouse.

"I'm not telling you again, girly! Move!"

"My name's not 'girly'." Ginnie frowned, trying to figure out what her dad or Uncle Ben would say or do. Both had a knack for staying calm in these kinds of situations.

The night Mr. Owens had come to the farmhouse to accuse Ginnie and Toran of blacking Pierce's eye, Dad had been the one to keep his head, diffusing the situation by appealing to Mr. Owens' better nature.

Unfortunately—at least as far as Ginnie could tell—his better nature had already hit the highway, probably hoping for greener pastures.

Knowing she had not inherited her dad's calm, Ginnie blew out a breath and leaned forward, hoping a Plan B would form before Mr. Owens could get past her and Calliope.

Mr. Owens raised his fist again.

Ginnie's prayer for inspiration was quickly detoured while she wondered where and how hard she would have to kick Mr. Owens to stop him from getting to the farmhouse.

62

COOKIES & DRAMA, ANYONE?

*T*illie looked up from the tiny heart-shaped sugar cookie she scooped off the miniature cookie sheet with the little purple spatula that came with her Easy-Bake oven.

Jasper sat perched in the blue leather bar stool seat, watching. "I can see why little girls love this toy, but I like Aunt Sadie's theory about big cookies better."

"What was that?" Tillie slid a flower-shaped cookie onto the cooling rack next to the heart.

"She made them huge so you don't need as many to fill you up." Jasper picked up the flower cookie, then dropped it and blew on his fingers. "I'm not sure why I didn't expect that to be hot."

Tillie laughed. "The light bulbs make the cookies hot—as well as the cookie sheet."

He winked in a playful manner. "I'll try to remember that."

She slid the last cookie onto the cooling rack, then stood back to admire the assortment of treats. She and Mysti had made two pans of brownies, one double-layer cake, and a batch of chocolate chip cookies before Mysti deserted her to play with the kittens.

The front porch screen door squeaked open. "Dad!" Toran's voice called. "Dad! Where are you?"

"Let go!" Mysti squealed. "You're squishing my arm."

"Sorry, Mysti." Toran's voice pitched louder. "Dad!"

Tillie turned toward the kitchen archway, surprised to see Pierce and his mom following Toran quickly through the dining room.

She swiveled toward the family room where DT sat looking at a scrapbook with Aunt Roni.

"Todd, Toran needs you," Jasper said about the same time DT heard the last "Dad" and stood, calling, "Coming."

Tillie rushed into the dining room. "What's wrong?"

"I—It's my husband. He's outside," Mrs. Owens said.

DT crossed into the dining room as Mrs. Owens' voice trembled. Aunt Roni followed close behind.

Jasper stood, clearly alarmed. "What's going on, Tilda?"

Tillie shrugged, panic rising when she saw dried blood on Pierce's face.

DT pulled out a dining room chair for Mrs. Owens. "Marsha, did he hurt you?"

"He tried to." Pierce sucked spit through his teeth, then touched his nose. "I stopped him."

"Stopped who?" Jasper dropped his jaw. "Your dad?"

Pierce nodded.

Jasper narrowed his eyes angrily as understanding lit them. He pointed to Tillie. "Stay here."

Aunt Roni circled a protesting Mysti into a protective hug. "Marsha, should I call the police?"

Dazed, Mrs. Owens shook her head. "I don't know."

"Mysti, stop fussing and mind Aunt Roni," DT scolded.

Mysti stuck her bottom lip out, but stopped whining and wriggling.

DT motioned toward the kitchen. "Toran, take everybody to the cellar and bolt the door shut if Ray comes in. Stay with them."

Toran nodded. "Yes, sir."

DT pointed at each child like he was counting heads.

First worry, then relief, crossed his features. "Ginnie's out riding Calliope—she should be fine."

Toran's eyes grew huge. "No, sir."

"No, sir, *what*?" DT demanded.

"Ginnie's not out riding Calliope, Dad. She's out front with Mr. Owens." Toran, DT, and Jasper swiveled toward the front door. "Mysti wouldn't come, so I brought her. I thought Ginnie would follow, but I guess she didn't."

"Stay here," DT and Jasper barked together, moving as one toward the hallway.

Tillie froze for a second, then caught sight of Pierce's bloody nose again. "I'll get a washcloth."

63

ANOTHER SIDE OF DAD

Glancing around, Ginnie searched for anything that might help her keep Mr. Owens from reaching his family ... or hers. No branches or rakes or anything useful littered the ground. Only a line of large decorative rocks separated the grass from the gravel in front of the parked cars.

Not that I could reach the rocks anyway.

Sitting straighter in the saddle, she felt the termites from last night gnaw her insides.

Mr. Owens made a beeline for the farmhouse, acting like he would go through her and Calliope if he needed to.

Ginnie kept Calliope even with him. "Why are you so mad? What're you going to do?"

His round face reddened, reminding her of an overripe tomato. "None of your business." He waved her away and stepped around Calliope.

Ginnie urged Calliope forward to match his steps, keeping her horse between the farmhouse and Mr. Owens. "Whatever it is, you don't need to hurt Pierce or his mom. You don't want to go back to jail, do you?"

The hate that filled his eyes took Ginnie's breath away.

"I still owe you for that. I have a right to discipline my own kid. You cost me a decent job for no good reason." A string of swear words flowed like a river from his lips.

No good reason? Mr. Owens' vile words made her mind go blank for a moment.

Recalling Pierce huddled on the floor in a ball as his dad kicked him fueled her own anger.

"Kicking isn't discipline. Pierce loves you, but I don't know why. You're just a big bully." She spat the words with as much contempt as she could muster. "He didn't deserve that!"

"You have a big mouth." He rushed toward her. "Maybe I'll help you shut it."

Sucking in a quick breath, Ginnie squeezed her eyes closed and tapped Calliope's sides firmly with her riding boots. She opened them when Calliope leaped forward.

Mr. Owens' eyes and mouth formed capital "O"s as her mare's right shoulder crashed into Mr. Owens' side, toppling him to the ground.

Ginnie wheeled Calliope sharply to the left, her rear hooves barely missing Mr. Owens' crumbling body.

The curse he swore hung in the air, silenced when the side of his head cracked against the gravel.

Grimacing, Ginnie stopped Calliope as they made a second loop to avoid Mr. Owens' flailed-out arm. His eyes closed as she leaned over to see him better.

I killed him! What do I do? Ginnie stood in the stirrups, then lifted her right boot so she could dismount.

"Stay!" Dad's sharp command reached her as she arched her leg over the saddle. "I mean it, Gin. Stay put!"

She felt for the stirrup while whirling toward the farmhouse.

Dad and Uncle Jasper rushed forward, her dad's pale face colored with worry and anger.

"S—sorry, Dad," Ginnie blurted, heart racing.

"Are you okay?" Dad's anxious eyes searched her face before glancing down.

He stopped running when he reached Mr. Owens and nudged the downed man's arm with his boot.

Mr. Owens moaned.

Uncle Jasper squatted next to Pierce's dad and lifted his head. "No blood, just a big knot." He smiled. "He's gonna have a headache when he comes to. Nice job. Wish I had a horse when my dad came at me."

Surprise at his approving tone squashed the anxiety rising in Ginnie—at least until she took another glance at Mr. Owens. "He was trying to get to the farmhouse. I didn't want him to hurt Pierce or his mom, or our family. Is he okay?"

"He'll be fine." Dad gave a dismissive glance to the man on the ground and reached his arms to Ginnie. "I'm more concerned about you."

He enveloped her in a strong hug and pulled her off Calliope. "Are you okay?"

Nodding, Ginnie circled his neck with her arms. "I—I'm sorry. I didn't know what else to do."

"*You* don't have anything to apologize for," Dad squeezed her harder. "You did the right thing."

"You're not mad?" Ginnie hugged him again, letting his words repeat in her mind.

"Of course not." Dad looked her in the eye. "If one of you has to be lying on the ground, I'm glad it's not you. He's a big guy, he can handle a tumble."

"I told him to calm down, but he didn't listen."

"He's pretty calm now," Uncle Jasper teased, shaking Mr. Owens slightly as he helped him sit up. "Aren't you?"

Mr. Owens groaned, pushed away Uncle Jasper's hand, and tried to stand, growling, "Get your mitts off me." He stumbled, his foot giving out under his weight, yelping "OW!"

"You might want to stay put." Uncle Jasper pushed him roughly into a sitting position and lost his teasing tone. "If I have to go to jail for the likes of you, I *will* make it worth my while." His jaw tightened. "I couldn't do much about my own lousy excuse for a father, but I'd be happy to pound some sense into *you*."

Mr. Owens lurched forward.

"Sit!" Uncle Jasper grabbed his shoulder and shoved him backward. "And just for your own light and knowledge, if you touch my niece, I'll turn you into hamburger and barbeque your—"

"Jasper! He gets the picture," Dad warned, setting Ginnie on her feet and then stepping in front of her. "Ginnie, please get him some water and an ice pack."

"Always the Eagle Scout, aren't you, Todd?" Jasper asked, eyes narrowing with disapproval. "He tries to hurt your kid and you're making nice with him?"

"He touches my daughter—I'll show you *both* how prepared this Boy Scout is to knock him into next week." The harsh protectiveness in Dad's tone surprised Ginnie ... in a good way.

She stepped around her dad, who pointed an angry finger at Mr. Owens. "Jasper's right, Ray. You'd do better to sit a minute and cool off, because if you try to harm my kid, I'll do to *you* what *you did* to Pierce. Understood?"

Mr. Owens muttered something underneath his breath.

Uncle Jasper shoved him. "There's a lady present. Watch your mouth."

Dad gave Ginnie's shoulder a gentle squeeze. "Please get the water and ice pack while we decide whether we need to involve the police." He nodded to the farmhouse before glaring at Mr. Owens. "And just so you know, Ray, I'm thinking we should call them."

"Yes, sir." Ginnie hugged her dad and bolted toward the front porch, liking this fiercer side of him.

64

R.I.P. ... NOT SO MUCH

Ginnie grabbed the container of ice out of the freezer and dumped half of it in a gallon-sized zip-top bag. Then she picked up the ice container to put it away.

"What are you doing?" Toran asked.

Startled, Ginnie spun toward her brother, spraying ice cubes from the container. "Sheesh, Tor! Don't sneak up on people!" She shoved the bowl at him. "I gotta go."

She whirled toward the cupboard and pulled out a glass.

"I didn't sneak. What's going on?"

"Calliope ran over Mr. Owens." She turned the faucet on. "I have to get ice for the knot on his head—and his ankle might be broke."

"That's not good." Toran's eyes went wide. "Unless it's keeping him from being a problem."

"It's keeping him on his rear—he can't stand up."

"Then that's good."

"For now." Ginnie turned off the faucet and grinned, realizing that her pulse had been racing like the lead horse at the Kentucky Derby. "Dad and Uncle Jasper are about to go Hulk all over him, so it might not be good for long ... at least for him."

"*Our* dad?"

Ginnie laughed at the shock on Toran's face. "Yeah. He's pretty mad—but it's not at me, so it's all good."

"What's going on?" Aunt Roni called from the bottom of the stairs in the family room that led to their basement.

"Calliope ran over Mr. Owens." Toran called back. "I guess he's not a problem anymore."

"Oh, my stars!" Aunt Roni raced up the stairs. "Is Ginnie okay?"

"I'm fine. Gotta go!" Ginnie gathered the glass and bag of ice and rushed through the house and out the front door onto the porch.

She stopped on the concrete stairs when she saw Uncle Jasper's fist cocked, ready to throw a punch into Mr. Owens' face. "I'm not telling you again. Stay put."

Mr. Owens spewed a fountain of swear words.

Ginnie froze.

The screen door slammed, jump-starting her brain as well as her feet.

She jogged to her dad and handed over the bag of ice and glass of water.

"Thanks, Gin. Please go in the house."

She turned to obey.

The screen door slammed again.

Toran, Tillie, Pierce, and Mrs. Owens stood on the porch, their faces a kaleidoscope of expressions ranging from mild shock to raging horror.

Aunt Roni stayed in the house, keeping a protesting Mysti from joining them.

Mrs. Owens hurried down the four steps. "Is he okay?"

"As long as he stays put," Uncle Jasper replied.

"You don't scare me," Mr. Owens barked, but with a lot less bite than he used earlier.

"Just give me a reason to show you how scary I can be." Jasper threatened, leaning into Mr. Owens' face. "You're the worst kind of garbage there is."

"Jasper!" Dad warned, nodding at Pierce and the others coming closer. "Stay back, kids."

Uncle Jasper glanced at each tween and Mrs. Owens, then pointed to Pierce. "Is he your kid?"

Mr. Owens glared. "What was your first clue?"

"His face." Uncle Jasper jabbed his thumb toward Pierce and narrowed his eyes at Mr. Owens. "There's a reason garbage like you don't do well in jail. Wanna know why?" Uncle Jasper didn't wait for an answer. "Because kids like your son grow up tired of being beat by the bullies who *should* be showing them how to be men. I know. I used to be him. He can't take you out, but *I* can. So please, go at me like you did him, and *make ... my ... millennium.*"

Mr. Owens lifted his fist, but dropped it when Uncle Jasper motioned his fingers in a "C'mon, let's do this" kind of way.

"That's what I thought. You're *pathetic.*" Uncle Jasper spit just past Mr. Owens' face. "You only pick fights with children so you know that you can win."

Still seated, Mr. Owens threw a punch with his right hand that Uncle Jasper caught with his left. He returned the punch with a quick jab, catching Mr. Owens square in the gut.

The heavier man lurched forward.

In a quick flurry of movement, Uncle Jasper grabbed the wider man's right arm and twisted it up behind his back until Mr. Owens yelped.

"Jasper, let go," Dad said.

"No way, Eagle Scout. I've got this." Uncle Jasper leaned his weight into the twisted arm and grabbed the other arm, pinning both behind Mr. Owens' back.

"Let go!" Mr. Owens huffed.

"You're hurting him!" Mrs. Owens screamed.

Uncle Jasper leaned in. "How many times did your son beg you for mercy that you didn't show him?"

Pierce sucked in a worried breath. "You're just gonna make him madder."

"I'm giving him a taste of his own medicine. It tastes a little bitter, huh, Ray?" Uncle Jasper asked, close to Mr. Owens' ear. "Even after treating him bad, your son's still worried about you. You should remember that the next time you go off on him."

"I'll have you arrested! Let go."

"You're not in a position to make threats."Uncle Jasper glanced at Pierce. "Want a free shot at him, kid?"

Wide-eyed, Pierce shook his head. Part of Ginnie wanted him to say "Yes".

"Jasper, that's enough," Dad said calmly.

"I don't think so, Eagle Scout, I'm just getting started."

"I said *that's enough*." This time, Dad's voice held the warning. He lowered his voice to barely audible. "You're scaring Tillie. He's not worth losing her over."

Ginnie searched for her BFF.

Tillie's eyes and mouth were open wide, horror plastered on her face.

"You're not worth the spit it would take to shine my shoes." Uncle Jasper jerked Mr. Owens' arm higher until he gasped in pain. "Just remember that there's always a bigger bully. You do that to your boy again, I'll find you and become your worst nightmare." Uncle Jasper pushed him roughly and stood. "That's a promise."

Mr. Owens rubbed his arms and glared, but stayed quiet, staring at Pierce's anguished face.

Ginnie swallowed hard, remembering that eventually Pierce would have to go home with the very angry man sitting on the ground.

The termite colony quadrupled.

Tillie turned to Pierce's dad. "Mr. Owens?" Her voice trembled with emotion.

Mr. Owens' face scrunched with disgust. "Yeah?"

Tillie stiffened against his sneer, seeming to gather the strength to say what she needed to say, but didn't want to. "Pierce really does love you." All the hesitation left Tillie's voice. "You're the only dad he has. Please be a good one." She glanced at Uncle Jasper and turned toward the house.

Mr. Owens harrumphed and snapped his gaze to his feet.

Pierce dropped his head, bright pink covering the yellow-green bruises on his cheeks.

"Tilda, wait." Uncle Jasper pointed a warning finger at Mr. Owens, walking around him to meet Tillie.

"Stay put and think about what she said," Dad advised, moving closer to Mr. Owens, standing between him and Uncle Jasper. "Nobody here wants to see your family destroyed, but you're the only one who can save it."

"That's true, Ray." Mrs. Owens wiped her eyes. "I can't keep doing this. You need help."

"If you wouldn't make me angry, we wouldn't have this problem," Mr. Owens growled.

"Dad, you're always angry—even when we don't do anything wrong." Pierce kicked the gravel. "When you're not, I like being with you. Today, you came home mad and took it out on Mom." Pierce straightened and looked at Tillie. He seemed to siphon some courage. "That's not fair."

"And even if they do make you mad, you don't get to hurt them," Dad insisted, locking his eyes on Mr. Owens'. "Pierce is a courageous kid. He might have learned that from you at some point, but right this minute, you're teaching him to continue the cycle of abuse you said just two days ago that you wanted to stop."

"He said that?" Pierce asked.

The surprise in his voice made Ginnie sad.

"He did, Pierce, and you were right to defend your mom, but you shouldn't have had to. *Real* men don't hit their wives, *ever*." Dad frowned at Mr. Owens. "Do yourself a favor, Ray, and hear what Pierce just said. He wants a dad he can depend on. It's your job to make his world safe. If you don't, who's going to?"

"Don't tell me how to raise my kid."

"Somebody has to," Uncle Jasper snapped, swiveling toward Mr. Owens. "Why not him? At least he lives what he preaches. Maybe though, even better, you should listen to *me*." He stepped closer. "I've been the kid your son is now, afraid of my old man, and I've been you

—the monster my wife and child feared. The big difference is I realized what I'd become and I did something about it."

"You don't know squat!" Mr. Owens declared.

"Oh, yeah?" Jasper reached past his shoulders, pulled his red polo over his head, and threw the shirt at Mr. Owens. He turned around, exposing several crisscrossing scars across his back. "Tell me again how I don't know squat."

Tillie gasped. "What happened?"

"My old man happened." He spun toward Mr. Owens. "Wanna know why?" Jasper rushed on without pausing for an answer. "Because I found my mother in a bloody, unconscious heap. It didn't take a genius to figure out my old man had been on a drunken rampage. Once the ambulance pulled away from the house, I got rid of all of my dad's liquor, thinking I'd gotten rid of the problem."

Toran inhaled quickly. "But your dad found out and got madder?"

"Exactly. Part of me knew he'd explode, but I thought even *he* had his limits. No such luck." Jasper squatted next to Mr. Owens and leaned into his face. "He decided I'd be paying him for the loss of his liquor with a literal pound of flesh." He hitched his thumb toward his back. "Add some stripped telephone wire to an angry drunk and you get this. Wanna tell me again how I don't know squat about dealing with a dad with anger management issues?"

"I've never done anything like that," Mr. Owens said.

"Says you. How long has it been since you beat your kid? Looks like at least a couple of weeks--I know--because that's what my face would look like. And he still has bruises?" Jasper stood, disgust chiseled on his features. "You're every bit as bad. Just like your kid said. My old man would be having a bad day and I became his punching bag. It wasn't fair then. It's *not* fair now, but *you* can change things for the better for *your* son."

With that, Jasper lifted his boot like he was going to kick Mr. Owens, but snatched his shirt and swiveled away from him at the last second. "My old man's dead. Good riddance. I hope he never rests in peace—he doesn't deserve to."

65

CRISS-CROSS APPLESAUCE

illie stood immobile, staring at Jasper's back. The crisscrossing scars varied between white and a darker shade of Jasper's skin tone. Some were barely noticeable, but three pinkish, rope-like scars reminded her of the thick yarn used for a child's art project.

Tillie gasped, sucking spit noisily through her teeth, realizing those "ropes" represented the most brutal of his wounds. She remembered Jasper's tale of Uncle Ben patching him up.

Realizing that these scars were the end result of Oscar Taylor's anger made her queasy.

"Angel, it's okay," Jasper said softly, his voice tinged with embarrassment. He slipped his shirt over his head, put his arms through, and then tucked in the hem. "It doesn't hurt anymore. Sorry you saw that."

She shook her head. "It's okay. I needed to see it."

"No, Tilda, *you* didn't." He grimaced, then nodded at Mr. Owens. "But *he* did."

"Yes, I did." She locked her eyes on him, needing him to believe her. "You never treated me like *that*."

"More importantly, I never—even once—*wanted* to." He held his hand out, seeking permission to hug her.

She nodded, letting him envelop her in a tight hug, blinking against hot tears she didn't understand.

His hug reassured her that she was right to reach out to him, though some uneasiness lingered.

"Todd, Tilda and I are going to step over there a minute." He grimaced at Mr. Owens. "Ray, stay put and ice your ankle." Jasper slipped his arm around Tillie's shoulder. "When Uncle Ben and Jake come, we'll take you to the clinic and have it looked at. I'll be watching, so don't get any ideas about leaving."

Mr. Owens gave a disgruntled wave of his hand.

Jasper chuckled, and then pointed at Calliope. "Ginnie, you should mount up and provide cover in case we need some extra backup before they get here."

Ginnie giggled. "Will do."

"Keep your nag away from me," Mr. Owens bellowed.

"I'll have you know, Ray, that horse is no nag," DT informed him. "Calliope and her mama and daddy have more impressive papers than you've got."

"Then I guess I know what to sue for!" Mr. Owens spat.

"Dad!" Ginnie protested. "Can he do that?"

"Only if he wants me to press charges for attacking a child." DT narrowed his eyes at Mr. Owens. "If you don't care enough about your wife and son to stay employed so you can provide for them, the cops can be here in no time to sort this out. I have Officer Malley's card from the other night."

"Ray, stop it," Mrs. Owens demanded, tears streaming down her cheeks. "Why is it that the West family cares more about your family than you do? Pierce and I deserve better. Maybe Todd should call the cops. You can tell them why you hit me and why you gave your son a bloody nose."

Jasper let go of Tillie and took a step closer to Mr. Owens.

Mrs. Owens sobbed into her hands.

Pierce started to reach for his mom, hesitating before he threw his arm awkwardly on his mother's shoulder. "It's okay, Mom. Don't cry."

His obvious discomfort was hard to watch.

"It's not okay." Mrs. Owens shook her head. "You shouldn't have to see your father like this." She lowered her hands and glanced angrily at her husband. "Why can't you see what you're doing to your own family?" She shook her head and broke into loud sobs. "I can't talk to you."

She whirled toward the front porch and walked quickly away.

"Marsha!" Mr. Owens tried to stand, but wobbled and fell down roaring, "OW! Marsha, come back here!"

Pierce shook his head with disgust. "Mom's right. We don't deserve the way you treat us."

The front porch screen door slammed.

"Watch your mouth, boy." Mr. Owens said. "I'm still your father. You don't get to talk back to me."

"What he said wasn't backtalk, Ray," Jasper argued. "It was the truth. He *doesn't* deserve to be treated badly. Being a father isn't about bossing and intimidating your kid. It's about teaching him how the world works."

"The world sucks," Mr. Owens slammed a fist on his knee. "If it didn't, I wouldn't be sitting here with a broken ankle."

"You think a broken ankle sucks? I drove almost three thousand miles to find out my wife and kid would rather be with him." Jasper jerked his thumb at DT and squatted next to Mr. Owens. "*That* sucks, but you don't see me whining and blaming everybody else."

Tillie wanted to protest his words, but knew she couldn't. She still wanted DT to marry her mom.

Ginnie arched a questioning eyebrow.

Tillie gave a slight nod. The relief on her BFF's face didn't make Tillie feel any better, part of her wondering if she and Mom should give Jasper another chance.

"He made their lives good when I couldn't."

"Jasper," DT said, sympathy coloring his tone.

"Don't say it, Todd." Jasper leaned closer to Mr. Owens and blew out a frustrated breath. "Of course, if my old man had cared more about me than his booze and his pride—and protected me from the evils of the world instead of inviting them into our home, my life would be very different now."

Jasper's words tore at the vulnerable place in Tillie that she spent a lot of time pretending didn't exist.

She searched for words to take away the pain she heard in Jasper's voice, surprising herself as unrehearsed words popped out of her mouth. "That *isn't* fair. His horrible dad didn't just ruin *his* life—he ruined my mom's and mine as well." Tillie stepped next to Jasper and slipped her hand in his. "I'm not gonna lie. Sometimes, he really scared me." Tillie swallowed hard, glanced at Jasper, "Sorry."

She plunged ahead before she talked herself out of saying anything more. Unable to meet Jasper's gaze, Tillie concentrated on Mr. Owens' open mouth instead. "But *now* at least I know he didn't *want* to be that angry dad. That makes me want to give him a chance to start over."

Jasper gave her hand a gentle squeeze. "Thanks, Tilda."

"You're welcome. I'm sorry I made it so hard for you last night."

The gratitude in his eyes sped up the tears in hers.

"No problem. I should have handled things differently ... long before last night." He smiled. "We've got a lifetime to figure things out."

Tillie smiled back, glancing from Pierce to Mr. Owens. "I'll bet Pierce would like to know if you really *want* to be a scary dad or if you just can't help it right now."

"Yeah, Dad." Pierce took a step closer. "We used to have fun together, but not much anymore. I know you didn't have a dad of your own, but if you did, would you want to be afraid of him?"

"Of course not," Mr. Owens said, eyes cast downward.

"Then do something about it, Ray." Jasper leaned toward him again, this time with compassion. "It's only too late if you hurt your family again or if you die before you fix things with them. I can hook you up with people to help you through this." He nodded in DT and Toran's direction. "And the Wests will help, too. Uncle Ben is compulsive that way. He gathers troubled people the way kids gather stray cats."

"He's a meddler," Mr. Owens muttered.

"Yep, he sure is ..." Jasper straightened, smiling wider. "He cares more about me than either of my folks ever did. If you give him half a chance, he'll help you fix things with *your* family." He cleared his throat. "Ray ... don't take this wrong, but you could use the help."

"Dad, please don't get mad," Pierce begged. "Don't make them call the police. I want us to be a good family. We don't have to do family sing-alongs and that kind of lame stuff, but I don't like being afraid of you."

Mr. Owens tightened his jaw and nodded.

Jasper pulled Tillie closer, hugging her against his hip. "Todd, you okay with him?"

"Of course." DT clamped an encouraging hand on Pierce's shoulder and smiled. "Ray and I'll do some male bonding while you and Tillie get reacquainted."

"Just shoot me now," Mr. Owens muttered.

"Too messy," DT joked. "But Calliope could take you out quick enough."

Fear, then anger, crossed Mr. Owens' face, quickly being replaced with resignation when he caught sight of Pierce. He let out a discouraged breath.

"Good, you're learning." Jasper motioned for Tillie to go ahead of him to his black sports car.

She stopped by the trunk.

Jasper glanced at Mr. Owens, then back at her, and spoke. "Thanks for your help with them."

Embarrassed, Tillie dropped her gaze to his work boots. "I didn't really do anything."

"You spoke the truth to people who needed to hear it. You gave Pierce the courage and the words to help him help his dad. That is huge. Who knows—maybe Ray will listen and change for the better."

"What if he doesn't?"

"Then I hope his wife and kid leave him. They don't need to be abused just because he doesn't appreciate what he has. I mean, just because you're related to a person doesn't mean that person is good for you."

"That makes sense."

"It's a really easy concept to understand when I thought about my folks." He sighed. "It wasn't so easy when I had to apply it to myself and you, Angel."

The sadness in his voice tugged at her. "Have you always called me Angel?"

"From the moment I held you in the delivery room." As he spoke, his whole countenance changed to a softer, kinder presence. "You were still fussing from the nurse cleaning you up after being born. Once she placed you in my arms, you quieted right down."

"Really?" Tillie tried to picture herself as a tiny baby.

He nodded. "You opened your eyes, looked into mine, then closed your eyes again and snuggled against my chest. Like you knew you could trust me. A feeling of unbelievable peace came over me."

Tillie smiled at the image.

"Since you brought me peace, I figured you were my own personal angel. You named yourself."

"That's a really sweet story."

His smile deepened. "And every bit of it is true."

Tires crunched in the gravel.

Both swiveled to the left.

Uncle Ben's older-than-dirt truck sped down the gravel lane.

Jasper whistled. "Uncle Ben's on a tear. There's gonna be trouble in River City, partner." He chuckled, nodding at Mr. Owens. "And since I know Uncle Ben's not gunning for me, this might be fun to watch."

"How do you know he's mad?"

"Todd called him after he sent Ginnie for ice and filled him in on Ray going after her. Uncle Ben has no patience for adults who hurt kids. Trust me—he'll have a few things to say." He chuckled harder and guided them closer to his GTO. "You'll probably want to witness this, but don't get too close."

The truck tore around the corner, sliding to a stop a few feet from Mr. Owens.

Tillie glued her eyes on Uncle Ben's furious, red face as he threw open his door, leaped out, and bolted toward Mr. Owens.

"What kind of thick do you have to be to understand you don't solve problems by hitting people?" He stabbed an angry finger at Mr. Owens. "*Especially children?* Do you ever use that muscle between your ears for anything besides giving shape to that bony skull of yours?"

Yikes, he's mad!

Tillie swallowed hard.

For the first time ever, she was concerned about what else Uncle Ben might say or do.

66

PIERCE'S THOUGHTS

Standing next to Tillie, Toran, and Ginnie, Pierce watched as Uncle Ben and Buzz helped his dad into Mom's minivan, not sure what to think or feel. Toran's Uncle Jake, climbed in next to him--probably to make sure his dad didn't do anything to hurt Uncle Ben.

Pierce looked between the man Toran's dad called "Jasper" and Tillie, realizing that he must be Tillie's real dad--the man Tillie had told him had hurt her and her mom--and left his family years ago. *He doesn't seem so scary--to me--though Dad looked like he didn't really want to mess with him.*

His jaw tight, Tillie's dad kept a careful eye on the process asking Uncle Jake, if he was sure he didn't want him to come along as well.

Uncle Jake nodded at Pierce. "I've got Ray. You and Todd hold down the fort here."

"Sure thing." Tillie's dad swiveled toward the kids as Uncle Jake closed the door, looking most intently at Pierce. He blew out a breath and offered Pierce a hesitant smile. "I hope I didn't make you too uncomfortable asking if you wanted to take a swing at your old man."

Alarm pulsed through Pierce, then defensiveness. He was used to fighting his own battles and didn't want the Wests' to think he was a wimp. Glancing around the circle of faces, he didn't see judgment, just kindness and concern. He let out a slow breath, calming as Tillie's dad continued.

"Personally, I would have loved to strike out at mine--but I didn't think about the awkward spot I was putting you in. I just wanted to give you a chance at some payback." He pointed at Pierce's cheek. "My dad bruised my face more times than I'd like to remember and I always wished I could have returned the favor."

Pierce gave a quick nod. "I've thought that too, but it wouldn't make things better." Pierce paused, trying to decide if he could really trust his new "friends"--and their dads. Toran's dad offered an encouraging smile. Pierce decided to trust him. "He'd just hurt me more."

Sighing, Pierce thought about something else Tillie 's dad had said. "Did you mean it when you said if my dad hurts me again, you'd make him pay?"

"Yes." Tillie's dad gave an emphatic nod. "That's a promise. I know what it's like to be someone's punching bag. I couldn't do much about my dad--but if your dad hurts you again--I *will seriously* motivate him to change his ways or leave. You don't deserve to be treated like that."

Concern shifted through Pierce. He didn't doubt Tillie's dad would make good on that threat.

Pierce glanced from him to Tillie. He liked that someone new was willing to take a stand for him. But he really didn't want to see his dad pounded to a pulp--well, maybe if he hurt Pierce again. But right now, he hoped a broken ankle would be enough to make his dad change. "Thanks. Maybe you just threatening him will be enough. He did look a little afraid of you."

"Trust me--if he hurts you again--he will be *a lot* afraid of me." He reached a hand to Pierce's shoulder and motioned his other one around the group. "Hopefully it won't come to that. You've got good friends here. Uncle Ben always says: '*Wests don't do friendship halfway.*' They have always come through for me. They will come through for you." His warm smile made Pierce believe him. "And I am a West by choice--if not by birth. So I will be looking out for you as well. That's a promise."

That assurance lightened the alarm in his belly. "Thanks. Toran has been really cool. And Austin." Pierce glanced at the girls, not fully resolved with his conflicting feelings about Ginnie. *But she did run over Dad with her horse to keep him away from Mom and me.* "And Ginnie and Tillie surprised me--" He turned to Tillie. "Thanks for sticking up for me with my dad. Maybe he will want to be better. He actually looked sorry he hurt me after you asked him to be a good dad."

Tillie offered an encouraging smile. "I hope he does. Sometimes people need to hear the truth from someone new to *really* hear it." She glanced at her dad and strengthened her smile.

He nodded his agreement, his smile also growing bigger, then he winked at Tillie.

Pierce recalled Tillie telling him how she had been afraid of her dad, finding it hard to believe this man standing in front of them was that same man. *She doesn't seem so afraid of him right now. She seems to really like him. Maybe if her dad can change, mine will too.*

The thought gave Pierce some hope.

He glanced at Toran's dad, who also smiled at Tillie, then turned his attention to Pierce. "Sometimes it's easier to be braver for someone else, than yourself. Tillie is a good friend, as are Ginnie and Toran. Now that you guys have resolved the differences between you and you four have spent some good time together, I hope you can see that we *all* care about you, Pierce. Oh, and to make the introductions official. This is Jasper Taylor, a very good friend I've known since I was your age." He nodded at Tillie's dad. "Jasper, this is Pierce Owens. His mom, Marsha, and he are the newest friends of our family."

"It's nice to meet you, Pierce--officially." Jasper Taylor offered a welcoming hand to shake. "Sorry it had to be because of something like this--but having walked in your shoes, I can assure you, this is the best place to be if you have to be going through hard things."

His other hand waved at their surroundings, taking in the house in front of them, the woods behind the main barn to their left, the cornfield behind them with the hay barn and the alfalfa to the right. "Heart of the Wests' farm is my favorite place to be. Good friends, good family." He winked at Pierce. "And when you're here, *you are* family. That's the best part."

His words surrounded Pierce like a favorite blanket, comfortable and right. "That's why Mom and I came here. Uncle Ben always seems to know how to handle my dad." He pointed to Toran's dad. "Him too."

"Yah. Todd is a lot like Uncle Ben." Jasper Taylor sighed, then looked at Ginnie. "Are you okay?"

She nodded as she stepped closer to Pierce. "I feel bad about hurting your dad. But he was so mad--I didn't want him to get to you and your mom. I was trying to keep him out here until Toran could get my dad and Uncle Jasper." She glanced between the two men. "But he tried to hit me, so Calliope knocked him down. It happened really fast. I didn't mean to hurt him. Only to keep him from getting to you."

Ginnie's confession made Pierce's heart stop for a second.

Realizing his dad had tried to hurt Ginnie really bothered Pierce. "I'm sorry he went after you. Thanks for keeping him away. Maybe he won't want to hurt anybody anymore--now that his ankle is probably broke"

"We can hope." Toran interjected, moving closer. "I'm glad Ginnie is a little crazy. It's annoying sometimes--but she means well." He smiled at his twin, who smirked back at him. "And Tillie made a bunch of cool treats this morning." He glanced at Tillie, his smile deepening. "Could we have some? All this excitement has made me a little hungry."

"That's a great idea." Tillie turned to Pierce. "Mysti and I made brownies, cookies, and a double layer chocolate cake earlier. They're tiny--but yummy."

"Speaking of Mysti--we should check on her, your mom, and Roni." Toran's dad said. "Lunch is in the crockpot. You got here at a good time, Pierce. Vi makes the best chicken alfredo."

Cheesy pasta sounded really good to Pierce. "Yum."

"Gin, why don't you pasture Calliope for now, then after lunch you can stable her or go for a ride," her dad suggested, sliding his arm around her waist and pulling her near. He dropped his hand, his expression surprised. "Why are your clothes all wet?"

"I accidentally--then on purpose --splashed Calliope while she was drinking." Ginnie chuckled. "Apparently, she didn't like it, so she pushed me into the creek."

Laughter rounded the group.

Ginnie pulled a cell phone out of her pocket. "And this broke. If one of us gets in trouble for it breaking--can it be *her*?" Ginnie hammed a concerned look, then rolled her eyes, and hitched a thumb toward her horse.

Everyone laughed louder.

Her dad shook his head, grinning big. "I think she redeemed herself by keeping the family safe. I'll give her--and you--a pass. You guys should probably take the time to order phone cases today so this doesn't happen again. We can put your sim card in Tillie's extra phone and get this one fixed."

Surprised that he didn't get mad about the broken phone, Pierce took a closer look at Ginnie's dad. He hugged her tight, seeming sincerely happy she was safe and sound. Wishing his dad could be more like hers, he glanced at Toran, who winked back at him.

And hey ... when did they all get cell phones?

67

THINKING CAN

BE OVER-RATED

*G*innie and Tillie stood at the horserack, wicking away water from Calliope's neck and side with squeegees. Ginnie offered her mare a quartered apple as a reward for acting so bravely.

"Wow, I can't believe you two ran over Pierce's dad!" Tillie stopped the squeegee on Calliope's shoulder and smiled. "I don't even care how bad that sounds. I'm still glad."

"Even better—Daddy's fine with it, so I'm not in trouble." Ginnie giggled, then remembered Mr. Owens stumbling to his minivan with Uncle Ben's help. "I hope his ankle isn't really broken."

Tillie smirked. "I hope it is. Then Pierce can outrun him if he holds a grudge about it."

Ginnie let out a huge grin remembering how Uncle Ben flew out of his truck, took one look at the downed Mr. Owens, and lit into him like a pack of wild dogs on a three-legged cat.

Uncle Ben was not one to embarrass people in public, but had made an exception for Mr. Owens.

Ginnie laughed. "I loved how everybody—and most especially—

how Uncle Jasper and Uncle Jake—gave Uncle Ben plenty of room."

"Yeah. They're probably two of the only people who've been on the receiving end of Uncle Ben's anger. I've never seen him that furious." Tillie laughed along. "But Jasper and Uncle Jake acted like they were waiting for Mr. Owens to threaten Uncle Ben—just so they'd have an excuse to pound him." Tillie pointed the horse scraper at Ginnie. "I almost wished he had, but I wouldn't want them to go to jail because of Mr. Owens."

"Me either." Ginnie wiped Calliope's flank, then blew out a quick breath. "Say, Tillie ..."

"Yeah?"

"Do you think you're ever gonna call Jasper 'Dad'? I mean, he wants me and Toran to call him 'uncle', so it seems a little weird for you to still call him just Jasper."

Tillie tightened her jaw and focused on Calliope's front leg, out of Ginnie's view.

Ginnie wished she hadn't said anything—though she figured "Uncle" Jasper would eventually ask Tillie the same question. "Sorry, Til. You don't have to answer."

"I don't know *how* to answer. I like Jasper a lot better now, but I don't want him to be my *only* dad. I still want the five of us to be a family." Tillie stepped into view again and lowered her voice. "I don't know if I can handle having two dads. If I let Jasper be my dad, what will *your* dad think?"

"For one, I don't think Uncle Jasper's gonna give you a choice. And two, since my dad is already planning to be your stepdad, *nothing* will change—he already loves you. I mean he gives you an allowance--just like me and Toran. He already thinks of you as his daughter." Ginnie set another apple piece on her palm and offered it to Calliope, smiling when her mare's velvety lips tickled her palm. "So you don't have anything to worry about."

"Yes, I do." The alarm in her voice made Ginnie turn toward her friend. "I don't want to hurt either of their feelings. I don't want your dad to think I don't want him anymore."

"Are you serious?" Ginnie wiped her palm on her jeans and

locked her eyes on her friend's. "My dad isn't letting you go anywhere. After hearing him threaten Pierce's dad for trying to hurt me, I realize he doesn't go looking for trouble, but he's pretty good about standing his ground if he finds it. And get this ... Uncle Jasper made a smart aleck remark and Dad about took his head off—and then Mr. Owens'. I never thought he'd stick up for me like that."

"Why not?" Tillie asked.

"Yeah, why not?" A deeper voice echoed.

Tillie and Ginnie turned as one toward the front of the horserack stall.

Dad and Uncle Jasper came around the wall, walking toward them. "I've never let anyone hurt you. Why would I start now?"

Tillie's eyes went wide.

"Because you don't like violence." Ginnie shrugged. "I've never heard you threaten anybody."

"Because I don't think violence solves *most* problems." Dad shrugged, then slid his hand down Calliope's neck. "But very occasionally, violence does solve *some* problems."

Tillie frowned. "Really?"

"Like when?" Ginnie asked, surprised at his answer.

"Like when idiot men attack kids. People like Ray Owens don't always understand the finer points of talking out disagreements. Sometimes it takes a heavier-handed approach." Dad chuckled. "Or in this case, a heavier-*hooved* approach. Like most bullies, Ray only threatened you because he's bigger than you, Gin. Calliope is bigger than *him* ... and so am I. Trust me, had he gotten to you before I did, a broken ankle would've been the least of his worries."

"Don't forget about me," Uncle Jasper reached a hand to stroke Calliope. "Had he touched you, he'd *still* be spitting out his teeth."

Ginnie swallowed, not as afraid of Uncle Jasper as she was disturbed about the image he described. "Do you think his ankle is really broken?"

Dad shrugged again. "Could be. I was too busy watching Ray's fist coming at you to see where Calliope's hooves stepped." He patted Calliope's back. "Thanks for keeping Ginnie safe, girl."

Calliope whinnied.

"That doesn't sound like you," Ginnie said, shaking her head.

She gave Calliope the last piece of apple.

"Yeah, Todd—it *doesn't* sound like you," Uncle Jasper agreed, offering an approving grin. "But you showed some real fire. Kinda surprised me. Before you got in Ray's face, I was seriously considering taking Tilda to Kentucky with me on Thursday."

Dad swiveled, pointing an angry finger close to Jasper's chin.

Ginnie and Tillie sucked in astonished, worried breaths.

Oh, man—this won't be good. Termites chomped determinedly in Ginnie's belly again. *But if it's gonna happen, I'm on Dad's side. Go, Daddy!*

"Like Ginnie said, just because I don't go looking for trouble doesn't mean I won't deal with it when I find it." Dad's tone became hard like a sledgehammer. "And just to be clear, *you* are *not* taking Tillie *anywhere*. You're welcome to be a part of her life, but that happens here." Dad punctuated each word with a downward tap of his finger. "On ... the ... Heart."

Uncle Jasper put his hands up in a "whoa" motion. "Back the bossy train up, Todd."

Dad waved away Uncle Jasper's warning. "I'm willing to make allowances because you're her birth father, but make no mistake, Jasper, in *my* mind, Tillie is as much my child as Ginnie and Toran are. If you try to take her away from Amanda and me, you *will* regret it. I didn't let Cabot take my kids, and I won't let *you*, either. You, Amanda, and I will share Tillie here on *The Heart* or *you* don't get to be a part of her life."

Tillie and Ginnie exchanged alarmed glances, each taking a step closer to the other.

They clasped hands, meeting in front of Calliope's head.

"Hold up, Todd." Uncle Jasper glanced at Tillie and frowned. "I only said I was *thinking* about taking her to Kentucky. But you stepped up like I needed you to. No need to make threats—unless you *want* this to get ugly."

"No, sir. It's *not* a threat." Dad shook his head and took a calming breath. "We might as well clear the air right here and now. If you think you're taking Tillie *anywhere,* now or in the future that Amanda doesn't give permission for, this *will* get ugly. You can consider *that* a promise."

"You said so yourself ... I'm her *real* dad. I have rights," Uncle Jasper countered, taking a step back from Dad.

"True, but so do I. Six years is a lot of time to invest in a child I love and care about very much." He pointed to Ginnie and Tillie. "Our daughters decided to make themselves sisters a long time ago-- and since Ginnie is my daughter, that makes Tillie my daughter as well."

"Except it really doesn't," Uncle Jasper protested.

"Uncle Ben says family is who you want them to be," Ginnie reminded them both. "And Uncle Jasper--you said this morning to Uncle Ben that you listen to him when he talks."

"I did," Uncle Jasper agreed, nodding. "But I left here thinking of your dad as my brother--which makes you two *cousins* rather than sisters." He pointed between the girls. "Tilda already has a dad. I'd rather Todd be her uncle--just like old times."

"Be that as it may be--things have changed." Dad softened his tone. "Your daughter is a West and as you know, we Wests take care of our own. *You included.* Uncle Ben and Aunt Sadie made you part of us and I will honor that decision, *Brother...*" Dad stood straighter, tapping his finger downward. "... as long as you do your visiting here on the Heart, everything stays friendly ... just like old times. When you are here--you *are* family. Only for you, when *you* are *not here*--you are *still* family ..." He pointed at Tillie and firmed his voice. "... *unless* you try to take Tillie anywhere else without permission from her mother. If that happens, all bets are off and you open a can of worms that you will *not* be able to close."

Dad crossed his arms and leaned forward, his six-foot-two frame seeming to tower over Uncle Jasper--even though he was only an inch taller.

Uncle Jasper fisted his hands, but clamped his jaw shut, corralling up his frustration, good and tight.

321

Dad winked at Tillie and then turned his attention back to Uncle Jasper. "Just so we're all on the same page, I'm willing to share her, but I *won't* give her up." Dad tapped his finger downward again. "Tillie stays *here*."

Uncle Jasper looked like he wanted to protest, but must have heard Tillie suck in a loud breath.

Ginnie squeezed her friend's hand.

Tillie returned the squeeze.

"For *now*." Uncle Jasper insisted, matching Dad's stance, then unfisted his hand.

"*Forever*," Dad countered.

After glancing at Tillie, Uncle Jasper blew out a frustrated breath. "Look, Todd. I just needed to know you weren't going to let that piece of trash run over the kids. Eagle Scout or not, you've never been one to put a dog in any fight. No offense, but you used to be a bit of a marshmallow. I can see that's changed."

"I'm glad you see that. Just to be clear--I'm in this fight for the long haul. *Nobody's* running over them." Dad stood straighter, but not less intimidating. "My last father-in-law taught me a lot of things he probably wishes he hadn't. I can handle this situation all the way around—including *you*."

"You're the one being aggressive." Jasper frowned, looking like he wanted to say more, but glanced at Tillie and seemed to make an effort to keep his words neutral. "I just want you to realize that I'm back to stay."

"You've made that crystal clear, Jasper. I respect that--and believe it or not--*I'm even happy about it*. I'm still your friend--the engagement hasn't changed that--though I understand that it has made everything more awkward and difficult."

"Ya think?" Uncle Jasper rolled his eyes and fisted his hands.

Ginnie squelched the urge to giggle as Tillie's eyes grew wider.

Dad ignored the slight. "Trust me, I'll do what I can to work this out. I believe you being part of her life will be good for Tillie." He glanced between Tillie and Uncle Jasper. "But I've been thinking about this from Tillie's perspective and I realize this parallels Quee-nie's situation somewhat."

Uncle Jasper grimaced. "How do you figure?"

"Cabot's biggest fault was he thought he knew what was best for his daughter *without* consulting her. He made up his mind that it would be his way or no way. Queenie didn't happen to agree--and he didn't give her the respect to at least hear her out. He waited until it was too late to fix something that was *very* fixable."

"Which has *what* to do with *my* daughter?"

Yeah, what? Curiosity piqued, it was all Ginnie could do not to blurt the question.

"Bear with me a minute. Cabot made Queenie choose between him and me, and it hurt her deeply. She just wanted us to get along. I was willing, but he wasn't."

Uncle Jasper shifted from one foot to the other.

Dad smiled at each girl. "Now that I have daughters, I understand his thinking better, but I'm not willing to put Tillie in a situation where *she* thinks she has to choose between you and me. As far as I'm concerned, she has two dads and a mom, with Amanda getting final decision-making authority."

Uncle Jasper glared at Dad. "Amanda will probably go along with whatever *you* want."

Shrugging, Dad lengthened his smile. "As long as we all want what's best for Tillie, I don't see where that has to be a problem."

"I'm sure *you* don't." Jasper shook his head, frustration staining his words. "Maybe I don't want to share my kid. You have two others."

"Too late, she's already *my* kid." Dad didn't hesitate and reached an arm to Tillie. "Maybe you should ask your daughter what *she* thinks."

After grimacing at Dad, Uncle Jasper turned to Tillie. "Well, Angel? What *do* you think?"

Ginnie peeked at her friend, whose eyes darted around and between each man like a bunny rabbit looking for a place to flee.

68

THE BUNNY TAKES A STAND

ou can do this. Tillie took in a determined breath, willing her racing heart to calm—preferably before it jumped out of her chest. *Now's your chance to say what you really think.*

Tillie puffed out a quick breath. *Which would be fine—if I actually knew what I wanted.*

"Take your time, Tillie. We'll wait." DT's quiet reassurance helped ease her jitters.

She nodded, and then licked her lips.

Ginnie offered her usual understanding smile while giving a silent nudge with a nod of her head.

There's nothing to be afraid of. Tillie peeked at DT and realized that was true.

Feeling more confident, Tillie turned her gaze to Jasper, surprised to see him looking vulnerable. *Wow, I didn't expect to feel so sorry for Jasper.*

But she did.

Tillie glanced between the two men—the dad she had chosen— and who had chosen her, and the dad she had feared for too long ... who now wanted her back.

Only right now, she didn't fear him—she pitied him.

More importantly, she understood his vulnerability.

Jasper reminded her of the last kid on the playground to get picked for the gym class soccer team. The kid nobody wanted because they weren't even half as good as the second-worst soccer player in school. The kid who pretended not to care ... but cared very much.

The kid she often was ... and didn't want to be.

She channeled some of her BFF's confidence and stepped toward Jasper, beaming the most welcoming smile she could muster. "I think his idea is a good one."

Jasper grimaced. "For *him*."

"For all of us." Tillie motioned to DT and Ginnie. "You heard Uncle Ben. We're all part of the same family."

"To be clear, I'm okay with Todd being your *uncle*." Jasper exhaled a frustrated sigh. "It's him being your stepdad I'm having issues with. Especially since he's dating your mother—*my* wife."

"Amanda is your *ex-wife*, Jasper," DT reminded him.

"My feelings for Amanda haven't changed, Todd. I only allowed the divorce because I couldn't be who she needed me to be four years ago. I *am* that person *now*. If she gives me a chance, I can prove it." Jasper sighed and gave a dismissive wave of his hand. "Never mind. I can't win. Any way you look at it, you get my family, and I get nothing. You win, I lose."

"That's not true." Tillie shook her head. "It's not exactly what you want, but it can still be good."

"How do you figure, Tilda? I came back with the intention of doing whatever it took to win you and your mom back only to find out that would be as likely as Gertrude the goat growing wings and learning to fly-fish." His voice broke. "I should've stayed in California."

"No, you shouldn't have." Tillie blurted the words without thinking, surprised she didn't agree with him. "I'm glad you came back."

Ginnie seemed equally mystified at her objection.

"Okay, I'll play," Jasper said, making an obvious effort to keep his voice even. "Why is it better to be rejected by my wife and daughter than to stay in California where I had made a new start?"

When he put it like that, Tillie questioned her protest.

It took a moment to figure out why she objected. Then it came to her. "If you'd stayed in California, I would never have wanted to get to know you ... but now I do."

"Why? What's changed?" He hung his thumb off his front jean pocket. "Besides me telling you I refuse to let you fire me as your dad? That isn't ideal for either of us."

"But now I know *why* you left. Everybody told me it was because you loved me, but I didn't believe them. You hurt me—"

"That was an *accident*! I've apologized seven ways to Sunday, Tilda." He shook his head. "I don't know how to fix it. I can only say I'm sorry it happened."

Tillie backed up from him. "That's not what I meant."

DT gave a slight shake of his head to Jasper, reaching a gentle hnd to Tillie's shoulder.

Jasper grimaced, then shrugged. "Then I'm lost, because I don't know either."

Not knowing what she *did* mean to say, Tillie blinked back the annoying tears that always seemed to surface at times like these. She jutted out her chin. "I thought you left because you didn't want me anymore. Now I know you really do care about me."

"I care about you very much." He sighed again. "You're my daughter. *I love you.*"

"I know that *now*," Tillie whispered, nodding. "That's what changed everything."

He dropped his jaw, seeming not to know what to say.

She pointed at DT and Ginnie. "No offense, but they've always been here. I love them, too. Ginnie's the best sister I could ask for—and even better, she's my best friend."

Ginnie hugged Tillie quickly. "Tillie's a great sister."

Tillie returned the hug, smiled at her friend, then moved closer to Jasper. "I know this is hard for you." Tillie glanced at Jasper while nodding at DT. "He's been here for me forever."

"*I'd* like to be here for you—from now on."

"I know. I want you to be ... as long as you want to be a good dad like you said." She wiped a tear. "I don't want to be afraid of you anymore."

His eyes widened. "I never wanted you to be afraid of me—*ever.* I'm sorry I made you feel that way."

"I want to believe you. I'm trying to remember the good times, but I still remember you hurting my mom. And that's hard for me."

Jasper gave a defeated nod. "I wish I could undo that."

"Me too, but you can't. Even so ... I want us to start over." Tillie locked her gaze on his, needing him to understand what she was about to say. His gaze stayed strong. "I also don't want you to make me choose between you and him. I know it's not what you want, but I ..." Tillie swallowed hard. "... I want ... you ... *both*."

Surprising herself, Tillie knew she meant every word.

69

THE END

*G*innie led Calliope into her stall. She stroked her mare's neck. "It's been a long, weird day, huh, girl?"

Calliope raised and lowered her head while whinnying.

"I know. Super weird."

Laughing, Ginnie latched the wooden door behind them. "But you were my hero. Thanks for saving me from Mr. Owens. I don't want to think about what would have happened if you weren't there."

"Yes, Calliope," Dad's voice agreed enthusiastically. "You definitely earned your keep today."

Ginnie turned, surprised to see him. "I thought you and Miss Amanda were going out."

"We are, but I wanted to give you something first." He opened the stall door and came through. "Tillie will be busy with Jasper and Uncle Ben tonight, so I thought you might like a good book to read."

"Um, Dad, Toran and I may be twins, but we aren't identical." She wiggled her braid. "I'm Ginnie. *Toran* is the bookworm, you know, the twin with short, curly hair."

"Fine, suit yourself." Dad held up an emerald-green book titled "Journal" in gold lettering and smirked. "I doubt it'll ever be a classic since the author was only ten when she wrote it, but I thought *you* might find it interesting."

"Umm ... uh ..." Ginnie dropped her jaw, unable to form a coherent thought for a few seconds. "That's Mama's?"

Dad nodded. "One of them. This was the oldest one I found. I gave the second-oldest to Toran. I thought you might like to start at the beginning. He'll catch up later."

Ginnie stared, trying to process her dad's words.

The book immobilized her, as if it cast a spell.

She couldn't believe how close she was to one of the journals she'd wanted him to return for weeks, or that she would soon be able to peek into the mind of the woman she barely remembered and yet, missed so much.

"I thought you didn't have time to read them yet," Ginnie said, reaching for the book.

He crossed the stall and handed it over. "I didn't. But I couldn't sleep last night with Jasper here, so I decided to check out the journals and keep my promise to you."

Gratitude filled Ginnie's heart. "Thanks. I've been missing her."

"I know." Dad sighed. "I thought this might help. I'm not sure how much you'll recognize of your mom as you read this, though—she was a child, and not a mom when she wrote it—but I found it enlightening. It helped me connect a few dots ... with her as well as with you."

"Really?"

He nodded. "Your personalities are very similar, so I got some insight into both of you. However, there are some big differences between you as well, for which I am very grateful."

His teasing tone piqued her curiosity. "Like what?"

"Like how you think about things. You aren't quite as impulsive as she was—though you have your moments." He gave a quick wink. "Like I said last night, I'm glad she was my wife, and *not* my kid. You give me a run for my money at times, but she made me feel a lot more sympathy for Cabot than I've had in a long time."

Ginnie giggled. "No way. How?"

"Let's just say she was a little focused on getting her own way ... *a lot*. Which reminds me ..." He locked his gaze on Ginnie, squeezing both of her shoulders firmly. "I'm not him and you are *not* her. She was a lot sassier and stubborn than I am comfortable with a child being. The woman I married is not the same girl you'll read about."

A little stunned at this revelation, Ginnie searched his face for more explanation. "What do you mean? Isn't Mama just Mama?"

He shrugged. "Let's just say that between the time she wrote this and when I met her, her outlook on life changed some, mellowing some of her less-desirable qualities while shaping and perfecting the traits I loved most about her."

"Like what?"

"Well, she was still pretty spirited when I met her, but she had more self-control. Her passion, her drive, her fearlessness—which sometimes shows up in her journal in a negative light—were more focused and admirable when I fell in love with her than they are in *this* book."

Ginnie giggled. "Are you trying to say she was a brat?"

"Don't put words in my mouth—she was still your mother--have some respect." He smiled, lightly tapping the tip of Ginnie's nose, then lifted his hands to air quote. "Let's just say she would have bene-fited greatly from Uncle Ben's 'creative consequences' in her forma-tive years."

"That would be a 'yes'." Giggling, Ginnie held the book more firmly, her desire to read it increasing exponentially. Reading "bratty mama" might be even more fun than she thought.

"Of course, the quality I loved most was how much she loved our children." Dad gently chucked her under the chin and continued in a more serious tone. "She threw her heart and soul into you, Toran, and me. She gave up a lot to be your mother, as well as my wife, and reading her journals reminds me of just how much."

The reverence in his voice made Ginnie search his face.

She nodded. "I'm glad she chose you over her dad."

"I'm sorry she had to choose between us at all." He took a step back from her, voice firming. "That should never have happened. It caused her a lot of pain, but once she married me, she didn't compromise what she wanted most of all—and that was a happy family. That's what I admired about her most." Dad steeled his eyes on Ginnie's. "She wanted heaven on earth for you and Toran especially, and while she was here, she made sure we *all* had that. Never once did she act like she regretted choosing us over him or her old life—which was pretty good, as you will see."

Ginnie pondered this new revelation about her mother.

"Anyway, realize she was only ten when she wrote this." He pointed at the journal. "People change. Things she thought were good ideas when she wrote this, she probably wouldn't have done at twenty." He shook his head, then chuckled softly. "On second thought, some of it she might have. She just would've used more flair."

Completely intrigued, Ginnie made a conscious effort to keep her growing grin under control. "So you're saying that Mama might be a bad influence on me?

"I'm saying she wrote about *her* life ... and Cabot's views on parenting are quite a bit different than mine. She made some choices I would rather *you* didn't make." Dad smiled, shaking his head at some memory he didn't seem inclined to share. His tone bore warning. "This isn't a parenting book of advice from a mother to a daughter—it's a ten year-old's thoughts on how life should be lived ... which may be better than reality in some ways, but in my opinion, not always the best way to go about things."

Ginnie grinned. "Says the stick-in-the-mud."

He motioned for Ginnie to hand him the brush she was rubbing Calliope's flank with. She gave it to him. He brushed the top of her back "Yes. Says the stick-in-the-mud," Dad agreed, returning her playful grin as he pointed the brush at her. "Who, by the way, has the authority to ground you until you're thirty and make you repaint the fence."

"Oh, man!" Ginnie teased. "How did you two ever get together? You were like complete opposites."

He chuckled harder. "You should pay more attention in science class—opposites attract."

"But you and Miss Amanda are like clones. What's your theory for that?"

"Maturity. I married a 'take-my-breath-away' hurricane the first time—whom I would still be happily married to if she were still here." Dad brushed the top of Calliope's back. "Now I'm engaged to the sweetest woman I could ever hope to know." He locked his gaze on Ginnie. "Just so you know, I love Amanda for herself, not as a substitute for your mom."

"I know that."

"Good, I'm glad. Amanda is amazing, thoughtful, kind ... and most importantly, she loves my children." He offered a playful wink. "I guess I'm a sucker for women who love you and Toran. Bonus, I get Tillie."

"Yeah, we're pretty awesome sauce."

"I concur." He nodded. "Fun fact—I'm the first West man in seven generations to have *two* daughters. I'd say *that's* pretty awesome sauce."

"And Tillie's the first West girl to have two dads." Ginnie returned his grin, then grimaced. "I'm not sure how well that's gonna work out."

"It'll work out." Dad's confidence spiked Ginnie's curiosity.

"How do you know?"

"Because I'll *make* it work out. Losing your mom so young really brought home to me is how precious life is." He stroked Calliope's back with the brush a couple times. "Now that I have decided to move forward with my life again, I really want it to be meaningful. I love Amanda and Tillie. I want them to be happy. I want you and Toran to be happy as well."

"What about Uncle Jasper? He's not very happy."

"Yeah, he's definitely on the losing end of this deal." He sighed. "I don't have all the answers, Gin. I'm torn about him, as is Amanda."

"I'm not. He should've gotten his life together a long time ago."

Ginnie stroked Calliope's neck, frowning. "I don't want to sound mean, but if you snooze, you lose."

"And that's a perfect example of what I meant about maturity and your mom. While that sentiment may be true, real life can be complicated. She would have said the same thing at twelve, but at twenty, she would have realized that you can't storm your way through other people's feelings."

Squelching the urge to roll her eyes, Ginnie stared at him. "Are you going to break off your engagement?"

"Of course not."

Ginnie smirked. "Then *you* think the same thing. *You* just want to sound nicer about it."

"Maybe, but it's complicated."

Shrugging, Ginnie steeled her gaze on her dad's. "Let me uncomplicate it for you. If *you* marry Miss Amanda, Uncle Jasper can't. Problem solved."

"Tillie said the same thing two nights ago."

"Brilliant. That's two votes." Ginnie cocked her head to the side and smiled. "Maybe people should listen to their inner twelve-year-olds—or better yet, to their daughters."

"Maybe so." Dad pretended to swat her with the brush. "However, *when* we marry is Amanda's decision. I don't want to pressure her."

"Dad, Dad, Dad," Ginnie teased, shaking her head in mock pity. "Why don't you go back to being an ostrich and iron your tuxedo or something? Tillie and I'll handle Miss Amanda and the wedding plans."

"Um, I think I can handle wooing and pursuing Amanda." He offered a sarcastic smirk. "If you remember correctly, she already said she'd marry me."

"True, but it's not a done deal until she says 'I do'. Let Tillie and me help you close the deal."

Dad backed up a step. "Now that's just creepy."

"What?"

"You using your mother's phrasing—my first wife—to help me marry my second wife."

Ginnie shrugged. "You're the one who said life is complicated. I'm just trying to help you focus on what's important—which—hint, hint ... is marrying Miss Amanda before Uncle Jasper can change her mind."

"That's not going to happen."

Ginnie frowned her disagreement. "You don't think he won't try to change her mind?'

"Oh, he'll try," Dad stated matter-of-factly, giving a quick shrug. "I just won't *let* him. I told you before, Cabot Stratton was a bigger menace to me than Jasper Taylor ever was or will be."

Ginnie considered his words and gripped the journal tighter, rethinking her position on his "lameness" and inability to protect his family. Dad had shown he was a force to be reckoned with—and *he* was the one going on a date in a few minutes with Miss Amanda, *not* Uncle Jasper.

Still, even though Ginnie didn't know Uncle Jasper very well, she was pretty certain he'd do his best to complicate matters.

After all, *she* would—if she was in his position.

Not wanting her dad to know she had doubts about the situation, she offered what she hoped was a confident nod.

His appreciative smile told her she had masked her doubts well enough for him to quit worrying about reassuring her. "Be good for Uncle Ben. Don't wait up. We'll be back late."

"Sure, Dad." She gave him a quick hug, adjusting the journal so it didn't slip out of her hand. "Mama will keep me busy. Thanks for giving this to me."

"You're welcome." He turned to leave, then swiveled back, an odd expression on his face.

He reached for the journal.

Ginnie gripped it firmly to her chest and backed up.

He stopped reaching. His lips hovered between a knowing smile and a worried grimace. "Don't make me regret giving that to you, okay?"

Forcing her amusement at his concern into an obedient nod,

Ginnie cleared her mind of the entertaining notions that might await her in Mama's journals. *You can go now.*

Dad seemed to read her mind.

His hand still froze in midair, like he was still considering snatching the journal back.

Hoping her expression projected innocence; Ginnie tried not to laugh at his definite misgivings and clutched the journal harder. "Have fun."

Her energetic wish seemed to jump-start his brain ... and his hand, which he dropped to his side. "You too. Just not too much."

"Got it."

After his eyes emitted a silent warning, he nodded, clamped his jaw shut, turned quickly, and made his way to the stall gate. He opened the door and went through.

She watched his frame grow smaller.

Ginnie corked her giggle until he disappeared around a corner.

As she released the bottled-up laugh, the journal dropped out of her hand, landing spine down on the straw and opened.

A few pages turned.

"Funny, there isn't a breeze." Ginnie leaned over the book to retrieve it, her gaze catching two-inch letters spelling the words: SHHHH! Secret Plan! If you aren't Ginnie Stratton, don't read this or YOU ... WILL ... BE ... CURSED! (that includes YOU, Roni!)

Ginnie stopped reaching, a little concerned at the bold warning—and the skull and crossbones—in bright red marker.

Then she shrugged, feeling a smile grow on her lips. "I'm Ginnie Stratton *West*. That's close enough."

After turning the page, Ginnie scanned it, dropping her jaw. "Wow, Mama. I can see why Daddy was a little worried about you. You make me look really, *really* good."

The entry pulsed with energizing excitement.

Ginnie laughed, a little in awe of her mother's daring.

Keeping her eyes glued on the next page, Ginnie backed into the corner of the stall where she had just made a fresh straw bed for Calliope and lowered herself onto it.

She braced against the wooden walls, determined to devour every word of the journal she now held before she left the barn tonight.

Soon Ginnie would know the mother she missed so much.

THE END--FOR NOW

Book 5 in the Ginnie West Adventures will be completed soon By Spring 2021.

Please check back to your favorite book retailer--it will be there full of new adventures.

AFTERWORD

A MESSAGE FROM
THE AUTHOR:

If you want personalized signed copies of any of my books, please visit my website:
 http://TheHeroInsideMe.com

Or message me on Facebook: I'd love to be Facebook friends! You can find me at:
 https://www.facebook.com/Author-Monique-Bucheger-193789017310198/
 or Author Monique Bucheger on Facebook.com

I hope you have enjoyed reading this book as much as I have enjoyed writing it. Writing empowering and entertaining books has always been a dream for me, so I truly appreciate your support.

If you like my books, I would really appreciate it if you would leave a review at Goodreads.com, Amazon.com, Audible.com, Barnesandnoble.com, or anywhere else reviews are given, I'd love to hear from you.

It's easy and would help me immensely.

Just type my name in the search bar: Monique Bucheger, and all of my books will show up. Please write a sentence or two about why you liked it. You can copy and paste the same review to all places. This would really help me reach new readers.

Thank you. -Monique Bucheger

For More Great Content
Including Free Downloads Visit:

https://TheHeroInsideMe.com

For more about about the illustrator,
Mikey Brooks, visit:

www.insidemikeysworld.com

ABOUT THE AUTHOR

MONIQUE BUCHEGER

When Monique isn't writing, you can find her playing taxi driver to one or more of her 12 children, plotting her next novel, scrapbooking, or being the "Mamarazzi" at any number of child-oriented events. Even though she realizes there will never be enough hours in any given day, Monique tries very hard to enjoy the journey that is her life. She shares it with a terrific husband, her dozen children, one adorable granddaughter, two cats, and many real and imaginary friends. She is the author of several books and hopes to write many more. You can find more about Monique and her works at:

www.moniquebucheger.blogspot.com

A new website is being built at: http://TheHeroInsideMe.com

Downloadable free content will be available as soon as the website is live.

OTHER BOOKS BY MONIQUE BUCHEGER

Trouble Blows West: A Ginnie West Adventure

Putting her body in motion before her brain is in gear creates a mountain of problems for 12 year-old Ginnie West. She is certain that defending her twin brother, Toran, from the biggest bully in sixth grade was the right thing to do. But Ginnie couldn't be more wrong. She quickly learns that Toran doesn't appreciate being rescued by a girl any better than Pierce likes being knocked down by one.

When Pierce seeks revenge on Ginnie, Toran sets aside his anger and helps her plot a payback prank at Pierce's house. Sadly, Ginnie learns that Pierce has a reason for being a bully when she sees his dad drop him to the floor like a ragdoll. Realizing he's a boy in big trouble, Ginnie decides to be his ally, because he won't let her be his friend.

Simply West of Heaven: A Ginnie West Adventure

Twelve-year-old BFFs Ginnie and Tillie are matchmaking geniuses. Sweet! Not long after they schemed to get Ginnie's widowed dad to fall in love with Tillie's divorced mom, Ginnie stumbled upon her late mom's journals, making life even more awesome sauce ... until her dad confiscated the journals, determined to protect Ginnie from a danger he won't name.

Ginnie is counting on her future sister's help to make Dad change his mind, but Tillie's not so sure the ghost of Ginnie's mom will make a good addition to their new family tree. The girls' world gets flipped upside-down when a blast from the past shows up and makes Tillie go nutburgers. Ginnie is torn between helping her best friend and what could be the answer to her deepest wish.

Being West is Best: A Ginnie West Adventure

Twelve-year-old BFFs, Ginnie West and Tillie Taylor, are matchmaking geniuses. Together, they maneuvered Ginnie's widower-dad into proposing to Tillie's divorcee-mom. Sweet! Certain they are well on their way to sisterhood, each girl is floored when Tillie's lousy-excuse-for-a-father puts in an appearance after a six year absence. Too bad "lousy dad repellant" doesn't come in a can.

Even though Tillie's dad has sobered up and is determined to make amends, Tillie would rather he just disappear again. If he stays, "Operation: Secret Sisters" may need to be renamed "Operation: Not Gonna Happen."

If that's not bad enough, the biggest bully in seventh grade comes over often and wishes he could call the West's farmhouse "home." When the bully's abusive dad shows up as well, Ginnie thinks it's time to change her family's motto from "When you're here, you're family" to "There's no more room at the West's."

The Ginnie West Adventure Collection

Multi-Book set (Featuring Books 1-3)

Popcorn: A Picture book featuring Ginnie and Toran when they were 3 1/2 years old

When hunger wakes little Ginnie from her dreams she sets out to make herself a midnight snack. Hilarity and trouble ensues as she wrecks the kitchen in her attempts to make homemade popcorn balls.

Child Abuse Resources

National Coalition to Prevent Child Sexual Abuse and Exploitation: www.preventtogether.org

Prevent Child Abuse America
 www.preventchildabuse.org

Healthy Families America
 www.Healthyfamiliesamerica.org

Stop It Now!
 www.stopitnow.org

Darkness to Light
 www.d2l.org

Association for the Treatment of Sexual Abusers (ATSA)
 www.atsa.com

Prevention Institute
 www.preventioninstitute.org

Child Help USA
 www.childhelp.org

Child Care Aware
 www.childcareaware.org

The National Child Traumatic Stress Network
 www.nctsn.org

National Children's Alliance
 www.nationalchildrensalliance.org

Kempe Center for Prevention of Child Abuse and Neglect
www.kempe.org

International Society for Traumatic Stress Studies
https://istss.org

National Children's Advocacy Center
www.nationalcac.org

National Alliance of Children's Trust and Prevention Funds
www.ctfalliance.org

Made in the USA
Monee, IL
26 January 2021

58008105R10204